The WIND the ROAD & the WAY

Reader's Comments

Join the Epic Order of the Seven on another rollicking good ride! During the team's new mission to spread Jesus' message of restoration, mercy, and love throughout the world, they witness life lessons which are as powerful today as they were 2,000 years ago. The Maker repeatedly shows Himself faithful, true, and ever-able to accomplish what He has promised.

—**Claire Roberts Foltz,** Cup of Cold Water for Women: Conference Speaker, Author and Storyteller, Atlanta, GA

The Wind, the Road & the Way is my favorite book in the series so far! I couldn't put it down. I was transported to another time and became absorbed with the story as each chapter took me on a journey with Paul to better understand his missionary journeys and the pain he endured. Once again, I fell in love with all the animal characters that have become like friends. Jenny L. Cote makes them come to life. I wanted the story to never end. Fantastic book!

—**Mitchell Carey,** 11, Southside Homeschool Academy, Amelia Courthouse, VA

I love following Max and Liz as they travel through Bible stories. In this book I like that they help to start the Church and spread the word of Jesus, seeing the miracles that happened. God still performs miracles on Earth and I have been witness to some of them! God's message came to life as if I were there to experience the trials and triumphs that Paul and the others experienced.

—**L. Lee Ramey,** 20, Adult Learning Program at Nova Scotia Community College, Nova Scotia, Canada

My son absolutely loves Max and Liz, and I love the way their tales bring the Bible to life. Following the disciples as they faced trials and persecution was fascinating. Some parts were a little tough to read because it broke my heart, but Jenny has a way of showing how even the worst situations are all part of God's perfect plan. This book was a great reminder that God is in control no matter what.

—**Ashley Rhodes,** Mom to Alex, 6, Gordonville Elementary, Gordonville, MO

Incredible! Jenny L. Cote has truly outdone herself with this book. I love how it explains the deep areas of the Bible that I had difficulty understanding before. This story has everything you could ask for: humor, adventure, suspense, fantasy, and most importantly, the Gospel.

—**Isabel DeSanno,** 11, Faith Academy, Victoria, TX

It wasn't until I read this book that the reality of the apostles' missions, especially Paul's, became clear to me. The dialogue, descriptions, and Mrs. Cote's writing style make this AMAZING series something worth reading. You truly are an effective and inspiring writer, Mrs. Cote. I simply can't wait for the next one!

—**Lily Calhoun,** 13, Homeschooled, Atlanta, GA

This book continues to prove how God is using Jenny to show kids of all ages God's word, making it more accessible and enjoyable. She is continuing to let His light shine through her and her writing.

–**Stephen (with a "ph") Moss,** 13, Outlook Academy, Prattville, AL

This fifth book by Jenny L. Cote continues the saga of Max, Liz, and their friends, as the animals journey with Paul, Peter, and other leaders of the early church. Filled with scriptural insights and fresh views on old stories, Jenny L. Cote makes the stories in the book of Acts come to life.

–**David Sampson,** 17, Homeschooled, Canterbury, New Zealand

The Wind, the Road & the Way was an adventure from the start! Jenny L. Cote uses her gifts to point to the Way by sharing her imaginative exploits of lovable animal characters to help tell the story. The story is rich with well-researched details that immerse the reader's heart to go deeper. Like C. S. Lewis, she crafts stories that can be enjoyed by young and old. These books will prove to be the "road" that helps many find a change in their hearts!

–**Lisa Stewart Barker,** Mother, Wife, Human Resources Director, Prince George, VA

Reading *The Wind, the Road & the Way* made me want to open my Bible and continue studying the missionary journeys of the apostles. It is a wonderful, powerful story where Jesus' genuine love shines and we learn about those who followed him. This is the best book I've ever read, and I want all of my friends and family to read this so they will know about the one, true God.

–**Kaitlyn Nicole Barker,** 10, South Elementary School, Prince George, VA

I have read every one of Jenny L. Cote's books! This book is really special because she has included characters named Nate & Noah. Those names represent the boys who were special friends to many of us, and we lost them suddenly in a terrible lake accident. I think it is wonderful that their legacy and memory have been included in this book for many to read and enjoy. Thank you, Mrs. Cote, for this incredible and funny tribute to my friends, now in heaven!

–**Tucker Hill,** 10, Cornerstone Academy, Morristown, TN

The Wind, the Road & the Way is another action-packed, triumphant treat—as sweet and satisfying as chocolate! Each character displays strengths and weaknesses, so everyone can relate to some or all. We have laughed and cried, as Jenny touches hearts and opens minds. Your heart will feel love and hurt as you journey through. A page-turner for sure! Come on, let's jump in the IAMISPHERE, *mon ami,* and be prepared to be AMAZED and ENTHRALLED!

–**The Hurley Family** (Caleb 14, CaLyn 12, & Sassy 10), Homeschool, Fort Polk, LA

Of all the Max and Liz books, *The Wind, the Road & the Way* is the most enthralling yet, which is quite a feat considering they are all phenomenal! The cliff-hanging chapter endings held me in great suspense, making the book nearly impossible to put down. I can't wait for the culmination of their time and travels with the Apostle Paul. I know it will be epic!

–**Gabriel McLeod,** 9, Homeschooled, Tallahassee, FLA

I never realized the extent of Paul's travels and hardships until I read this book. In the Bible the incidents and journeys are spread out over chapters and books; here they are one after another, making me realize the full extent of what Paul and the apostles went through to develop the early church. If you want to see the Bible in a new way, read this book. Follow *The Wind, the Road, & the Way* and let the Lord reveal to you what he desires through the pen of his faithful servant, Jenny L. Cote.

—**Grace Flint,** 17, Columbus Christian School, Columbus, IN

A delightful and thrilling adventure! The book came alive as I travelled through historic Bible events with lots of humor, mysteries, and faith. An amazing book that I couldn't put down, catching up with Max, Liz, and the gang on their new mission with Paul and friends, unlocking new mysteries and pointing The Way!

—**Jessica Modarelli,** 14, Australian Christian College, Sydney, Australia

The Wind, the Road & the Way is truly one of the very best things I have ever read! I especially liked Noah the monkey and Nate the lizard. I also learned a lot about Paul. It is amazing!

—**Brian Brown,** 9, Jupiter Christian School, Jupiter, FLA

Once again, Jenny L. Cote has woven a beautiful story, this time covering the early Church. Her brilliant writing makes her characters leap off the pages and into your hearts. Her plot will enthrall you. *The Wind, The Road & The Way* is another must-read addition to the Epic Order of The Seven.

—**Gabe Fox,** 12, Homeschooled (Ridgecrest Christian Academy), Newton, AL

Jenny L. Cote has done it again! Every time I read the next book and think it cannot get better, I am always wrong! She made all of the biblical characters I've read about in Acts come alive. I laughed, cried, shouted, and stared in shock at how Jenny has written this masterpiece! I am amazed. Jenny, you truly have "beautiful feet"! (Isaiah 52:7)

—**Lily Deal,** 13, Homeschooled, Knoxville, TN

In *The Wind, the Road & the Way*, Mrs. Cote brings to life the beginnings of the Church and missionary work. We read about Christians being persecuted for spreading the truth, and it inspired me to stay strong in the faith even in the midst of hard times. Thank you, Mrs. Cote for your hard work to make our history come to life!

—**Megan Jones,** 15, Metrolina Christian Academy, Waxhaw, NC

Normally when I read these stories, I think, "I've heard all of this before," but Jenny L. Cote makes them exciting to read. She makes sure we understand what is fictional and what is not, and mentions profound things with symbolism that I never noticed before. Reading about how Liz, Max, and others "happen" to always be there when Paul, Peter or anyone needs them reminds me that God will always be there when I need him. Her writing seems to make God more approachable. I'd often see Him as the great and powerful I Am; in this book He is powerful, but has the gentleness of a lamb.

—**Kaitlyn Sien,** 15, San Mateo High School, Foster City, CA

I think Liz and Max learned an important lesson: God can use ANYONE as a part of his plan. This book left me on a cliffhanger, and I am so excited to see how it plays out in the next book! Congratulations, Mrs. Cote!

—**Faith Brunner,** 13, Homeschooled, La Veta, CO

With Jenny L. Cote's books, the past comes alive in vibrant and colorful tales. I began reading these books to my daughter for her benefit, but soon found that I was anticipating each new adventure as much as she did! While reading *The Wind, the Road & the Way*, I felt the presence of the Holy Spirit at work and I began to see the disciples and Paul as real people as I struggled along with them. Jenny writes with incredible passion and emotion, balanced with just the right amount of humor and fantasy.

–**Beth Woods,** Homeschooling mom of five for 18 years, Winston Salem, NC

The Wind, the Road & the Way makes me feel joyous, glad, sad, and lots of different emotions. Jenny L. Cote brings out the joy of life with the Holy Spirit in her best book yet! My favorite character is Al with his innocently profound remarks and goofy humor.

–**Hannah Woods,** 9, Homeschooled, Winston Salem, NC

My favorite part of the book was the missionary travels of Paul, Silas, and Barnabas. They made me feel like I was right there with them, experiencing their successes and struggles. I also enjoyed learning about what it was like to be a missionary back in their times. Their lives encourage me to be a better missionary kid.

–**Sophia Kim,** 10, Missionary Homeschooled, Koutiala, Mali, Africa

What a wonderful way to share the gospel with your family! *The Wind, the Road & the Way* is an easy read for younger readers, while Jenny's blend of the biblical story and her historical knowledge makes the reader feel they are actually in the story, appealing to the older readers. Every time I read the newest edition of this series, it quickly becomes my new favorite, and this was no exception. Looking forward to reading a second time to catch details I missed.

–**Debora Hamerly,** 56, Retired, Olympia WA

This is my favorite book out of the series. My favorite part is when the Holy Spirit came down and into the lives of the disciples and others. I love the adventures of Max and Liz.

–**Jacob McCollum,** 13, Homeschooled, Montgomery, AL

The Wind, the Road & the Way teaches New Testament history and deep biblical insights in a simple and enjoyable way. I love the way Jenny L. Cote masterfully weaves events like the missionary journeys of Paul and the founding of the First Century Christian Church into a truly fantastic story. Each member of the Order of the Seven has a fun, unique personality, which adds a lot of depth to the book. Another magnificent book in an outstanding series!

–**Jeremiah Shultz,** 15, The Master's Study, Whitestown, IN

I enjoyed reading *The Wind, the Road & the Way* because it showed the lives of the apostles in a fun, new way. Max, Liz, and their friends help make the Bible come alive to me. I would recommend this book to everybody.

–**Payton Jones,** 8, Manchester Elementary School, North Manchester, IN

Another amazing adventure! I love the way you are able to transport me back into Bible times. I feel like I am there, experiencing events from the Bible that have been told and taught to me. Al continues to be my favorite character. He always adds humor, like trying to steal the fish from the baskets, even when it is a difficult time in the story. As long as you keep writing books I will keep reading them!

–**Carolina Cuomo,** 11, The King's Academy, West Palm Beach, FL

I love this book, because it is like all of my favorite things in one book. The problem is more people need to know about Jesus and the solution is to tell them! This book is a magical way of telling people about Jesus, and it inspires me to write.

–**William J. Sotelo,** 10, Westview Elementary School, Chattanooga, Tennessee, USA

These books are exciting adventures to re-read over and over again! I like how *The Wind, the Road & the Way* mentions "Berea" ten times because that is where I got my name! Paul and Timothy were men who searched the scriptures daily to be sure what they were told aligned with God's word. My name is a reminder to do the same.

–**Berea Boerrigter,** 10, Homeschooled, Colorado Springs, CO

I love the Epic Order of the Seven. I enjoy getting a new perspective of the Bible from these books. They make me laugh, cry, and have a surprise at the turn of every page.

–**Libbie Ligon,** 13, Bradley Middle School, San Antonio, TX

The Wind, the Road & the Way changed my point of view on Paul and the disciples. I felt their pain, fear and joy and experienced feelings in book has ever produced in me before. It's truly magical!

–**Emma Sebastiani,** 11, Homeschooled, Jasper, GA

I learned new things and saw stories from the Bible from many new and different perspectives. It felt like God was speaking through the words of this book. I really liked how Jenny used Aesop's Tortoise and Hare fable as a parallel to human behavior in our spiritual journeys. The words were really powerful all throughout the book. Five star rating!

–**Ella Dines,** 13, Nunawading Christian College, Melbourne, Victoria, Australia

Wow! *The Wind the Road & the Way* was another incredible look on biblical history through the unique eyes of Max, Liz, and the Epic Order of Seven. It was so amazing to read about Bible stories from such a perspective that makes them so much more alive and real. Once again, another book that takes God's truth, and makes it so much more personal, so much more real.

–**Sacha Gragg,** 16, Loudoun Valley High School, Purcellville, VA.

I absolutely love the way Jenny L. Cote writes. Describing how the disciples feel gives me a way to relate easily. It also gives me new perspectives on the Bible. When I read her books, God becomes more intimate to me.

–**Destiny Twohill,** 15, Berean Christian School, West Palm Beach, FLA

Jenny L. Cote is one of my all-time favorite authors EVER! All of her books are a perfect blend of excitement, adventure, suspense, and thrilling Bible stories. Her newest book, *The Wind, the Road & the Way* is my favorite book so far! I love how all the animals get to spend time with the disciples and Jesus! Keep up the great work, Jenny!

–**Taylor Olson,** 14, Homeschooled, Wasilla, AK

The Wind, the Road & the Way is an awesome book that challenged me to do the things I never thought I could. I realized that not only do you have to trust Him with everything but you also have to listen to His every word.

–**Kaitlyn Clark,** 14, Homeschooled, Coshocton, OH

The Wind, the Road & the Way is awesome! It shows what Christians went through during Paul's time; and how much we should stand for God while we're still young. Jenny's books blend humor, spiritual truths, history and most importantly God in them. This is a great series for anyone; even those who struggle with reading.

–**Shiloh Phinney,** 14, Homeschooled , Norway, IA

Br-r-rilliant account of the birth of the church and the apostles as they spread the gospel of Christ. As always, Jenny refreshes and grows my knowledge of the Scriptures. Her research and dedication amaze with her descriptive detail of the local cultures, scenery, and traditions. *The Wind, the Road & the Way* has been an excellent reminder to me that God's plans are at work behind all things (good or bad) and that He is always in control!

–**Lori Smith,** 2nd grade teacher, Portsmouth Christian School, Portsmouth, VA

This book was definitely one of Jenny's finest—well written, fun and exciting! When I read the Bible, I can't help but imagine that the animals are somehow involved. Now I am more interested in reading about Paul and the Apostles. I cannot wait to see what Jenny has in store for *The Fire, the Revelation & the Fall!*

–**Maggie Pena,** 12, Homeschooled, Kansas City, MO

The Wind, the Road & the Way is a captivating work of fiction that will transport you to AD 54, to Paul's life. Filled with suspense, love, humor, animal conflicts, and more, this book is hard to put down! Can't wait for *The Fire, the Revelation & the Fall!*

–**Samuel Katz,** 14, Homeschooled, Dunwoody GA

This book takes Bible stories you have heard and gives you a different point of view to see them, through lovable characters surrounded by those who are against them. Everyone should read this heart-warming book.

–**Katie Vidinich,** 12, Sutherland Elementary School, Chicago, IL

Jenny L. Cote has been given a gift of bringing the Bible to people of all ages in a fun, clear, endearing way. Once you meet the heartwarming cast of characters you will want to follow them to the end of time—literally! There is always something to learn about the Bible and God in Jenny's books no matter your age. Wonderful to read as a family as well!

–**Mary Vidinich,** Katie's mom, Accountant and Youth Worker, Chicago, IL

The Wind, the Road & the Way is a heartwarming story of adventure and the true story of Paul and the Disciples. I knew Paul went on a journey but did not know the details. Mrs. Cote's books are very good for those just learning about Jesus and God because they leave you wanting to read the Bible and become more spiritual. I can't wait for the sequel!

–**Emerson Hamm,** 10, Homeschooled, Blue Ridge, GA

A beautiful and inspiring story that leads right back to the gospel.

–**Anna McClure,** 14, Homeschooled, Northam, Western Australia

Delightful, playful, entertaining, educational, enlightening—all of these words describe this book well. It covers biblical history during the time of Acts and shows how God uses even persecution to spread the news of His salvation around the world. It shows the importance of understanding and memorizing Scripture when sharing the Gospel. And it shows the importance of waiting on God's timing. Overall, this story does a great job teaching kids how to follow God when bad things happen in a fun, enjoyable way.

–**Jamie Kimmons,** Homeschool Instructor, Glad Tidings Bible Camp, Bloomfield, NE

The Wind, the Road & the Way brings Paul to life! Jenny L. Cote excels at articulating the life of Paul. I felt like I was introduced to an old friend. This book, like all of hers challenges me. It makes me ask the question, "What am I doing to spread the Good News about Jesus?"

–**Jenny Keeton,** Lead Teacher at Mount Pisgah Christian School, Johns Creek, GA

I have really enjoyed how Jenny brought Paul to life, showing him dealing with hard situations and yet showing us how to stay strong and obedient to the Lord. While the author may intend these books for a younger audience, they are enjoyable for all ages, and a great way for parents to start discussions of biblical truths with their children.

–**Lyndy Britt,** 49, Johns Creek, GA

Amazing, I couldn't put it down! I learned a lot of things I didn't know. My favorite character is Al. *The Wind the Road & the Way* is the best book in the Order of the Seven so far. Jenny L. Cote is a great Author!

–**Jonah Huckel,** 8, Homeschooled, Adelaide, Australia

Awesome book! My favorite characters are Max, Noah, and Nate. I learned quite a few things like the Olympic Games are split into 4 sections that make up the Olympiad. It's a good book, but I would mostly recommend it to someone who has read the other four books. Altogether it's the greatest book in the series. As always I cannot wait for the next book.

–**Benjamin Huckel,** 11, Homeschooled, Adelaide, South Australia

I am floored by the research, insight, and inspiration that has gone into this novel. The style of writing and attention to detail put me right in the middle of the action of the first believers. This book is so rich and full of potential for our family's use as God-honoring reading material for our children, a springboard for family devotions. Our children are blessed to have these books on their shelves. As parents we are delighted to read along and patiently (ahem!) share the books with them! Thank you so much, Jenny L. Cote, for your immense and inspired work to bring this to us. Please. Do. Not. Stop!

–**Sal Huckel,** Homeschooling parent, Adelaide, South Australia

EPIC ORDER OF THE SEVEN

The WIND the ROAD & the WAY

JENNY L. COTE

LIVING
INK
BOOKS
Writing Worth Reading™

Epic Order of the Seven®
The Wind, The Road, and the Way

Copyright © 2014 by Jenny L. Cote

Published by Living Ink Books, an imprint of AMG Publishers, Chattanooga, Tennessee
(www.LivingInkBooks.com).

Print Edition   ISBN 13: 978-0-89957-793-7
ePUB Edition   ISBN 13: 978-1-61715-358-7
Mobi Edition   ISBN 13: 978-1-61715-359-4
ePDF Edition   ISBN 13: 978-1-61715-360-0

First AMG Printing—January 2014

EPIC ORDER OF THE SEVEN is a trademark of Jenny L. Cote.

Cover and internal illustrations by Rob Moffitt, Chicago, Illinois.
Interior design by KLOPublishing.com and theDESKonline.com.
Editing and proofreading by Rich Cairnes and Rick Steele

Printed in Canada

20 21 22 23 24 - M - 10 9 8 7 6

To Noah and Nate

You finished your race earlier than we expected
and certainly earlier than we wanted. But we know that we'll
see you again, because death is indeed swallowed up in victory.
In the meantime, may we live like you when it comes to loving,
serving, and following Jesus with reckless abandon.
May we always remember to live like that.

Nate Lynam 2001–2012 | Noah Winstead 2002–2012

From the Families of Noah and Nate

As Noah's father, I am truly grateful to see how God continues to use these two boys to touch many lives by living on through these characters. God worked through Jenny's writing to make their personalities spot on.

–Todd Winstead (Noah's dad)

To give a small comment in a book with such great meaning for us is almost impossible. We have seen these characters come alive in such a way that only an author filled with the Holy Spirit could achieve. You will be blessed and encouraged. The characters of Nate and Noah were an amazing addition to the already amazing cast of characters. We are eternally grateful.

–Travis and Kelly Lynam (Nate's parents)

This book is very adventurous and true to Scripture. I love how Noah's and Nate's characters are exactly like them.

–Haleigh Raye Winstead (Noah's sister)

I will never again read about Paul's conversion without the visual that Jenny painted through her writing and without remembering the encouraging words that the tiny mouse, Nigel, offered Paul before he regained his sight: *"You see, old boy, once you get past this painful first step of dealing with your past, it will be time to get on with your future . . . You will have much to share."* The Lord's anointing was upon Jenny as she developed the story line to include Noah the capuchin monkey, and Nate, the plumed basilisk lizard. I am still amazed at how God directed her to weave their distinct personalities into *The Wind, the Road & the Way* and am humbled by His great love for us as demonstrated by this great gift.

— Denise Voccola (Nate's Grandmother)

Jenny brought Noah and Nate to life in my mind. She captured them. It was as if Todd was telling me a story about what the boys had done. I laughed and cried all at the same time! On one of the last visits I had with Noah, I pulled into the driveway with my sunroof open. I heard Noah say "Hi Aunt Dee." He had climbed up in a tree and was looking at me from up above through my sunroof. Our little monkey! I still look for him...

–-Dee Winstead (Noah's aunt)

This book contains fact, fiction, fantasy, allegory, and truth.
For the entire true story,
read Acts and the rest of the New Testament.

. . . he marked out their appointed times in history . . .
Acts 17:26 (TNIV)

CONTENTS

PART THREE: TO THE ENDS OF THE EARTH

Acknowledgments

My Trinitarian Boss

Thank you, God, Jesus, and Holy Spirit for saving my life in November 2012. Obviously you're not finished with me. Thank you for moving my pen to write this book. This little dictation girl prays she heard you accurately and that you are pleased with the end result. Holy Spirit, I hope I captured your debut in riveting form. I love and appreciate your daily presence as I write. Sorry I was a little slow to get your message that you wanted to split this work into two books. But thanks for the just-in-time text from Claire. Feel free to text me anytime!

Family

Casey and Alex, thank you for your love and for support while I wear my other hats of author, speaker, and researcher, in addition to wife and mom. Dad and Mom, I'm so grateful to you for being there for every phone call and reading. Max and Liz, much love, me wee ones.

The Wise Guys

If you marvel at the deep spiritual insights in my books, please know it certainly isn't all me! Believe me, I *wish* I was that wise! I am deeply indebted to the amazing Bible commentators and authors whose biographies give me invaluable insight and understanding to bring my characters alive. I weave those insights into the dialogue of my characters and the historical background of my stories. I always list my resources in the bibliographies of my books, so if you wish to study in greater detail the characters in my books, please seek out these wonderful works. My main commentary heroes for this book are Dr. Chuck Swindoll, William Barclay, F. F. Bruce, F. B. Meyer, John Stott, and John Pollock. And thank you to my awesome Dad, Dr. Paul Mims, for preaching through Acts as I was writing through Acts. Your sermons were timely and the best around, as usual. (See the link to his sermons in the Bibliography.)

Supporting Friends

Do you believe God sends texts? I do now. After days of being stuck on determining a strong ending, which kept my pen either still or backspacing over everything I wrote, I got a text from Claire Roberts Foltz. This was after I had felt that I should call her to help me talk through my plot line. I hadn't talked with her in a while, but for each and every book I've written, this girl has given me a crucial idea or a pivotal nudge. I also had this impression to check my mailbox, but I didn't. So while I was sitting there NOT checking my mail or calling her (my bad), wallowing in writer's block, she texted ME this message: "LORD, please give her clarity of thought, bright ideas, and let her be a conduit for YOUR words." We were on the phone within minutes and after an hour of brainstorming I had the ending I had been searching for. Claire told me she had just returned from Europe and was exhausted and lying down to take a nap when the Lord told her not just to text me, but to text me those specific words! Thank you, God, for your text and your faithfulness to answer my prayer to finish your book well. And thank you, Claire—my dear friend and fellow author—for your obedience to the Lord! You helped me just when I needed it, and this will be a phenomenal book because of you. Oh, and when I finally checked my mail that night, there was a postcard from Claire sent from Scotland.

My gratitude to friend Tom Luckett who we tragically lost during the editing of this book. He gave me Pollock's incredible book on Paul which became the primary text in shaping my concept of Paul's character. I may not have found that vital resource if Tom hadn't passed it along. I grieve that you aren't here to see your name printed in my book, but I know you've already seen your name in a far greater text: the Lamb's Book of Life. Tell Paul hello, and keep heaven chuckling, my friend.

Ann McColl, my right (and sometimes left) arm! Thank you for helping me tell the world about the Epic Order of the Seven, and getting kids excited about writing by scheduling all my events. You are a God-sent friend.

Prayer warriors—you know who you are. Thank you for praying me through the writing of this book, and the tough physical year I've had. You pulled me across the finish line.

Critique Team

These awesome people keep me going with feedback and encouragement as I write. Love and appreciation to Paul and Janice Mims, Claire Roberts Foltz, Lisa Hockman, Lori Marett, Faith McColl, and Gabe Fox.

Publishing Team

An EPIC thank you to the people who take what comes out of my pen and turn it into something so beautiful to hold and read! Illustrator Rob Moffitt, Editor Rich Cairnes, Interior Designer Katherine Lloyd, Literary Agent Paul Shepherd, and the AMG Publishing Team: Dale Anderson, Rick Steele, Trevor Overcash, Warren Baker, Mike Oldham, Gin Chasteen, Amanda Donnahoe, Donna Coker, and the support staff.

Readers

To say I am overwhelmed by the messages you send me is an understatement. Thank you for your prayers, encouraging notes, letters, pictures, cards, e-mails, and Facebook posts! I frequently have tears with a big smile as I read your words. I'm honored that you love the books and that they inspire you to pursue God and dig into the Bible to discover the true stories behind mine (and to make sure I get things right.) Please let me know how you like this book at jenny@epicorderoftheseven.com. I'll keep writing as long as you keep reading! Epic love to you!

Main Character Profiles

ORDER OF THE SEVEN

Max: a Scottish Terrier from (where else?) Scotland. Full name is Maximillian Braveheart the Bruce. Short, black, with a large head, always ready to take on the bad guys. Faithful leader of the team who started with their first mission on Noah's Ark in *The Ark, the Reed, and the Fire Cloud.* Loves to mess with Al, "encouraging" him to work on his bravery. Immortal.

Liz: a petite, French, black cat from Normandy. Full name is Lizette Brilliante Aloysius. Brilliant, refined, and strategic leader of the team, beginning with Noah's Ark. Loves the study of history, science, the written word, culture, and languages. Prides herself on knowing the meanings of names, and simply adores gardens. Immortal.

Al: a well-fed, Irish, orange cat. Full name is Albert Aloysius, also called "Big Al" by his close friends. Hopelessly in love with his mate, Liz, since Noah's Ark. Simple-minded, but often holds the key to gaining access to impossible places, and figuring out things everyone else misses, including deep spiritual truths. Lives to eat and sleep. Afraid of everything. Immortal.

Kate: a white West Highland Terrier, also from Scotland. The love of Max's life ever since they 'wed' on the way to the Ark. Has a sweetness that disarms everyone she meets. Is also a fiery lass, unafraid to speak her mind. Always sees the good in others, and sticks up for the underdog. Immortal.

Nigel: a jolly, British, white mouse with impeccable manners and speech. Wears spectacles and is on the same intellectual level as Liz, joining her in the thrill of discovery. An expert Egyptologist who joined the team on their mission to Egypt with Joseph in *The Dreamer, the Schemer, and the Robe.* Taught Liz all about Egypt, giving her the affectionate term "my pet"—the mouse was the teacher and the cat was his pet. Able to travel quickly and easily via carrier pigeon. Does spying to help carry out missions. Immortal.

Gillamon: a wise, kind mountain goat from Switzerland. Moved to Scotland, where he raised Max (an orphan) and served as his mentor. Died before the Flood, but serves as a spiritual being who delivers mission assignments from the Maker to the team. Can take any shape or form, and shows up when least expected.

Clarie: a sweet little lamb from Judea. Shepherds gave her to Mary and Joseph as a gift for Baby Jesus in *The Prophet, the Shepherd, and the Star.* Enabled the family to escape to Egypt without harm and joined Gillamon as a spiritual being member of the team. Serves as all-knowing guide in the IAMISPHERE when the team goes back in time to observe historical events. Can take any shape or form.

Open your ears to what I am saying,
for I will speak to you in a parable.

I will teach you hidden lessons from our past—
stories we have heard and known,

Stories our ancestors handed down to us.

We will not hide these truths from our children;
we will tell the next generation about the glorious deeds
of the Lord, *about his power and his mighty wonders.*

—Psalm 78:2–4 (nlt)

PROLOGUE

AND THEN THERE WAS ONE

AD 95

No more for you, old man!" The Roman soldier backhanded the prisoner on the cheek, causing the elderly man to crumple and fall back onto the ship's deck with a muffled groan. The wooden cup fell out of the prisoner's hand and tumbled over to rest at the angry soldier's feet. The Roman picked up the cup and gripped it tightly as he leaned over the prisoner with a snarl on his face. "You and your kind have been nothing but trouble for Rome," he growled. A rogue wave suddenly splashed over the side of the ship, soaking the prisoner and this hardened soldier. The Roman grabbed the railing to steady himself, wiping the sea spray off his face. He looked out to sea and glimpsed the island looming larger on the horizon. A cruel grin grew on the soldier's face as he looked down at the shivering, wet prisoner. "It's your misfortune you didn't die quickly in Rome. A slow death from hunger and thirst will teach you Christians to defy the emperor." He kicked the old man in the gut before he stormed away, leaving the prisoner curled up in a ball, gripping his stomach in pain.

Prochorus tightened his manacled fists in anger but waited until the Roman had walked down the deck before he rushed to the old man's side. "John! Are you all right?!" This fellow prisoner, not much younger than John, helped his friend sit up with his back resting beneath the railing. Their iron shackles clanked together as they moved about.

John winced but put his hand on Prochorus's shoulder. "I'm all right. Just let me catch my breath." He leaned his head back and closed his eyes. The sound of the sea lapping against the hull of the ship had a comforting rhythm to it. He breathed in the salt air and wiped back the stringy grey hair stuck to his face. Prochorus frowned and lowered his head at their hopeless situation.

"If you find the godless world is hating you, remember it got its start hating me. If you lived on the world's terms, the world would love you as one of its own. But since I picked you to live on God's terms and no longer on the world's terms, the world is going to hate you," John muttered softly. "*When* that happens, remember this: Servants don't get better treatment than their masters. If they beat on me, they will certainly beat on you."

Prochorus raised his gaze and looked at John. "Did he . . . did our Lord say that?"

John nodded and a sad smile appeared at the corners of his mouth. "The night he was arrested." John slowly rubbed his aching stomach and continued quoting Jesus' words from memory. "I've told you these things to prepare you for rough times ahead. They are going to throw you out of the synagogues. There will even come a time when anyone who kills you will think he's doing God a favor. They will do these things because they never really understood the Father. I've told you these things so that when the time comes and they start in on you, you'll be well-warned and ready for them."

A rush of wind blew across the two old men. "How I wish you had written all these things down." Prochorus rubbed his aching upper arms and pulled his knees into his chest. "He wanted to prepare us for times like this, didn't he? Do you think the Roman is right? Will we die of hunger and thirst?"

John reached his wrinkled hand up to the railing and slowly lifted himself to stand. His gaze drifted back toward his beloved Ephesus, some twenty-four miles away and getting smaller in the distance. His past was slipping away. He turned to see the rocky island getting closer with each passing moment. This was his future. The sea would separate him from all that he loved.

John's body was old but his mind was as sharp and on fire for truth as it was on that last night with the Master. He took in a deep breath, closed his eyes, and tried to remember the young faces of the eleven others there that night: Peter, James, Andrew, Matthew, Nathaniel, Philip, James the Less, Thaddeus, Thomas, Simon . . . John frowned as the face of Judas entered his mind. He opened his eyes to clear away the betrayer's image. "The others who were with me that night have all died, some in horrible ways." John frowned, shaking his head in grief. He peered into the blue sea below.

Prochorus joined John at the railing. A massive, shadowy figure glided past the ship deep under the turquoise water and John stared at the mysterious image. It seemed too big to be a shark. He looked back up at the island and could now see men standing on a pier, waiting for them. "I'm the last one left of the original twelve. It matters not how, where, or when I die. I'll join the others when my work on Earth is complete," John said with a broken voice.

"There's a reason you didn't die in Rome," Prochorus affirmed.

The Roman soldiers began shouting at the more heavily guarded prisoners near the front of the ship, getting everyone to stand as they approached the craggy shoreline. It was time for them to disembark. A scuffle began and the soldiers quickly brought the prisoners under control with whips and clubs. The sound of screams and clanking chains echoed off the cliffs of this desolate place.

This volcanic island of exile was reserved for Rome's worst enemies. Murderers, thieves, and other common criminals labeled by Rome as the scum of the earth were doomed to live out their remaining days with hard labor. Political prisoners who had defied or angered the emperor faced a different fate. John and Prochorus fell into this second group. They were doomed to total abandonment, left to find their own food, water, and shelter. They were given no clothing or medical care. All they had was the clothes on their backs. Regardless of what kind of prisoner you were, escape was impossible, as had been proved time and again by prisoners who risked climbing down the sharp rocks only to be slammed back into them by the strong currents of the angry sea.

"I don't feel much like a Son of Thunder anymore," John lamented, watching the angry Roman soldier making his way back to where they stood, a bloodied whip in his hand. The old man clung to Jesus' words as he was roughly pushed along to the plank that led down to the dock. *"I have told you these things, so that in me you may have peace. In this world you will have trouble. But take heart! I have overcome the world."*

The island prison guards immediately began barking orders at

xxvii

the prisoners, separating them into two groups there on the gravelly shoreline. The second group consisted of only John and Prochorus. A grimy, pot-bellied guard with several missing teeth walked along the row of twenty or so hardened criminals, resting a club on his shoulder as he inspected the prisoners. "Listen well, you scum. You now belong to me," he taunted with a sinister smile, getting eye-to-eye with the toughest-looking prisoner of the lot. "First, you will be scourged. Then you will be worked to the bone every day until I tell you to stop. Soon you will be begging the gods for death." The tough prisoner seemed to melt under the gaze of this guard and hung his head to look at the iron fetters around his feet. The grimy guard was pleased at the prisoner's submissive, defeated response.

A group of prison guards surrounded the terrified criminals and led them down a stony path toward their cruel fate. John and Prochorus stood quietly by, wondering what they were supposed to do.

The Roman guard from the ship came over and jingled a ring of keys in the faces of the two elderly men. "Consider yourselves lucky, Christians." He proceeded to roughly unlock the fetters from their wrists, tossing the chains on the ground to be collected by another soldier.

John and Prochorus rubbed their sore wrists, and looked up to the barren hillside dotted with caves. The Roman turned and walked back to the ship. Prochorus stepped forward. "Excuse me, sir, but where are we to live? Where can we find food and water?"

The Roman turned around and with a mocking tone replied, "Why don't you ask that invisible God of yours? He's all you've got, now. Isn't there a tale about how he miraculously made countless loaves of bread and fish just appear out of nowhere?"

The other soldiers laughed and together they prepared the ship for departure, leaving the two old men standing on the beach. They were exiled, alone and left to fend for themselves.

As the ship shoved off into deeper water, the Roman soldier laughed and called back to the old men, "Welcome to Patmos!"

PART ONE

In Jerusalem

ACTS TO COME

JERUSALEM, AD 31

"Shhhh! Hurry!" Clarie the lamb urged as the animals made their way into the garden courtyard. "Find a hiding spot. He's coming!"

The animals each found a place to hide. The big Irish cat lifted his head, startled by what he saw. "What's wrong with him?" Al asked.

His mate, Liz, gasped and put a paw to her mouth. "Oh, no! Achilles has been wounded!"

The magnificent grey stallion lay on his side, breathing heavily. His body shuddered and he struggled to lift up his front leg. Achilles was in pain.

Armandus walked into the courtyard with a poultice and knelt down by his beloved horse. "Here you go, my friend. Let's see if this brings you any comfort."

"His leg," Liz observed sadly. "It is swollen due to an injury. *C'est tragique!* Armandus may have to put Achilles down."

Armandus winced as Achilles grunted from the pain. He sat down next to his horse on the richly tiled terrace floor of his parents' grand home in Jerusalem. He looked around at what was once a happy place for him. When his parents moved back to Rome, they agreed to allow Armandus to keep the property for his use, knowing he would be stationed in this region for an indefinite period of time. It was eerily quiet as he looked around the neglected garden, which had been his mother's pride and joy. It was her place of solace. There in the middle of the garden was the carved statue of Libertas, bearing the likeness of his mother's face, with a carved cat figure at the base. Armandus laughed sadly. "If the Jewish leaders knew that this idol was within the walls of Jerusalem, they would be banging down the doors, demanding its removal," he said to Achilles. "But I won't let them in. I won't let anyone in. No one is going to take you from me."

When Pilate assigned Centurion Armandus Antonius back to Herod Antipas, he sent word that Armandus had performed extraordinarily well in "that Jesus matter." As a reward, Herod gave Armandus two days' leave. When Armandus gratefully returned to the Antonia Fortress, the Roman army's headquarters, he was horrified to see that Achilles had suffered this leg injury when the earthquake hit on Friday. All the horses rose up in alarm that day, and Achilles's leg fell into a crack, leaving him wounded. Armandus immediately brought the lame horse here, where he could privately care for him. But it appeared there was nothing he could do.

Tears filled Armandus's eyes as he pulled back the poultice. It was hopeless. His horse was wounded beyond hope. He shook his head. Too much grief. Too much death. Too much loss. "I don't think I can take losing you, too."

Suddenly he heard someone banging at his door and immediately wiped his eyes and got to his feet, running to see who it was. As he opened the window latch, there stood his two legionnaires, Velius and Ulixes. Their eyes were wild with fear.

"Sir!" Velius exclaimed as Armandus opened the door. "We've just come from guard duty and have some disturbing news to report."

"What has happened?" Armandus demanded with his hands on his hips.

"Pilate appointed us to guard the tomb of that Jesus of Nazareth, along with one of the Jews' temple guards," Ulixes explained. "This morning at the tomb . . ." He stopped and looked at Velius.

"Well, get on with it!" Armandus shouted.

4

"Sir, there was an earthquake, and we saw a man who looked as bright as lightning suddenly appear," Velius continued.

"He rolled away the stone in front of the tomb, and sat on it," Ulixes jumped in. "Sir, the body just vanished. Jesus is gone."

"Did someone take the body?" Armandus asked, wide-eyed at this incredible report.

The two soldiers looked at one another. "No, his graveclothes were there neatly in place, like he just disappeared out of them," Velius explained. "And that bright man who rolled away the stone—he wasn't human. He looked like a god. And he had the strength of a god."

"We went with the temple guard to first report to the Jewish leaders," Ulixes added. "They gave us a huge sum of money and told us to report that we had fallen asleep and that Jesus' disciples came and stole the body."

"They vowed to protect us should this word get back to Pilate," Velius further explained.

"But that story doesn't even make sense," Armandus pointed out with a frown. "If you were asleep, how would you know that Jesus' disciples had stolen the body? And for a Roman soldier to fall asleep on duty is punishable by death!"

"Sir, we know!" Ulixes pleaded. "We know what happened, but we took the money and agreed to spread the story as the Jewish leaders instructed us. We didn't know what else to do."

"Go back to the Antonia Fortress and wait for me there," Armandus instructed them. "And speak of this to no one."

"Yes, Sir!" the two soldiers exclaimed, respectfully saluting their commanding officer before turning to leave.

Armandus returned their salute, shut the door, and rubbed his face with his hands. His mind was reeling with this news. Jesus had claimed he would rise from the dead. Could it be true? The centurion shook his head. Rising from the dead was impossible. There must be some other explanation. As he walked back to where Achilles lay, he stopped and stared at the statue of Libertas. She represented freedom. Armandus looked at her longingly, wishing he could be free. He felt imprisoned by guilt, pain, sorrow, and the impossible burdens placed before him. If

5

only this goddess were real. But now, after Jesus, Armandus doubted all of Rome's gods and theology. He had come to feel there was only one true God. But he had killed God's Son. Surely the pit of Hades was all that awaited him now.

Achilles snorted in pain, and Armandus ran over to him. The horse was sweating and clearly in agony. It was time to get back to his men and his duty, but Achilles was not physically able to return with him. He knew what he must do. Armandus pulled his sword from its sheath as his eyes filled with tears at the horrible task before him. He fell over his horse to embrace him one last time, weeping and softly whispering, "I'm sorry, my friend. I'm so sorry."

"Why are you crying?" a voice from behind him asked.

Armandus quickly turned around with his sword raised, startled at the presence of an invader in his home. There stood Jesus. Armandus's eyes filled with fear, and his throat tightened so much he couldn't say a word.

6

Jesus simply smiled. "Put away your sword." He proceeded to kneel down next to Achilles and placed his hand on the horse's leg.

Armandus watched in disbelief as he saw Jesus' pierced hands now tenderly touching Achilles. *How is this possible?!* he wondered.

Suddenly Achilles whinnied and rose up to stand tall on his feet, strong and completely healed. He stomped his foot and vigorously nodded his head, as if to say, "Thank you!"

Armandus dropped to his knees and bowed low before Jesus, swimming in a sea of emotions. "Thank you, my Lord! Thank you for healing Achilles! Oh, please forgive me! Forgive me for all I've done."

"I already have, remember?" Jesus put his hands on Armandus's shoulders. Armandus turned his gaze to look upon this man who was indeed the resurrected Son of God. Jesus gripped him by the hand and helped him to his feet. Armandus immediately embraced Jesus, overcome with gratitude. For the first time, he was experiencing the grace and forgiveness of the one true God, and it was unlike anything he had ever known. "I've got you," Jesus smiled and said.

Armandus wept for joy and leaned back. "Yes, you do, my King. Please, tell me how I can be one of your disciples."

"When you return to Capernaum, find Peter," Jesus replied. "He'll show you how."

"I will, but where are you going? You're alive now! Won't you stay here and establish your kingdom?" Armandus asked. "No one can doubt any longer that you are the Son of God! You have the power to come back from the dead."

"My kingdom is not an earthly kingdom, but will be composed of men just like you," Jesus said. "I will be here for a short while after I meet with my disciples and others, including some now on the road to Emmaus. Then I will return to my Father in heaven."

"I don't understand," Armandus said.

"You will, with time," Jesus replied. He looked around the court-yard and reminisced, smiling. "Our parents were friends. You and I met here as children."

"Yes, I know," Armandus replied sadly. "The day you died, I finally understood who you were."

"Armandus, tell your father. Tell him about me and all that has happened," Jesus urged. "He has grieved these many years over what he did to the children of Bethlehem that horrible night so long ago. Tell him the child he saved has now saved the world."

Armandus bowed his head and nodded. "I will, my Lord. I will tell him."

When he looked up, Jesus was gone. Armandus looked around the courtyard and raised his hands toward the heavens. "Thank you, my King!" He ran over and embraced Achilles. "Oh, Achilles, you are well! I don't have to lose you. I will ride you out of here!" Jesus had given Armandus everything: forgiveness, healing, hope, a future, and a mes-sage. Armandus would not let Jesus down.

"Stay here, Achilles. Let me get my things and together we'll ride to the Fortress!" Armandus exulted.

The animals stayed put in their hiding places, but Liz thought she saw something strange out of the corner of her eye. Her tail started twitching back and forth, as was her habit when something had her full attention.

The white Westie named Kate noticed. "Wha's troublin' ye, Liz?"

7

Liz shook her head, rubbed her eyes, and again stared intently at the Libertas statue. "I could have sworn . . ."

Armandus rushed back into the courtyard and lifted the saddle up onto Achilles. "I never thought I'd ever be able to put this on you again." He secured the saddle and walked Achilles out of the courtyard, smiling and shaking his head in wonder and awe. Armandus climbed up in the saddle once they were outside. "Long live the King! *Magna est veritas et praevalebit!*" Armandus exclaimed as he squeezed Achilles with his heels and the horse galloped off.

"Wha' did the lad say when he were r-r-ridin' off then?" Max asked.

"Great is the truth and it will prevail," Nigel translated in his punctuated British accent, preening his whiskers. "Splendid sentiment, I must say!"

"Oh, this were wonderful ta see! Jesus healed Achilles an' gave hope ta Armandus," Kate noted happily.

"Aye, an' that lad will give hope ta his father," Max added. "There's nothin' as powerful as gr-r-race ta give ta those who feel they be unforgivable."

Liz said nothing but jumped down from the garden wall and cautiously walked over to the Libertas statue, slinking up to it as slowly as a jungle panther toward its prey.

The other animals stopped talking and watched the petite black cat.

"What's me lass doin'?" Al whispered.

"She sees somethin'," Max answered, his spine stiffening as he, too, felt something strange in the air. "I best join her if tr-r-rouble be br-r-rewin'." The Scottish terrier quietly trotted over to join Liz.

Al gulped, his paws up to his mouth, cowering behind Kate. "Trouble?"

Liz suddenly stopped. Her fur stood on end as she gasped and pointed. "Max, did you see that?"

Max furrowed his brow and looked in the direction Liz pointed. "I didn't see anythin' but I *feel* somethin'. Wha' did ye see, lass?"

"The statue! Libertas! It . . . it moved!" Liz managed to stutter, clearly shaken.

The Scottie's eyes widened before they narrowed and he addressed the statue. "All r-r-right! I know ye're in ther-r-re! Whoever ye be, ye best make yer presence known!"

The animals heard a crackling sound and suddenly the statue stretched out its arms and let out a sigh of relief. Liz jumped behind Max. Kate jumped behind Clarie. Nigel wiped clear his spectacles. Al fainted.

"Oh, how good it feels to stretch out my arms," the statue said, smiling and bending down to the animals. "Happy Resurrection morning, everyone!"

Max exhaled loudly and shook his head in relief. "Gillamon! Ye aboot scar-r-red us out of our fur, ye did. Wha' in the name of Pete are ye doin' in the statue?"

Gillamon chuckled and straightened up, raising his marble arms to look them over for good form. "I must say, that sculptor did a beautiful job with this statue."

9

"Gillamon!" Max grumbled, wanting an answer.

"Patience, young friend. I wanted to try out a new form." Gillamon, a mountain goat in real life, was now a spiritual being and head of the Order of the Seven team. He could take any shape or form. "I've always found it fascinating how statues seem so lifelike. Plus, it will be an easy way to communicate with you in the years to come."

Liz shook her head good-humoredly. "You never cease to amaze us, the way you show up, no? Where will we be going to see such statues?"

"Greece. Rome. Turkey. Deep into Gentile territory," Gillamon relayed. "It's time for the next phase of your mission."

"Fantastic! I find the pagans utterly fascinating!" Nigel said, straightening his tiny gold spectacles atop his tiny mouse nose. "So much culture, art, literature, and the like. But sadly also dastardly behavior, I'm afraid."

Kate hurried up to the group. "Gillamon, will we get ta see Jesus again? We've been just missin' him all mornin' as he's appeared ta people."

The statue smiled warmly. "Yes, little Kate. Jesus will be here on Earth forty more days, and you will most certainly get to see him before he departs for heaven. His appearances will be elusive but frequent. Rest assured he wants to see all of you alone."

Max smiled excitedly. "That's gr-r-rand news! Wha' are we ta do next?"

"You will be privileged to watch the apostles as they boldly carry to the rest of the world the good news of what Jesus has done," Gillamon explained, lifting his arm, "to the north, the south, the east, and the west. Then it will be up to you to make sure their story is told for future generations."

"Well, right now the chaps are frozen and hiding in fear," Nigel noted, marveling at the moving statue. "That will be quite the act for them to pull off."

"Indeed, Nigel," Gillamon agreed. "But you will marvel at watching the transformation of Jesus' disciples. They will change just as I've made this frozen Libertas statue change. You will see many unexpected acts of the apostles. Perhaps the greatest act will be one new apostle turning from a murderous tyrant into the model of what a Christ-follower should be."

Max furrowed his brow. "A *mur-r-rderer?* Who is he, Gillamon?"

"You will know in time," Gillamon assured him. "Just as a sculptor chips away stone to bring a desired image out of the cold, hard marble, so too will the Maker sculpt this cold, hard soul."

"Gillamon, how are we to tell their story for future generations?" Liz posed. "With the written word, I presume?"

"Precisely, Liz!" the statue nodded. "You and Nigel will once again influence some of history's most important writings to inspire generations of believers to come. It's time to bring a New Testament into being, from the writings of the apostles."

Liz's eyes brightened. *"C'est bon!* Another writing assignment!"

"Right! I say, I remember you telling us Matthew would wield his pen for such a purpose," Nigel remembered, tapping his fingers on his chin. "And you told us another one of the twelve would also write down Jesus' story. Might we know which one?"

"Of course you might, Nigel," Gillamon teased. "When the time is right."

10

"It's all aboot the timin', all the time," Kate reminded them.

"Max, you and Kate will need to protect the apostles and their writings as this movement gets off the ground," Gillamon instructed. A grim look appeared on the statue's face. "Very dark days lie ahead. A time will come when protection will be beyond your control. The Enemy will take many forms and seek to eliminate anyone who follows Christ."

"Aye, we'll be r-r-ready," Max agreed with a look of determination shared with Kate.

Clarie nudged Al, who regained consciousness and sat up. He looked over at the statue with terror in his eyes.

"Nice of you to join us, Al," Gillamon smirked.

Al held up a paw and whispered to Clarie, "That statue be talkin' to me, Lass!"

Clarie rolled her eyes and nudged the scaredy cat. "It's *Gillamon*, Al. Go on over and see him."

The expression of fear on Al's face melted as he stood up and cleared his throat. "O' course it is!" The plump cat trotted over and looked up at the statue. "Top o' the mornin' to ye, Gillamon. Ye be lookin' quite, uh . . . statue-y."

The statue chuckled. "Indeed. I recall some wise words you once said about this statue in this very garden. Do you remember what they were?"

Al massaged his head for a moment but threw up his paws. "Beats me, lad. I can't remember all the profound things that come out o' me mouth."

"Liz was worried about posing as the cat for the sculpting of this statue since it was for the image of a Roman goddess," Gillamon reminded him. "You wisely said that the Maker can bring good out of anything, even an image that's bad."

Al sat there with a goofy grin on his face, shrugging his shoulders. "Sounds like somethin' I'd say."

"And so it is, with images *and* men." Slowly the statue of Libertas crackled and resumed its original form. "The Maker can take any-thing—or anyone—and bring good out of them, even when it looks as if they are set in stone. Watch the Divine Sculptor and his Acts to come."

The Libertas statue stood there in the garden, quiet and motionless once again. Gillamon was gone.

"We best split up," Clarie suggested, wagging her fleecy tail. "Jesus will be quite busy today!" The lamb was also a spiritual member of the Order of the Seven team. Like Gillamon, she could take any shape or form, and she guided the animals on their missions.

"Where are we going, *mon amie?*" Liz asked excitedly.

"Max and Kate, you two get back to the Garden tomb. You've seen Mary and the women with the angels, but you won't want to miss the next encounter there," Clarie instructed. "Liz and Al, you head to the Upper Room, where we'll all meet tonight. The disciples are gathering there, and the women are on their way there now."

"And where might I go, my dear?" Nigel asked, his paws clasped behind his back.

"To observe some clueless humans," Clarie teased, "on the road to Emmaus."

12

AND PETER

eter slowly ascended the stairs leading to the Upper Room, where the disciples had shared one last meal with Jesus. The fisherman's feet felt heavy with every step, but nothing matched the heaviness of despair in his heart and the heaviness of confusion in his mind. He and John had just been to the Garden tomb, following the teary report by Mary Magdalene that someone had removed Jesus' body. She didn't know where they had taken him. Peter and John immediately ran to see the tomb for themselves and, indeed, Jesus wasn't there.

As John peeled off to go get Jesus' mother, Mary, to join the other disciples in the Upper Room, he enthusiastically went on and on muttering something about Jesus rising from the dead. Peter heard John's voice, but not his words. Peter was consumed with his own inner turmoil, and was extremely sleep-deprived from the last few days. He didn't remember sleeping at all, although he felt as if he were in a living nightmare. He hadn't eaten either. Everything was foggy. Nothing made sense. He couldn't concentrate on anything but what a failure he was.

I failed three times to keep watch with the Master in Gethsemane as he repeatedly asked. He asked me to pray. The weight of the world was on Jesus' shoulders and all he asked me to do was to pray for him. But what did I do? I slept! Peter accused himself repeatedly, shaking his head. When he did take action to protect Jesus with a sword, Jesus told him to stop and had to take measures to fix the tense situation Peter had caused. But then the worst failure came. Three times he publicly denied knowing Jesus. And Jesus had locked eyes with him the third time, driving home the fact that his prediction of Peter's denials had come true.

For three days Peter had done nothing but relive these failures over and over and over again in his mind. He was sick to his stomach and wanted to die from the grief of it all. He felt as if Jesus' missing body was almost further proof of his failure, as the miserable disciple would even be kept from having a physical place to grieve his Master's death.

Liz and Al watched from behind the water pots as Peter entered the Upper Room. All the other disciples except John were already there, talking in hushed voices lest the Jewish leaders find out their location and come after them as well. Peter half-wished they would come and take him away. Death would be welcome at this point. He stood a moment and stared at the spot at the table where Jesus had sat that last night and predicted his denials. Peter blinked back the tears and meekly went over to sit alone on the floor, his head in his hands, sobbing quietly.

"*Quel dommage!*" Liz said softly, also blinking back tears. "Peter is blind with grief. He's seen the empty tomb and yet he still doesn't understand that Jesus is alive."

Al wrinkled his brow, trying to understand why Peter and the other disciples didn't get it. "Well, when ye go lookin' for the dead among the dead, o' course ye won't find the livin' there."

Matthew went over and squatted down next to his friend, putting his hand on the defeated man's shoulder. "Peter . . ." He couldn't muster much more than that. What was there to say?

Suddenly they heard the voices of women outside the door, followed by their noisy entrance into the room. Their faces were jubilant and their voices cheerful as they gushed out what had just happened. Mary, Salome, Joanna, and the others were talking a mile a minute. Matthew stood and put his hands up to shush them. "Keep your voices down! Now what is this all about?"

"We've seen him! We've seen the Lord!" they announced all the louder, drawing looks of disbelief and confusion from the disciples.

"What do you mean?" Andrew asked as he and the other men stood up at hearing this news. Only Peter remained seated.

"When we went to the tomb with our spices, the stone was rolled away," Salome began.

"Mary Magdalene told us the same thing," Peter chimed in harshly. "John and I went to the tomb and Jesus' body wasn't there."

"Yes, but didn't you see the angel?" Joanna asked him excitedly.

Peter simply shook his head "no."

Salome piped up. "He said Jesus was alive and told us to come tell all of you this news, and that Jesus would meet you in Galilee! Then when we left the tomb we saw Jesus himself!"

"Yes, just briefly but it was he!" the other women readily agreed.

The men looked at one another and mumbled among themselves. "They're delusional in their grief."

At that moment, Mary Magdalene burst into the room with John and Mary, the mother of Jesus. The three of them were giddy with joy and joined the voices of the others.

15

"He's alive!" Mary Magdalene declared. "I've seen the Master myself! When I went back to the tomb, Peter, he was there! I thought he was the gardener but he spoke my name: 'Mary!'"

Peter looked up for the first time with a hint of alertness in his eyes. Mary Magdalene had been with the women when they first approached the tomb, but had run off in fear to find Peter and John while the other women went into the tomb and encountered the angel. Upon hearing her news the men had run to the tomb while she backtracked slowly behind, as there was nowhere else to really go. The men saw neither angels nor Jesus, yet John wasn't full of despair. What did John know that Peter didn't? This was all very confusing to Peter. *Why didn't I see anyone? More failure*, he thought. *I'm not worthy of an angelic encounter. I'm no better than Judas.*

Joanna went over to Peter and gripped his arm. "Peter, the angel mentioned *you* by name!"

"*What?*" Peter asked in disbelief. "What did he say?"

"He told us to come tell the disciples, *and Peter*," she recounted with a hopeful smile.

Peter looked at her and wrinkled his forehead. "The angel . . . the angel said my name?" With that he immediately got to his feet and looked at John, who smiled warmly and simply told his friend, "Go."

Mary, Jesus' mother, nodded silently as Peter made his way out the door.

The other disciples looked at the women and John but didn't believe what they were hearing. "Everyone is hysterical," Thomas mumbled.

Liz's tail was twitching back and forth with such force that she hit Al in the face. *"C'est ridicule!* These dense men do not believe the women! But they do not believe *John's* account either! And *I* cannot believe their response to this happy news! What is wrong with them?!"

Al shook his head sadly. "They must be daft."

∝

Peter couldn't run fast enough. He tripped twice over rocks in the road, falling face-first in the gravel. He didn't even notice that his lip was bleeding when he got back to the Garden tomb.

"Looks like Peter's come back," Max said when he saw Peter run inside the tomb. He and Kate were hidden behind a plant, waiting for this encounter to unfold.

"Clarie didn't tell us who else would encounter Jesus here," Kate noted. Her eyes welled up. "Oh, for Peter ta see Jesus alone! How he needs the Master's touch."

Peter was on his knees next to the empty slab, weeping with gut-wrenching sobs. No angel was here to greet him. And Jesus wasn't here. The grave was silent and empty. He was alone. *What did the angel mean, "Tell the disciples and Peter?"* Peter wondered. A sudden realization hit the weary man. *Maybe the angel meant I'm not worthy to be counted as a disciple any longer because of what I've done! Oh, what a wretch I am!* This thought felt as if the grave stone was rolling over his heart, crushing his chest.

Peter threw himself onto the slab where Jesus' graveclothes still lay undisturbed. He gathered the linen with his arms and buried his face into the pile of garments that once had embraced the dead body of his Lord. He breathed in the sweet aroma of spices and wished he could disappear into the cloth. His cries were muffled yet heard by the One they were intended for.

"Jesus, Jesus, Jesus! I'm so sorry," Peter repeated over and over, gasping for breath and soaking the cloth with his tears. "Please, please. Forgive me. Oh, Jesus, Jesus, Jesus!"

Peter rocked violently back and forth, holding the cloth to his face as he cried and sobbed. But after a few moments he was spent with grief and grew very still. He leaned over and put his head on the ground, pulling his knees into his chest while still clutching the graveclothes to his heart. He simply wanted to die right there and go wherever his Lord was.

Suddenly he heard footsteps slowly walking toward him. He didn't care who it was. He didn't plan on moving. They would have to carry him out of the tomb.

The footsteps stopped, yet whoever it was didn't say a word. Peter could feel the warmth of another person standing right by his head. His eyes fluttered open and tears stung his eyes. Standing next to him were nail-pierced feet.

A sob deep within this broken man slowly rose but stuck in his throat. He rolled over with his face in the dirt. Peter couldn't bear to look up. He was shackled to his shame.

"Simon," Jesus said softly.

Peter shook his head and continued to sob silently. He couldn't muster a response.

"Simon," Jesus said again, this time stooping down to place his hand on Peter's head. "Simon."

The warmth of Jesus' touch and the gentleness of his voice made all the nerves in Peter's body tingle, as if willing him to respond lest they had to shout out themselves. But Jesus waited there in the quietness. He wasn't going anywhere.

"Master," was all Peter could finally utter in a broken voice.

"Your groans have spoken volumes, Simon," Jesus replied.

He keeps calling me 'Simon,' not Peter, Peter painfully realized. *I can't blame him. I'm no rock. I wouldn't want to use me anymore, either, after what I've done.*

Peter opened his eyes and slowly lifted his head, locking eyes with Jesus for the first time since that devastating moment of denial. But in those eyes he saw no judgment, no condemnation, no anger. He only saw love. And he only felt hope.

Supernatural strength filled Peter's mind and heart. His lip trembled at the miracle of grace entering his spirit. Slowly he sat up and rose to his feet to stand eye-to-eye with Jesus. "Forgive me, oh, please forgive me, Master."

"All is forgiven," Jesus replied. "Now you will understand true grace. Now you finally will grasp every word I've taught you. You, who strayed as a sheep, now have returned to the Shepherd, the Guardian of your soul."

Peter continued to weep, but now the tears sprung from the well of hope and gratitude. "I once judged Matthew as the prodigal son. I was the arrogant, resentful brother who didn't want him home. But now *I'm* the prodigal son!"

"No longer," Jesus affirmed with his piercing eyes of love and grace. "Welcome home, *Peter.*"

Peter put his hands to his eyes and covered his face for a moment. Such grace, mercy, and forgiveness were almost too much to take in. He wiped away his tears, but when he opened his eyes, Jesus was gone. Peter gripped the graveclothes once more to his face and fell to his knees in praise to God. Raising his hands in the air he shouted, "Blessed be the God and Father of our Lord Jesus Christ!" His breathing was fast and his voice was shaky with emotion. "You are full of mercy! You have given me hope! You have raised Jesus from the dead!" Peter fell forward with his face on the ground, rejoicing in awe and wonder of what was happening to him.

"The women were right," Peter muttered to himself. "*John* was right. But he knew without an angel or Jesus to tell him. He believed on faith what Jesus had been trying to tell all of us all along." Peter sat up and held the graveclothes to his face. They meant nothing now. Jesus didn't need them anymore. And neither did Peter. Jesus was alive! Peter tossed the graveclothes on the ground and ran out of the tomb.

Max and Kate slowly entered the tomb for one last look around, deeply moved by what they had just witnessed with Jesus and Peter.

"I don't think words could ever truly describe wha' jest happened here," Kate said, wiping away her tears of joy. "Do ye think Peter will tell anyone wha' he an' Jesus said here?"

Max walked to stand over the unneeded graveclothes. "I don't think the lad has ta share everythin'. Some things are jest better kept between Jesus an' yerself alone."

"Jesus secrets," Kate said thoughtfully.

"Aye, Lass," Max smiled. "Jesus secrets."

19

SEVEN MILES

T here they are!" Nigel exclaimed, grabbing the hare's long ears to halt the fast-running jackrabbit. "Whoa, my dear! Stop, I say!"

The brown hare slowed its frantic pace and hopped behind a large rock next to the road. "Good eye, Nigel," Clarie whispered and panted from the energetic run. "We should be able to hear them easily as they walk along to Emmaus."

"I jolly well should hope so." Nigel chuckled as he eyed the exaggerated size of Clarie's thin ears that twitched back and forth. They appeared bright pink with the sun shining behind them, and were as long as her furry brown body. "It was simply brilliant for you to become a hare for this excursion. We have camouflage and stupendous *'haring'* with those huge ears," the mouse quipped.

Clarie wiggled her fluffy white tail and thumped her big feet. "And speed!"

"Shhhh! Here they come," Nigel hoarsely whispered. He sat on Clarie's head between her long ears as she slowly peered around the rock. Two men were walking toward them.

Cleopas frowned and dug his walking stick into the ground with each step. "The women's account of the empty tomb and angels talking to them is a bit much to believe."

"But what of John?" Jacob posed. "Even *he* thinks Jesus is alive, although he didn't see him. He was there at the cross and saw for a fact that Jesus died. Perhaps he, too, is so grief-stricken he can't think straight."

"Well, even I don't know what to think anymore," Cleopas sighed. "Nothing we thought was going to happen has happened. Jesus had an adoring crowd on Sunday when he entered Jerusalem. Everything was perfect for him to assume the role of Messiah."

"Yes, he could have taken control of everything with the power he possessed. We ourselves *saw* the miracles he performed!" Jacob reminded his friend, gesturing wildly with his hands. "He healed the incurable. He even made a blind man see! Any prophet who can do that surely could assume the throne and be as great as King David."

"It should have been Israel's time. He was our hope for Messiah," Cleopas commiserated.

"Sounds like *they* are the blind men who need their eyes opened," Nigel observed with a frown.

"They are mourning the death of their dreams as much as the death of Jesus," Clarie added. "They're only looking at things from a human perspective, not God's."

"Their failure to grasp the Resurrection will keep them blind to everything," Nigel realized.

Just then, a man came up to join the men on the road. "What are you discussing together as you walk along?"

"It's Jesus!" Nigel squeaked, then clamped his paws over his mouth. "They are blind indeed! They don't even recognize him!"

"I told you they were clueless," Clarie answered him.

The men stopped and stared at the stranger, their faces full of sadness. Cleopas furrowed his brow. "Are you the only one visiting Jerusalem who does not know the things that have happened there in these days?"

"What things?" Jesus asked.

"About Jesus of Nazareth," they replied in unison, looking at one another in amazement at this man's lack of awareness.

"He was a prophet, powerful in word and deed before God and all the people," Cleopas explained. "The chief priests and our rulers handed him over to be sentenced to death, and they crucified him; but we had hoped that he was the one who was going to redeem Israel. And what is more, it is the third day since all this took place."

Jacob was eager to get a word in. "In addition, some of our women amazed us. They went to the tomb early this morning but didn't find Jesus' body. They came and told us they had seen a vision of angels, who said he was alive. Then some of our companions went to the tomb and found it just as the women had said, but they did not see Jesus."

Jesus looked at the men in amazement at *their* lack of awareness. "How foolish you are, and how slow to believe all that the prophets have spoken! Did not the Messiah have to suffer these things and then enter his glory?"

"Hear, hear!" Nigel exclaimed with his tiny fist in the air. "Give them what for and all that, Jesus!"

"Better hold on, Nigel," Clarie told her mouse passenger. "It's time to move."

22

Jesus began walking and captivated the men with the fact that he not only knew about all that had been going on—he could explain why. Beginning with Moses and all the Prophets, he explained to them what was said in all the Scriptures concerning himself.

Clarie and Nigel hopped along quietly for seven miles from Jerusalem all the way to the outskirts of Emmaus, listening intently to Jesus.

Nigel provided running commentary of his thoughts as they went along, but grew especially animated as Jesus discussed Isaiah's prophecies.

"Isaiah continually talked about 'the Servant of the Lord,'" Jesus explained. "He said clearly what this Servant would do: bring justice to the world, . . ."

"Isaiah 42," Nigel referenced with his arms folded across his chest, nodding.

". . . lead his people into a new, right relationship with God, . . ." Jesus continued.

Nigel preened his whiskers. "Isaiah 49:5."

". . . enlighten the nations and make salvation available to everyone, . . ."

"Isaiah 49:6." Nigel emphasized the "6" with a finger raised.

". . . endure unjust humiliation and take on the divine punishment deserved by others," Jesus added, hoping that some light would go off in the heads of these men.

Nigel fumed when the men's blank expressions remained. "Blast it all, can't they see these truths betwixt Isaiah 50:6 and 52–53?"

"Steady, Mousie," Clarie said.

Jesus continued with Isaiah's description of the suffering Servant. "He would be led as a lamb to the slaughter for a sin offering. Don't you see? God originally meant for the temple sacrifice to teach Israel that sin is costly and ultimately leads to death. One lamb slain for one person as the atonement. But God is establishing a new covenant and a new way to deal with sin. One Lamb for all people, for all time. Everything has changed!"

As they approached the village of Emmaus, the men stopped to head home. Jesus continued on as if he were going farther. The sun was beginning its descent.

23

Cleopas and Jacob weren't ready for this conversation to stop. Cleopas respectfully took the stranger by the arm. "Please, stay with us, for it is nearly evening; the day is almost over."

"Yes, please," Jacob also implored. "Come, dine with us."

Jesus hesitated but then smiled and nodded slowly. "Very well, I'll join you."

As Jesus followed the men and entered the home of Cleopas, Nigel surveyed the house. "We simply must get inside."

"This way," Clarie said as she hopped around the side of the house to find an open window above them. "Up there, Nigel."

"Splendid! Do you mind if I pop on up then?" Nigel asked as he jumped off the jackrabbit.

"Not at all," Clarie wriggled her nose. "I think I'll be able to hear everything just fine."

"Right!" Nigel cheered as he climbed up the stucco wall to reach the window. Inside was a long table lined with baskets of bread and platters of food. Oil lamps gave the room a soft glow as the family gathered around the table. Jesus took his place at the head of the table as the honored guest in their home.

"Please, will you bless our meal?" Cleopas asked Jesus.

Jesus took a piece of the bread and held it up to bless it. "O Lord, we give you thanks for this food. You are the giver of all good gifts: food to the hungry, strength to the weary, and sight to the blind. Amen."

Nigel watched as Jesus then broke the bread and handed pieces to each of the men. As Cleopas and Jacob took the bread from Jesus' hands, they suddenly saw the nail scars. Their eyes locked as they both instantly understood. More than seeing the scars, the veil that was over their spiritual eyesight was lifted. They finally recognized that the man in their midst was indeed not only Jesus, but Messiah.

"By Jove, I think they've got it!" Nigel cheered.

In that same instant Jesus disappeared from their sight.

The people gasped at the empty seat at their table. While the women started talking a mile a minute about what was going on, Cleopas and Jacob talked as if no one else were in the room.

24

"Were not our hearts burning within us while he talked with us on the road and opened the Scriptures to us?" Cleopas asked, putting his head in his hands, not believing his stupidity.

"How could we have been so blind?" Jacob added, shaking his head.

The two men hurriedly got up from the table and put on their cloaks, leaving their food untouched.

"Where are you going? And who was that?!" the women cried.

"To Jerusalem!" Cleopas announced, running out the door.

"It was the Lord!" Jacob echoed, following him. "He's alive!"

"Then shall the eyes of the blind be opened," Nigel said with a pleased grin. "Isaiah 35:5."

4

Missing Doubt

Nigel held on for dear life to Clarie's big ears, flying with his legs dangling in the air behind him as she raced the seven miles back to Jerusalem. The mouse was exuberant with the thrill of the ride in the cool night air. When finally they stopped near the house where the Upper Room was located, Nigel's tiny feet drifted back down to rest on Clarie's back.

"I SAY!" Nigel exclaimed, jumping off the hare. "Now THAT took the biscuit! I must travel like this again soon."

"Glad you enjoyed the ride, Nigel," Clarie said with a grin. "I'll leave you here to meet the others."

"Are you not coming inside then?" Nigel asked, pointing upstairs.

"Time for me to be hopping along," Clarie joked as she started down the road. "Go join the others. I'll see you all soon in Galilee."

Nigel stood and watched Clarie disappear into the darkened street. "Ta-ta!" he called after her before scurrying up the outer steps to the Upper Room. He looked back down to the street and grinned upon seeing Cleopas and Jacob heading toward the house.

"Pssst!" Al signaled when he saw Nigel sneak in the room through a hole in the wall. "Over here, Mousie."

"How was your walk to Emmaus?" Liz asked her mouse friend.

"It was more of a *hare-ied* run, I assure you," Nigel quipped, drawing a puzzled look from Liz. "Clarie took the form of a long-eared rabbit for our journey. But the two gentlemen were quite dense, I'm afraid. They were completely oblivious to the fact that it was Jesus walking along the road with them as he talked for seven miles, explaining why Messiah had to come as he did. It wasn't until Jesus popped off into thin air that they realized who he was. Curious, the mind of a human, isn't it?"

Liz's eyes grew wide. "Pardon, but 'popped off into thin air'?"

"Right. Jesus broke the bread at supper and when the men finally recognized him, he simply vanished in front of their eyes," Nigel explained. "Brilliant!"

"Oui, mon ami," Liz marveled. "I am fascinated by Jesus' ability to move about. His resurrection body is almost like a living IAMI-SPHERE." Liz was referring to the vehicle the animals used to travel in time and space when necessary. "But where is Clarie?"

"She said she'd see us in Galilee," Nigel explained. He looked around the room and spotted Max and Kate sitting next to a very happy Peter. "I say, Peter looks like quite a new man."

"Aye, he saw Jesus!" Al reported. "He told the lads all aboot seein' him at the tomb. Good thing ringleader o' doubt Thomas left. Sure, and he were bringin' everybody down."

"Max and Kate decided it would be okay if they made their presence known to Peter, since he had seen them here in Jerusalem anyway," Liz relayed. "Albert is right. We listened to these men all day, arguing with each other over the reports from the women and how deranged they must be. But when Peter arrived with his happy news they finally began to believe that what the women had told them was true. Thomas stormed out, saying he couldn't listen to any more of such talk."

"What a pity. So Thomas isn't here?" Nigel asked, looking around the room. "I hate for him to miss Jesus because of his doubt."

"It appears doubting hearts have missed Jesus all day, even when they've seen him, no?" Liz pointed out.

Suddenly there came a bang on the door. Philip got up and cautiously asked, "Who is it?" The disciples were so afraid of the Jewish leaders rounding them up they had locked themselves in.

"Cleopas and Jacob," came the reply. Philip quickly unlocked the door and let the men in. They were covered in dust and sweat, having hurried the seven miles back to Jerusalem from Emmaus. "We had to get back and tell you," Cleopas gushed, out of breath. "Jesus is alive!"

"Yes, it's true! The Lord has risen and has appeared to Peter," Matthew announced gleefully.

Peter nodded and smiled. "Please, tell us what happened when you saw him."

"We were on our way to Emmaus when he joined us on the road. We were discussing all that had happened, but we thought he was a stranger!" related Jacob. "We didn't recognize him! He started teaching us about why Messiah had to come the way he did, explaining everything from Moses and the Prophets."

"Yes, and our hearts burned as he spoke, but we didn't recognize him until he broke the bread in my home," Cleopas added. "We then saw his hands." Tears welled up in Cleopas's eyes and he shook his head at the miracle of their risen Savior. "It was as if a veil of doubt was lifted from our eyes to recognize him at last."

27

"What happened then?" James wanted to know.

"He disappeared!" Jacob exclaimed with his hands in the air. "He was just . . . gone! So we rushed right here to tell you."

The disciples' mouths hung open at this news. Max and Kate suddenly looked at one another as their fur stood on end. "Somethin's here, Lass," Max whispered in Kate's ear.

"Aye," Kate replied, looking around the room. "Or some*one.*"

Suddenly Jesus himself stood right there in the room in front of them. "Peace be with you!"

The men fell back onto the floor in fear. "It's a ghost!" someone cried out.

"Aye, it *were* someone!" Max whispered. "Why do the laddies always say "ghost" when Jesus shows up unexpectedly? I heard them yellin' like that when we were out walkin' on the water."

Kate nodded. "Aye, humans can be daft that way, bein' scared of Jesus."

Jesus walked closer to them and held up his hands. He looked each one of them in the eye with a reassuring look. "Don't be upset, and don't let all these doubts and questions take over. Look at my hands; look at my feet—it's really me." He smiled and stood in front of Matthew. "Touch me. Look me over from head to toe. A ghost doesn't have muscle and bone like this."

"They still can't believe what they are seeing, no? It is too much; it seems too good to be true," Liz whispered to Al and Nigel. *"Ooh-la-la, but doubt is a powerful thing to weakened hearts."*

"He'll get them to come around, I have *no* doubt," Nigel answered, adjusting his spectacles.

Jesus saw that the men had finished supper. "Do you have any food here?" He proceeded to sit down next to Nathaniel and gave him a reassuring smile.

Thaddeus put a piece of leftover fish on a plate and slowly set it in front of Jesus, staring in awe at his hands.

"Thank you, Thaddeus." Jesus picked up the fish, took a bite, and looked around the room. "Delicious."

"C'est incredible!" Liz marveled. "He can pass through walls like a spirit yet still eat like a man."

Al's mouth watered. "I love how Jesus always teaches with fish." He stepped out from behind the water jar and went right up to Jesus, begging for a bite.

"Where did the cat come from?" Andrew asked. They were surprised to see the hungry, fish-loving cat show up after they lost track of the old man Gillamon and his animals the day of the Last Supper with Jesus in this very room.

Jesus laughed and broke off a piece for Al. "Nice to see you, Ari."

Al gobbled down the fish and headbutted Jesus, meowing, *"Aye, I'm glad to see ye alive then."*

"Ah, well, I suppose I can join him," Liz said happily, sauntering over to Jesus.

"And you, little Zilla," Jesus said, picking Liz up and holding her to his cheek with affection.

Liz's eyes filled with joyful tears, meowing, *"Cher Jesus! Welcome back, mon Roi."*

"Merci, Liz," Jesus whispered in her ear. "I am happy to be back."

The disciples relaxed at seeing Jesus act the way he always did. He was sitting down, eating, and interacting with the animals he loved. He was actually alive! Jesus saw Max and Kate sitting next to Peter, wagging their tails. "You, too, Tovah and Chavah. Come on over and say hello."

Max and Kate ran up to Jesus and he enveloped them with hugs and laughter. *"Ah, Jesus, I never lived a longer thr-r-ree days,"* Max barked, happily licking Jesus' face.

"How we love ye, Jesus," Kate added, nuzzling Jesus.

"I'm happy to see you this side of the cross," Jesus whispered in their ears. "I love you, too."

Matthew leaned over to Peter. "What happened to Gillamon? The old man with the donkey? These were his animals, weren't they?"

Peter just shrugged, smiling. Nothing seemed to matter to him except Jesus.

After Jesus finished the fish, he wiped off his hands and started teaching the group, picking right up where he had left off the night he was arrested. Max, Liz, Kate, and Al settled in around his feet. "Everything I told you while I was with you comes to this: All the things written about me in the Law of Moses, in the Prophets, and in the Psalms have to be fulfilled."

"Just like you explained to us on the road to Emmaus," Cleopas offered. "Forgive us for not recognizing you, Master. We were blind to not see who you were."

"No one has been able to see me for who I really am until now, Cleopas," Jesus replied, looking around the table. "None of you could fully understand my teachings before about the kingdom of heaven and why I came from my Father to Earth. Open your eyes, all of you! You must look at everything differently from now on. You must see everything through God's eyes in his Word. Surrender your worldly, human eyesight and expectations of Messiah, and ask God to help you understand his plan. Believe in me and what I've done through the cross. But more than that, stake your future on my resurrection and never doubt my words. Then you won't be blind to anything anymore."

The disciples looked at one another in awe as their minds began

29

exploding with understanding. They suddenly longed to go back and remember every single word Jesus had taught them over the past three years. Everything would make sense now. Every parable he told, every encounter he had, every miracle he worked. All of it would come into focus as their spiritual eyes started to open.

Jesus went through the prophecies of Messiah to paint a clear picture of how it all came together. "That is how it was written, and that is why it was inevitable that Christ should suffer, and rise from the dead on the third day. So must the change of heart which leads to the forgiveness of sins be proclaimed in his name to all nations, beginning at Jerusalem."

The disciples looked at one another with a newfound sense of purpose. They were part of the unfolding story of Messiah, and they would be responsible for proclaiming this good news of forgiveness to all the nations. But how? A general feeling of impossibility crept into their minds.

At that moment Jesus once again disappeared from their sight. They hoped he would be back, but for now, the disciples had reached the limit they could absorb in one day.

A knock came again at the door and everyone's hearts skipped a beat. Philip went to the door and saw it was Thomas. As the doubting disciple entered the room he looked around and noticed that everyone was quiet, yet a sense of peace was there that hadn't been present earlier in the day.

Thomas furrowed his brow. "Did I miss something?"

Nigel shook his head and planted his face into his paw.

The Fish,
the Tortoise,
and the Hare

U nless I see the nail marks in his hands and put my finger
where the nails were, and put my hand into his side, I will
not believe,'" Nigel recounted, shaking his head. "That's what
doubting Thomas said when the disciples told him they'd seen you."

Jesus smiled and stirred the embers of the fire with a stick. A spark
popped and rose into the cool night air. "That's why I told him to
touch his finger to my hands and my side. Some followers need more
confirmation than others. But as I shared with them, Thomas believed
because he saw me. A greater blessing will come to those who have not
seen and yet have believed."

"Aye, but at least he came ar-r-round then," Max agreed. "He never
lacked courage. He jest were a natural pessimist."

"*Oui,* but he was honest," Liz added. "He would not say he understood when he did not, or that he believed when he did not. But now
that he truly understands and believes, he is fully on board with you,
Jesus."

Jesus gave Liz a loving rub on the cheek. "Very true, Liz."

"Hear, hear!" Nigel piped up, preening his whiskers. "When a man

31

fights to gain victory over his doubts that you are indeed his 'Lord and his God,' as Thomas so aptly *finally* claimed, nothing can shake his certainty again."

"I do believe Thomas finally got it," Jesus quipped to Nigel in an impeccable British accent.

"Jolly good accent," Nigel cheered. "Sadly, I shall miss interacting with you like this, Jesus."

"Sure, and we all will," Al said with big mopey eyes and a quivering lip.

"Aye," Kate agreed, nuzzling up to Jesus.

Jesus leaned over and hugged Kate on one side and Al on the other. "I'll miss times like this, too. It has been a joy to spend some of my time here on Earth with you. It won't be long until we're together again, for all eternity."

"Aye, but ye have a r-r-really different outlook on time than we do," Max said with a frown. "It's all the same for ye, but here on Earth, time can be a wee bit slower."

"Yes, Max, I do see time differently, but you're going to be so busy helping my disciples spread the Good News that time will pass quickly." Jesus looked at the Sea of Galilee, making out the darkened shapes of men on a fishing boat. "And I'll always be with you in Spirit."

"So when will you be leaving us?" Liz asked sadly.

"After I get my disciples back on track, and give them instructions they'll need," Jesus answered. "Thomas is in a good place now that his doubt is gone. Now I must restore Peter. He needs to know he will still be my chosen leader for these men, but he needs to completely submit his heart to me before he can accomplish anything."

The first pink rays of dawn crept up onto the horizon. Max squinted to locate the seven fishermen. "Do ye think they've caught anythin'?"

"Not yet. From here on out, they have to learn they won't catch anything without listening to my instructions," Jesus said, standing up, "and obeying them exactly."

Al tugged on Jesus' garment, drooling and staring at the fish cooking on the fire. "In that case, can I have some o' yers?"

Peter stood up to stretch his sore muscles and let loose a grumbly moan. "Nothing. All night, and not one fish."

Andrew rubbed his stiff neck and gave a good yawn. "Well, at least we tried, brother."

"Yes, and at least fishing made you stop sitting around the house going crazy with waiting on the Lord," Thomas said, looking into the deep water. "Jesus said he'd meet us here in Galilee. So he will. We just have to wait for his perfect time."

John smiled and lowered his head, thinking how far Thomas had come, from the chief doubter to the chief believer.

But Peter's mind had been swirling for a week, wondering what he was supposed to do now. Yes, Jesus had forgiven him, but Peter had determined that the Lord couldn't or wouldn't want to use him anymore. He thought he would spend the rest of his life following Jesus, but then Jesus' ministry was cut short, and Peter had blown it. Everything had changed and Peter was in a place he didn't expect to be. Jesus had told Peter to follow him, and he would make him a fisher of men. That was a lost opportunity now. All Peter knew was fishing, so he decided he'd just return to what he knew. But on his first time back to regular fishing, he had failed. Sadly, it wasn't just the one thing Peter knew—it was what he truly loved.

Peter gazed out to sea. How the burly man regretted his rash behavior! His loud mouth and his bold actions had repeatedly got him into trouble. One night he had jumped overboard and walked on this very water to get to Jesus, yet sank when he took his eyes off the Lord. Jesus called him "faint heart." Peter shook his head, replaying another regrettable moment in his mind. *Even if all fall away on account of you, I never will.* Peter knew how long that bold statement lasted. A few pitiful hours. *I'm such a fool! What's the matter with me? Why can't I stick to anything with the Lord? What am I missing?* Jesus' words of affirmation on the night of Peter's betrayal haunted him. When *you have turned back, strengthen your brothers . . . He knew I would betray him and he knew I would turn back. So what else does he know about my future?* Peter was restless to find out.

The sun's early morning glow grew over the hillsides surrounding the lake. The men were only a hundred yards off the beach.

33

"Who's that?" Nathaniel asked, pointing to a man standing next to a fire on the shore.

James and Matthew looked up but didn't realize it was Jesus. "Who knows?"

Jesus cupped his hand over his mouth and called out to them, "Friends, haven't you any fish?"

Peter snorted a sarcastic laugh, pulling in their nets from the left side of the boat.

"No," several of the men answered, helping Peter.

"Throw your net on the right side of the boat and you will find some."

"Maybe he can see some fish schooling from the shore," Andrew offered.

The weary men didn't balk at the stranger's suggestion but lifted the nets over to the other side of the boat. The nets splashed on the surface of the water, sending ripples out in every direction. As the nets slowly descended into the depths, something jerked the boat. Suddenly they were reliving a scene just like this, long ago. Their nets immediately grew so full of fish they couldn't pull them into the boat. Last time their nets had broken. They pulled with all their might, wondering if the nets would hold this time.

John knew immediately what was going on. He smiled and elbowed Peter. "It's the Lord!"

Peter's head snapped up and he looked toward shore. The man was sitting by the fire, cooking breakfast. Peter quickly wrapped his outer garment around him and jumped into the water. His heart was pounding as he swam to shore.

"Looks like the lad went overboard again," Al observed with a grin.

Max replied, "Aye, but this time he's not walkin' on the water, he's swimmin' thr-r-rough it with all his might."

"He must be really hungry," guessed Al.

Jesus chuckled. "Yes, Al, but not for food."

Peter waded in to shore and sloshed up to the campfire. He dropped to his knees in the sand.

"Good morning," Jesus greeted him with a warm smile, handing Peter a piece of baked fish.

Peter smiled and gratefully took the fish. "Thank you, my Lord." He peeled off the skin and simply sat there, eating fish he hadn't caught. He didn't know what else to say, so he said nothing for once.

The other disciples neared the beach towing the net full of fish, but were struggling to get the huge catch in to shore.

"I think your friends need you," Jesus suggested, standing.

Peter jumped up from the fire, wiping his hands on his wet clothes, and ran back to the water. He waded to the boat to help drag the net ashore. He locked eyes with John and they shared a knowing grin. "The nets didn't tear," John said, giving Peter a cheerful pat on the back. The men pulled the flopping fish up onto the beach, and counted them out.

Jesus waved the men over to the fire. "Come and have breakfast. Bring some of the fish you've just caught."

By this point, none of the disciples needed ask him, "Who are you?" They knew he was the Lord. Jesus proceeded to hand them some bread and the fish he had already cooked. Then he laid some of their freshly caught fish on the coals.

35

As the men ate, the animals walked over to the enormous catch of fish lying on the beach. Liz surveyed the catch calmly while Al ran around in frenzied excitement, exclaiming, "SO MANY FISH!"

"*Ooh-la-la,* but there are 153 of them, no?" Liz finally exclaimed. "Do you know what this means?"

"Aye! I get to stuff me face!" Al cheered, trying to get his paws around a fish that kept slipping out of his arms.

"This number is significant," Nigel marveled, adjusting his spectacles to inspect the various kinds of fish the men had pulled in to shore.

"Wha' do it mean then?" Kate asked as she and Max looked around at the flopping fish.

"Humans only know of 153 types of fish in the sea," Liz explained. "Jesus has not only provided this catch by telling the disciples exactly what to do, he is teaching them something very important with this number."

Al's face was planted in the sand next to Max as he chased the slippery fish. He sat up with a goofy grin, spitting sand all over Max. "Aye! Jesus be teachin' with fish again!"

Max frowned and bopped Al on the head. "Daft kitty!"

Nigel's whiskers quivered with excitement. "Actually, our fish-crazed feline is spot on. Jesus is teaching his disciples that when they follow his instructions, they will catch every kind of person in the world!"

"Aye, an' their nets won't break," Kate added with her perky grin.

"PUT ME DOWN!" the fish shouted as it slapped Al across the face and flopped out of his arms. Suddenly the fish rolled over and over in the sand until it was completely covered.

Al's eyes widened as he hid behind Max. "That fish don't like me."

Max rolled his eyes. "Ye *think?* Now *there's* a mystery."

Together the animals watched the fish shake off the sand to reveal that it was no longer a fish, but a tortoise. It stretched out its neck and slowly walked over to Kate, Liz, and Nigel. "Right you are, Kate," the tortoise said. "Jesus' net will have a name: the *church.*"

Liz giggled. "I thought that was you, *mon amie.* Please tell us more, Clarie."

Al gave a weak grin. "I shoulda known then."

"Jesus' followers will make up a body of believers called the Church. Once the promised Spirit of God comes—very soon—to believers, they will all be connected in their minds and hearts," Clarie explained. "Peter and the disciples are the first ropes he'll use to weave his net, and it will grow as others join them."

"An' nothin' will be able ta br-r-reak this net," Max chimed in. "It will be str-r-rong an' big enough ta hold as many fish as can swim in."

"Exactly, Max," Clarie agreed with a smile. "If you remember, the last time Jesus performed this fish-catching miracle, the nets broke, but that was before the cross. Peter and the others broke before Jesus went to the cross."

"Brilliant!" Nigel exclaimed with his fist in the air. "But *this* time, the nets held. Now on this side of the cross, the disciples will not break. Ergo, they will hold, and truly become fishers of men!"

"Right, but Jesus has to mend one part of the net so it will continue to hold," Clarie said, leading the animals back to the fire. "The Peter part. Watch."

The disciples were full from the breakfast Jesus had made. James, Andrew, Thomas, Matthew, and Nathaniel stretched out around the fire, closing their eyes after their sleepless night of fishing. The fire crackled and popped as Jesus, Peter, and John sat there quietly, staring into the comforting embers.

Jesus pointed to the men and then to the last bit of fish cooking on the coals. "Simon son of John, do you love me more than these?"

Peter looked at his fellow disciples, a symbol of his leadership. He looked at the fish, a symbol of his life's work up until now. And he looked at the fire, a symbol of where he had betrayed Christ while warming himself in the courtyard of the high priest. Jesus never failed to create learning opportunities from the settings around him.

"Yes, Lord," Peter said eagerly, "you know that I love you."

Jesus nodded. "Feed my lambs."

A few moments passed as the men sat quietly by the fire. Peter felt a glimmer of hope that Jesus would ask him to do something for him. But Jesus was calling him Simon.

37

Again Jesus asked, "Simon son of John, do you love me?"

Peter leaned forward and put his hands on his chest, imploring Jesus with a look of genuine emotion. "Yes, Lord, you *know* that I love you."

Jesus stirred the embers and nodded. "Take care of my sheep."

"Curious," Liz whispered. "Jesus asked Peter twice if he loved him, using the word *agape,* which means "supreme love." But Peter replied with the word *phileo,* which means "brotherly love." It is a lower form of love. Why would he do that?"

"Maybe he doesn't feel like boastin' anymore," Max whispered back. "Maybe Peter's finally realized he ought not claim he's the best of all by usin' the highest word."

Jesus turned and looked Peter right in the eye. "Simon son of John, do you love me?"

Peter furrowed his brow and his eyes expressed the hurt he felt. When Jesus asked him the third time, he used the *phileo* word for love, as Peter had used twice in reply to him. Jesus had come down to Peter's verbal level to pull him back up. Peter felt emptied of himself at that moment, and he finally realized what his trouble had been all along.

He always fell short in word and deed because he had never been fully devoted to Jesus alone. Whether in leading the men or in fishing, he held on to his own desires and aspirations, and every time he took his eyes off his Lord, he sank. Peter never wanted to experience that again. Jesus was calling him Simon once again because Peter was acting like Simon once again. He needed to act like Peter, the rock, but this time with his heart fully surrendered to Jesus. Peter's lip trembled and he spilled out in relieved anguish, "Lord, you know all things; you know that I love you."

Jesus smiled and stood up. "Feed my sheep." He started walking away from the fire and Peter jumped up to follow him.

Liz's eyes brimmed with tears. "Peter finally used the highest form of love in his reply to Jesus: *agape.*"

"Thrice denied, and thrice restored," Nigel added, wiping back his whiskers. "Such poetic love, *agape.* It attends to every detail."

38

Jesus and Peter slowly walked along the beach. "I tell you truly, Peter, that when you were younger, you used to dress yourself and go where you liked, but when you are an old man, you are going to stretch out your hands and someone else will dress you and take you where you do not want to go." Jesus stopped and looked Peter in the eye. "You must follow me."

Peter lowered his gaze and nodded slowly. Jesus was once again telling Peter about his future. Peter would follow Jesus not only in his life. He would follow him in his death, dying the same way Jesus had died. This was no small directive. Jesus was asking big things of him. He had forgiven him and was placing on his shoulders the responsibility of shepherding his flock of believers. His obedience would be costly, but Peter's steadfast love for the Lord would enable to him to do anything. Peter looked up and turned his gaze back to see John following them. "Lord, what about him?"

Jesus put his hand up to Peter's face to return the disciple's gaze back to himself. "If I want him to remain alive until I return, what is that to you? You must follow me."

"Peter best learn to keep his gaze on Jesus alone," Al said. "Or he'll keep sinkin'."

The animals looked in awe at Al's profound insight. Liz kissed Al on the cheek.

"And Jesus' questions to Peter now demand a response," Clarie added. "If you truly love me, prove it. Do something to show others that kind of love. Feed them, take care of them, and show them the way."

"The only way ta really show we love Jesus is by lovin' others," Kate realized.

"Precisely, my dear," Nigel agreed. "And we are each called to love others with the specific tasks he gives us to do. Jesus told Peter exactly what to do, as I'm sure he'll tell John exactly what to do."

"Aye, jest like he told the laddies exactly wha' ta do with their nets," Max said.

"That he will, Nigel and Max." Clarie smiled, thinking of John's future. She lovingly looked at Peter. "And now that Jesus' net is repaired, it's ready to catch lots of fish."

"Clarie, might I ask why you have taken the form of a tortoise?" Liz asked, studying Clarie's beautifully patterned shell.

"I too wish to know," Nigel said, adjusting his spectacles. "When you left us in Jerusalem you were a speedy hare."

"This sounds familiar," Al said, tapping his chin in deep thought. "Somethin' aboot fast and slow beasties."

Liz put her dainty paw up to her head. "Of course! *Cher* Albert, you have reminded me."

"I say, you don't mean Aesop's ancient fable? The tortoise and the hare?" Nigel supposed, also realizing that Clarie was now teaching *them* a lesson, using animals.

"Very good!" Clarie said, stretching her neck out proud and long. "Some people are fast to come to the truth, but rush into it without fully understanding what it's all about."

"Like Peter then?" Max asked. "He were fast ta say who Jesus were an' how he'd serve him, but he really didn't understand wha' it meant. An' he fell off the trail for a bit."

Clarie nodded. "Others may be slower in coming around to the truth, but when they do, they might be farther along in their journey because they've really asked questions to *understand* the truth."

"Like Thomas!" Kate declared. "He may have been labeled a doubter at first, but when he finally declared Jesus as Messiah, he meant it an' understood it better than Peter did at first."

"You all are quite right," Clarie affirmed with a smile. "Peter was like the hare, and Thomas was like the tortoise, but thankfully both are securely across the finish line of trusting Jesus. Now he can use them to catch fish."

"This is good for us to understand as we go forward with these men, no?" Liz said. "I am sure we will keep encountering both kinds of humans with these animal traits as we go forward in time."

"Aye, those who get it at first an' those who don't," Max agreed. "Tortoises and hares."

"Merci for our object lesson, *mon amie,"* Liz said, gently patting Clarie on her shell.

"Weren't we jest talkin' aboot nets and fish? And now we're talkin' aboot tortoise and hare beasties?" Al looked puzzled. "There's jest one thing I don't understand."

"Just one thing?" Nigel teased.

Al scratched his head. "How's Jesus goin' to use tortoises and hares to catch fish?"

I Am with You Always

Jesus' gaze was fixed on Jerusalem. He studied the city carefully, wanting to remember every inch of its beauty. It wasn't because he would no longer be here to see the city. He knew that in the not-too-distant future Jerusalem would be destroyed. And the thought broke his heart. "Oh Jerusalem, dear Jerusalem. It didn't need to be this way. If only you had believed in my first coming," Jesus lamented over his beloved city. "But I will restore you again, as promised long ago. I give you my word."

A warm spring breeze wafted through the air and Jesus closed his eyes to inhale the sweet fragrance of the flowers here on the Mount of Olives.

"Is he prayin'?" Max asked quietly as the animals climbed up the hill toward Jesus.

"Shhhh, let's not disturb him," Liz whispered, holding her paw up to her mouth as Al was about to speak. Al stopped with his mouth open and sat down on the grass, rolling onto his back.

Nigel nodded. "We'll just wait until he is finished."

"Aye," Kate said quietly, sitting down next to Max.

Jesus grinned with his eyes still closed as he heard the animals surrounding him on the hillside. "And Father, please especially be with

41

my dear friends Max, Kate, Liz, Al, and Nigel. Be with them as they continue to serve me by helping my disciples with the mission I will soon give them. Keep them brave when dangers come, and keep them strong when they encounter situations that seem beyond their control. Protect them from the Evil One. And I ask most of all that you help them know they are so very loved by me, and that they are indeed able to do all that they need to do in this mission. Amen."

"A-MEN THEN!" Al said loudly, startling them all. Al gave a weak smile.

Jesus opened his eyes and chuckled at Al's exclamation. "I'm glad you were here as I prayed over you," he said as he looked around at each of his animal friends. He took in a deep breath and sighed. "I will miss you so."

Liz's eyes filled quickly. "So this is indeed our last time with you, no?"

42

Jesus picked Liz up and held her close to his heart, feeling her gentle purr. *"Oui, mon amie.* Keep being my intelligent little one. The world needs to know what you know and how to make sense of everything that is coming. I know you won't let me down." He kissed her on the head.

"I shall, *cher* Jesus," Liz replied, gently rubbing Jesus' chin. "Always and forever, *pour vous."*

Kate and Max softly walked over and placed their heads on Jesus' lap. He leaned down and hugged them both. "My brave little warriors. Keep the rest of the team safe as you've done across time. And don't fear the threats of the Enemy. Max, just as you had to let my time come, please understand that you will need to let my disciples' times come as well. Don't worry as to how you'll know. I'll make sure your heart knows when to let go."

Max sniffed and cleared his throat with a broken, "Aye."

"Sweet Kate, you always look out for the underdogs of this world," Jesus said with a smile. "How we need more hearts like yours to stand up for those who are rejected and downtrodden. Never give up your spirited defense and fierce love. I'm proud of how you share part of me with others."

Kate wiped her eyes. "I'll love everyone jest like ye'd love them, Jesus. I promise."

Nigel walked up to stand before Jesus, who held out his hand for the little mouse, who jumped up. Jesus lifted Nigel to his shoulder as he had done countless times since childhood. "I will miss having a little British mouse on my shoulder."

"Indeed," Nigel sniffed, wiping his eyes behind his spectacles. "It's not only been an honor, my Liege, it's been utterly splendid fun to hide in your cloak all these years. Nothing shall ever take the biscuit more than riding on your shoulder."

Jesus nodded fondly. "Nigel, you are truly one of a kind. I shall miss your brilliant sense of humor. You and Liz will have to help people write many books in the future, and you shall become quite the musical aficionado. Someday you'll help to tell my story in song."

Nigel's eyes grew wide. "Is that so, my Lord? I shall especially look forward to that, I assure you! I do hope you'll be pleased with my work."

43

"I will, Nigel," Jesus grinned. "And don't be surprised if you hear extra loud applause in the audience one day."

Suddenly Al grasped Jesus' legs, wailing and hiding his face in Jesus' cloak. "No! No! You can't go! Pleeeeeeeease don't go! Wahhhh!"

Although Al was genuinely grieving in his own way, his dramatic outburst brought a bit of comic relief to the others' heavy hearts. Jesus leaned over, pulled Al's claws off his garment, and lifted him to his other shoulder. Al continued to cry as Jesus gently stroked the lovable, big cat's back. "It's okay, laddie. I'll always be in your heart, just like you'll always be in mine. Never stop making everyone laugh. Never stop being you. And you know what?"

Al sniffed and stopped sobbing for a moment. "What?" Sniff. Sniff.

"I know you're smarter than you let on," Jesus whispered in his ear. "But always keep them guessing."

A big, goofy grin broke out on Al's face. "Aye, laddie. That I can do."

Jesus set Al down in his lap to keep consoling him while he addressed the group. "I'm glad you're here to see me off. It's been a very emotional week for me. I said goodbye to my mother and to my brother James. Shortly I'll be telling my disciples farewell. But I'm glad to tell you a few more things before I go."

"Please do, *cher* Jesus," Liz asked, wiping her eyes. "We want to remember everything you have to say."

"These last forty days I've given plenty of appearances and proof of my resurrection, including the five hundred I saw as a group in Galilee," Jesus began. "It was important that a good number of people see me at the same time so they would be encouraged and know that what they saw was real. Going forward you must always remember that even though I am not physically here, my work continues. I'm simply moving my headquarters."

"Right! From Capernaum to heaven," Nigel enthused. "Brilliant strategy."

"Yes, to the right hand of my Father. You've heard the voice of my Father, and you've seen me on Earth as the Son. Now you will have the honor of feeling the third member of our Trinity," Jesus explained. "The Holy Spirit will come in ten days, and when he does, the real work of spreading the good news about what I've done here will begin."

"C'est bon!" Liz exclaimed. "How will he appear?"

"I'll leave that as a surprise," Jesus replied. "But it will be a day like none other in history, and you will watch my disciples change before your very eyes."

"Aye, sounds gr-r-rand ta me," Max enthused. "Now ye're sure these lads can do all ye're goin' ta ask them ta do?"

Jesus nodded. "Remember, Max. There is no 'Plan B.' These eleven men will be responsible to start my church and begin the spread of the gospel until my name is known around the world. We're going to take back the world that Satan took in the Garden of Eden, one heart at a time."

"Bravo! We'll give that old snake what-for and all of that!" Nigel exulted with a fist of victory raised in the air.

"Understand that I've already defeated him at the cross. He lost the war, but he will continue fighting and trying to stop my believers every step of the way." Jesus' face grew serious. "And this fighting will be unlike anything you've ever seen against my people. Much sorrow, pain, and death is coming as the Enemy goes down fighting. But from the blood of the martyrs will spring up an army of believers to take their places and proclaim my truth. The more he tries to silence my people, the louder they will get. And you all will be there across the ages, helping to encourage believers to let their voices be heard."

"This is indeed war," Liz said, wrinkling her brow. "Much like the Romans who are conquering the world for their emperor."

"Yes, but my kingdom will be set up in the hearts of people as the Holy Spirit moves into their lives. My kingdom will be spread not by soldiers but by witnesses, not by war, but by a gospel of peace. My witnesses will tell what I did in my first coming and summon people to turn their lives around in preparation for my second coming," Jesus explained. "My kingdom will grow through the work of the Spirit, not by force, politics, or violence. And understand that the kingdom of God will collide with the kingdom of Caesar."

45

"I know who'll win," Al offered up, sitting proudly, pointing back at Jesus.

Jesus smiled and mussed the fur on Al's head. "I already have won, but many times enemies keep fighting to the bitter end. And until the day I come back to you on this very mountainside and establish the physical kingdom to go with the spiritual kingdom, the war will continue. I have explained all this to my disciples, but they will soon understand what it means. So, dear friends, be strong. Fight the good fight, Order of the Seven. Remember, I am with you always."

The animals all gathered around Jesus' feet, bowing to him in reverence. Nigel put his foot forward with his paw draped across his chest. "Your humble servants, my Liege."

"And now, I have to tell you and them farewell." Jesus saw the group of eleven disciples making their way up the hillside. "Before the Spirit can come, the Son must go."

Jesus gave each of the animals a final petting before walking over to welcome the men who gathered around him. The animals hugged one another with a newfound sense of destiny. One phase of their long-standing mission with Messiah was ending, yet another was beginning.

And so it was also with these eleven men, who would have the entire world put into their hands.

"The time has come, my friends," Jesus said, making eye contact with each of the eleven. Remember what I told you. Do not leave Jerusalem, but wait for the gift my Father promised, which you have heard me speak about. For John baptized with water, but in a few days you will be baptized with the Holy Spirit."

"Lord, are you at this time going to restore the kingdom to Israel?" Simon the Zealot asked.

Jesus knew how eager these men were for an earthly kingdom where Israel would return to its glory days of David and Solomon. Still, how little they understood about the kingdom of God! He knew that the Holy Spirit would bring them to understand that the spiritual kingdom far outweighed an earthly one. Still, the long-foretold promises of Messiah's physical reign on Earth would indeed be fulfilled at Jesus' second coming. For now, there would be a grace period for all Jews and Gentiles to come to his light. And it would be up to these men, his disciples, alone to start the process of gathering believers into the kingdom.

"It is not for you to know the times or dates the Father has set by his own authority. But you will receive power when the Holy Spirit comes on you," Jesus explained. "And you will be my witnesses in Jerusalem, and in all Judea and Samaria, and to the ends of the earth."

"Brilliant! He's given them a roadmap of how to spread the Good News," Nigel cheered.

"*Oui,* but this Great Commission will be not only for the group but for each heart," Liz added. "I believe he means that everyone will have a Jerusalem, a Judea and Samaria, and an Earth to reach for Jesus."

"How do ye mean then?" Kate asked. "Wha' be someone's Jerusalem?"

"That would be those closest to you, *mon amie.* Your family and friends, no?" Liz answered.

Kate's smile brightened. "I see wha' ye mean then! An' Judea an' Samaria would be their community where they live?"

"Precisely! And of course, the ends of the earth is wherever else the Spirit leads you to go," Nigel added. "I say, this is utterly thrilling to think about being ambassadors to tread the green sod of lands near and far in the name of our King."

"That it be, Mousie," Max agreed enthusiastically. "We're goin' ta make Jesus pr-r-roud."

"I like the power part!" Al said. "Makes me not feel so scaredy."

Liz smiled at her lovable mate. *"Cher* Albert, Jesus' words will help these disciples not feel so scaredy also. To hear something like this is very stunning for these men who live in a world where power is never put in the hands of ordinary people. In this world, no one ever receives power. It is taken by force or by earning it."

"Bravo! And, the KING is sharing his power," Nigel added. "Jesus has just told his followers that the very same resurrection power he possesses will be *theirs* when the Holy Spirit comes into their hearts. Utterly smashing! I, for one, can't wait to watch what these ordinary fishermen do."

"Ye mean to tell me that the power that made Jesus come back to life will be given to anybody who believes in and follows him?" Al asked, wide-eyed. "That means they can do the impossible!"

"Aye, laddie," Max agreed, nudging the big cat. "An' so can even a kitty like ye."

Jesus placed his hand on Peter's shoulder. "Peter, remember who you are and the name I gave you. Be the rock for my church." He stared intently into Peter's eyes. "And keep your gaze always on me."

"I will, Master. I won't let you down," Peter stated resolutely, gripping Jesus' nail-scarred hand with his own.

Jesus smiled and moved on to John, placing his hand on the disciple's face. "Dear John, you will care for not only my mother, but many new children in my church. Your words will move heaven and earth."

John swallowed back a lump of love and deep emotion. "Thank you, my Lord. I am yours for all time."

Jesus proceeded to go down the line of men, blessing each of them with a specific word to encourage his heart in the way he individually needed. Then he stepped back from them and opened his arms wide. As he was speaking, he began to rise off the ground. Up above him, the fire cloud gloriously filled the sky.

"All authority in heaven and on earth has been given to me. Therefore go and make disciples of all nations, baptizing them in the name of the Father and of the Son and of the Holy Spirit, and teaching them to obey everything I have commanded you. And surely I am with you always, to the very end of the age."

Jesus' words powerfully resounded as he disappeared into the cloud. The men clung to one another and rejoiced in awe over what they had just witnessed. Jesus had ascended into heaven, right before their eyes!

"The fire cloud!" Al exclaimed, pointing up to the sky.

"Aye, there it be again!" rejoiced Max.

Liz, beaming, looked up to marvel at the incredible glory of the powerful presence of God in the fire cloud that enveloped his Son. "Jesus has done this to let his disciples know he is truly gone. He has been appearing to them for forty days. Now it is time for them to wait for someone new."

"Look!" Kate shouted. "Angels!"

As the men were looking intently up into the sky, suddenly two men dressed in white stood beside them. "Men of Galilee," they said, "why do you stand here looking into the sky? This same Jesus, who has been taken from you into heaven, will come back in the same way you have seen him go into heaven."

With that, the band of eleven brothers hugged one another as they turned and walked back down the mountainside toward Jerusalem. It was all up to them now. But they knew they wouldn't be alone.

Jesus would be with them. Always.

CIRCLE OF TWELVE, TONGUES OF FIRE

Mary sat in the corner of the large upper room belonging to her friend Mary, mother of John Mark, or "Mark" for short. The animals surrounded her and she breathed in contentedly as she softly stroked Liz, who was curled up purring in her lap. Max, Kate, and Al napped while Nigel peered out from a hole in the wall next to them. Although the animals did not speak to Mary, Jesus had told his mother that these were special animals on mission for God. Mary didn't understand, nor did she have to. She had loved these four-legged friends since before Jesus was born, and considered it a blessing to be with them whenever they reappeared. Mary called them by their Hebrew names, and had taken charge of their care since they appeared on Resurrection night.

"My little Zilla," Mary said with a smile as she tickled Liz under the chin, "I am a blessed woman. Although Jesus is gone, I am witness to what is happening with his followers." Mary looked around the room where 120 of Jesus' faithful followers sat together, talking, praying, and enjoying fellowship. Together with the eleven disciples, men and women who had followed Jesus' earthly ministry now gathered to wait expectantly for the Holy Spirit as Jesus had instructed them. Jesus' brothers— James, Jude, Joses, and Simon—were some of his most eager new followers. "And Jesus' brothers finally believe he is indeed Messiah. It took Jesus' resurrection for them to finally believe the truth."

"I know your heart is happy that your children now believe what you have known to be true for so long," Liz meowed. *"How hard it must have been to see them doubt Jesus and you,* mon amie."

Mary smiled at Liz. "I don't understand what you say to me, but I'm certain you understand what I say to *you,* my little shadow." She looked over at her son James. "Jesus spoke with James a long time before he left. I have a feeling James will play an important role in the church. I'm so proud to see such joy in his eyes."

The eleven—Peter, John, James, Andrew, Philip, Thomas, Nathaniel, Matthew, James the Less, Simon the Zealot, and Thaddeus—were huddled together discussing something. Peter nodded and stood, holding up his hands to get the attention of everyone gathered in the room. "Friends, long ago the Holy Spirit spoke through David regarding Judas, who became the guide to those who arrested Jesus. That Scripture had to be fulfilled, and now has been. Judas was one of us and had his assigned place in this ministry. For it is written in the Book of Psalms: 'May his place be deserted; let there be no one to dwell in it,' and, 'May another take his place of leadership.'"

Liz got up from Mary's lap and walked over to stand beside Nigel. "Who do you think it will be?"

"I'm not certain, but well done, Peter! The old boy tied the prophecies to Judas the betrayer," Nigel said to Liz quietly, adjusting his spectacles. "I'm quite pleased."

"Judas must now be replaced," Peter said, looking around the room. "The replacement must come from the company of men who stayed together with us from the time Jesus was baptized by John up to the day of his ascension, designated along with us as a witness to his resurrection."

James the Disciple stood and walked over to two men, placing his hands on their shoulders to stand. "We nominate Joseph Barsabbas, nicknamed Justus, and Matthias." The two men smiled and humbly stood before the group of believers.

Peter closed his eyes and prayed. "You, O God, know every one of us inside and out. Make plain which of these two men you choose to take the place in this ministry and leadership that Judas threw away in order to go his own way."

John held a bag of stones in his hand. "Only one stone is marked with the symbol of a fish. Whoever draws that marked stone will be the chosen new disciple. May the Lord guide his chosen one to the stone."

Justus and Matthias nodded and took turns slowly drawing out stones, but the first few were not marked.

"Each is a splendid choice, no?" Liz whispered. "This old method of casting lots to determine the Maker's will is true to Scripture, but I wonder if things will be different when the Holy Spirit comes."

"Quite true, my dear. I suspect that this type of decision-making process will no longer be needed, but for now, there we are," Nigel whispered. "I daresay the suspense is killing me!"

51

Matthias put his hand into the bag and slowly pulled out the marked stone. His heart swelled when he saw the sign of the fish. He smiled and looked up, handing the stone to John.

John held up the stone to show it to everyone. "Matthias it is! He will be one of the twelve."

Peter hugged the young man. "God be praised! Welcome, Matthias!"

The eleven gathered around the new disciple, enveloping him with love and open embraces.

"*Bon!* Now there are twelve," Liz said. "Judas needed to be replaced, not because of his death, but because he abandoned his post. Jesus said his twelve disciples would represent the new order of Israel and will someday judge the twelve tribes of Israel."

"Indeed, Matthias has just gained a throne to sit upon with the eleven," Nigel added. "What a splendid day for the young lad!"

"*Oui.* Jesus has returned to heaven, and the circle of twelve is once again complete," Liz pointed out, looking around the room. "Only one thing is missing."

"The Holy Spirit," Liz and Nigel uttered at the same time.

The Upper Room was buzzing with activity as the group of believers returned from the temple area. Over the past ten days they had been going to the temple, praying and praising. But today was a day of celebration and joy as they took their offerings of loaves to the temple and returned here to the Upper Room to enjoy the Feast of Weeks.

Al pouted, plopping down on the floor of the Upper Room. "Why couldn't I have any o' that bread?"

"Those loaves of bread are offerings for the Feast of Weeks," Liz explained. "Do not worry, *cher* Albert, you will have plenty to eat at the celebration feast tonight."

Kate put her paw on Al's back. "Can ye explain the festival ta the hungry kitty? Might help him ta wait then."

"Certainly," Nigel piped in, straightening his glasses. "The Feast of Weeks, also known as Pentecost, is a joyous festival celebrating the completion of the harvest season. You may recall that all able-bodied Jewish males are required to attend three major festivals each year."

52

"Aye, I r-r-remember this one," Max offered. "Passover, Pentecost, an' the Feast of Tabernacles."

"This is correct, *mon ami,*" Liz affirmed. "Pentecost is celebrated as a sabbath, with rest from work and a sacred assembly. This is why Jerusalem is bursting at the seams with people, no? There are Jews who have traveled from nations all over the Roman Empire to be here in Jerusalem for the festival."

"Aye, I never heard so many different languages spoken in one place," Kate said. "It were like standin' at Babel when the humans were confused an' scattered for tryin' ta reach heaven with their tower."

"Interesting observation, Kate," Liz agreed, curling her tail up and down in thought.

"So, the people are to count seven weeks from Firstfruits of harvest and then on the next day this feast is to be observed," Nigel continued. "Seven weeks are forty-nine days plus one additional day to make fifty days. *Pentecost* means "the fiftieth day" in Greek."

"Bread. Fifty days. Pentecost. Firstfruits," Liz thought out loud. "Do you realize that today marks fifty days since Jesus' resurrection?"

"Aye, so it be, Lass," Max nodded. "An' Jesus were the br-r-read of life."

"*And* the firstfruits of his sacrifice!" Nigel cheered, his whiskers shaking excitedly. "Look how perfectly the Maker once again has brought new meaning to the traditional feasts! Jesus was slain on the day of the Passover when the sacrificial lambs were offered to pay for the sins of the people. And he rose on the day after Firstfruits, being the first one to rise to new life!"

"*Mon Dieu! C'est incredible!*" Liz exclaimed. "Jesus is in the middle of everything!"

Some cloth hanging in the rafters of the Upper Room started to move. The fur of all the animals rose as they felt electricity in the air. Suddenly a sound like the blowing of a violent wind came from heaven and filled the whole house where the believers were sitting. They looked up and slowly stood to be enveloped in the middle of what seemed to be tongues of fire that came to rest on each of them. All of them were filled with the Holy Spirit and began to speak in other tongues as the Spirit enabled them. The room was aglow in glory.

Max, Kate, Nigel, Liz, and Al hugged one another in awe as they watched the disciples and the other believers in the room. They were singing and praising God in multiple languages. It was a miracle as the Holy Spirit permeated every heart and gave the room an unmistakable feeling of holiness, warmth, and love. It was as if Jesus himself were standing in the room.

"Wha' were we jest sayin' aboot the Tower of Babel?" Kate asked with her peppy grin.

"*Oui, Liz. C'est vrai!*" Al exclaimed in impeccable French. His eyes grew wide as he surprised himself, clasping his paws over his mouth. "*Je parle français! Je parle français! Je parle français!*"

"*Oui, mon cher!*" Liz marveled in reply. She couldn't believe what she was hearing. Al was speaking in French!

"Never in a millennium did I think I'd ever hear the lad speak like ye, Lass," Max chuckled.

That alone was a miracle, but as Liz looked around the room, it

53

dawned on her that an even greater miracle was happening. "Why else would the Holy Spirit give these believers the ability to speak in all these languages unless they were meant to use it for the Maker's purposes?"

Nigel scurried up to the window when he heard noises coming from outside. "I believe their opportunity has already come," Nigel called from the window. "People from all the nations where these languages are spoken are standing outside below the house! I believe they've heard the holy ruckus going on inside!"

"Sounds like a Babel reversal!" Kate exclaimed. "Instead of the nations scatterin' from confused languages, they all be comin' together."

"Aye, the Holy Spirit be br-r-ringin' heaven down ta the humans this time," Max declared.

"*Oui,* the Holy Spirit is just like Jesus, so he had to come to Earth to all men, just like Jesus," Liz thought out loud. "At Babel, humans arrogantly tried to climb to reach heaven. Now, heaven is humbly descending to reach Earth."

54

Nigel joined the animals back on the floor. "And it's happening here in Jerusalem! I've just realized something quite profound. What Bethlehem, known as 'house of bread,' was to Jesus' birth, Jerusalem is to the Holy Spirit today on Pentecost, celebrated with *bread* offerings. It's another bread incarnation, but this time with the spiritual member of the Trinity. The Holy Spirit shall feed hungry hearts with the Bread of Life from within. Brilliant!"

"*Oui! Le pain!*" Al exclaimed in French, running toward the door. "*Allons-y!*"

"Is he hurtin' then?" Kate asked, worried.

"No, *mon amie,*" Liz giggled. "*Le pain* means 'the bread.'"

"Well, I hope Big Al starts speakin' with his Ir-r-rish accent again soon," Max said, shaking his head. "Or he'll be a *livin' pain* if he keeps this up."

The contagious joy and energy was overflowing from the 120 people in the room. Peter ran to the door and the others followed him to run downstairs and meet the crowd outside. The animals ran after them with Al leading the way, continuing to shout, 'Let's go,' in French, "*Allons-y!*"

But Mary stayed behind a moment and Liz stopped to watch her while the others left the room. Mary stood with her eyes closed, nodding with tears of joy slowly streaming down her cheeks. She held her hands over her heart, gently tapping her chest. "Ah, yes, that's him. That's him."

Liz's eyes filled with tears with the sudden realization of what Mary was feeling. *Mary is the only one to ever have felt the presence of the Holy Spirit when he hovered over her and she became pregnant with Jesus. Mary felt him before as the baby she birthed. Now he has hovered over these believers in this room.*

It was a holy moment to witness this with Mary. Liz walked over and wrapped her tail around Mary's legs in affection. Mary smiled and reached down to pick the little cat up, holding Liz next to her heart.

"Il est ici, mon amie," Mary said to Liz, much to the surprise of them both.

"He is here indeed," Liz replied.

55

Liz smiled and Mary kissed her. Together they walked outside to witness an entirely new birth. The birth of the church.

8

3,000

Outside was holy, blessed chaos. The 120 believers were spreading out through the crowd filling the temple area, joyously sharing the good news of Jesus to everyone they saw. The people were shocked and amazed at hearing their own languages spoken by these believers. The crowd included Parthians, Medes, and Elamites; visitors from Mesopotamia, Judea, and Cappadocia, Pontus and Asia, Phrygia and Pamphylia, Egypt and the parts of Libya belonging to Cyrene; immigrants from Rome, both Jews and proselytes; even Cretans and Arabs.

One after another, these people shouted, "Aren't these all Galileans? How come we're hearing them talk in our various mother tongues?"

"They're speaking our languages, describing God's mighty works!" they exclaimed.

"Their heads be spinnin'," Max said with a big grin. "These humans can't make heads or tails of how it be happenin' but they sure can understand the message then."

"Aye, look at them talkin' back an' forth, happy but confused as can be!" Kate echoed, wagging her tail.

Somebody in the crowd shouted out, "They're drunk on cheap wine!"

"Blast it all! Peter needs to explain what has happened!" Nigel ranted, scanning the crowd.

Suddenly Peter and the other eleven disciples made their way up some steps to stand on an elevated portico. The men held out their hands to silence the crowd and the murmuring simmered down. Once it was quiet, Peter started to speak.

"Fellow Jews, all of you who are visiting Jerusalem, listen carefully and get this story straight. These people aren't drunk as some of you suspect. They haven't had time to get drunk—it's only nine o'clock in the morning," Peter said with his hands to his head, laughing at himself and the crowd joining him.

"This is what the prophet Joel announced would happen:

'In the Last Days,' God says,
'I will pour out my Spirit
    on every kind of people:
Your sons will prophesy,
    also your daughters;
Your young men will see visions,
    your old men dream dreams.
When the time comes,
    I'll pour out my Spirit
On those who serve me, men and women both,
    and they'll prophesy.
I'll set wonders in the sky above
    and signs on the earth below,
Blood and fire and billowing smoke,
    the sun turning black and the moon blood-red,
Before the Day of the Lord arrives,
    the Day tremendous and marvelous;
And whoever calls out for help
    to me, God, will be saved.'"

57

Peter grew even more animated as the Holy Spirit flowed through him and gave him the words he needed to address the crowd. "Fellow Israelites, listen carefully to these words: Jesus the Nazarene, a man thoroughly accredited by God to you—the miracles and wonders and signs that God did through him are common knowledge—this Jesus, following the deliberate and well-thought-out plan of God, was betrayed by men who took the law into their own hands, and was handed over to you. And you pinned him to a cross and killed him."

Once outside, Mary set Liz down and the petite black cat made her way over to join the animals on a wall as they watched this incredible scene unfold. Her tail whipped back and forth as she watched a group of men dressed in their priestly robes. "Those trouble makers are at it again. The same ones who took Jesus to Pilate and called for him to be crucified."

"Oh dear, you are most certainly right," Nigel lamented. A frown grew on his face. "I suppose I shall once again have to see what they're up to!" The mouse scurried off to make his way over to where the men stood.

Zeeb, Jarib, and Saar were Pharisees, and Nahshon was a Sadducee. They stood in the back of the crowd with sour expressions and arms folded over their chests as they listened to Peter and watched the people. They looked at one another in disgust.

"Do you hear this lowlife rabble accusing us?" Jarib scowled.

Zeeb held his hand up to silence his fellow Pharisee. "Wait. Listen."

"But God untied the death ropes and raised him up," Peter continued. "Death was no match for him. David said it all:

'I saw the Lord always before me.
    Because he is at my right hand,
    I will not be shaken.
Therefore my heart is glad and my tongue rejoices;
    my body also will rest in hope,
because you will not abandon me to the realm of the dead,
    you will not let your holy one see decay.
You have made known to me the paths of life;
    you will fill me with joy in your presence.'

"Fellow Israelites, I can tell you confidently that the patriarch David died and was buried, and his tomb is here to this day. But he was a prophet and knew that God had promised him on oath that he would place one of his descendants on his throne. Seeing what was to come, he spoke of the resurrection of the Messiah, that he was not abandoned to the realm of the dead, nor did his body see decay." Peter held his hand up to the heavens and smiled broadly. "God has raised this Jesus to life, and we are all witnesses of it. Exalted to the right hand of God, he has received from the Father the promised Holy Spirit and has poured out what you now see and hear. For David did not ascend to heaven, and yet he said,

"'The Lord said to my Lord:
"Sit at my right hand
until I make your enemies
a footstool for your feet.'"

"Therefore let all Israel be assured of this: God has made this Jesus, whom you crucified, both Lord and Messiah."

59

When the people heard this, they were cut to the heart. "What shall we do?" one of the men in the crowd cried out.

"Yes, please, tell us!" another echoed, followed by a unified voice of broken hearts moved by the Holy Spirit. They swarmed up to Peter and the disciples, begging them for guidance.

"Repent and be baptized, every one of you, in the name of Jesus Christ for the forgiveness of your sins. And you will receive the gift of the Holy Spirit," Peter explained. "The promise is for you and your children and for all who are far off—for all whom the Lord our God will call."

Peter looked right at the Pharisees. "Save yourselves from this corrupt generation."

As the crowd erupted in joy, those who believed ran to the pools surrounding the temple area. The disciples immediately started baptizing them and the joy of the people spread like wildfire through the crowd.

"Do you realize we have just witnessed the birth of Jesus' church?" Liz exclaimed, holding a paw to her face in wonder. "And look again at how precisely everything is happening! One hundred twenty has always been the number of people required to establish a local body of religious authority in Israel!"

"Aye, but wha' started with 120 looks like it's gr-r-rown way past that today," Max observed, scanning the crowd.

"Three thousand to be precise," came a voice from behind them.

The animals turned to see a beautiful young lady sitting on the wall next to them, smiling.

"Clarie?" Kate asked, cocking her head. "It's hard ta keep up with all yer disguises, Lass!"

Clarie giggled. "I know, but I enjoy it. You have just seen one of the most important days in history, my friends. In one day, the church was born and has grown by a huge percentage!"

Al wrinkled his forehead, rubbing it with his paw, trying to do the math. "What times 120 equals 3,000?" He put his paw in the air, trying to calculate it on an invisible tablet. He shook his head repeatedly. "Sure, it beats me."

"That would be 2,500 percent, old boy," Nigel said, rejoining the group. "It appears the Holy Spirit only gifted you briefly with language, not math." His whiskers shook as he chuckled.

"Nigel, what did you learn about the Pharisees?" Liz asked her mouse friend.

"Right. Well, of course you can imagine they are none too pleased with what they heard Peter say, and what the crowd is now doing," Nigel explained, wiping off his spectacles on Clarie's cloak. "They've already assigned the temple guards to watch the disciples, especially Peter. I followed them to their chambers and heard a new fellow, quite bold in his speech and knowledge. He insisted that they monitor these believers and their movements in Jerusalem. A chap by the name of Saul."

"Oh, dear, this is jest like it were when they spied on Jesus," Kate said with a frown. "Didn't they learn ye can't stop Jesus?"

"Aye, an' they can't stop his followers!" Max muttered gruffly.

"Sounds like *déjà vu* to me," Al said, growing a goofy grin. "At least I still got a little French in me. But I knew that before the Holy Spirit came then."

"You're going to see many things that will repeat what Jesus said and did," Clarie explained. "You will also see those opposing Jesus' church try to silence them, just as they tried to silence Jesus."

"*Oui,* Jesus told us this would happen," Liz agreed. "So what are we to do now?"

"For now, we'll watch this baby church as it grows," Clarie said, jumping off the wall. "Come on, time to get to the pools. There's a big baptism party going on!"

"Aye, time ta dive in!" Max cheered, now happy to get in the water.

"*Allons-y!*" Al started running ahead of the others. "Last one in is a rotten Pharisee!"

"Oh, dear, I think we'll have to work on Al's theology," Nigel quipped.

Liz grinned, watching her lovable mate running along with Max to his baptism. "At least he wants to be 3,001."

9

The Name

*K*oinonia? Wha' do that mean, Liz?" Kate asked in a hushed voice. She and Liz watched Peter yawn and tell the last of their fellow believers "Good night," handing them a blanket. The tired disciple walked over to the other side of the room, stretched out long and hard, and mussed his hair with both hands. He knelt down on his mat and said a prayer before lying down and quickly falling asleep.

Liz also stretched out on the floor, gently curling the end of her tail up and down. *"Koinonia* is a Greek word that means 'common'," she answered, yawning. "The new church is sharing their common belongings with one another, so no one has need for anything. They share food, money, places to stay . . ." Liz stopped, yawning again. ". . . blankets."

Kate caught Liz's yawn as she also grew sleepy. "I see. But they also share faith in Jesus an' enjoyin' each other, too. They pray for one another an' lift each other up in love. That's *koinonia* of the heart, right?"

"Oui, Kate." Liz smiled and yawned again, her eyelids growing heavy. She spoke slowly and softly. "Peter and the apostles have made this home and many others around Jerusalem a safe, happy place for believers to come fellowship together. No one is jealous, no one has pride. The poor don't feel ashamed, and the rich don't act above the

others." She yawned again, and closed her eyes as she curled up in a cozy ball next to Al, who was fast asleep. Nigel was tucked in between Al's front legs, dreaming of adventure. "It is a beautiful thing, no?"

"The people seem ta think so. New believers keep comin' ta worship an' visit every day. Aye, I like *koinonia*. It's a bonnie thing," Kate whispered. Liz closed her eyes and Kate smiled as she watched her friend purr and start drifting to sleep. "Night, Lass. Looks like we have sleepiness in common, too." Kate stretched and put her head down next to Max, who was running in his sleep.

Everyone in the house felt full, safe, happy, and loved.

Clarie hummed merrily and swung her basket side-to-side as she walked with the animals on the way to the temple area. It was a beautiful, sunshiny day, and everyone felt happy. The church was growing, and people were eager to believe Jesus and follow him. The apostles enjoyed sharing the truths about what Christ had done, and meeting the needs of people.

63

"My dear, I hate to be a bother, but could you not swing the basket so very far to and fro," Nigel said, hanging on the rim with one paw and holding his head with the other. "I'm afraid I'm getting dizzy."

"Sorry, Nigel," Clarie giggled. "We'll stop here and rest by the Beautiful Gate. There's something wonderful for us to see here soon." She set her basket on a low wall and took a seat, dangling her legs over the side.

"I'm most grateful," Nigel said, steadying himself. He climbed out of the basket to stand on the wall. "Ah yes, the Beautiful Gate. What a magnificent entryway! It's the only gate in the city made of Corinthian bronze and carved with such exquisite artistry."

"Looks like some heavy doors ta open an' close every night," Max observed. "It must take a couple of dozen laddies ta move them."

"You are correct, Max. Those double doors are seventy-five feet high," Nigel explained. "The other nine gates in Jerusalem are plated with silver and gold, but none has finer craftsmanship than this one."

"*Oui,* the touch of a master has made this gate too pretty to have silver and gold detract from its beauty," Liz added, smiling with a memory. "Speaking of the touch of a Master, I remember being here with Jesus when he was a boy, watching him trace his fingers along the intricate carvings of this gate."

"He loved this gate, indeed," Nigel remembered fondly. "Correction, *loves* this gate!"

"Exactly, Nigel," agreed Clarie. "Many beggars come here, so they love this gate as well. It's situated as a main entry point for worshippers going to the temple. Rabbis teach the people three main things of faith: reading the Torah, worship of God, and showing kindness and charity to others."

"An' the people know one of the best ways ta show charity is ta give money ta the poor beggars," Kate said. "So the poor laddies sit here beggin' for alms."

"Yes, Kate, and sadly this is as far as the lame can get into the temple area," Clarie frowned. "Not just because they cannot walk, but because they are viewed as unworthy. I know how they feel."

Kate was incensed. "Ye mean ta tell me the Jewish leaders teach showin' kindness by givin' these poor lads money, but they won't show kindness by helpin' them ta worship?!"

"*Oui,* this is part of the old order of things," Liz explained. "And precisely one of the things Jesus set out to change. All are welcomed with open arms in *his* church."

Al pointed to a trio of men. Two men were carrying another man who had his arms around their shoulders while they linked their arms under his knees. "Looks like some poor laddie be comin' now."

Clarie looked up at the sun's position in the sky. "Three o'clock. Right on time."

"I say, I've seen this chap many times," Nigel observed, adjusting his spectacles. "The poor man has been crippled since birth, suffering for forty years. I always wondered why Jesus didn't heal him."

"An' here come Peter an' John," Max noted. "Must be goin' ta the temple ta pr-r-ray."

"They are faithful to the old disciplines of prayer at the temple," Clarie said. "Even though their new faith in Jesus frees them to pray anytime and anywhere, the apostles realize that their new faith and the old disciplines can walk hand-in-hand."

"Aye, they be prayin' at three o'clock jest like Daniel did in Babylon!" Kate realized. "Remember how he wouldn't stop, even if it meant he'd be thrown ta the lions? He went out on his balcony an' prayed anyway."

"And he pulled down the curtain that Mousie put up for him to pray behind," Al remembered. "Daniel knew there were no right way to do the wrong thing."

"Aye, an' the Maker took care of the lad, lions an' all," Max added. He nudged Al with a wide grin. "Ye were in the lions' den ta see it, Big Al."

Al smiled weakly. "Aye, and I thought I had closed the beasties' mouths by talkin' to them. Glad it were an angel after all. I don't know if I could handle havin' so much power."

65

The lame beggar held up his hand as he saw Peter and John about to enter the Beautiful Gate, but kept his gaze eye level with his place on the ground. It was easier not to make eye contact in case he was rejected. "Alms! Please, help me! God bless you for helping a lame man!"

Peter and John stopped and looked at one another before looking straight at the lame man. "Look at us!" Peter demanded.

The man turned his gaze up to them expectantly, hoping they would give him something. Peter studied his face and his sad condition sitting here by the Beautiful Gate. Peter put his hand on the intricate carving of the gate, knowing it lacked silver and gold, but was far more valuable because of the master artisan's touch. He realized he had something far more valuable than silver and gold to give this poor man as well.

"If you are expecting silver or gold," Peter told him, turning his gaze back to meet the eyes of this suffering man, "I have neither, but what I have I will certainly give you. In the name of Jesus Christ of Nazareth, walk!"

Taking him by his outstretched right hand, Peter helped the lame man up. Instantly the man's feet and ankles became strong. He jumped to his feet and began to walk.

The people who were gathered around the Beautiful Gate gaped and cried out in awe as this lame beggar began to walk and jump around. They had seen him sit at this gate for years, so they knew that a miracle had just occurred.

"Look at me! Look at me! Look at me!" he cried, trembling with indescribable joy. "I can walk! Heaven be praised!"

Kate and Liz clung to Clarie as this beautiful miracle unfolded, their hearts bursting with joy and their eyes filling with tears at the goodness of God. "Peter helped him to stand just as Jesus did when he healed the lame."

"Right! I suppose Jesus waited until now to heal him," Nigel exclaimed. "'*Then the lame man will leap like a deer.*' Isaiah 35:6."

"Aye, the power were from Jesus' name, r-r-right through Peter's hand inta the lad's legs," Max marveled.

Peter and John smiled as the man went with them into the temple courts, walking and jumping, and praising God.

"Let's go see what happens next," suggested Clarie, jumping off the wall and walking ahead of the animals, who quickly fell in line behind her. "Our lame friend is experiencing physical *and* spiritual healing. He finally gets to worship in the temple."

The man held on to Peter and John with joy as they walked into the temple court area. They headed to Solomon's Porch, made of a double row of marble columns topped by a cedar roof that ran along the eastern wall of the outer court. The people were amazed and ran over to see them, chattering a mile a minute about the miracle as their voices echoed off the marble columns.

Peter saw the reaction of the people and held up his hands to calm them down. "Fellow Israelites, why are you surprised at this, and why do you stare at us? Do you think that it was by means of our own power or godliness that we made this man walk? The God of Abraham, Isaac, and Jacob, the God of our ancestors, has given divine glory to his Servant Jesus. But you handed him over to the authorities, and you rejected him in Pilate's presence, even after Pilate had decided to set him free. He was holy and good, but you rejected him, and instead you asked Pilate to do you the favor of turning loose a murderer. You killed the one who leads to life, but God raised him from death—and we are witnesses to this."

Liz turned her attention to the back of the crowd where some priests, the officer in charge of the temple guards, and some Sadducees arrived. They immediately saw the healed condition of the lame man and furiously talked among themselves.

Peter pointed to the lame man and smiled broadly. "It was the power of his name that gave strength to this lame man. What you see and know was done by faith in his name; it was faith in Jesus that has made him well, as you can all see."

The lame man held up his hands and danced around in a circle, laughing with joy. He clasped his hands together in front of his face and turned his head up to heaven in gratitude. Tears slipped down his cheeks as he closed his eyes and smiled.

The Jewish leaders angrily crossed their arms and stared down their noses at Peter. Liz's tail slowly curled up and down as she studied the sour faces of the Jewish leaders. "They look like angry *chats* with raised fur, no?"

"And now, my friends, I know that what you and your leaders did to Jesus was due to your ignorance," Peter offered. "God announced long ago through all the prophets that his Messiah had to suffer; and he made it come true in this way. Repent, then, and turn to God, so that he will forgive your sins. If you do, times of spiritual strength will come from the Lord, and he will send Jesus, who is the Messiah he has already chosen for you."

"Brilliant move, Peter!" Nigel cheered. "He's offering even the angry cats a second chance."

"How do ye mean?" Kate asked.

Al wrinkled his brow. "Aye, I don't see any angry cats around."

"No, old boy, I was simply using your bride's analogy of those Jewish leaders who look like angry cats," Nigel explained. "Kate, ignorant sins are considered forgivable and are distinguished from deliberate sins. There are means of making amends for sins that are committed unintentionally. Jesus himself said the Jews and especially the Romans didn't know what they were doing when they crucified him."

"Aye, they didn't know wha' they were doin', but God did," Kate added. "So Peter has ta explain how God used wha' they did for his plan."

"*Oui*, Peter is not excusing their sin or saying forgiveness is not necessary for what they did," Liz interjected.

"They didn't know it then, but they best know it now," Max relayed. "They r-r-rejected Jesus the first time 'cause they didn't know better, so they best ask for forgiveness."

"Right. If they reject Jesus a second time, it's an entirely different matter," Nigel noted with a serious expression. "If they reject him after hearing the truth, it will be . . . unforgivable."

"He must remain in heaven until the time comes for all things to be made new, as God announced through his holy prophets of long ago," Peter continued. "For Moses said, 'The Lord your God will send you a prophet, just as he sent me, and he will be one of your own people. You are to obey everything that he tells you to do. Anyone who does not obey that prophet shall be separated from God's people and destroyed.' And all the prophets who had a message, including Samuel and those who came after him, also announced what has been happening these days. The promises of God through his prophets are for you, and you share in the covenant which God made with your ancestors. As he said to Abraham, 'Through your descendants I will bless all the people on earth.' And so God chose his Servant and sent him to you first, to bless you by making every one of you turn away from your wicked ways."

Liz saw the Jewish leaders call the temple guards and point at Peter and John. Her tail was angrily swishing back and forth. "This is not good. They are angry at Peter's words. The Sadducees don't believe in resurrection and an afterlife."

"That's why they're *sad, ye see,*" Al quipped.

"I believe that Peter is only holding the Jerusalem Jews account-able for what happened to Jesus," Nigel suggested. "Not the Jewish people in general. And these Jewish leaders in Jerusalem are cozy with the Romans. They do not wish to do anything to upset their positions of power allowed by Rome. Such revolutionary talk is a threat to their authority. That's the real reason they killed Jesus."

The guards not only arrested Peter and John, but also the lame man they had healed. "Now they will come after Jesus' followers," Clarie added. "It's late in the day, so the men will spend the night in jail until they can stand before the Sanhedrin tomorrow morning."

"The devil can't stand for the name of Jesus to be exalted, so he has stirred up the Sanhedrin," Liz spat, her fur rising on end in anger as she watched the Jewish leaders quickly file out of the temple courts.

"Looks like ye're the angry *chat* now," Al said, looking at Liz. He turned and puffed up his fur at what these Jewish leaders were doing all over again, just as they had with Jesus. "That makes two o' us."

"Seven, actually," a voice said from the marble column.

10

THROWING
THE STONE

T he crowds dispersed quickly from Solomon's Porch after Peter, John, and the lame man were carried away. The animals gathered around the marble column as the face of Gillamon appeared. "Greetings!" Al almost fainted to see the mountain goat's marbled face move, but the plump kitty held on to Max. "I thought I'd try out a column since statues aren't allowed here."

"Gillamon, ye done scared the kitty lad," Max said. "Aye, but wha's goin' ta happen ta Peter an' John?"

"Aye, an' the poor lame laddie?" Kate implored. "Well, he's not lame anymore."

"I know we are all upset, and yes, angry. But this is a significant event, my friends. You are witnessing the very first persecution of Jesus' church," Gillamon explained. "You will begin to see a steady pattern emerge between the apostles and forces opposing The Way. In Jerusalem, it will be the Sanhedrin. In Judea and Samaria, it will be the Jews and the Greeks, and as for the rest of the world, Gentiles will lead the charge. This jailing of Peter and John is just the beginning."

"This is intolerable!" Nigel fumed, pacing back and forth.

"Oui, are we to just stand by and do nothing?!" Liz added, her anger rising.

"Remember that things are different now. The Holy Spirit has come, so these men are not alone," Gillamon assured them. "But the war has begun. And the Enemy will use four weapons against the church: persecution, moral compromise, distractions, and false teaching."

"Oh, dear, and so it begins with persecution," Nigel lamented.

A low growl rumbled in Max's throat. "Aye, an' physical violence be the cr-r-rudest way ta persecute anyone."

"I want you to watch for these four weapons of the Enemy," Gillamon continued. "You will see them used over and over again, and you will soon see that these weapons will be used on individual believers as well as the church as a whole. Learn how the Enemy operates, for you will see this repeated until Jesus comes again."

Kate looked at Liz. "I guess now there be a new kind of *koinonia.* The believers will have attacks in common, aye?"

71

"But remember the thing they have most in common, dear Kate," Gillamon reminded her as his face disappeared from the column. His voice echoed throughout the marble colonnade. "Jesus."

"Oui, and he's already prepared his soldiers for battle," Liz said, still angry but, after Gillamon's visit, understanding better what was taking place.

"Nigel, go check on Peter and John tonight," Clarie suggested. "The rest of us will sneak into the room where the Sanhedrin will bring them in the morning. We'll meet you there."

"Right!" Nigel immediately agreed. "I shall keep watch over our brave warriors tonight and see you in the morning."

As soon as Nigel scurried off to the jail, Clarie ducked behind a column as the beautiful young girl, and reemerged on the other side in the likeness of a temple guard.

Max grinned. "Guess ye can walk inta any r-r-room ye want then, Lass."

"That's the idea," Clarie said in a brusque male voice. "Come, let's get you hidden. You're not going to want to miss this."

The temple guard pushed Peter, John, and the lame man into the damp prison cell. "You better think about what you've said today and more importantly, what you'll say tomorrow. The entire Sanhedrin will be very interested in every word." He slammed the door and the men heard him lock it behind them.

The lame man trembled and sank to his knees in despair. "How can one day be filled with such miracles and joy, yet end up like this?"

John went over and put his hand on the man's shoulder. "Please tell us your name."

"Jethro," the man replied. He looked at John and smiled. "No one's cared to ask me my name for a long time."

"Ah, your name means 'overflowing abundance,'" John said with a smile. "I'd say that is the exact kind of day you've had, friend. So don't lose heart. The Lord who healed you today has a plan."

Peter paced back and forth. "The Sanhedrin are within their right to question us, according to the law. Do you remember what Moses spelled out in Deuteronomy?

'Prophets or interpreters of dreams may promise a miracle or a wonder, in order to lead you to worship and serve gods that you have not worshiped before. Even if what they promise comes true, do not pay any attention to them. The Lord your God is using them to test you, to see if you love the Lord with all your heart. Follow the Lord and honor him; obey him and keep his commands; worship him and be faithful to him. But put to death any interpreters of dreams or prophets that tell you to rebel against the Lord, who rescued you from Egypt, where you were slaves. Such people are evil and are trying to lead you away from the life that the Lord has commanded you to live. They must be put to death, in order to rid yourselves of this evil.'

"So they need to understand that we are not telling them to rebel against the Lord, but to follow him, but in the new way," John determined.

72

"Will they put us to death?!" Jethro cried in panic, putting his hands up to his head.

"Not you, my friend, for you have said nothing," Peter assured him. "You are a witness as we healed you. I think they want to frighten you away from our teachings. But John and I have spoken boldly about the Resurrection, and this is something the Sadducees can't accept. They see such statements as leading away from the Lord."

"So we can expect stones from the Sadducees," John said, wrinkling his brow.

Peter continued to pace back and forth across the dirty floor. The men grew silent as they contemplated what tomorrow could hold. Suddenly Peter stopped and a huge smile appeared on his face. He clapped his hands together and sat down next to John and Jethro. "This is exactly what Jesus told us about! John, don't you remember what he said would happen? 'Suddenly . . .'" He stopped and lifted his head, closed his eyes, and mumbled as he tried to recall the words. He quickly opened his eyes and grew animated with his hands as the words came rushing back to him. "'You will be arrested and persecuted; you will be handed over to be tried in synagogues and be put in prison; you will be brought before kings and rulers for my sake . . .'"

John nodded and his face brightened as he, too, remembered the words of Jesus. "Of course! The Master said, 'This will be your chance to tell the Good News. Make up your minds ahead of time not to worry about how you will defend yourselves, because I will give you such words and wisdom that none of your enemies will be able to refute or contradict what you say.' The Sanhedrin don't realize what they've done by arresting us! They've given us an audience with the most powerful men in Jerusalem to share the Good News! Perhaps the leaders of Israel will listen!"

"I fear their ears will hear, but their hearts will not," Peter replied with a frown. "But at least we will be told what to say to them, and whether they believe is not our responsibility."

"But the *people* hear you," Jethro said.

"He's right, Peter," John said with a hand on Peter's shoulder. "Look what happened just today when you spoke. Two thousand men

73

embraced your words to accept Jesus as Messiah. Two thousand!"

Peter shook his head in wonder. "We now have five thousand believers in the church. How can it be that my Lord would use such a man as me for his work? Only a few weeks ago I publicly denied him."

Nigel sat in a crack in the jail cell wall, listening to the men. *Now, dear Peter, you will get to publicly defend him.*

Jethro jumped when he heard loud voices outside their cell. The jailer's keys jingled and scraped as he unlocked the door. Jethro leaned over to shake Peter and John. "They're here!"

"Get up!" the jailer barked, rousing the men with his foot. "Time to go explain yourselves."

Peter and John sat up and quickly got to their feet. They offered Jethro a hand but he declined. "I need the practice of getting up by myself." Jethro pushed himself up and shook his head at the ease with which he did so. "I still can't believe it," he whispered as he stared at his strong legs.

Peter and John shared a smile. Just being reminded of where this man sat this time yesterday was a boost to their spirits. Suddenly Jesus' words came pouring into their minds: "I am with you always."

Peter walked ahead of the jailer. "Well, come on, let's get going."

"Bravo!" Nigel exclaimed with a fist in the air. He climbed down the wall and scurried along behind the men as they made their way to the room where the leaders of Israel were assembling.

The rulers, religious leaders, and teachers of the law were assembled in the room, forming a semicircle. Both Sadducees and Pharisees were present and murmured among themselves as Annas, the former high priest, and members of his family filed into the room. Annas took the main chair; his son-in-law Caiaphas sat next to him. Two scribes sat at desks in front of the leaders, ready to write down a report of the proceedings.

"I thought Caiaphas were the high priest," Max whispered from the hiding place where Clarie had situated them.

"He is, but remember that his father-in-law, Annas, retains utmost power as former high priest and head of the family," Liz answered. Her tail was already switching back and forth. "For Annas to be called to this meeting is significant. Jesus was first brought to him on the night he was arrested."

"Gillamon were r-r-right," Max replied. "This be a *big* moment."

"Bring them in," Annas ordered a temple guard, who gave the signal to the guards at the door.

The doors opened and in walked Peter and John, followed by Jethro. The guards stood Peter and John in the middle of the room, but placed Jethro to the side. He breathed a sigh of relief that Peter was right. He was only to serve as a witness.

"Morning, all," Nigel whispered, coming up behind the animals. "I do believe our chaps are ready. They know that their Wonderful Counselor is in court with them today."

"But of course he is," Liz replied with a smile. "Jesus told them they wouldn't be alone."

Annas looked Jethro up and down with a scowl. He lifted his hand toward the once-lame beggar now standing before him on two strong feet, but turned his gaze on Peter and John. "Who put you in charge here? What business do you have doing this?"

Peter felt a jolt of strength, mental clarity, and confidence surge through him, and Psalm 118 popped into his mind: *"The Lord is my strength and my defense." Of course!* Peter thought to himself. He knew exactly what to say. "Rulers and leaders of the people, if we have been brought to trial today for helping a sick man, put under investigation regarding this healing, I'll be completely frank with you—we have nothing to hide." He looked over at Jethro and shared a knowing smile with the healed beggar. Then he turned his fiery gaze onto the leaders of Israel. "By the name of Jesus Christ of Nazareth, the One you killed on a cross, the One God raised from the dead, by means of his name this man stands before you healthy and whole. Jesus is 'the stone you masons threw out, which is now the cornerstone.' Salvation comes no other way; no other name has been or will be given to us by which we can be saved, only this one."

John stood there and nodded with an air of confidence and gazed at the seventy-one leaders who did nothing but look at Peter and John, dumbstruck.

"Brilliant strategy!" Nigel cheered. "Peter has immediately gone on the attack, using the stone reference from Psalm 118."

"I thought he wouldn't want them to be thinkin' aboot stones," Al said, confused.

"No, the stone the builders rejected is in this psalm but also in Isaiah," Liz explained. "Every man in this room knows the story, dating back to the building of Solomon's Temple. All stones were cut off site so there would be no noises from hammers and axes to disturb the holiness of the area. One day a huge, strangely shaped stone was delivered that had clearly been cut with great care, but the builders didn't know where to put it. They did not understand the place it was meant to fill, so they set it aside where it soon became forgotten."

"Right, until the time came for the building to rise from the ground and they needed a cornerstone of a particular shape," Nigel chimed in, preening his whiskers. "It was then that someone remembered the stone. It filled the gap exactly."

"Aye! So Peter be usin' the story ta fit it in this case," Kate realized. "The Jewish leaders be the first builders who rejected the stone. Now Peter, John, an' all the new believers be the ones who know wha' the stone needs ta be."

"Precisely, my dear!" Nigel eagerly affirmed. "Jesus is that stone, and his followers have put him in the key position as his church has started to rise."

"Peter also realized somethin' else then," Max jumped in. "The Sanhedrin said they didn't want the stone, but Jesus said, 'Whoever falls on this stone will be cut ta pieces; an' if the stone falls on someone, it will cr-r-rush him ta dust.'"

"*Oui,* Max, this is why Peter said there is no salvation for men apart from Christ," Liz added, marveling at Peter's insight. "*C'est magnifique!*"

"Looks like Peter threw a stone at the Sanhedrin instead o' the other way around," mused Al. The animals looked at the orange cat, completely amazed. Meanwhile, the leaders were equally amazed when they realized these two were laymen who possessed no formal training in Scripture and no formal education. They recognized Peter and John as companions of Jesus, but with Jethro standing before them, well and healed, what could they say? "Now the *chat's* got their tongue."

Annas motioned for the guards to take the three men out of the room. Peter, John, and Jethro walked confidently away from the assem-bly while the Sanhedrin immediately began discussing what they were going to do about them. As usual, Zeeb, Jarib, and Saar the Pharisees and Nahshon the Sadducee took the lead in the discussion.

"What can we do with these men? By now it's known all over town that a miracle has occurred, and that they are behind it. There is no way we can refute that," Jarib pointed out. "The people won't stand for us keeping these men in jail. They are out there praising God over what's happened with that lame beggar."

"Have you seen how the people go after these men?" Saar scowled. "We were there during Pentecost when the masses were swept into a frenzy and started getting baptized in the name of this Jesus!"

"How do these uneducated men speak as they do, referencing the Scriptures?" Nahshon spat in frustration.

"They've been with Jesus for three years, that's how," Nicodemus spoke up boldly. "And this chamber has not refuted the claim of Jesus' resurrection."

"We are divided on the issue of resurrection, but if we could refute the claim that Jesus rose from the dead, this new movement would col-lapse," Joseph of Arimathea added to the shock of his peers. He looked around at these most learned of all men in Israel and his eyes landed on Zeeb and his companions. "Even bribing some Roman soldiers to convince the people otherwise with stories of Jesus' stolen body, the truth is that no one in this room *can* refute it."

Everyone paused and looked over at Nicodemus and Joseph. It was well known that these two respected members of the Sanhedrin disap-proved of Jesus' execution. No one wanted to begin a debate between the Sadducees and the Pharisees on the issue of resurrection, much less Jesus' resurrection. And silently, the Sanhedrin knew they were right about this dividing point. Zeeb glared at Joseph and cleared his throat. "Well, the reality facing us is that we'll have more trouble with this Jesus *after* his death than before, if these followers keep it up."

The young Pharisee named Saul leaned over and whispered in Nahshon's ear. "I know I am a guest of this prestigious assembly, having accompanied my teacher Gamaliel here today to observe the Sanhe-drin. But may I be so bold as to make a suggestion? So that it doesn't go any further, I would silence these men with threats so they won't dare to use Jesus' name ever again with anyone."

Nahshon nodded and rose to his feet. "Perhaps we should silence these men by threatening them to never use Jesus' name again."

A quiet murmuring with nodding heads filled the room. Zeeb and the others raised their eyebrows in approval of Saul's suggestion. Every-one looked to Annas for his opinion. "Very well. Bring them back in."

Once Peter and John stood before them again, Annas pointed his finger at them with an intimidating stare. "You are on no account ever again to speak or teach in the name of Jesus."

John immediately answered him right back, "Whether it's right in God's eyes to listen to you rather than to God, you decide. As for us, there's no question—we can't keep quiet about what we've seen and heard."

Peter nodded calmly and held his head high. "We will not reject the cornerstone."

Immediately the assembly started shouting threats at Peter and John to intimidate them but the two stood there, resolute and calmly confident. Finally, Annas stood and motioned to the temple guards. "Release them." He stormed out of the room, followed by Caiaphas and the others.

As Peter and John left the room, they put their arms around Jethro, and grinned from ear to ear. "God was true to his word!" John enthused.

"He told us exactly what to say," Peter agreed. "The leaders didn't know how to even respond. Let's go share the good news with everyone!"

Saul glared at the jubilant apostles with unmasked hatred. He clasped his hands tightly, wishing he had stones to hurl at them. Zeeb came up to the young Pharisee and smiled. "It is clear you take our point of view on this Jesus matter."

Saul bowed humbly. "Thank you, sir. I am passionate about the law, and these rebels must be stopped! However I can be of assistance, I am willing."

Zeeb shared knowing looks of approval with Jarib, Saar, and Nah-shon. He smiled insidiously at Saul. "You have a future with us, Saul." He put his hand on Saul's back and together they walked out of the room.

The animals stayed behind until the humans cleared out, but they were hugging one another to celebrate this huge victory in the first battle of persecution.

"There be two types of courage," Max said. "The reckless kind that don't understand the dangers ahead, an' the cool kind that knows the dangers but refuses ta back down. Peter had cool courage today. I'm pr-r-roud of the lad! He's come a long way."

"Jest like David an' Goliath!" Kate remembered. "Peter an' John were the little guys up against the most powerful giants in Israel."

"David threw a stone and took out his giant, too," Al noted. "Sure, and I'm glad stones can sometimes be on our side."

"Ah, but not just any stone," Liz pointed out. "*The* Stone. And the new church builders put it firmly in place today."

"We'll return to this room again," Clarie announced as she led the animals out of the Sanhedrin's chambers. She stepped around a column and turned from a temple guard back into a beautiful young girl. "But for now, we have a builder's party to attend."

11

TROUBLE WITHIN AND THREATS WITHOUT

E veryone was on their knees in the upper room, praying for Peter and John. Waves of varied emotions had swept over the group since they learned of yesterday's arrest: fear, anxiety, discouragement, sadness, uncertainty. The heaviness in the room was unbearable at times, but still this infant church prayed for their leaders, hoping beyond hope that what happened to Jesus wasn't happening all over again to his followers at the hands of the same men.

Mary lifted her head when she heard footsteps coming up the outside staircase. Her heart began to race and she put her hand up to her neck. "Please let it be them," she prayed silently.

Suddenly Peter and John burst into the room with radiant smiles. Mary closed her eyes and smiled in relief.

"We're free!" John exclaimed. "And so is our new brother, Jethro!" John stood him in front of the group. "His body is free from lameness but his heart is also now free in Christ. Welcome him into our fellowship."

James the disciple and the others joyfully got to their feet and surrounded the three men. "Welcome, Jethro. Praise God you are healed!"

He put his hand on Peter. "And praise God you and John are safe. We haven't stopped praying for you."

Matthew ran up to embrace Peter and John. "Tell us what happened!"

"Everything Jesus said would happen," Peter answered with a wide grin. "He told us we would face persecution, which we did. But he told us he would give us the words to say, which he did."

The women poured cups of water for the men to drink, and ushered them over to sit down while they busily prepared something for them to eat. The men eagerly drank the water and the rest of the people sat down around them, excited to hear their news. Clarie and the animals slipped in the door unnoticed.

"Thank you," Jethro said as he took some bread and sat among his new friends, overwhelmed with gratitude. "Thank you all for welcoming me here."

"The Holy Spirit gave Peter the exact words to boldly speak to the Sanhedrin, who asked by what authority we healed Jethro," John explained, wiping his chin. "He boldly declared that Jesus whom they had killed had risen and was alive and well as the cornerstone they had rejected."

"Well done, brother!" Andrew said, shaking Peter by the shoulder. "How did they respond?"

Peter swallowed a bite of bread. "At first they were speechless and sent us out of the room to think of what to say. Then they brought us back and told us that we were never again to speak the name of Jesus."

"And?" Thomas eagerly implored.

"We told them that wouldn't work for us," gushed John. "We told them we must obey God alone, not them."

"We made it clear we would not reject the Cornerstone," Peter added, his finger in the air to make a point. "I thank God that *this* time, I was able to publicly, proudly say I am indeed a follower of Jesus."

Jesus' brother James and the others were caught up in the joy of hearing this incredible report. James lifted his hands to lead them in prayer. "Lord, you are God, who made heaven and earth and the sea, and all that is in them, who by the mouth of your servant David have said:

'Why did the nations rage, and the people plot vain things? The kings of the earth took their stand, and the rulers were gathered together against the Lord and against his Christ.'"

"He's quoting Psalm 2," Liz whispered to Nigel. "I'm so happy they now see Jesus everywhere in the Scriptures!"

"Jolly good!" Nigel whispered back. "He's on every page! I do believe they're getting it."

James the disciple continued. "For truly against your holy servant Jesus whom you anointed, both Herod and Pontius Pilate, with the Gentiles and the people of Israel were gathered together to do whatever your hand and your purpose determined before to be done."

Nathaniel joined in. "Now, Lord, look on their threats, and grant to your servants that with all boldness they may speak your word . . ."

". . . By stretching out your hand to heal, and that signs and wonders may be done through the name of your holy servant Jesus," Philip continued.

Liz welled up. *C'est bon!* They haven't asked to be delivered from the threats of the Enemy, only to have the courage to keep speaking boldly and to continue to heal others in Jesus' name."

Max and Kate looked at one another with caution. "Wait for it," Max whispered, feeling something in the air.

Suddenly the bread started vibrating across the plate and the water in the cups rippled with movement. Everyone looked up at the rafters as dust fell from the ceiling. The people locked eyes with one another as the room began to shake. But instead of fear, their hearts burst with joy as they were filled anew with the Holy Spirit. They hugged one another and started to sing a hymn of praise.

"How . . . utterly . . . splendid!" Nigel grunted, pulling himself out of Al's terrified grip. "Look how pleased the Maker is with these people, giving them such an affirming show of his presence."

Al let Nigel go, not realizing he had seized the little mouse in fear of the room's shaking. "Ye mean that weren't an earthquake?" A goofy grin grew on his round face. "So that's what it sounds like when the Maker claps his hands."

The ladies rose to their feet and Mary, mother of John Mark, exclaimed, "We will have a feast tonight to celebrate what God has done!" She quickly led the women to begin preparing the food.

Mary got up and went over to the animals, petting Al on the head as she heard him meowing. "Clarie, isn't it?" Mary asked the young girl. "I know you are one of our new members but I haven't gotten to speak with you. I'm Mary, Jesus' mother."

Clarie smiled. "Yes, yes, I know who you are," Clarie answered awkwardly. *If Mary only knew.* "I'm so happy to be here with you, and the others of course."

"Yes, it's a wonderful day," Mary said with a squeeze to Clarie's arm. "Hmmm, Clarie. I hope you won't be offended but I once had a little lamb by your name. Her fleece was as white as snow."

The animals looked at one another and giggled. "I'm honored you had a lamb by my name, Mary," Clarie said warmly. "I know she was very happy to be yours."

"Well, we were happy she was ours, and she . . ." Mary stopped and looked at Clarie's penetrating blue eyes, and how she sat comfortably among the animals. Mary wore a puzzled expression for a moment, reaching over to pet Liz. "She was good friends with all these animals."

"Well these are special animals, aren't they?" Clarie answered quickly, standing to go help the women. "I should see how I can help the others. Excuse me."

As Clarie walked over to assist the women in preparing food to celebrate the safe return of Peter and John, Mary picked Liz up and held her close. "If I didn't know better, Zilla," she whispered in Liz's ear, "I'd say this Clarie is one and the same. I wouldn't put anything past my Jesus, especially now with the Holy Spirit."

Liz gazed up at Mary and smiled affectionately. *"Oui, chère Mary,"* she meowed. *"Expect the unexpected, no?"*

"They're both," Al gulped, "dead?"

"Sad but true, I'm afraid," Nigel replied, wiping off his spectacles and placing them back on his head. "Ananias and his wife, Sapphira, have been severely punished by the Maker for their deception. They each dropped dead after Peter confronted them. I daresay, Peter was just as shocked as anyone."

The animals were gathered in an alcove off Solomon's Porch, where the apostles now met regularly to teach and worship in public. Crowds were gathered around listening to them boldly preach the good news about Jesus.

"But why did the Maker take such dr-r-rastic steps then?" Max asked with a furrowed brow. "Seems a bit harsh. Wha' exactly were their cr-r-rimes?"

"As you know, this new church family is made up of believers who share everything so no one lacks food, shelter, or clothing," Nigel explained.

"Aye, *koinonia,*" Kate affirmed. "Everythin' in common."

"Precisely, but all this sharing is completely voluntary. No one is forced to do anything to help but does so out of love for fellow believers," Nigel relayed. "Some of the believers who own land have sold it to give the money to help the church."

"Aye, like Barnabas, the new apostle from Cyprus," Kate interjected. "His kindness stunned everyone when he brought all that money ta Peter ta help feed so many. I like Barnabas a bonnie bunch. He always be helpin' others."

Liz put her dainty paw on Kate's shoulder. "*Bien sûr*, of course you do, *mon amie*, for you are very much like him with your big heart. The apostles gave him the nickname *Barnabas,* which means 'son of encouragement.' His real name is Joseph."

"So what happened to the dead, bad couple?" Al wanted to know, eager for the story to continue.

"Right. Well after seeing how well received Barnabas was for generously giving money from the land he sold, Ananias and Sapphira evidently wanted to experience the same praise for their good works.

They also sold a piece of property, but didn't bring all the money to the apostles. They secretly kept some of it," Nigel continued.

"The land and the money were theirs to keep or to do with as they wished, no?" Liz pointed out. "The problem was not that they did not give all the money to the church, but that they lied about it. If they had simply been honest all would have been fine. *Quel dommage!*"

"Precisely right, my dear," Nigel said. "They told Peter they were bringing all the money they made from the land. They didn't just lie to Peter, they lied to God, and therein rests the dreadful truth of their crime."

Al's eyes widened. "They *lied* to the Maker? Did they not think he knew anyway?" The big cat waved his paw in disgust. "Even *I* know that he knows what I'm doin' even when I don't want him to know that I don't know what I'm doin'."

The animals sat a moment and stared at Al, trying to follow what he just said.

Nigel shook his head. "Anyway, when Peter confronted them sepa-rately, they both denied it. Peter asked Ananias how Satan had so filled his mind that he could cheat the Holy Spirit. Ananias was overcome with fear and dropped dead on the spot!"

"*Oui,* so after the men returned from burying Ananias, Sapphira came to Peter, knowing none of this," Liz added. "She repeated the lie and also dropped dead. The Maker wanted to show how serious this was and to let the church know that there must be no such behavior among his believers. The Maker is not impressed when humans try to impress other humans through sin."

"Sounds jest like Judas," Max frowned. "Satan got inta his heart an' made it all aboot the money with that lad, too. An' we all know how he ended up."

Al wore a look of horror. "Sure, and I didn't know money could be so deadly! I'd rather be a poor kitty than die from money!"

"Money itself is certainly not deadly, old boy, but how one uses it becomes the issue," Nigel said. "Money is good when in the right hands, such as Barnabas's. And the Maker blesses those who

85

can bless others with it."

"It's the second weapon!" Kate realized. "Clarie said the second weapon of the Enemy were moral compromise. He's weaseled inta the church by gettin' inta the heart of its members. This were a crime of the heart."

"That's right, Kate," Clarie said. "So far we've seen persecution without and moral compromise within. So the Maker had to take this drastic step to stop the Enemy in his tracks. The Maker needs his church to understand that they need to truly be one heart and live in complete trust with each other. Where there is unity and trust, the church will only thrive. But if there is deception and division, it will fail."

"Aye, if this keeps up, people might think the church has a bunch o' hypocrites in it then," Al pointed out.

"At least only true believers now dare to come join the church, as news of this event has put the fear of the Maker in humans," Nigel said. "The Maker will use this incident to help his new church get well established with strong, truthful people."

"How it angers me that this beautiful new paradise of the church has been invaded by that serpent, just like in the Garden," Liz said with a frown, her tail whipping back and forth.

"Yes, but it was expected. This is a brand new war, remember," Clarie reminded them. "And as this war begins we will see things hap-pen with this early church that may not be repeated as history rolls on. Some things are to serve as examples and guides for followers to come. The Maker can do whatever he wants, whenever he wants, but most likely the events of causing people to drop dead, bringing earthquakes and tongues of fire, and even healing by Peter's shadow will be unique to this new church."

"I say, that last bit has been terribly thrilling to watch!" Nigel said, preening his whiskers excitedly. "The people have brought their sick and possessed loved ones to the apostles and some have actually been healed just by sitting there when Peter's shadow walked by. Brilliant!"

"Aye, an' everyone who comes has been healed," Kate noted. "Jest like when Jesus were here an' the people came ta him. It's a grand thing ta see!"

Max stood up and growled, watching some of the Jewish leaders roaming the courtyard area, looking in the direction of the apostles. "The most gr-r-rand thing of all has been that the lads have kept r-r-right on pr-r-reachin' in the name of Jesus. They don't care a camel's spit aboot how those r-r-rats thr-r-reatened 'em."

Liz turned her gaze to where Max looked and saw a group of Sad-ducees and temple guards, clustered with their heads together. The same bunch of scheming Pharisees joined them. "I can only imagine the anger and jealousy those men now have, watching the apostles blatantly ignore their threats and continue to teach and heal in Jesus' name."

Suddenly a group of twenty armed temple guards entered the tem-ple courtyard and marched straight toward the apostles in Solomon's Porch. Yelling and screaming ensued as they arrested all twelve apostles, carrying them off to the prison. The people scattered in all directions. Two of the schemers walked over to stand by the columns where Peter and the others were preaching just moments before.

87

"I see now that the biggest mistake last time was to arrest Peter and John and quickly release them with only threats," Saul sighed, resting his hand on the marble column right in front of where the animals hid. "It has only emboldened these Jesus-followers."

"Indeed," Nahshon replied with a frown. "Mere threats won't stop them. It's time we back up our threats with action. Come with me, Saul. Zeeb asked me to bring you to his chambers."

As the men walked off, it was all Max could do to not run after them and bite their ankles. "Steady, Max," Kate cautioned, putting her paw on his shoulder.

"No! Not again!" Liz lamented.

"It be almost like *déjà vu* all over again," Al whined.

"Blast it all, they're off to prison again, but this time all *twelve* of them!" Nigel shouted, pacing back and forth. "Once again, this is intolerable! And who is this Saul fellow anyway?!"

"This is persecution, round 2, with many more rounds to come, so you best get used to it." A big smile grew on Clarie's face. She slipped behind a column. "But if you thought round 1 ended well, just wait 'til you see how this round goes."

The animals looked at one another when Clarie didn't reappear. Liz stepped cautiously forward. *"Mon amie?"* Liz walked completely around the column and back to the animals. "She is gone."

"Where did she go now?" Kate asked. "An' where should we go?"

"I believe we should return to comfort the others in the upper room," Liz suggested. "I'm sure Mary would appreciate our presence until tomorrow."

"Aye," Max agreed. "But at least from wha' Clarie said, I bet tomorrow will be somethin' gr-r-rand ta see."

88

"Right, well I shall resume my post and give you a full report in the morning," Nigel remarked, scurrying off. "It's back to prison for this churchmouse."

12

UNEXPECTED ALLIES

I n you go!" the jailer shouted, shoving Matthias into the prison cell with the others. The jailer looked over at Peter and John. "You two must like being in here. Decided to bring some friends with you this time, I see!" the grimy man laughed as he slammed the door behind him, locking it with one of his jingling keys.

"You two are to guard these men tonight," the chief temple guard instructed his men outside the cell. "No one is allowed in or out of this cell until I send for them in the morning. Is that clear?"

"Sir!" the guards each affirmed, putting their heels together, standing at attention with spear and shield in hand. They remained at attention while their superior officer peered into the dimly lit cell to count his prisoners.

"Twelve," he muttered before turning to walk down the corridor, making the mounted wall torches flicker as he passed.

"Peter, what do we do?" Matthias asked nervously, joining the others seated on the dirty floor.

Peter put his arm around the young man's shoulder and smiled. "We pray and we trust the Lord for what he will bring from this."

Matthew looked around the dank cell, lit by a single torch hanging on the wall. He pulled his cloak up around his shoulders. "Do you suppose this is where they kept Jesus that night?"

John gazed at the dingy walls and nodded grimly. "More than likely, after the temple guards had brutally beaten him. After Jesus appeared before Annas and the Sanhedrin illegally in the night, they locked him up until they could have a legal hearing at dawn."

"Then I feel honored to be kept where they put our Lord," Thomas said. "And if they see fit to give us the same sentence," he swallowed hard, "so be it."

"I don't think it will come to that, Thomas, at least not right away," Peter smiled reassuringly. "They gave direct orders to only John and me not to speak in the name of Jesus, which we have willfully disobeyed, just as we told them we would. By now their anger has reached a boiling point when they see the two of us defying their authority."

"The Sanhedrin is afraid of the people who support us and keep adding to our numbers daily," James added. "They cannot refute the healing miracles they've seen the Lord provide through us on the temple grounds."

"And as our gatherings have been peaceful they cannot accuse us of causing a disturbance in the temple," Andrew pointed out.

Peter looked at the eleven men gathered around him. "The most important thing to realize is not what these men have in mind, but what God has in mind. As before, he will tell us exactly what to say and do. Let us seek his will."

The men bowed their heads and entered into a time of fervent prayer. After their prayers were concluded they quietly lay down on the straw scattered around on the floor, closed their eyes, and drifted off to sleep, resting fully in the Lord's peace alone.

Nigel yawned from his nook in the prison cell wall once he saw that the men were finally asleep. "I suppose I shall do the same." The little mouse took off his spectacles and set them down, yawning again. "We all need our sleep for the big day tomorrow." He curled up in a ball and quickly fell asleep.

Nigel's whiskers twitched as he heard a voice, but he didn't want to leave his dream of playing the harp with his finest student, Benipe, back in Egypt.

"Nigel! Nigel, wake up!" the voice whispered.

The mouse rolled over away from the voice. "That's it, my boy," he spoke in his sleep. "Keep practicing."

"NIGEL!" the voice whispered insistently.

Nigel finally opened his eyes but they were blurry without his spectacles. He groped for them while he rolled over to see a face hovering right over him.

"Who goes there?!" Nigel demanded uneasily, still groping for his glasses. His tiny paws grasped them at last and he quickly put them on to see two beautiful blue eyes staring at him.

"Shhh, it's me," Clarie answered, putting a finger to her mouth. "We're going to help break the twelve out of prison. An angel is coming now to wake them."

Nigel quickly stood up and saw that Clarie was dressed like a beautiful angel. She wore a white robe that cascaded over her in layers with satin sashes criss-crossed over her shoulders and tied at her waist. Her curly blonde hair rested on her shoulders. "My dear, you look radiant!"

91

"Thank you, Nigel," Clarie smiled. "This is a great privilege for me to work with an actual angel so I wanted to look the part! The men won't be able to see me. Now, I'm going to open the prison doors while the angel leads the men out of here. I need for you to keep watch over the prison guards, and make sure they do not awaken until the temple guards arrive. I'll keep an eye out at the other end of the corridor."

"Right! What jolly good fun!" Nigel chuckled. His eyes then widened. "I say, how exactly am I supposed to accomplish such a feat?"

"Serenade them if need be," she replied, walking over to the door. "I'm sure you'll think of something."

"What shall become of our twelve friends here?" Nigel asked as he scurried down the wall and over to the already opened door.

"You'll see," Clarie told him with a smile before dashing down the corridor.

Suddenly an angel appeared standing by Peter's head. He bent down to gently shake Peter's shoulder. When he opened his eyes, he quickly put his finger to his mouth. "Come," he whispered. "Bring the others."

Peter immediately tapped each man on the shoulder, instructing them to remain quiet. Once they were on their feet, the angel motioned for them to follow him out the open door. They looked at one another in awe and cautious excitement, and did as instructed. One by one they tiptoed past the sleeping guards and made their way down the corridor.

Once they were clear, Nigel hopped up onto the stone bench where the sleeping guards sat with their heads propped against the wall. He crossed his arms and tapped his finger on his chin. "How does one keep two human guardsmen asleep?"

The angel turned the corner and led the twelve apostles up the steps leading out of the prison. Once they were out of earshot of the guards, he turned and faced them. "Go and stand in the temple complex, and tell the people all about this life." He smiled and nodded to them and disappeared into the night.

Peter grinned at the apostles and they all hugged one another over this miraculous deliverance. "Back to Solomon's Porch!"

92

❮⟩

"How you, men of Athens, have been affected by my accusers, I do not know; but I, for my part, almost forgot my own identity, so persuasively did they talk; and yet there is hardly a word of truth in what they have said. But I was most amazed by one of the many lies that they told—when they said that you must be on your guard not to be deceived by me, because I was a clever speaker." Nigel strolled back and forth between the guards, lifting his hands for emphasis as he recited ancient Greek literature. He looked up to check on the guards to see if this was working. One guard dropped his head back down to his chest while the other started snoring.

"Oh, Plato, old chap, forgive my using your splendid work for such a belittling purpose as this, but I had to find something to bore the uneducated mind," Nigel said to himself, preening his whiskers. "Now where was I? Oh, yes . . . *For I thought it the most shameless part of their conduct that they are not ashamed because they will immediately be convicted by me of falsehood by the evidence of fact, when I show myself to be not in the least a clever speaker, unless indeed they call him a clever speaker who speaks the truth; for if this is what they mean, I would agree that I am an orator—not after their fashion. Now they, as I say, have said little or nothing true; but you shall hear from me nothing but the truth."*

Clarie peeked around the corner and listened to Nigel for a minute, unable to contain a giggle. "Well done, Nigel," she whispered, walking over to quietly close the cell door and lock it back securely. "You can stop now. It's almost daylight."

Nigel held his chin in the air, clasped his paws behind his back, and rolled up and down on his toes and heels. "Plato's Apology," the mouse quipped with a grin. "Hypnotic to the uneducated mind."

Nahshon raised his hand to motion for Saul when he saw the young man enter the chamber of the Sanhedrin. All the Jewish leaders were gathering together, waiting for the arrival of the high priest and his close associates. Saul smiled and made his way over to sit next to Nahshon and the others. While not yet a member of the Sanhedrin, his status as a well-educated Pharisee and student of the respected Gamaliel afforded him the opportunity to attend as part of his training.

"Glad you could make it," Nahshon said. "This morning should prove to be most interesting."

"I certainly hope so," Saul eagerly answered. "Having Jesus' inner circle of followers in custody certainly will lead to the stamping out of this blasphemous sect."

Suddenly Caiaphas the high priest entered the chamber and all grew quiet. "Bring the men to us," he instructed the chief temple guard. The man bowed and instructed his men to go get the prisoners. Caiaphas took his seat and looked around the room at the Sadducees and Pharisees, knowing full well this would be a heated session.

The guards yawned and shook their heads as they slowly awoke. One looked over at the other. "I had the strangest dream."

"Shhh!" the other guard responded, quickly getting to his feet. "Last thing we need to talk about is how we fell asleep!"

They heard the footsteps of the temple guards coming down the corridor, and the unmistakable sound of jingling keys belonging to the jailer in front of them. The two guards straightened their caps, grabbed their spears, and stood at attention by the cell door.

The jailer put the key into the cell door, which creaked loudly as he pushed it open. "Alright, wake up you . . ." He stopped suddenly. "They're gone!"

Nigel chuckled from his hole. "'*We are twice armed if we fight with faith*' . . . Bravo, Plato."

"We found the jail securely locked, with the guards standing in front of the doors, but when we opened them, we found no one inside!" the temple guard reported when he returned to the chamber of the Sanhedrin.

The assembly broke out in murmurs expressing shock and unsettled anger as the men huddled together to discuss the situation.

"They must have someone working for them on the inside," Zeeb muttered through gritted teeth.

"Precisely," Nigel said softly from his position, now sitting directly behind this band of schemers.

"I agree, perhaps someone with the temple Guard?" Jarib suggested.

"Maybe they've paid off the jailer," Saar suggested. "He would be an unexpected ally."

Caiaphas leaned over to the chief temple guard and whispered brusquely, "How did this happen!? Where will this end?" The chief guard was at a loss for words, struggling to come up with a reply, when they heard someone entering the chamber.

"Look! The men you put in jail are standing in the temple complex and teaching the people!" The messenger was dressed in the common garb of a Jewish man, with a brown robe and burgundy head wrap.

Caiaphas and the chief temple guard turned to see the messenger but didn't recognize him. "Bring. Them. Here. NOW," Caiaphas sternly ordered the chief guard.

"Yes, sir Caiaphas," the guard answered quickly, heading to the door. He nodded an unspoken "Thank you" when he walked by the messenger. As he walked off toward the temple he puzzled about the stranger. *Blue eyes?* He shook off the thought and called to his group of guards, "Follow me, but do not threaten the people. They might stone us if we try to coerce the men."

The messenger spotted Nigel and winked as he was quickly ushered out of the chamber. Nigel smiled and shook his head in wonder at his ingenious friend Clarie.

Peter's voice echoed off the columns of Solomon's Porch. "I asked Jesus, 'Lord, how many times shall I forgive my brother or sister who sins against me? Up to seven times?' and the Master answered, 'I tell you, not seven times, but seventy-seven times.' So you see, my brothers and sisters, we are to forgive others generously." He looked up and saw the temple guards heading toward them and stopped speaking. He motioned to the other apostles to be calm and let him handle this.

95

"Peter," the chief guard said humbly. "I need you and your men to accompany me to give audience to Caiaphas."

Peter breathed in deeply and nodded. "Very well." He motioned for the others to follow him and together they walked with the chief temple guard and his men to see the Sanhedrin.

The guards brought the twelve men in, and stood them before the assembly. Saul and the others were incensed to see how confident these men looked after having not only defied the high council but somehow escaped from prison.

"Didn't we strictly order you *not* to teach in this name?" Caiaphas started in on them. "And look, you have filled Jerusalem with your teaching and are determined to bring this man's blood on us!"

Nigel planted his face in his paw, shook his head, and looked back up in disbelief. "He really did *not* just say that! These scoundrels *told* the people to call for Jesus' blood to be on them and their children! This is madness!"

Peter held out his hands, motioning toward the others to indicate he was speaking for them as well as himself. "We must obey God rather than men. The God of our fathers raised up Jesus, whom you had murdered by hanging Him on a tree." Peter paused a moment and bore his gaze right into the faces of the leaders of Israel. "God exalted this man to His right hand as ruler and Savior, to grant repentance to Israel, and forgiveness of sins. We are witnesses of these things, and so is the Holy Spirit whom God has given to those who obey Him."

When they heard this, the assembly erupted in anger. The Sadducees shouted threats. "Stone them! Death to these blasphemers!"

The apostles remained calm and quiet. They held their heads up high and looked around at the angry faces shouting at them.

A Pharisee named Gamaliel, a teacher of the law who was respected by all the people, stood up. "Please take these men outside for a little while," he ordered calmly.

While the guards escorted the Twelve back out of the chamber, Saul leaned over to Nahshon. "My teacher will talk some sense into everyone." He sat back and smiled, eager to hear what Gamaliel had to say.

"Men of Israel, be careful about what you're going to do to these men," Gamaliel began, his finger up in warning. "Not long ago Theudas rose up, claiming to be somebody, and a group of about four hundred men rallied to him. He was killed, and all his partisans were dispersed and came to nothing. After this man, Judas the Galilean rose up in the days of the census and attracted a following. That man also perished, and all his partisans were scattered."

Gamaliel turned his gaze to Saul, Zeeb, Jarib, Nahshon, and the others. "And now, I tell you, stay away from these men and leave them alone. For if this plan or this work is of men, it will be overthrown; but if it is of God, you will not be able to overthrow them. You may even be found fighting against God."

The assembly once again started murmuring as the old Pharisee took his seat. Caiaphas raised his hands to quiet them. "As usual, Gamaliel has spoken wisdom. Bring them back in," he ordered the chief temple guard.

Saul crossed his arms and frowned, clearly disappointed with his teacher. He was hoping for Gamaliel's voice to join his in a call for death to these rebels.

Nigel raised his eyebrows in delight. "Well, well, well, it appears that the unexpected ally is sitting in the middle of the Sanhedrin."

Peter, James, John, Andrew, Matthew, Thomas, Philip, Nathaniel, Matthias, Simon, James the Less, and Thaddeus filed back into the room and stood before the assembly. Caiaphas looked down the row of men with a stern expression. "I shall warn you one last time. You are *not* to speak in the name of Jesus again. I will send you off with a reminder so you will not soon forget my words." He stood and motioned for the chief temple guard. "Forty lashes minus one for each of them."

The members of the assembly watched as the twelve followers of Jesus hugged one another, and rejoiced at their sentence.

"Praise God! We are worthy to suffer for our Lord!" Peter exclaimed as the men were ushered out of the room.

Saul balled up his fists until his knuckles turned white. "They must be mad! How can these rebels possibly talk this way?!" he fumed.

"Because, you blind, pathetic creature," Nigel said behind him, preening his whiskers, "they have an *expected* Ally."

13

Seven Chosen

Clarie were dressed like an angel?" Kate wanted to know. "She must have been a bonnie lass!"

Nigel clasped his hands together in delight. "Yes, yes, yes, she was indeed! I believe she rather enjoyed the jailbreak, being the lamb who pulled the wool over the wolf's eyes and all that sort of thing."

"I cannot believe that Caiaphas did not bring up the question of how the twelve escaped," Liz remarked. "The embarrassed Sanhedrin wished to skip over their obvious powerlessness, no?"

"Indeed, never a word from the much-chagrined high priest," Nigel related. "It was utter madness, yet Peter once again offered up the message of salvation through Jesus to them. Alas, it only angered them and made them issue death threats."

"Ow!" Matthew yelped.

Stephen winced, pulling back the bloody cloth. "I'm sorry, Matthew, but I have to clean these wounds."

Matthew buried his face in the pillow, mumbling. "I know, I know. Thank you, brother."

The twelve apostles were spread out across the room, receiving first aid for their bloody wounds. Each had thirty-nine stripes on his chest and back. Some sat up while they were attended to by this group of believers.

Liz wore a look of sadness as she gazed at the wounded apostles. "How proud Jesus must be of their courage!"

"Cool courage," Al agreed, lip trembling to watch Peter grunt in pain.

"Aye, not jest their courage but their attitude aboot it all," Kate noted.

"I have to admit it was terribly inspiring to see them rejoice in the presence of the Sanhedrin that they were worthy to suffer for their Lord," Nigel said, adjusting his spectacles. "Their open defiance didn't set too well with the religious leaders, as you can imagine. There's an especially worrisome chap named Saul who gets cheekier every time I see him."

"Were he the lad I wanted ta bite standin' next ta the column?" Max grumbled. "I'd like ta r-r-rip his beard off while I were at it!"

"Steady, *mon ami,*" Liz cautioned. "Jesus warned us these days were coming, so we all must maintain self-control. Peter and the apostles are setting a fine example of how to be conscientious citizens yet object to leaders that misuse their God-given authority."

"Precisely, my dear," Nigel agreed. "If rulers command what the Maker forbids, or forbid what the Maker commands, then it is the duty of a believer to disobey human authority and obey a higher one."

"I must get up and go teach," Peter said, trying to lift himself up off the floor. "The people must see we will not be stopped in proclaiming Jesus, even after this beating."

"No, Peter! You rest. I'll go," Stephen ordered him. "All of you need to heal and regain your strength. Allow us to fill in for you and minister to your needs."

"He's right, Peter," John said, trying to lean against the wall but jumping at the pain. He grunted as Prochorus came over to attend to his wounds. "Let these men go for us until we are able to be back on our feet."

"Besides, others are supposed to spread the word besides us," James reminded them. "This is a great opportunity for them to let their voices be heard."

"I'll go with Stephen," Philip spoke up. "And we'll check on the other houses around Jerusalem to make sure there is enough food for the people."

99

"Very well." Peter closed his eyes, lying down on his side to rest. "Thank you, brothers."

Stephen and Philip smiled at one another, pleased they could help in a greater way.

$$\propto\hspace{-0.5em}\!<$$

"Thank you all for coming," Peter welcomed the group of believers to the upper room. "As you know the Lord has blessed us with thousands of new believers over the past several months as we've been out every day preaching in the name of Jesus."

"With no arrests!" Matthew called out from the back of the room. The crowd there cheered for this blessed fact. Despite the warnings of the Sanhedrin, the apostles and other believers had been preaching in the temple, in the many synagogues around Jerusalem, and in private homes. Gamaliel's words of advice to do nothing to these men had been heeded by the Jewish leaders and the temple guard.

100

Peter smiled broadly. "Indeed, Matthew! No arrests, praise God! So, we have a huge number of people to not only minister to with the Word, but to minister to by providing them with food. It has come to my attention that the Greek-speaking believers in our community have been overlooked with the daily food provision, specifically the widows."

"Yes, Peter, I've heard this in the synagogue where I primarily go to discuss the Good News," Stephen interjected. "I know we would never disregard them on purpose, but perhaps the language barrier is causing poor communication with the widows."

"Unfortunately, this has caused a lot of hard feelings with our Greek friends," Philip added.

"Which is why the twelve of us have asked you all here today to come up with a solution to stop this division in the church," James explained.

"It wouldn't be right for us to abandon our responsibilities for preaching and teaching the Word of God to help with the care of the poor," Peter advised. "So, friends, choose seven men from among you whom everyone trusts, men full of the Holy Spirit and good sense, and we'll assign them this task. Meanwhile, we'll stick to our assigned tasks of prayer and speaking God's Word."

Those gathered in the room were very pleased with this idea and started talking among themselves. The animals were in their usual corner of the upper room, watching all that was going on.

"But this is a fantastic idea, no?" Liz said excitedly. "I can see how the third weapon of the Enemy has started its work on the church."

"Aye, distr-r-raction," Max agreed. "If the twelve apostle lads are kept busy takin' food all around Jerusalem, they won't have time ta pr-r-reach wha' they know."

"They be the ones who were with Jesus so they need ta share the most," Kate added.

Nigel nodded eagerly. "Precisely. I daresay this is a brilliant plan to divide the *work* of the church so as to not divide the *heart* of the church."

"Did ye notice they be pickin' seven?" Al asked proudly. "Jest like us then. Since the Maker be pleased with how we do on our missions, maybe he told Peter that seven were a good number."

After several minutes, seven men were chosen and stood before the group: Stephen, Philip, Prochorus, Nicanor, Timon, Parmenas, and Nicolas. The twelve apostles stood up behind them, placing their hands on their shoulders.

Peter closed his eyes. "Let us pray. O God, we present to you these seven men who will now serve the church by meeting the needs of its members. Give them strength, wisdom, and hearts of compassion to carry out this charge. May the work of their hands be pleasing in your sight. We ask that you would protect the church from any more of this division and hard feelings. Holy Spirit, please fill the hearts and minds of everyone these men encounter, so your peace will spread across Jerusalem. Amen."

The twelve and the seven embraced, and the church celebrated the early stages of an organized ministry of caring for God's people.

"All seven men are Greek," Liz observed. "This not only makes perfect sense for the Greek-speaking believers, but I believe we are witnessing the beginnings of the Good News going beyond the Jewish community."

101

"How so, Liz?" Kate asked.

"When Jesus told the disciples to go to Jerusalem, Judea and Samaria, and the rest of the world, he did not just mean geographically," Liz explained.

"Right! I see your meaning," Nigel jumped in. "The Good News must cross land barriers but also cultural, racial, national, and religious barriers as well. The Greek-speaking believers here in Jerusalem are truly different from the Hebrew believers, so choosing these seven Greek gentlemen is a brilliant strategy to help overcome such barriers."

"I'm happy the Enemy's third weapon were quickly put down then," Kate said, wagging her tail. "Jesus' church is goin' ta keep growin' an' growin'!"

Stephen looked over and saw Kate. He walked over with a big smile and squatted down to pet her on the head. "Looks like you approve, little bit." He reached over to also pet Max, Liz, and Al. Nigel hid behind a plant. Stephen reached into a bag tied around his waist and pulled out some morsels of dried fruit. "Are you hungry? Here, why don't I start with you four? You may as well be considered part of the church, even if you are from a different race!" Stephen's deep brown eyes radiated joy as he laughed and put the morsels on the floor for them. He was a handsome young man with a pronounced jaw line, long, narrow nose, and curly black hair. He cocked his head to one side as he considered these little animals. Kate, Max, and Al happily gobbled up the morsels while Liz studied him with eyes full of affection. Stephen told her, "There's something special about you, little bits, but I don't know what it is."

"Stephen, let's talk about tomorrow's food distribution," Philip called over to him.

"Coming," Stephen responded as he winked at the animals and mussed the fur on Kate's head one more time. The seven new church servants gathered in a circle on the floor to map out how to best minister to the people.

"I like Stephen," Kate said happily. "He's a dear lad."

"An utterly splendid fellow," Nigel agreed as he popped back over, picking up a tasty morsel. "The Holy Spirit is strong with him. He has performed many miracles among the people, which is extraordinary.

Only the twelve have had this power before now. I say, how do you spell his name? With a 'v' or with a 'ph'?"

"Stephen with a 'ph.'" Liz's tail curled up and down slowly as she studied Stephen. *"Oui,* because the Holy Spirit is strong with him, I believe this is why he senses something special about us."

"I thought it were because o' me charm," Al joked with a goofy grin, patting his fluffy belly.

Max playfully bonked Al on the head. "Daft kitty."

"There is something special about Stephen, too," Liz said. "He has that mark of destiny about him, with sweetness and strength rolled into one heart."

"Things are going very well with the young church. The Maker is very pleased," Clarie told the group of animals. They were enjoying a beautiful sunset on the Mount of Olives. Once again in the form of a beautiful young girl, she sat with them in the grove of olive trees.

"Aye, the humans be doin' a gr-r-rand job with the church," Max affirmed. "But me an' the others were wonderin' when we are supposed ta *do* somethin'. Seems all we do is sit ar-r-round an' watch."

"Yes, and not that we aren't grateful to be witnesses of the thrilling growth of the church these last years," Nigel added. "But we do wish there was something we could contribute to the effort."

Clarie put her hand on Max's back. "You've been faithful to be patient, watch, and learn. Sometimes that is the most important thing to do when serving the Maker, especially when you are witnesses to great history in the making." Her face suddenly grew serious. "However, things are getting ready to change. Be on your guard as the Enemy is preparing a new wave of attacks. Much sadness is coming, so prepare your hearts as well as your minds."

Liz wrinkled her brow. "Of course we do not wish to hear this, but it has been expected, no? Gillamon told Nigel and me we would help with the written word."

"Aye, Kate an' me are supposed ta help protect the apostles' writin's," Max added.

"And dare I add that we are to see a murderer's turnaround?" Nigel reminded them.

"All of this is coming. Soon I will tell you more, but this part of the mission will be similar to the one you had with Joseph in Egypt," Clarie replied. "Remember that you each had to go separate ways to your various posts for quite some time. Very soon you will need to split up and go where you are needed."

Kate nuzzled Max. "I hate the thought of bein' away from ye, but we made it through last time."

"Aye," Max sighed. "I had ta open me big mouth then aboot not doin' anythin'. Okay, Lass, we'll be r-r-ready."

Al grabbed Liz and whimpered, "Don't say we have to be apart! Don't say it!"

"There, there, *cher* Albert," Liz consoled him.

"Might I once again be of service with the communication between us all?" Nigel offered, preening his whiskers. "I am the most mobile of the group, with pigeons waiting in the wings."

"Good one, Mousie," Al brightened, chuckling. "Pigeons waitin' in the *wings.*"

"You each will be given assignments that match your skills, and will cross paths back and forth on the way to your ultimate destination for this mission," Clarie explained. "Specifics from Gillamon are coming soon."

"*Bon.* Although I hate to see the coming sadness, we will be ready to serve the Maker however he chooses," stated Liz.

"Very well," Clarie said, getting to her feet. She breathed in deeply and let out her breath slowly. "We best get going. I need to get you all in place for tomorrow."

The animals started following Clarie down the hillside. She slipped around an olive tree and once more became a temple guard. Liz swallowed, immediately assuming the worst. "Oh no, are we going back to the Sanhedrin?"

Clarie nodded grimly. "Yes, but this time, *they* will be the ones on trial."

14

THE FIRST TO DIE

D on't you see, my brothers?" Stephen pleaded. "When Jesus said he would destroy the temple and rebuild it in three days, he spoke not of the place where we worship, but of *his body!* When the Sanhedrin convicted him they didn't understand this, but isn't it clear now, after Jesus' resurrection?"

"Anyone who dares talk against the temple is suspect in my mind," a Greek-speaking Jew named Egan grunted.

"Yes, you know that the temple and the law are our two most important treasures as men of Israel!" Talus argued. "Wasn't Jesus ignoring our laws when he broke them? Healing on the Sabbath, for instance?"

Stephen shook his head and looked around the synagogue at this group of Hellenistic Jews—Greek-speaking Jews who had settled in Jerusalem but were descended from those scattered from the *Diaspora,* the Babylonian exile. They were so hungry for the truth but were blinded by their traditions.

"Jesus didn't come to do away with the law but to fulfill it!" Stephen argued. "Look, many of you are former slaves. You understand what it is like to not have your freedom. God gave us ten laws with Moses yet the Jewish leaders have added so many burdensome details to the laws that the people are enslaved to the law! Laws are meant to bring freedom, not slavery. Time and time again, Jesus showed how wrong it was to bend to man-made traditions that went against the original intent of God's law."

"Give us one example if you can!" some of the men there argued.

"Was it wrong for Jesus to heal on the Sabbath a lame man who had suffered for so long?" Stephen asked. "The commandment to rest on the Sabbath was never intended to keep us from doing good to others. The Pharisees reason that you can feed a donkey but you can't heal a hurting man on the Sabbath. Come now, think! This is the kind of backward thinking Jesus tried to get them to be aware of and avoid. Have we reached the point of worshipping the man-made laws? What about worshipping the man-made temple? Remember that idols are also man-made. Anything we place ahead of God can become an idol!"

The men looked at one another, unable to reply on this issue. Saul sat in the back of the room, for this was the synagogue he attended with other men from his area of Cilicia. He was fuming as he listened to Stephen, having reached the limits of what he could tolerate with this Jesus movement. *Gamaliel was wrong! They must be stopped!* he thought to himself. "These Jesus-followers are out to destroy Israel! And this one, this Stephen . . . he sounds like that Jesus himself," Saul muttered to the man, named Lander, sitting next to him.

"I couldn't agree more," Lander answered calmly. He leaned over and whispered in Saul's ear. "A group of us could be persuaded to help you stop them, if the price is right."

Saul looked Lander in the eye and narrowed his gaze as he studied the man's face for a moment. Lander's eyes were dark and a chill ran up Saul's spine to think of what he meant. "Do you mean stir up the people?"

"Stir up the people, certainly," Lander replied in an arrogant tone. "After we've stirred up the Sanhedrin."

"You revere the temple as should we all, but revering it as a holy place to pray and worship is one thing," Stephen continued. "Using it to try to lock God in a building is another. He is the Maker of everything! He can't be contained in a building! In the past we have come to the temple to meet God, but when Jesus died, the veil was torn in two, from top to bottom. The message is clear, my brothers. We need not go to the temple to reach God any longer. We need not make sacrifices any longer. Jesus was the one sacrificial Lamb who provided the way to reach God in the temple of our hearts."

The room erupted in anger. Saul clenched his jaw, looked at Lander, and nodded. "I will approve of whatever you do, and I'll make sure you are well paid." Saul stood and slipped away from the group.

Lander gave a sinister smile as he watched Saul quickly leave the synagogue. He walked over to a group of angry men in the back of the room. Suddenly they ran over to where Stephen sat, grabbed him by the arms, and dragged him out of the synagogue. "We'll see what the Sanhedrin have to say about your blasphemy!"

The animals sat anxiously in their hiding place within the Sanhedrin's chambers. Nigel paced back and forth.

"I don't know how much longer I can handle this suspense," Liz said with a frown. "Especially for something that seems so ominous."

Suddenly the chamber doors opened and in walked the seventy-one members of the Sanhedrin. The animals peeked around a pot to see what was happening. Max's fur suddenly rose and a low growl entered his throat. "That scoundr-r-rel Saul be doin' somethin'."

They watched as Saul went up to speak to Zeeb, Saar, Jarib, and Nahshon. They huddled together and gave Saul an eager, approving nod. Saul turned and quickly left the chamber.

"Wha's he doin', Clarie?" Kate wondered.

Clarie looked straight ahead, guarding the area where they hid. "Setting things in place."

They soon heard the sounds of shouting from a mob of people coming down the corridor leading to the chamber. The doors opened and their hearts immediately sank.

"Oh no, not Stephen!" Kate cried.

"Who are those men with him?" Liz wanted to know, her tail swishing back and forth.

"Greek-speaking Jews from the local synagogue," Nigel relayed. "I've been there several times."

Caiaphas motioned for a group of men to bring Stephen to stand in front of his elevated chair while they remained to present their case before the Sanhedrin.

Liz saw one of the men who remained in the back of the crowd nod to Saul, who by now was seated next to Nahshon. Her fur rose on end as she gazed at him. "One of the men isn't coming forward with the others to accuse Stephen," Liz said, pointing to the man. "But he looks like the ring leader with this mob. Who is he?"

Nigel put his paw up to his spectacles and studied him closely. "I believe his name is Lander."

Liz's heart skipped a beat. "Lander is Greek for 'lion.'"

"Proceed," Caiaphas instructed. "Why have you brought this man to us?"

"This man," they said, taking turns speaking, "is always talking against our sacred temple and the Law of Moses. We heard him say that this Jesus of Nazareth will tear down the temple and change all the customs that have come down to us from Moses!"

"Look at his face," Kate said, welling up. "He looks like an angel."

The council members stared at Stephen with wonder. Liz whispered softly, looking around the room. "They all can see this, too."

"Even though he is being charged with blasphemy," Nigel observed, "he is serene and full of peace."

Caiaphas wore a sour frown and looked at Stephen. "Is this true?"

Stephen held out his hands to answer them. "Brothers and fathers, listen to me! Before our ancestor Abraham had gone to live in Haran, the God of glory appeared to him in Mesopotamia and said to him, 'Leave your family and country and go to the land that I will show you.' And so he left his country and went to live in Haran. After Abraham's father died, God made him move to this land where you now live. God did not then give Abraham any part of it as his own, not even a square foot of ground, but God promised to give it to him, and that it would belong to him and to his descendants. At the time God made this promise, Abraham had no children. This is what God said to him: 'Your descendants will live in a foreign country, where they will be slaves and will be badly treated for four hundred years. But I will pass judgment on the people that they will serve, and afterward your descendants will come out of that country and will worship me in this place.' Then God gave to Abraham the ceremony of circumcision as a sign of the covenant. So Abraham circumcised Isaac a week after he was born; Isaac circumcised his son Jacob, and Jacob circumcised his twelve sons, the famous ancestors of our race."

"Wha's this got ta do with wha' they've charged the lad with?" Max asked with a frown.

"He is setting up his case," Nigel said. "I believe I know what he's doing but let's hear more."

"Jacob's sons became jealous of their brother Joseph and sold him to be a slave in Egypt. But God was with him and brought him safely through all his troubles. When Joseph appeared before the king of Egypt, God gave him a pleasing manner and wisdom, and the king made Joseph governor over the country and the royal household. Then there was a famine all over Egypt and Canaan, which caused much suffering. Our ancestors could not find any food, and when Jacob heard that there was grain in Egypt, he sent his sons, our ancestors, on their first visit there. On the second visit Joseph made himself known to his brothers, and the king of Egypt came to know about Joseph's family. So Joseph sent a message to his father Jacob, telling him and the whole family, seventy-five people in all, to come to Egypt. Then Jacob went to Egypt, where he and his sons died. Their bodies were taken to Shechem, where they were buried in the grave which Abraham had bought from the clan of Hamor for a sum of money."

109

"Just hearin' those memories of our time with Joseph makes me wish he were here ta stand up for Stephen!" Kate lamented.

Stephen started walking up and down before the assembly, growing more animated. "When the time drew near for God to keep the promise he had made to Abraham, the number of our people in Egypt had grown much larger. At last a king who did not know about Joseph began to rule in Egypt. He tricked our ancestors and was cruel to them, forcing them to put their babies out of their homes, so that they would die. It was at this time that Moses was born, a very beautiful child. He was cared for at home for three months, and when he was put out of his home, the king's daughter adopted him and brought him up as her own son. He was taught all the wisdom of the Egyptians and became a great man in words and deeds.

"When Moses was forty years old, he decided to find out how his fellow Israelites were being treated. He saw one of them being mistreated by an Egyptian, so he went to his help and took revenge on the Egyptian by killing him. He thought that his own people would understand that God was going to use him to set them free, but they did not understand. The next day he saw two Israelites fighting, and he tried to make peace between them. 'Listen, men,' he said, 'you are fellow Israelites; why are you fighting like this?' But the one who was mistreating the other pushed Moses aside. 'Who made you ruler and judge over us?' he asked. 'Do you want to kill me, just as you killed that Egyptian yesterday?' When Moses heard this, he fled from Egypt and went to live in the land of Midian. There he had two sons."

"Aye, that were a long spell in the wilderness with Moses," Max remembered. "But wha' a gr-r-rand day it were when the burnin' bush appeared."

"After forty years had passed, an angel appeared to Moses in the flames of a burning bush in the desert near Mount Sinai. Moses was amazed by what he saw, and went near the bush to get a better look. But he heard the Lord's voice: 'I am the God of your ancestors, the God of Abraham, Isaac, and Jacob.' Moses trembled with fear and dared not look. The Lord said to him, 'Take your sandals off, for the place where you are standing is holy ground. I have seen the cruel suffering of my people in Egypt. I have heard their groans, and I have come down to set them free. Come now; I will send you to Egypt.'

"Moses is the one who was rejected by the people of Israel. 'Who made you ruler and judge over us?' they asked. He is the one whom God sent to rule the people and set them free with the help of the angel who appeared to him in the burning bush. He led the people out of Egypt, performing miracles and wonders in Egypt and at the Red Sea and for forty years in the desert. Moses is the one who said to the people of Israel, 'God will send you a prophet, just as he sent me, and he will be one of your own people.' He is the one who was with the people of Israel assembled in the desert; he was there with our ancestors and with the angel who spoke to him on Mount Sinai, and he received God's living messages to pass on to us."

"I believe I see what Stephen is setting up here," Nigel noted. "He has made the case that the Maker was never tied down to any given land or place, with his people able to worship him as they went along. And the Maker can make any spot on earth 'holy' with his presence, not just Israel."

Stephen lifted his gaze and stared into the faces of the Sanhedrin. "But our ancestors refused to obey him; they pushed him aside and wished that they could go back to Egypt. So they said to Aaron, 'Make us some gods who will lead us. We do not know what has happened to that man Moses, who brought us out of Egypt.' It was then that they made an idol in the shape of a bull, offered sacrifice to it, and had a feast in honor of what they themselves had made. So God turned away from them and gave them over to worship the stars of heaven, as it is written in the book of the prophets:

'People of Israel! It was not to me that you slaughtered and sacrificed animals for forty years in the desert. It was the tent of the god Molech that you carried, and the image of Rephan, your star god; they were idols that you had made to worship. And so I will send you into exile beyond Babylon.'

"Our ancestors had the Tent of God's presence with them in the desert. It had been made as God had told Moses to make it, according to the pattern that Moses had been shown. Later on, our ancestors who received the tent from their fathers carried it with them when they went with Joshua and took over the land from the nations that God drove out as they advanced. And it stayed there until the time of David. He won God's favor and asked God to allow him to provide a dwelling place for the God of Jacob. But it was Solomon who built him a house.

"But the Most High God does not live in houses built by human hands; as the prophet says,

'Heaven is my throne, says the Lord, and the earth is my footstool. What kind of house would you build for me? Where is the place for me to live in? Did not I myself make all these things?'"

"Right! Now he has set up Israel's pattern of constantly resisting and rejecting God's appointed leaders and repeatedly breaking God's laws with idolatry," Nigel explained.

"Israel's past now points to its present, no?" Liz added. "Joseph was not recognized by his brothers on their first visit. It wasn't until their second encounter that they truly realized who he was."

"Aye, an' Moses were r-r-rejected by his people the first time he tr-r-ried ta help them," Max continued the train of thought. "When he came ta Egypt a second time they recognized him as the one ta deliver 'em."

"And they kept killin' the poor prophet laddies 'til the Maker stopped sendin' 'em," Al jumped in.

"Until Jesus," Nigel said with great seriousness. "They killed and rejected him on his first visit, too."

"How stubborn you are!" Stephen went on to say. "How heathen your hearts, how deaf you are to God's message! You are just like your ancestors: you too have always resisted the Holy Spirit! Was there any prophet that your ancestors did not persecute? They killed God's messengers, who long ago announced the coming of his righteous Servant. And now you have betrayed and murdered him. You are the ones who received God's law, that was handed down by angels—yet you have not obeyed it!"

As the members of the Council listened to Stephen, they became furious and ground their teeth at him in anger.

"He has turned this trial around to accuse the Sanhedrin, just as you said, Clarie," Liz realized. "He hasn't tried to defend himself."

"He's only cared aboot defendin' the tr-r-ruth," Max said. "Now that's br-r-rave."

"To reject God's messengers is to reject God," Nigel added. "And Stephen has boldly accused Israel of this very thing. They are guilty of sinning against God and his Law."

While the Sanhedrin began shouting curses at Stephen, he stood there with his eyes fixed upward, and a smile of wonder on his face. He was filled with the Holy Spirit. He couldn't hear them. And he only could see an inexplicable scene of grace.

"I will allow you to see what Stephen is seeing," Clarie said to the animals. "Open the eyes of your heart."

The animals looked to where Stephen gazed and could scarcely take it in. Their hearts caught in their throats.

112

"Look!" Stephen said in a broken, emotional voice. A single tear slipped down his cheek. "I see heaven opened and the Son of Man standing at the right side of God!"

"It's Jesus!" Liz's eyes filled with tears. "He stood in this very place and told these very leaders, 'But from now on, the Son of Man will be seated at the right hand of the mighty God.' Yet now he stands."

"The proper position for a witness in court is for them to stand," Nigel pointed out. "Stephen is being condemned by an earthly court, so has appealed to a higher Court," he said in awe. "Jesus is standing up for Stephen in front of heaven for what he has done here today."

With a loud cry the Council members covered their ears with their hands after hearing Stephen's vision. They all rushed at him at once, and chaos broke out. The mob viciously grabbed Stephen and rushed him out of the chambers, not waiting on any official word from Caiaphas or the other leaders. Liz watched Saul run out with Lander.

"Come quickly," Clarie urged them. "We don't have much time." She led them down a back passageway outside.

The animals could hear the roar of the mob as they dragged Stephen through the streets and outside the city walls. Liz, Max, and the others were running blind as their eyes filled with grief-stricken tears at what was happening.

"Shouldn't we be stoppin' this?!" Max cried when they finally reached the hillside where the crowd gathered.

"If we do, the gospel will not spread outside Jerusalem," Clarie said, wiping away her tears.

They looked on as the men who spoke up as witnesses threw Stephen down the hill. He landed with a grunt and rolled over to see an audience of angry faces peering down at him. Stephen slowly rose to his feet, waiting for the inevitable. The witnesses quickly took off their cloaks and laid them at Saul's feet. Saul simply stood there, arms crossed, watching the angry people do what they came for.

"I can't watch," Kate cried as she buried her face in Max's fur.

One of the witnesses heaved a large boulder down the hill and hit Stephen in the leg, causing him to drop to his knees. The next witness picked up a huge stone and hurled it down at Stephen, hitting him in the face. Suddenly all the people picked up stones and rained them down on Stephen. The sickening thuds of stones finding their mark filled the air.

Stephen struggled to hold his bloodied arms to his face as they heard him call out in anguish, "Lord Jesus, receive my spirit."

"The Psalm 31:5 child's prayer Jesus prayed on the cross," Liz observed, her lip trembling. "But Stephen is now praying it to Jesus."

Stephen couldn't withstand the blows any longer. He fell over into the now bloody dust and curled his legs into his chest, crying, "Lord, do not hold this sin against them."

Stephen became still and they knew he was gone. Only then did the stones stop falling.

"Jesus uttered those words from the cross as well," Nigel reminded them with a broken voice. "To the very last word, to the very last breath, Stephen . . . the first martyr . . . acted just like Jesus."

Run for Your Lives

Saul's gaze was fixed on Stephen's dead body. Liz studied Saul as he studied Stephen. For a brief moment she thought she saw deep emotion in Saul's eyes. But it soon left him as the witnesses walked back up the hill to claim their cloaks that sat at his feet. The men congratulated one another and shook the dust off their cloaks. A group of Stephen's Greek-speaking Jewish friends ran down the hill having just heard of this mob-induced murder. They threw themselves on his lifeless body and wept over their friend. Liz bristled when the dark-eyed man named Lander put his hand on Saul's shoulder.

"Mission accomplished," Lander smugly exclaimed, holding out his hand for payment.

Saul coolly handed him a small bag of money but kept his gaze on the scene below. Someone made their way down the hillside with a sheet and together they respectfully picked up Stephen's body to carry away for burial. Saul turned and looked Lander in the eye. "On the contrary. It's only begun." Saul left him and strode off to the city gates. Lander watched him for a moment, smiling, before joining his fellow witnesses to divide up their ill-gotten gains.

"More blood money," Liz spat with disgust. "Those witnesses were bribed to testify in court against Stephen. Lander led the witnesses and Saul led the Sanhedrin to this horrific crime."

The animals were filled with righteous anger as they watched Saul head back to the city.

"And Stephen led the charge that will finally take Jesus' gospel out of Jerusalem," Gillamon stated from a broken boulder next to them. His face formed above a row of craggy white stone that resembled his goatee. "Stephen understood that which the apostles have been slow to grasp. The church is not a building like the temple or a city like Jerusalem, but people who believe in the good news of Jesus, wherever they may be. Jesus told the Twelve to begin sharing that good news in Jerusalem, and so they have. Thousands of believers have come to Jesus here. But it's time to move on to the next phase."

"Ah, Gillamon, ye always be there when we need ye then," Max said, glad to hear his wise mentor's voice. "So how were Stephen leadin' the charge out of Jerusalem?"

"Stephen's blood has been spilled outside the gates of Jerusalem, which is a picture of what is to come. The blood of martyrs is like seeds going into the ground," Gillamon replied.

"Seeds have to be planted and die before a harvest of new growth can appear, no?" Liz pointed out, remembering her beloved garden from long-ago France. "But what will this picture look like?"

"The opposition against the church from the Jewish leaders began first as a warning, then a flogging, and now a death supported by the people," Gillamon explained. "The Sanhedrin now have a champion to take this persecution to the next level, going after more believers in Jerusalem to try to crush the young church."

"That no-good, dir-r-rty, r-r-rotten scoundr-r-rel Saul!" Max growled.

"He's on his way to the Sanhedrin now with a suggestion of how to squash this Jesus movement in Jerusalem," Gillamon informed them. "Get ready for some perilous days here, but understand that this is how the spread of the gospel will begin."

"But if the believers be afraid, they'll run away from Jerusalem!" Al worried with his paws up to his mouth.

"Exactly, Al," Gillamon smiled at the simple-minded yet spot-on cat. "And as they run away, they will not only carry with them their possessions, but their beliefs."

Al nodded with growing understanding. "Makes sense to me."

"Stephen led the charge in that Saul and the Sanhedrin will go after other Greek-speaking Jewish believers first," Clarie explained. "They are the ones who share the views Stephen proclaimed today about the temple."

"*Oui, je comprends.* Stephen has understood the depth of Jesus' message before the apostles did, that because the new way has come, the old must go," Liz realized.

Nigel held up his paw for emphasis. "And I'm afraid Saul has understood the counter to that: because the old must stay, the new must go."

"Saul will lead that persecution movement starting today," Gillamon told them.

"So the bad guy will be used to spread good?" Al wondered.

"Jest like when Joseph told his brothers that wha' they meant for bad, the Maker would use for good," Kate remembered.

"Gillamon, Clarie told us our team would be soon splittin' up. Be it time?" Max asked.

"Yes, but first you will assist believers as they escape Jerusalem, and help comfort the Twelve. Clarie will lead the escape effort. But they need a secret code to communicate with one another in safety, so you are charged to make that happen," Gillamon explained.

Liz and Nigel shared an enthusiastic grin. "*C'est bon!* Our study of hieroglyphs in Egypt should come in handy with such an assignment."

"After Saul has rounded up believers here in Jerusalem, he will take his rampage on the road," Gillamon answered. "That is when Max and Liz will follow Saul while the others remain here with the Twelve. When the Twelve finally understand that they must leave Jerusalem, Al, you will be assigned to Peter, and, Kate, you will be assigned to John. Nigel, you will serve as a go-between with everyone as well as have side missions."

"I shall fly with honor to keep the Order of the Seven well informed," Nigel proclaimed with a fist in the air.

"At least I'll be with a fisherman. He knows I like fish," Al said hopefully.

Max perked up. "Aye, so we'll stop that r-r-rotten Saul before he gets ta wherever he's goin', r-r-right?"

Gillamon smiled. "He must certainly be stopped, Max. And you'll be there to assist. For now, get back to the upper room. Nigel, I suggest you go hear Saul's plans and report back to the others. You have a big mission ahead, but remember what I've always told you."

"We be loved and able!" Al exclaimed proudly.

Gillamon chuckled as his face disappeared from the rock. "Indeed you are."

◯⟨

"I fear the Romans will come down on us for this death today," Caiaphas scowled, pointing his finger on the table. "This mob action is the exact thing Rome will not allow in its provinces! You know we are not allowed to execute anyone."

"But Caiaphas, aren't you pleased with the outcome?" Zeeb implored. "That blasphemer is dead, and his death will serve as a warning to others."

"Well, *Jesus'* death didn't serve as a warning to others, did it, you cheeky little man?!" Nigel squeaked from a hiding place in the wall of Caiaphas's private chambers.

"Of course, I'm pleased," Caiaphas replied. "But I must have an answer for Rome."

"May I?" Saul spoke up. "What happened today with Stephen was perfectly legal by Roman law."

Zeeb, Saar, Jarib, and Nahshon raised their eyebrows in delight, as did Caiaphas. "Go on," the high priest instructed with a wave of his hand.

"When Judea became a Roman province, the Sanhedrin was indeed deprived of administering capital punishment," Saul began. "As you know that power was given to the Roman prefect. As you recall from that Jesus matter, it was quite difficult to convince Pilate to carry out your wishes."

Caiaphas snapped at the unpleasant reminder of their powerlessness to execute Jesus themselves. "Yes, this we know, Saul. What is your point?"

"In studying the law there is one area where Rome allows the Sanhedrin to maintain power of execution. If violators in word or deed affect the holiness of the temple, you have the power to execute the violator by stoning," Saul continued.

"Yes, but we tried this approach to kill Jesus and it didn't work!" Caiaphas shouted.

"Forgive me, Caiaphas, but if you recall, the primary charges brought against Jesus before Pilate were blasphemy and Jesus' claim to be the king of the Jews," Saul reminded them. "I believe this entire business could have been handled differently. You could have simply limited the charges to violating the holiness of the temple and handled it yourselves by stoning him."

The men looked at one another in disbelief. Zeeb spoke up. "Our Saul here has studied the law well."

Caiaphas frowned and tapped his hands on his chin. "So this stoning today was within our legal jurisdiction in the eyes of Rome?"

"I think because Stephen's words were so specific in violating the temple, yes, I believe our case is solid," Saul explained. "Which leads me to my next point, in that all of the Hellenist followers of the Way agree with Stephen, and can be charged with the same crime. I suggest we strike while the iron is hot and use this point to stamp out this movement while Rome allows us the power."

"Of course, we know that their true crime is blasphemy by saying that Jesus was the Messiah," Saar pointed out. "The absurdity of thinking a man hung on a tree could possibly be the Messiah is laughable. Such a man is cursed by God himself in the Scriptures of Deuteronomy!"

"So we need to kill this movement in any way we can," Saul suggested, leaning back in his chair confidently. "I am prepared to round up these blasphemers and put them on trial. Of course, we need not stone them all. Prison should suffice to make them turn back to our ways. After all, we don't want the people to think we are heartless killers."

"Indeed we don't," Caiaphas agreed sternly. "We are charged with the well-being of the people, but we cannot allow this evil blasphemy to continue to divide us. Very well, Saul. Proceed with quashing this heretical movement and I will see to it that you obtain your rightful place in the Sanhedrin."

Saul's face lit up with delight. "I will accomplish it with zeal, Caiaphas."

Nigel shook his head gravely as the men broke up their meeting and left the room. "There's nothing more vicious than a religious terrorist who thinks he acts in the name of God."

"Twenty more were arrested by Saul and the temple guards last night," Andrew reported as he and James slipped into the upper room. "All Greeks."

120

"Saul is making a house-to-house search, breaking up house church gatherings, and carrying men and women off to prison," James added. "He's demanding that believers renounce Jesus on pain of torture and imprisonment."

"But several have also been stoned to death," Matthew said, rubbing his hands through his hair in dismay.

"Many of the Greeks have started fleeing Jerusalem," John reported.

"I'm telling you I think we need to leave before we're arrested, too!" Thomas declared.

Peter gripped his hands together and lowered his head, shaking it sadly. "No, I see what Saul is doing. He's only going after the Greek-speaking believers for their violation of the temple. We Hebrew believers have not done so. For now, that is the only thing Saul can succeed with. For the time being, we must stand our ground and remain in Jerusalem. We must help our brothers and sisters who remain, and keep the Jerusalem church alive. When we faced storms in the sea with the Master, he was there with us, and he is with us now. He will not allow his church to sink in this storm of persecution."

"Well, Saul is proceeding exactly as you heard him say he would do," sighed Liz. "Clarie has been out on the streets at night helping divert the guards' attention while the Greeks escape the city."

"Aye, that Saul be chargin' at believers like a lion tearin' its prey," Kate lamented. "Not like Marcus or Armandus Antonius when they had ta carry out orders that were so cruel. Those Roman lads had a sad efficiency aboot them. Saul be actin' like a crazy beast!"

"Power's gone to his head." Al lay on his belly, picking his teeth with a fish bone following dinner. He noticed a fly land in the bowl of salt and reached over to shoo it away.

"Well, I wish they would let us tr-r-ry ta stop that evil man now, but I understand why the believers need ta leave Jerusalem ta spr-r-read the Good News," Max grumbled. "I can't wait ta finally get me paws on that no-good, r-r-rotten, scoundr-r-rel!"

"It's all simply dreadful! Utterly intolerable!" Nigel fumed. "So we must, as Gillamon instructed, come up with a communication code for the believers to use. They must have a safe way to let others know they are believers."

121

"*Oui*, some sort of symbol," Liz suggested. "The Egyptians used hieroglyphs—symbols that portrayed words—so something like that would work."

Al's paw landed in the salt and a goofy grin appeared on his face when we saw the impression of his paw print. He took the fish bone and drew claws onto his paw print in the salt. "Look, Max! Reminds me of when we drew pictures in the sand in Egypt! Look at my lion paw. GRRRR!"

"Aye, somethin' *simple,* that even this kitty here could draw." Max frowned as Al got his fur in the salt. "Speakin' of Egypt, ye r-r-remember it were yer playin' in Pharaoh's food that caused all that tr-r-rouble. That poor baker laddie."

Al ignored Max's insult and kept drawing in the salt with his fishbone. "Well, these laddies be fishermen not kings, so I don't think I'll be gettin' into trouble with them. I think Peter even likes me since he gave me this fish for supper," holding up the fish bone. "Sure, or what's left o' it."

Liz studied Al and her eyes widened. "*C'est ça!* That's it! Albert, you are a genius!" She reached over and kissed her mate on the cheek, studying his salt drawing. "May I?" she asked, taking the fish bone out of his paw.

Al smiled gleefully at her praise and her kiss. "Anythin' ye want, me little lass."

Liz held up the fish bone. "Jesus told these fishermen he would make them fishers of men. So what would be more perfect than the symbol of a fish?" She proceeded to draw a simple fish in the salt.

All the animals leaned in to look at Liz's drawing. "I say, that will work brilliantly!" Nigel enthused. "But in order for this to work as a secret symbol, might I suggest that one person draw the upper arc of the fish and the other person draw the lower arc to confirm they are fellow believers? Allow me to demonstrate. May I?"

"Bien sûr, mon ami," Liz replied, handing the fish bone over to Nigel.

"Jolly good," Nigel replied, taking the fish bone. He scurried over to the salt and smoothed it so he could start a fresh picture. "If I draw the first arc like so . . ." He then handed the fish bone to Liz.

"Oui, and I draw the second arc like so . . ." Liz added to the picture. *"Voila!"*

"Aye, so if the second person ain't a believer they won't know wha' ta dr-r-raw next," Max pointed out.

"An' when they be done with the secret code, they can jest wipe it away," Kate added, putting her paw in the salt to clear away the picture of the fish.

"By Jove, I think we've got it!" Nigel celebrated, his whiskers shaking excitedly. "I shall inform Clarie posthaste so she can relay this code to the humans. Bravo, everyone!" The little mouse scurried off to find the beautiful young girl.

"Me work here be finished," Al told the others, yawning and stretching out long. "I think this kitty's earned a nap."

Mary walked over with a tray to clean up the food from the table. As she leaned over to pick up the dish of salt, she noticed it had orange, black, and white fur in it. She frowned and put her hand on her hip. "Who's been playing in my salt?"

Max, Kate, Liz, and Al looked at one another sheepishly. *"It was all for the cause, mon amie,"* Liz meowed.

Mary smiled and reached down to scratch Liz under the chin. "Never mind then. You four are worth your salt to me." She stood and picked out the fur from the salt as she walked away.

"Wha' did she mean by that?" Max asked.

"To be 'worth one's salt' means to be worth one's pay," Liz explained. "The Latin word *sal* is the root word for "salary," and Roman soldiers are given wages to buy their salt."

"Well, I think settin' up a secret code for believers runnin' for their lives be worth a dish o' furry salt any day," Al stated with a goofy grin. "That's what *I* always say."

123

PART TWO

In All Judea and Samaria

16

THE GREAT
EQUALIZER

I f you'd be so kind, my dear, please set down in one of those trees
just there," Nigel pointed.

"Next to that well?" Naomi the pigeon asked.

"Yes, that will be splendid," Nigel replied, smiling as he looked
down to see Philip walking along on the road leading into Samaria.
"Looks like we've beat him here."

Naomi flapped her wings as she came in for a landing on a thick
branch of an acacia tree. Its widely spaced branches spread out to bring
shade to the dusty patch of road.

"Ah, that was a wonderful flight! Thank you, Naomi," Nigel said,
climbing off the pigeon. He proceeded to whisk back his whiskers
to make himself presentable after their thirty-five mile flight from
Jerusalem.

"You're welcome, Nigel," Naomi replied with her sweet smile. "I'm
so happy to be able to help you again. It's been a long time."

"Indeed, I haven't traveled far from Jerusalem in recent years, but I
shall once more be on the road quite a bit, if you wish to be my 'pigeon
designee.'" Nigel rubbed his paw along the trunk of the acacia tree.

"Of course, Nigel!" Naomi replied happily. "I'd be honored."

"Very well," Nigel said. "Do you realize Noah built his ark out of this type of tree? I was most privileged to go see it when I was last in the Ararat Mountains. Simply astounding how Noah constructed that vessel! I can only imagine how many of these trees he must have used!"

"Philip's coming!" Naomi whispered.

Nigel snapped to attention as the evangelist walked up to the well. He was sweaty and covered in dust. He lifted his knapsack from his shoulder with a grunt and peered down into the well. He didn't have anything to draw the water with, so he decided to just rest a moment. He wiped his forehead with the back of his hand.

"By Jove, I don't believe it!" Nigel exclaimed, spotting a woman walking up to the well. "We couldn't have timed this better if we tried. It's she!"

"Who?" Naomi asked.

"The woman who met Jesus at this very well," Nigel replied in serendipitous delight. "She was the first one Jesus told he was Messiah. But she looks quite different now with a proper headdress. And she looks happy." Nigel smiled as he recalled that day long ago when Jesus and his disciples stopped at this well. "Jesus gave her living water."

Philip stood and smiled as the woman approached the well and put her jar on a rope to draw out some water. "Good day. May I trouble you for a drink of water?"

"Are you thirsty?" the woman asked him, setting her jar on the side of the well.

"Of course I am! Yes, please, thank you," Philip replied excitedly, digging in his knapsack for a wooden cup. He dipped the cup in the jar and gulped the cool water in relief. "Ah, that's good and cold."

The woman smiled at him. "I always ask that question. Ever since it was asked of me here."

"Who asked you?" Philip asked her, taking another cup full of water.

"A man who told me he was Messiah. He told me everything I'd ever done," she recalled sadly. "We were so hopeful he was the One. But I heard a rumor that that man died a few years ago."

Philip wiped his mouth with his sleeve and smiled broadly. "I'm here to tell you some good news. That man you met? His name was Jesus, wasn't it?"

Her eyes widened. "Yes! How did you know? What good news?"

"Because I'm his follower. And he's very much alive!" Philip explained. "I've come to Samaria to share this good news with the people here."

Tears filled her eyes as she held her hands to her face. "He's alive? But how?"

Philip put his knapsack back on his shoulder. "If you take me with you into town, I'll be glad to tell you and your friends all about it."

"Yes, please, you must come with me," she said eagerly. "Oh, my heart is so happy with this news! I wish for my mother-in-law to meet you. She cannot walk, so we must go to our home and I will invite my friends over to hear you."

Nigel and Naomi watched as Philip and the Samaritan woman walked into town, talking a mile a minute. "And so the spread of the gospel begins with the first person whom Jesus told that he was Messiah. I cannot wait to share this happy news with the others! Come, let's follow Philip and the woman."

129

Nigel and Naomi flew above to follow them to the woman's simple stone and wood house, where they softly landed on the thatched roof. Nigel scurried inside and remained in the rafters. He looked around the room and saw an old woman lying on a pallet with a blanket over her legs. A young girl played at the woman's feet before coming over to hug a burly man sitting on a rug by a low table. Nigel smiled at the family below him. "Oh, how splendid! She did turn her life around indeed."

"Mother, Husband, this is Philip, from Jerusalem," the woman said happily, setting down her jar as she walked in with Philip. "He has good news about Messiah." The child ran over to her and she embraced her. "Hello, my little one!"

"Messiah? The last time you brought someone here claiming he was Messiah, he ended up being a false one," the husband replied, eyeing Philip suspiciously. He looked over Philip's Greek-style attire of light brown, knee-length *chiton* with leather belt and thin headband. "And aren't you a Greek?"

"Actually, he was indeed the true Messiah, Jesus of Nazareth,"

Philip smiled and said, sitting down next to the man. "I'm one of his followers and have traveled from the church in Jerusalem to share the good news about Jesus. I'm a Hellenist Jew, so, yes, I speak Greek. But what I'm going to share with you is for the Jew, the Samaritan, the Greek, and even all others."

People came to the door and the woman ushered them in. "Please, come in, come in," she eagerly greeted them. Soon the room was packed with people.

"The very same Jesus who visited your city several years ago was the long-awaited Messiah, just as he told you," Philip began. "He taught us God's truth and shared how he had come to fulfill the long-foretold prophecies of why he had to be a suffering Messiah."

The people were glued to Philip's words as he proceeded to give an account of history leading up to Messiah very much like Stephen's speech before the Sanhedrin. Their hearts were moved and their faces lit up with Philip's message. He shared that baptism was part of professing Jesus as Savior, to publicly show others what had happened in one's heart by going down into the water.

The woman's mother-in-law lifted her hands. "But I cannot walk to be baptized."

Philip looked at her with compassion and walked over to where she sat. Praying silently he then knelt down by her and smiled, staring deeply into her eyes. "In the name of Jesus Christ, get up and walk."

Suddenly the old woman felt warmth running up and down her legs. She looked around with nervous excitement as Philip stood and held out his hand for her. She put her hand cautiously in his and slowly got to her feet, taking several steps. The Samaritan woman and her husband rushed over to embrace the old woman and the crowd of people erupted in joy.

"Mother! It's a miracle!" the Samaritan woman cried out. "She's been unable to walk for three years! Thank you, Philip, oh thank you!"

Philip held up his hands humbly. "Please, it was Jesus who healed her, not me. He alone gets the glory."

"Bravo, Philip!" Nigel squeaked from up in the rafters.

"Jesus is Messiah!" they exclaimed. "Please, Philip, baptize us now!"

"Certainly, let's go," Philip agreed, his heart full to see the Holy

Spirit work through him to do what only the apostles and Stephen had done up 'til now.

As the people filed out of the house to head to a nearby spring, Nigel watched a tall, skinny, strange-looking fellow in the back of the crowd. His eyes were wide and he shook his head in awe of what Philip had done. Nigel decided he would especially keep an eye on this one.

"From what I've learned, his name is Simon, and he is a magician who has long practiced sorcery here in Samaria," Nigel explained with a frown to Naomi. "He amazes the people and has boasted he is some-one great, so all the people, both high and low, have followed him and call him, 'The Great Power of God.' This Simon is nothing more than a cheeky charlatan with his bag of magic tricks."

"But since they have believed Philip's message of the Good News, they've been baptized and wish to follow Jesus now. Wasn't Simon him-self baptized?" the pigeon asked.

131

Nigel crossed his arms over his chest. "Yes, he was, but I assume he doesn't truly believe in the Good News. Or, he may believe but his heart doesn't appear to be transformed by the power of the Holy Spirit. I fear he may be just saying the words and going through the motions. But he follows Philip everywhere, continually astonished by the great signs and miracles he sees Philip doing here in Samaria." Nigel tapped his chin thoughtfully. "Come to think of it, something strange is going on here. The people believe and have been baptized, but the Holy Spirit does not seem to have come over the people. I think we need to fly back and tell the others the good news, of course, but also of this strange lack of the Holy Spirit. Clarie can let Peter and the others know she received word from Samaria."

"I'm ready," Naomi said, flapping her wings. "Let's go!"

"Praise God! This is great news! Philip has taken the Good News to Samaria, just as Jesus asked," Peter exclaimed, pacing around the room excitedly.

"And the people have accepted it!" John added. "Who would ever have dreamt that Samaria would be the first place outside of Jerusalem to accept Jesus?"

"Well, I think Peter and John should go to Samaria to help determine what is going on with the Holy Spirit not resting on the people," James, Jesus' brother, suggested. "You two can affirm the people and bridge the gap that has so long divided our people."

Peter and John looked at one another and nodded in agreement. "Yes, but remember the last time we were there, you and your brother James asked Jesus if you should call down fire from heaven on one of the Samarian villages for *not* accepting us. We'll have no more of that this time," Peter teased, grabbing John by the shoulder in a big bear hug.

"I promise not to be a 'Son of Thunder' in Samaria," John joked back. "All I want is for the Holy Spirit to come down from heaven on them."

"Well done, Nigel!" Liz said to the others in the back of the room. "How exciting to see all of this happening in Samaria. And to think the same woman who met Jesus at the well was there again. *C'est magnifique!*"

Kate nudged Liz. "Well, remember wha' we always said aboot her. Lassie power!"

∝<

As soon as Peter and John arrived in Samaria, Philip called together the group of new believers. The apostles hugged and celebrated what God was already doing here. A feeling of excitement swept over the assembly of people who met in a large courtyard since the houses were too small.

Peter stood and lifted his hands. "Please, pray with me. Oh Lord, we have done as you asked, and brought the Good News to the people of Samaria. They have believed with their hearts and have been obedient to follow your words to be baptized. Now, we ask you, promised Holy Spirit, please come and fill these people so they will truly know the full experience of your indwelling Spirit in their hearts. Amen."

Peter and John walked among the crowd of people, placing their hands on them. The Holy Spirit came and descended on the people and they immediately cheered with the joy they felt in their hearts.

When Simon saw that the Spirit was given at the laying on of the apostles' hands, he went up to Peter and John. Wearing a slimy smile he handed them a bag of money. "Give me also this ability so that everyone on whom I lay my hands may receive the Holy Spirit. I can pay handsomely for it."

Peter's facial expression changed immediately from joy to disgust. "May your money perish with you, because you thought you could buy the gift of God with money! You have no part or share in this ministry, because your heart is not right before God. Repent of this wickedness and pray to the Lord in the hope that he may forgive you for having such a thought in your heart. For I see that you are full of bitterness and captive to sin."

A look of terror came over Simon, and he cried, "Pray to the Lord for me so that nothing you have said may happen to me."

133

"It is you who must pray to the Lord and set your heart right," Peter admonished him. "This business can only be settled between you and he alone. You alone are accountable and he alone can forgive you."

Peter, John, and Philip walked away, leaving Simon with his thoughts. "Men must go directly to God for forgiveness," Peter said. "I still marvel at this new way that Jesus has provided."

"I've been considering why the Holy Spirit had not yet come to Samaria, even though the people had accepted Jesus and been baptized," John shared. "Could it be that since Jews and Samaritans have been such bitter enemies for centuries that the people needed to first see such a visible touch of peace and unity from us Jews who represent the first church in Jerusalem?"

"Almost like the debut of the Holy Spirit outside Jerusalem coming to bind our two peoples?" Peter wondered. "Could be, John. The gospel is the great equalizer. All I know is that just as it was with Jesus, we must continue to expect the unexpected with the Holy Spirit!"

"Well, let's move on to more Samaritan villages on our way back to Jerusalem," Philip suggested. "I know Jesus expects *us* to keep spreading the word."

"While we go, let me show you something," John said with a smile. He took his foot and drew an arc in the dirt. Peter took his foot and drew the other arc to make a fish. "It's called the sign of the fish. It's for believers to identify themselves to other believers if they find themselves in hostile territory."

"Like Jerusalem?" Philip raised his eyebrows in delight. "I like it. How very clever!"

Peter swiped the fish away with this foot. "Come, let's go fishing."

Philip's eyes opened suddenly and he sat up on his mat, his heart pounding. He looked around the upper room in Jerusalem. Everyone was still asleep. He picked up his knapsack and walked over to where Peter lay sleeping. "Peter," he whispered. "Peter, wake up. I must be going."

Peter slowly opened his eyes and looked at Philip through a sleepy haze, trying to come awake. "Is something wrong?"

Philip smiled and squeezed Peter's arm. "No, I've just received my next assignment. An angel of the Lord spoke to me. He said, 'Go south to the road—the desert road—that goes down from Jerusalem to Gaza.' I don't know what awaits me there, but I know I must leave."

Peter sat up and nodded approvingly. "Go with God, my friend. We will continue to pray for your work."

"As I will continue to pray for yours," Philip replied. "I think it best I leave before sunrise so Saul's henchmen don't find me. Farewell, Peter."

"Remember the fish," Peter whispered, putting his hands on Philip's shoulders. "Godspeed."

As Philip quietly made his way out the door, Liz nudged Nigel awake. "Nigel, wake up. I think you need to follow Philip. An angel told him to head south to Gaza."

Nigel reached for his spectacles and clumsily put them on his face crookedly. Liz giggled at her little mouse friend's groggy, disheveled appearance.

"Right," Nigel yawned, rubbing his eyes under his spectacles. "I'll catch the next flight to Gaza."

"Bon vol, mon ami," Liz encouraged him with her dainty paw on his shoulder. "A missionary mouse's work is never done."

Nigel preened back his whiskers, now waking up. "I should certainly hope not!"

Philip heard the sounds of iron chariot wheels grinding down the rocky road. He turned around to see a cloud of dust kicking up behind an ornate chariot pulled by two heavily adorned horses. Behind the chariot was a small caravan of travelers from far off Ethiopia coming up behind him. He kept walking straight ahead and was soon passed by the ornately decorated passenger chariot. Philip raised his eyes at the beautiful caravan of color passing by.

The blue chariot was trimmed in gold filigree with a red-fringed canopy. Seated facing backward on the passenger seat was a richly dressed man with the dark skin of the Ethiopians. He wore a purple robe and a tall golden cylindrical hat. Across his chest was a leopard-skin sash, and on his hands were the rings of wealth and prestige. And in those hands the man held an unfurled scroll. He bellowed with a loud, thick accent as he slowly read aloud.

"He was led like a sheep to the . . . sl- . . . slaugh-ter—yes, that's it—slaughter," the African man said out loud, tracing his finger along the words of the scroll. He did his best to keep his place as he was jostled by the movement of the chariot along the bumpy road. "And as a lamb before its shearer is silent, so he did not open his mouth. In his hu- . . . hu-mil- . . . i- . . . hu-mil-i-a-tion—yes, that's it—humiliation, he was deprived of justice. Who can speak of his descendants? For his life was taken from the earth." The man set the scroll on his lap and looked out of the chariot with a puzzled look on his face.

Philip studied the man, who was obviously an important representative of the royal court of the queen of Ethiopia. He raised his eyebrows at hearing this foreigner read from Isaiah 53. At that moment, the Holy Spirit whispered in Philip's mind, "Go to that chariot and stay near it."

Philip ran up to the chariot and smiled. "Do you understand what you are reading?"

"How can I," he said, "unless someone explains it to me?"

"I can help you, if you like," Philip offered.

"Stop!" the man ordered his driver. The horses immediately stopped and whinnied in the road next to Philip. The man smiled broadly with beautiful white teeth that contrasted against his dark skin. "Please, come, come sit with me," he asked Philip, waving him up to sit with him in the chariot.

Philip climbed up on the platform and took a seat next to the colorfully dressed character. Once he was situated, the man instructed the driver to resume their travel. Nigel jumped off Naomi's back and landed lightly on the canopy. He peered through the red fringe to watch the two men.

"I am the queen's officer of the treasury for all of Ethiopia, and I have been to Jerusalem for a festival," the man explained. "My mind is quick with numbers, but not with the words of this prophet. I fear God and wish to learn more about his truths. Please, please," he smiled, handing the scroll to Philip. "Tell me, please, who is the prophet talking about, himself or someone else?"

Philip read the familiar words of Isaiah and smiled. Jesus had identified himself as the one Isaiah wrote about, explaining the prophecies in detail. "Isaiah was writing about Jesus, and I am one of his followers."

Then Philip began with that very passage of Scripture and told him the good news about Jesus. Nigel smiled as he stared at the Isaiah scroll, remembering how he and Liz had sat on Isaiah's desk to read those words when the ink was still wet on Isaiah's parchment. He wondered if he would have more opportunities through time to see Isaiah's words shared with people of other nations. "Bravo, Isaiah!" he said to himself quietly. "And bravo, Philip! You have shared the Good News with groups of people and now one on one. You have shared it with a mixed race of outcast Samaritans and now this foreigner from Ethiopia. You have shared it with ordinary people and now a royal official. You have changed your method but not your message. Bravo, indeed, old boy! The great equalizer is blazing a trail!"

As they traveled along, they came to a desert spring of water near the side of the road. Date palm trees lined the shoreline. The Ethiopian clapped his hands excitedly and pointed. "Look, here is water. What can stand in the way of my being baptized? Stop the chariot!"

Nigel swung back and forth on a string of fringe as the chariot came to an abrupt halt. He quickly scurried back up to the top of the canopy to watch Philip and the man walk down to the water's edge. The servants didn't understand what the man was doing, but they rushed down to the water with him. He took off his hat, his leopard sash and his rich purple tunic, handing them to his servant while he walked with Philip into the water in his white linen undergarment.

When they were waist deep, Philip lifted his hand and prayed, "Oh, Lord, welcome this new believer into your kingdom, and Holy Spirit, please come to him now. Amen." With that, Philip leaned the man back into the water and he sprung up with his arms spread wide, laughing with joy. Beads of water ran down his animated, happy face.

"I am your brother now, yes?" the man exuberantly claimed. "This is a good day!"

137

"Yes, my brother, you are," Philip said with a big smile as the man grabbed his shoulder with excitement. "And yes, it is a good day."

As the two men walked out of the water, the servants held out the man's purple robe. When he turned around from getting dressed, Philip was gone. "Where did he go?" the man asked, looking around. "Well, he must be a busy man. But he stopped for me, thank the Lord. Let's be on our way," the man ordered his entourage. "I have more reading to do! I think I will be able to understand things more clearly now."

Nigel flew off on Naomi's back, looking everywhere along the road for Philip, but there was no sign of him. "This is extremely curious, but I don't put anything past our Maker. We've got more exciting news to share. Back to Jerusalem!"

THE ROAD
TO DAMASCUS

"D o you understand that you have been arrested for heresy and blasphemy against the temple and the law?" Saul questioned in a brusque voice. The veins in his temple pulsated with anger as he gazed on this group of Jewish followers of the Way. Despite his attempts to intimidate them, they stood there before him, unafraid and unmoved. "Well, what do you have to say for yourselves?" Saul demanded.

"I have something to argue in favor of my acquittal," one of the men calmly offered.

Saul plopped down in a chair, exhaled loudly, and rubbed his temple with one hand while lifting his other hand in an exaggerated show of irritation. "Yes, enough of this standard, allowable, rote reply. Tell me your specific answer to these charges. Are you guilty?"

"If you charge me with believing that Jesus Christ is the Messiah . . ." the uneducated, common man began before Saul interrupted him.

"WAS! *Was* the Messiah," Saul corrected him, shaking his head at the absurdity of the words "Messiah" and "Jesus" in the same sentence.

The man's face showed no impatience or fear. He continued, unfazed by Saul's rude attempt at intimidation. "I heard Jesus once tell a story about a man who had two sons. One son asked for his inheritance early and went off to a foreign land and spent it all on wild living. One day as he was feeding the pigs . . ."

Saul slammed his fist on the table. "Yes, I've heard this story countless times!" He turned the pitch of his voice high and mockingly continued the story. "The son comes to his senses, returns home, and is lovingly embraced by his father who forgives everything the worthless son had done and throws him a big party while the righteous older brother whines because he gets nothing. Yes, I could recite this and many of this Jesus' other stories!" Saul got up from his chair and stormed over to the man, but being so short he had to lift his finger to make his point in the man's face. "I bring the likes of you in here on serious charges against the law and the temple and you ignore them and try to spill this heretic's teaching into my ears?! Do you think I care about *anything* the man had to say? Answer the charges!"

The man looked Saul in the eye, but there was no anger or bitterness in the man's face. Only peace and confidence. "Yes, then, I am guilty. I am guilty of having a heart transformed by the loving power of grace," the man easily replied. "I am guilty of believing a man who said my sins were forgiven. I am guilty of believing Jesus is the long-awaited, prophesied Messiah and that he was crucified for my sins and rose from the grave. And I am guilty of wanting to continue to share the good news."

139

Saul's full, oval face turned red and blotchy. Beads of sweat covered his bushy eyebrows, and he was almost blind with hatred. "ENOUGH!" he screamed. "Guilty, you confess, and guilty, you will be punished! Guards, take these men away and scourge them with the maximum penalty. Then throw them in the deepest pit of a cell we have. Maybe some time among the rats will purge this heresy out of them."

The guards surrounded the believers and shoved them out of the room, but they didn't resist. They were calmly led away. On impulse, Saul thought, *Like a sheep led to the slaughter,* but he immediately dismissed Isaiah's words that these heretics dared to attribute to Jesus and his sacrifice. Saul cringed as he heard one of them call back, "We don't hold this against you, Saul."

He plopped back into the chair, put his elbows on the table, closed his eyes, and put his hands over his face. *AHHHHH! What am I missing?! What secret do they have that allows them to be unmoved by torture, stoning, and imprisonment? What? What? It's as if they are being told what to say.*

"Sir, I have news from Samaria and Damascus," a temple guard announced, walking up to Saul's table. He held out a scroll.

Saul opened his eyes, let his arms drop to the table, and held out his hand for the scroll. He exhaled as he took the scroll and unrolled it. The temple guard stood at attention as Saul read its contents. Saul's expression soured and he screeched back his chair on the tiled floor as he stood up. He clenched his jaw and then gave a sarcastic laugh. "Fleeing believers are spreading their doctrines with *outstanding* success in Samaria and northward to Damascus." He crumpled the scroll tightly in his hand. "Where is Caiaphas?"

The temple guard replied, "Sir, he is in his chambers. Do you wish a meeting with him?"

"No, I thought I'd go take a nice *nap!*" Saul glared at the guard. "*Of course* I want a meeting with him, NOW! I'll go get them all and kill them here in Jerusalem!" Saul stormed out of the room, leaving the temple guard standing there.

"I say, that was quite the temper tantrum!" Nigel mused, peering out from the hat on the head of Clarie the temple guard. "His face was like unto the shade of a rotten tomato."

The temple guard snickered. "You're not lying, Nigel. Not only do his arrests make no difference to the people he puts on trial, the mass exodus of believers fleeing has backfired. Saul knows his actions are actually spreading the Good News!"

"Liz will be most pleased with Saul's response to her scroll," Nigel said with a jolly chuckle. "If only she had been here to see it."

"Well, let's get to Caiaphas so you can give her the full story of Saul's temper tantrum." Clarie the temple guard and Nigel hurried to follow Saul.

"I ask that you give me letters to go arrest these followers of the Way who have fled to Damascus," Saul pleaded. "The Romans have granted a great amount of self-government to two huge communities there: Arabs who owe allegiance to their Nabatean king in Petra and Jews who owe their allegiance to the Sanhedrin. Let me go put a stop to the spread of this . . . disease . . . before it goes any farther."

Caiaphas nodded as he considered Saul's request. "You've done a remarkable job squashing this religious rebellion here in Jerusalem. I have no doubt you can do the same in Damascus."

"Thank you, Caiaphas. Of course I won't stop there. I will continue to Phoenicia and Antioch," Saul added.

"When can you be ready to depart?" Caiaphas asked.

"I'm ready now," Saul told him, gripping the scroll. "I'll leave as soon as I get the supplies we need and as soon as you have prepared the necessary letters for me to present in the synagogues when I arrive. I will need to take at least three temple guards, horses, and of course a pack animal for supplies."

"Very well," Caiaphas stood up and said. He walked over to Saul and looked him in the eye. "We'll trust you to put a stop to this Jesus matter once and for all."

141

"No one wants that more than I," Saul replied, now smiling with great satisfaction. "I won't let you down."

The men nodded and parted company, Saul to make preparations and Caiaphas to write letters.

"Let's go get packed ourselves," Clarie whispered to Nigel as she strode out of Caiaphas' chamber. "And Max and Liz need to say their goodbyes."

Al's lip trembled. "When will I be seein' ye again?"

Liz wiped away a tear. "I do not know, *cher* Albert. But I shall carry you in my heart." She leaned over to kiss him. "Be my noble, brave warrior until we meet again. And try not to eat all of Peter's fish."

"I'll try," Al said, giving Liz a big, smothering embrace.

Kate and Max nudged heads. "Be me str-r-rong lass an' take good care of John then. He'll be needin' ye ta look after Mary."

"I'll be happy ta watch Jesus' mum," Kate replied. "An' Max, be patient with those ye meet who need yer love. Stick up for the under-dogs then."

"Aye, I'll try ta think of wha' me bonnie lass would do," Max assured her.

Nigel cleared his throat. "Right, well I hate to break up this farewell but we really must be going. Clarie is waiting."

With that, Max and Liz gave one final kiss to Kate and Al. "All r-r-right, Mousie," Max said. "Let's get goin.' We've got ta stop a mur-r-rder-r-rer in his tr-r-racks."

Liz followed Max and Nigel along the road and wrinkled her brow as a thought crossed her mind. *Murderer? Gillamon said, "Perhaps the greatest act will be watching one new apostle turn from a murderous tyrant into the model of what a Christ-follower should be." But how could Saul possibly be the one the Maker would use?* Liz brushed away the very idea. It was unthinkable that Saul of Tarsus could ever be anything more than a killer of those who loved Jesus.

142

"Good, you're here," Clarie told them, appearing as a temple guard. "You will need to follow along, but stay out of sight until we get near Damascus. I'll be one of Saul's traveling companions. I'll make sure to find you at night and give you food as well as updates. It will take us about six days to travel the 140 miles."

"Understood, *mon amie,*" Liz said. "But what are we expected to do once we arrive?"

"Aye, shouldn't we figure out our plan of attack?" Max asked deter-minedly. "We can't let that scoundr-r-rel get far."

"All will become clear when things go dark." Clarie smiled and scratched her stubbly beard. "I'll never get used to human beards." She walked away from them, not answering their questions.

"I suppose we'll have to wait and see," Nigel offered. "But I plan to be a little closer to the action. I shall see you this evening." The little mouse ran off and caught up with Clarie, scurrying up the outside of her tunic as she took the reins of a donkey loaded with provisions for the trip.

Max and Liz looked at one another with puzzled expressions. "Sounds like a nighttime attack," Max said, trotting along.

"Hmmm . . ." Liz wondered aloud, following him. "With Clarie and Gillamon, you never know."

Saul mounted his black stallion and took the reins in his grip. A thrill coursed through his veins as they began their righteous mission and proceeded down the road. He looked back at the beautiful gates of Jerusalem and smiled to himself. He couldn't wait to bring back a string of manacled blasphemers and march them through those gates in shame. His smile faded as they passed the spot of Stephen's execution. *"Lord, do not hold this sin against them."* Stephen's words haunted him, and the upturned, angelic face of the martyr filled Saul's mind every night. *How could such a bad man die like that?* he repeatedly asked himself. Saul shook his head and set his gaze on the road ahead. *Jesus was a blasphemous impostor and he is dead. I know I'm right and they are wrong. Just wait until I prove it.* But even as he mentally justified himself once again, he realized the one he most needed to prove his righteousness to was he himself.

143

$$\propto$$

"Oh, look!" Liz exclaimed happily as they walked over the crest of a hill. "The Sea of Galilee! Oh, how this brings back happy memories! It seems like forever since we roamed these hills with Jesus."

"Aye, it were some of the happiest days of me life," Max replied. "Looks like a storm be br-r-rewin'."

The Wind was blowing steadily over the green hillside down to the lake. "So it appears," Liz responded. "Do you remember what Jesus told you when you walked with him out on the lake that stormy night?"

"He said it were time ta face me fears once an' for all," Max remembered.

"Oui, but he also said you would one day be in a far worse storm, and would need to encourage one of his greatest servants to be brave," Liz reminded him.

Max breathed in deeply. "Aye, I wonder who it could be. An' where."

"No, I do *not* want to stop here for the night!" Saul shouted up ahead. "The last thing I wish to do is hear more retellings of Jesus' miracles on this hillside by these uneducated people! We keep moving!"

Max growled. "Looks like the angr-r-ry little man be havin' another tantr-r-rum. I'd like ta encourage *him* by sinkin' me teeth inta his leg. I hope it comes ta that."

Liz frowned. "Come now, *mon ami*. You're better than that. Don't let your anger lead you to act just like Saul."

"Aye, ye're r-r-right," Max replied. "Kate wouldn't like me talkin' like that, no matter how bad the lad acts."

"Mount Hermon is getting smaller in the distance behind us," Clarie said, giving a few pieces of fish to Liz and Max. "We're nearly to Damascus."

144

The group looked behind them. The beautiful landscape of wildflowers blanketed the brown foothills, bursting with signs of spring. But rising from the foothills were the snow-capped peaks of Mount Hermon, still untouched by the spring temperatures.

"I shall never forget being up on that mountain the day Jesus was transfigured," Nigel said, lifting his gaze and clasping his paws behind him. "I daresay I have never seen such brilliant light in my life."

Liz smiled, remembering it well. "Peter was so shocked to see Jesus illuminated there with Moses and Elijah, he rambled on about building shelters for them all, not knowing what else to do. I have often thought that seeing Jesus like that was important for Peter, James, and John. They needed to see the divine nature of who Jesus really is. Bright with light in heavenly glory."

"Aye, it must have been like Jesus liftin' back his human mask ta show who he r-r-really be," Max added. "I didn't get ta see it like ye two did, but I imagine that's how it were."

"Precisely so, old boy," Nigel replied, tapping Max's front leg affirmingly. The sun peeked over the horizon and glared off Nigel's spectacles. "Perhaps one day you shall. Now, speaking of bright light, I suggest we all take our positions, as the sun is up and we'll be on our way shortly."

Clarie told them, "Look lively, everyone. It's going to be a day full of things that are illuminating for us all." She held out her hand and put Nigel up on her shoulder. He scurried up into her hat.

Max and Liz looked at one another and shrugged their shoulders as Clarie walked back to the caravan that was packing up to start again on its trek to Damascus.

The white dust kicked up behind Saul's horse as he led the way, riding up ahead of the small caravan. This patch of road was dry and almost white, contrasted with the brilliant blue sky overhead. Two temple guards also rode horses while Clarie walked along in the rear with the supply-laden donkey. Max and Liz darted in and around rocks along the side of the road to stay out of sight. The sun was directly overhead.

For no apparent reason Saul's horse pulled back its ears, and signaled its uneasiness by snorting, neighing, and trotting in place. Saul frowned and turned around to look at the other men. Their horses were also acting up. The men looked at one another and reached over to settle their mounts. The fur on Max and Liz stood on end and they stopped in their tracks. "Wha's happenin'?" Max growled.

Suddenly a blinding light from the sky flashed around them, causing the entire landscape to vanish from view. The horses violently reared up on their back legs in terror, knocking their riders off onto the dusty ground. Saul's horse took off running back down the road while the temple guards struggled to their feet to grab hold of the reins of their horses. Clarie held the donkey securely while it brayed violently in fear.

Saul's heart was pounding and he held his hands up to his face. The blinding light held some physical power over his being, as if a hand were pinning him to the ground. He couldn't move from where he lay. But his eyes were fixed on a face emerging from the center of the light. It was a man in his thirties with penetrating green eyes. His full body appeared as he stood before Saul of Tarsus in radiant glory.

"Saul, Saul! Why do you persecute me?" came a voice so powerful it made his nerves tingle from head to toe.

145

"Who are you, Lord?" Saul replied with a trembling voice. His stomach felt as if falling, as if he had jumped off a cliff.

"I am Jesus, whom you persecute," the man said. He lifted his hands and pointed at Saul. "It is hard for you, this kicking against the goads. But get up and go into the city, where you will be told what you must do."

Saul's throat tightened when he looked at the hands of the man who spoke to him. They were pierced! In an instant, Saul's world came crashing down around him. All of his intellect, theology, ideas, self-righteousness, reputation, and training evaporated as if he were held over a refining fire. Yet not one word of condemnation was spoken. Jesus' pointing hands weren't accusing him, they were holding him in the blazing fire of truth, and Jesus' eyes bored into Saul's darkened soul to rid it of everything that held no value. Saul felt as if dross were falling off of him, just like the needless refuse from gold and silver when those precious metals are refined. As painful as the reality of this moment was, Saul's heart was then plunged into the cooling waters of sensations he had long craved but never understood—unconditional love and inexplicable grace.

Saul trembled, overcome with the experience. The blinding light instantly vanished. His shaky hands went to the ground to push himself up, but as he rose to his feet, he couldn't see anything around him. No Damascus Road. No blue sky. No men. No horses. Only the image of Jesus' face encased in light remained in his eyes.

The temple guards looked at one another in confusion. "What was that noise?" they asked Clarie as they held onto the jumpy horses. Clarie walked over to the men and handed the reins of the donkey to one of the guards. "Whatever it was, it's gone now. Here, take this beast."

Clarie went over and took Saul's groping hands into hers. "I've got you," she told him quietly. "Just lean on me." Saul nodded, not able to utter a word after what had just happened.

"His letters from the Sanhedrin were in his horse's saddlebags," one of the temple guards realized, looking behind him. "One of us better go get that horse."

Clarie called over to the men. "One of you ride and get Saul's horse.

The other of you, tie the donkey to your horse and go on ahead of us into Damascus. Let our contact there know we are coming and have them prepare a room for Saul."

The two men nodded and split up as directed. When they were gone, Clarie motioned for Max and Liz to catch up to her as she led Saul slowly down the road.

Max's jaw hung there for a moment. He was speechless. He, Liz, and Nigel had been privy to Saul's vision.

"Now you don't have to wonder what Jesus looked like in his trans-figuration," an awestruck Nigel told his friend.

"And I don't have to wonder about who our murderous tyrant is," Liz added with great emotion.

"Ye don't mean . . . Gillamon were talkin' aboot . . . *Saul?*" Max asked incredulously. "*Saul* be the one who's supposed ta show the world wha' a Christ-follower should be?!"

Liz gazed at the now humbled, helpless man who stumbled along blindly, holding onto Clarie. "It appears that the only arrest of a blas-phemer on this trip was made today, no? And Jesus is the one who did the arresting."

147

18

STRAIGHT STREET

The sweet aroma of apricots tickled Saul's nose as they passed through the massive entry gate and along the colonnaded street into Damascus. He could hear the spice merchants calling out their wares and the sound of a wooden cart with a creaky wheel passing them by. A woman was arguing with a vendor about the price of barley, and a donkey brayed in the distance. The distinct smack of shutters opening to slam back against the cream-colored stone houses above the street sounded overhead. The colorful city was coming back to life after its midday rest.

"Judas lives on the western end of Straight Street," Clarie told Saul. "We're to follow along the colonnade until we see a three-story apartment next to his rug shop. Evidently he is a wealthy Jewish merchant here in Damascus."

"Yes, thank you," Saul muttered humbly. "He was referred to me by an elder in the Sanhedrin as someone who could provide proper accommodations. All I want is to lie down, please."

"Certainly. We'll get you there soon," Clarie encouraged him. "The other temple guard should be there waiting for us." She looked behind her to make sure Max and Liz were keeping up in the throngs of people weaving in and out of this busy city.

"I do believe we've entered quite the melting pot of culture in this frontier city," Nigel remarked, riding on the back of Max's neck. "What

148

a colorful menagerie of Arabs, Jews, Parthians, and Romans mingling together."

"This is a far cry from how Saul expected to make his entrance into Damascus," Liz said, watching Saul meekly trail a step behind Clarie as she led him by the arm. "He had planned to proudly ride his horse along this road with the caravan, making sure everyone knew he had arrived."

"Aye, he must be a humbled gr-r-rumbler by now," Max added. "I still cannot believe wha' we're seein' with the lad. This weren't wha' *we* expected either."

"We didn't expect this turn of events, but of course, it was well planned by the Maker, no?" Liz offered. "I believe we will begin to see the reason for his choice of Saul with time, just as Saul will hopefully regain his sight."

"There, just up ahead," Clarie announced to Saul. "I see the rug shop and our donkey and horses standing outside. I will get you situated. Do you wish for me to instruct the temple guards?"

149

Saul wrinkled his brow. "The reason for our coming no longer exists. Once I am settled, leave me and return to Jerusalem." He thought a moment. "Leave my knapsack, please."

"What should we tell the high priest?" Clarie asked, motioning for the animals to hide as they reached the house of Judas.

"Tell him I've had a change of plans, nothing more," Saul instructed. "And thank you for your kindness to lead me here."

Clarie raised her eyebrows in surprised delight to already see a change in Saul's temperament. "Certainly, sir. Leave everything to me," she said, walking up to the waiting temple guards. "Good, you retrieved Saul's knapsack. I'll take that. Stay here for a moment while I get him situated inside."

She led Saul inside the house of Judas here on Straight Street. The temple guards looked at one another with confusion over Saul's condition, but did as they were told.

A servant greeted them, opening the door and leading them to the guest room prepared for Saul. "I have water here and dinner will be served . . ." she started to say.

"Nothing for me, thank you," Saul said. "Just rest, please. I wish to rest. I'll call for food when I'm ready. Please give my appreciation to Judas. I will hopefully see him soon."

"Very well," the servant said. "Judas has instructed me to do as you direct, so I will leave you with it. You may come and go as you wish through the outer door."

"Thank you," Clarie said, dismissing the servant with a coin. "We'll manage from here."

Clarie helped Saul onto the bed. He breathed a sigh of relief, and rolled over to face the wall. "Shalom and safe journey," Saul muttered, pulling the coarse blanket up around his shoulders.

"Shalom," Clarie said with an unseen smile, setting down his knapsack. "May Jehovah bless you and keep you."

Clarie stepped outside and instructed the other guards to head back to Jerusalem. She bid the men farewell, making excuses why she would stay behind. After the men rode off, she motioned for Max, Liz, and Nigel to join her. "Come on, let's go see Gillamon."

"Aye, he's got some explainin' ta do!" Max nodded.

Clarie dipped around a column and took the appearance of an Arab man wrapped in a colorful striped robe like countless others roaming along Straight Street. She had a white headdress tied with a black sash that streamed down the back of her head. She scratched her face and winked. "I kept the beard."

"I don't believe this chameleon work ever gets old for you, does it, my dear?" Nigel quipped with a jolly laugh.

"Never," Clarie said with a big grin. She walked ahead and they came to an enormous Roman complex.

"By Jove, it's the Temple of Jupiter," Nigel marveled as he stared at the massive columns and archways.

"By Jove is right, *mon ami,* since Jove is another name for Jupiter, Roman king of the gods and god of sky and thunder," Liz teased. "What would Jupiter think about how you British use his name in vain?"

Nigel laughed, sweeping back his whiskers. "I think I'm quite safe, seeing how Jupiter is part of Roman mythology and is no more alive than this block of stone." The small mouse tapped a stone frieze of ornate leaves, geometric shapes, and lions' heads. The lions were carved with flowing manes and opened mouths that served as drainage downspouts on the wall.

"Aye, but the R-r-romans think he's alive enough," Max added.

Suddenly the lion moved.

"Sometimes stone can come alive," Gillamon's voice came from the lion's head right above Nigel.

Nigel jumped and put his tiny paw over his heart. "Oh, my dear chap, you caused my heart to jump!"

The stone lion became animated, moving its mouth and eyes. Clarie stood with hands on hips to hide the talking lion's head from the view of passersby.

Gillamon chuckled, and even his stony lion's eyes were smiling to resemble their mountain goat friend's. "Remember what I told you in Jerusalem. Just as a sculptor chips away stone to bring a desired image out of the cold, hard marble, so too will the Maker sculpt the cold, hard soul of your assigned human. Are you surprised he is Saul?"

"Sur-r-rpr-r-rised would be puttin' it lightly, Gillamon!" Max replied. "Up 'til now, I've wanted ta do nothin' but bite his backside. He's been a r-r-rotten scoundr-r-rel!"

"*Oui,* but no more," Liz reminded him. "Gillamon, now that we have seen how Jesus appeared to him on the road to Damascus, please tell us why Saul was chosen. How can he possibly be the one to spread the good news of Jesus?"

"Saul was selected for this assignment before the foundation of the world," Gillamon began. "Look around you at this busy city. Saul was raised in a similar city of Tarsus, unlike the twelve apostles, who came from rural areas. These Roman cities scattered around the empire are giant melting pots of people from all cultures. Saul has been exposed to international cultures his entire life. His father is a tentmaker and has Roman citizenship, so Saul is both a Jew and a Roman."

"*C'est magnifique!*" Liz exclaimed. "So Saul would feel very comfortable traveling to such cities, and knows how to interact with people from many backgrounds. He has many rights as a Roman citizen, no?

He has the protection of Rome, including a fair public trial and exemption from certain forms of punishment."

"To claim to be a citizen of Rome when you are not one is a serious crime, so this must be true for Saul to claim it," Nigel added. "I agree he is a brilliant choice to spread the gospel to the Gentiles. Who but a Roman citizen could mingle among them so easily?"

"I'm glad you see the plan behind his upbringing," Gillamon continued. "And he was raised in strict adherence to Jewish law. He knows the history of Israel and how the laws came into being better than any Jew around."

"Don't we know it," Max smirked. "All he does is thr-r-row the law at believers, sayin' they be br-r-reakin' it."

"Yes, but because he knows it so well, now he can fully understand why Jesus had to come and die as the type of Messiah he did. He will be able to argue both sides of the law with a quick reply," Gillamon explained. "He's had an unusual zeal to please God by keeping the law, but has led a frustrating life of never achieving perfection. I can tell you he actually feels relieved that he doesn't have to live that way any longer. The deep chipping away at his soul by the Maker will be painful for Saul as he wrestles with his past sins of persecuting Jesus' followers. He will learn that when Jesus' followers suffer, Jesus suffers, and this will break Saul's heart. But he will soon learn how grace is the new thing to throw at believers and unbelievers alike."

"I'm sure he will be the first to share that everyone has a dark side, but that changing one's life around is possible, no matter what they've done," stated Nigel. "Even the dirtiest scoundrel can be forgiven and start again."

"*C'est vrai.* Saul also has been well educated in languages. He knows Greek, Latin, and Aramaic. And isn't he also a tentmaker like his father?" Liz asked.

"Yes, we have prepared him with his speech, with safety in Roman citizenship, and with the ability to sustain himself by tentmaking, which he can do everywhere he travels," Gillamon explained. "Max, you'll be pleased to know he can make a living from the long hair of mountain goats. I've watched him grow up, right under his nose as a mountain goat."

Max grinned. "Ye've been gettin' this lad r-r-ready for a long time. If ye had a part in his upbr-r-ringin' then I know he'll turn out ta be a gr-r-rand lad after all. But I've been wantin' ta ask aboot wha' Jesus said when he appeared in the br-r-right light. Wha' did he mean that Saul were kickin' against the goats?"

Suddenly a man wheeled by in his cart and stopped to look at Max, Liz, and Clarie standing by the lion. Gillamon's lion face froze until the man had passed.

Liz and Nigel giggled while Gillamon's face broke into a big smile. "*Goads,* Max, not goats. Goads are wooden sticks that farmers use to prod their oxen along. When the ox pushes back against the farmer, he hurts himself by resisting instruction. The Maker had prodded Saul along with several goads, trying to steer him to the light of truth."

"Brilliant! I see it all now," Nigel enthused. "Some goads for Saul have been Stephen's words and death, the inexplicable courage of Jesus' followers, and Jesus' life and words themselves. I watched how these things nearly drove Saul completely mental as he fought against them. The goads led him to his colorful temper tantrums."

"*Oui,* now he is suffering from finally being stopped in his tracks," Liz added. "But suffering has long been the Maker's way to turn raging bulls into gentle lambs."

"Indeed, or in our statue terms, from an ugly block of cold stone to a beautiful work of art. With a mighty first blow of the Maker's chisel, Saul's conversion was immediate, but sculpting him into an intricately detailed champion for Christ will take a lifetime to achieve. But the Maker is a patient sculptor," Gillamon added. "Now, for the matter at hand, Saul will remain blind for three days. He will spend that time primarily in prayer with the Maker and Jesus, coming to grips with the revelation that Jesus is exactly who he claimed to be."

Nigel twirled his whiskers slowly, shaking his head. "What a terrible discovery for Saul to realize that what he has felt to be his solemn duty to the Maker has been one long sin against the Maker's dearest plans."

"A believer here in Damascus by the name of Ananias will come help Paul after the Lord instructs him," Gillamon informed them.

"Uh, ye said Paul, lad," Max corrected his mentor. "His name be *Saul.*"

153

"Not for long," the talking lion's head shared with a smile. "He'll begin using his Roman name of Paul right away. It's part of his new identity as a Christ-follower. It was part of the Maker's sculpting design to give him two names at birth with his Roman citizenship."

"So even his name will help open doors as he seeks to reach Gentiles," Liz marveled. "How are we to help S- . . . I mean Paul?"

"He will soon leave Damascus for an intense time of isolation and preparation in the Arabian desert. You will go to protect him there," Gillamon explained. "But you need to witness these initial sculpting moves with Ananias and other believers here in Damascus. For now, Paul can't see you, so feel free to go pay him a visit . . . and talk to him if you wish."

Max, Liz, and Nigel shared a startled look. "How splendid!" enthused Nigel. "It will be like when I was able to converse with my blind harp student, Benipe, long ago in Egypt for our Joseph mission. Extraordinary!"

154

"*Oui!* And I haven't spoken to a human besides Jesus, Isaiah, and briefly to Mary," Liz echoed.

"Very well," the lion carving announced with a wide smile. "Go enjoy watching the Maker's finest new statue come to life. But it's time to shut the mouth of this lion."

The lion sculpture grew still once more, and Gillamon was gone.

"Are you ready to meet Paul?" Clarie asked them.

Max furrowed his brow. "Aye, I don't know wha' he'll be thinkin' aboot me accent, but I'll be glad ta give the lad a word."

Clarie leaned down and mussed the fur on Max's head. "Well, I'm sure Paul will be glad you're only going to give him a word, and not your teeth in his blind backside."

"How utterly poetic that the street where Paul will begin his new life is called *Straight!*" Nigel cheered as they began walking back toward Judas's house.

Liz frowned. "*Oui,* and how equally poetic that the house where he will begin this new life belongs to a man called . . . Judas."

19

SURPRISING DEVELOPMENTS

A small wooden table held an untouched pitcher of water, a bowl of fruit, and a terra cotta oil lamp that the house servant would light at dusk. Saul didn't bother to turn over from facing the wall, allowing the servant to believe he was asleep. Light from the lamp danced off the beautifully tiled walls and archway above Saul's bed, but such a sight was lost on him. The bed where he lay was on an elevated nook in an alcove of this guest chamber designed for the privacy of both the host and the guest. The room had two doors. One door led from his room to the rest of Judas's house, and one door led directly outside to Straight Street. Saul could hear the goings-on of the city through the street front door. He heard the rumble of carts along the paved Roman road, the conversations of people walking along, and the enthusiastic cries of merchants selling their wares. But all these sounds became background noise to the thoughts bombarding his mind.

Tears rolled down from his sightless eyes. Saul grieved, not for his loss of sight, but for the stark reality of what he had done to so many people. He was a murderer, plain and simple. He had thought he was doing the Lord's work and that, as such, he was justified in his actions.

He had thought he was an important instrument of righteousness. Shame engulfed him as he now understood the depths of his cruelty. He had blasphemed and persecuted the Lord, not protected him. *"I am Jesus, whom you persecute."* It was one thing to persecute Jesus' followers, but Jesus told him he had persecuted Jesus himself. *Touch them, and you touch me* was the essence of what Jesus had said.

"Forgive me, Lord Jesus! Oh, please forgive me!" Saul cried out with deep, gut-wrenching sobs of despair. He didn't hear the soft knock on the door leading out to Straight Street.

Clarie slowly opened the door and entered with Max, Liz, and Nigel behind her. She had decided she would remain quiet while the others had their time with Saul. They didn't know what they would say, but felt they could help him understand they were there to help encourage his grieving spirit.

"Who's there?" Saul inquired weakly, lifting his head off the pillow.

"Friends," Nigel offered, looking at Max and Liz, shrugging his shoulders. "We've come to give you words of encouragement."

Saul wrinkled his brow. "I don't recognize your accent. Thank you for coming but I wish to be alone."

"Oui, we won't stay long," Liz joined in. "We can only imagine how you must be feeling. This is not at all how you expected things to turn out in Damascus. You came to invade and were invaded, *n'est ce pas?* Jesus is not one you can easily ignore when he wants your attention."

Saul turned over to face his mysterious guests. He appeared to gaze in their direction, but could not see them. Alarm was written across his face. "And you—a woman—I don't know what language you mix in with your speech. How do you know about me? How could you possibly know about . . . Jesus? I have told no one what happened!"

Liz looked at the others, uncertain of how to reply. "Do not concern yourself with how we speak, *mon ami.* Let us just say we are ambassadors of Jesus."

Saul slowly put his head back on the pillow, lying on his back. He wiped away the tears that continued to stream down his face. "I didn't know what I was doing when I persecuted them. When I murdered them. Stephen's words haunt me."

"Those words linger in your mind for your highest good, dear boy," Nigel offered. "Stephen asked that what you did would not be held against you. Stephen has already forgiven you."

"How could you know that, unless you were there?" asked Saul.

"Aye," Max agreed, drawing a puzzled look from Saul as he heard yet another strange accent. "But ye best be understandin' that ye can get past yer failures. Ye've got important things ta do."

"You are not the only one who has ever grieved over such a horrific crime as murder," Liz said, an idea coming to her mind. "David grieved before the Lord, and wrote down his words:

Have mercy on me, O God, according to your unfailing love; according to your great compassion blot out my transgressions. Wash away all my iniquity and cleanse me from my sin. For I know my transgressions, and my sin is always before me. Against you, you only, have I sinned and done what is evil in your sight; so you are right in your verdict and justified when you judge."

157

Saul picked up where Liz left off.

"Cleanse me with hyssop, and I will be clean; wash me, and I will be whiter than snow. Let me hear joy and gladness; let the bones you have crushed rejoice. Hide your face from my sins and blot out all my iniquity. Create in me a pure heart, O God, and renew a steadfast spirit within me. Do not cast me from your presence or take your Holy Spirit from me. Restore to me the joy of your salvation and grant me a willing spirit, to sustain me."

His voice broke with emotion as the words of David's Fifty-First Psalm engulfed him with a feeling of relief. David was a God-fearing man who had murdered to cover up sin, not in a zealous yet misguided attempt to serve God, as Saul had. Saul felt David's words in a way he had never felt them before. They became real to him. God called David "a man after my own heart." Could it be that Saul the murderer could also find forgiveness?

Liz continued. *"Then I will teach transgressors your ways, so that sinners will turn back to you."*

"You see, old boy, once you get past this painful first step of dealing with your past, it will be time to get on with your future," Nigel encouraged him. "You will have much to share."

Saul wiped his eyes. "How could the Lord ever use anyone who has done the things I've done?"

Saul's comment tugged at Max's heartstrings, carrying him back to the day Noah opened the door of the ark. He remembered asking himself the same thing, after he had lost his way from the Maker. An endearing sympathy came over Max, helping him forgive Saul in his own heart. "Tr-r-rust me, lad. He will. An' ye can do it. Know that ye're loved an' ye're able."

Clarie motioned that it was time for them to go. She put a finger up to her mouth and opened the door. The animals looked at the broken man who for now was in the dark night of the soul, and their hearts went out to him. Such was the transforming power of grace to have compassion on a wounded soul longing for forgiveness. They filed out into the street and Clarie closed the door softly behind them.

"It will take a miracle for me to ever believe that," Saul answered sadly. He lifted his head from the pillow when he didn't receive a reply. "Are you still there?" No response. Saul rolled over and pulled his covers around his shoulders. He drew a quick breath when a thought came to him. *Could I have just been visited by angels? Just like Abraham when he didn't know it? Angels unawares.*

Ananias lay on his bed, half awake in his house at the other end of Straight Street. He had had restless sleep for two nights, so although he was tired, he couldn't quite fall asleep. Some fellow believers in Damascus had discovered a plot from the Sanhedrin to arrest the Jesus-followers in the city. The ringleader was a man by the name of Saul, who had traveled there with marching orders to round the Christians up and carry them back to Jerusalem. No follower of Jesus was resting well in the city of Damascus tonight.

While in this twilight haze of sleepiness, a voice of authority called to him. "Ananias!"

"Yes, Lord," he answered immediately.

"Go to the house of Judas on Straight Street and ask for a man from Tarsus named Saul, for he is praying. In a vision he has seen a man named Ananias come and place his hands on him to restore his sight."

"Lord," Ananias answered, "I have heard many reports about this man and all the harm he has done to your holy people in Jerusalem. And he has come here with authority from the chief priests to arrest all who call on your name."

"Go! This man is my chosen instrument to proclaim my name to the Gentiles and their kings and to the people of Israel. I will show him how much he must suffer for my name."

Ananias came to a full state of awakening with a racing heart. He sat up on the side of his bed and pulled his fingers through his long, gray hair. Fear filled his mind. He was supposed to seek out the very man from whom believers were now in hiding? How could this be? Yet the Lord had spoken to him, of that the faithful Ananias had no doubt. *God's surprises are one of the ways he leads,* he reminded himself.

159

Ananias stood up and walked to the window. He pulled back the curtain and saw that the sun was beginning to rise. He looked around his room and realized he might never return to his home. Saul could take him away to Jerusalem once Ananias helped restore his sight. The Lord didn't tell Ananias *when* Saul would proclaim the Good News to others. Perhaps it would be after he had persecuted all of Damascus. His hands trembled, so he clasped them tightly together to steady them. *Very well, I will do as my Lord has asked, and trust what comes.*

With that, the old man put on his cloak, looked around his room one last time, and stepped out the door.

Clarie was standing outside next to a cart where she had hidden the animals under a tarp. Still dressed as an Arab man, she smiled when she saw nervous Ananias walking toward them. "Here he comes," she whispered to the animals.

Ananias saw the sign for rugs and closed his eyes tightly as he placed his hand on his heart to settle himself down. He walked over to the house and Clarie greeted him. "Are you looking for someone?"

Ananias jumped, wondering if this Arab was a spy for Saul of Tarsus. Still, he had to press on with his assignment. "Is this the house of Judas? I'm looking for Saul of Tarsus."

"Yes, he's here," Clarie answered, walking to the door. "I'll let you in."

The old man's palms were sweating and he rubbed them on his cloak. He nodded uneasily. "Th-th-thank you," he stammered, walking over to cautiously enter the door.

"The poor chap is beside himself with fear!" Nigel whispered from underneath the tarp.

"Wouldn't *you* be, if you had been asked to go see a murderer who was out to arrest you?" Liz posed.

As Ananias walked into the room, he was surprised to see the form of a small, defeated man kneeling at the side of his bed, praying. His shoulders were hunched over and he shook with soulful sobs. This caught Ananias off guard, but in a hopeful way. He slowly walked over to Saul, his heart pounding out of his chest. He knelt down next to Saul and placed his hand on the once-zealous Pharisee's shoulder.

"Saul, brother," he began, swallowing a gulp of relief mixed with joy, "the Lord—Jesus, who appeared to you on the road as you were coming here—has sent me so that you may see again and be filled with the Holy Spirit."

As Saul turned to face Ananias, something like scales fell from his eyes. He rubbed them slowly before opening them. And the first thing he saw was the face of a follower of Jesus. Tears quickened in Saul's eyes and his lip trembled. "I can see!" He put his hand on Ananias's arm. "Thank you, my . . . brother," he said, haltingly. "Pharisees have never spoken with such affection."

"The God of our fathers has chosen you, Saul. You were chosen to see the face of Jesus and hear words straight from his lips," Ananias assured him. "You are to be a witness to both Jew and Gentile alike, telling them about these things. You, Saul, have been chosen to become Christ's ambassador to the world."

Saul looked at him in overwhelming agreement, nodding slowly. "Even though it is hard for me to grasp why he would choose me, I am his servant and will do whatever he tells me to do. But please, I now wish to go by my Roman name of Paul."

Ananias smiled. "Paul it is. And I am Ananias. Now that your eyes have been opened, you must go open the eyes of others. But the first thing you must do is be baptized as Jesus commanded his believers."

"Yes, please, let's go at once," Paul urged, eager to rise to his feet. He faltered and Ananias had to catch him. He was lightheaded from having no food or water for three days.

Ananias saw the untouched food and water on the table. "You are weak."

"It doesn't matter, I must be baptized first," Paul insisted. "Take me to the river, please."

"Very well," Ananias said, holding Paul's elbow. "Lean on me."

Together they stepped outside. Paul immediately put his hand up to shield his sensitized eyes from the bright sunlight before he opened them. He smiled and slowly allowed them to adjust. Ananias walked ahead, and Paul gazed at the busy street called Straight. The sights and sounds and smells of this dynamic city filled Paul with energy. He silently thanked God for sparing him from entering this city as a vengeful zealot. They walked a half mile to the beautiful Abana River. Never had water looked so clear and beautiful to Paul. He and Ananias shared a knowing smile as they made their way down the grassy bank to the fast-flowing waters.

Clarie and the animals stood under a lush green tree, the branches of which swayed in the breeze over the cool water. They looked at one another with joy. This was a beautiful moment.

Ananias held his hand up and closed his eyes to pray. "Lord Jesus, I have done as you asked. Now here stands with me my brother Paul. Accept him into the fold of believers as he washes away the life of Saul to rise as your servant Paul. I baptize you, my brother, in the name of the Father, the Son, and the Holy Spirit." Ananias helped lean Paul back into the waters.

Paul came out of the water, smiling with his head back and his faced kissed by the warm sun. Immediately the Holy Spirit entered Paul and a rush of physical well-being and emotional wholeness came to him. Ananias gave a joy-filled laugh and enveloped Paul with a big bear hug. "Welcome, my brother."

"Oh, how beautiful!" Liz cried, watching this former murderer embraced by one he had come to arrest. "Jesus is hugging Paul through Ananias, I am sure!"

"Jesus came and rescued the persecutor," Nigel observed with emotion. "Extraordinary."

"Aye, amazin' gr-r-race," Max added.

"Come, let's get you something to eat," Ananias told Paul, patting him on the back. "And tonight, you will meet more brothers and sisters."

"I'm accepted, just like that?" Paul asked, marveling at this overwhelming feeling of love and grace.

162

"Just like that, Paul," Ananias said with a wide grin. "Just like that."

∝

A group of half a dozen men and women sat at a long table in the home of one of the believers, enjoying laughter and fellowship around the hearth, where a fire blazed. Ananias and Paul came in through the open courtyard to join them.

"Greetings, everyone," Ananias announced. "I have someone to introduce to you. This is Paul, a new fellow believer."

Two of the men got to their feet and shared angry glances. They took defensive postures and stood in front of the others. "This is Saul! He's the one who's come to Damascus to arrest us!" they reported in alarm. "We suffered at the hand of his whip before fleeing Jerusalem."

Ananias held up his hands and smiled. "Indeed, but his plans have changed. He has not only changed his name, but his heart." Ananias put his arm around Paul and brought him over to the others.

"I met Jesus, you see, and everything has changed," Paul told them joyfully. "Here, these are the letters I brought with me for the purposes you mentioned." He handed them over to the men who took them cautiously from his hand.

The men put their heads together to read the mandate signed by Caiaphas himself. They looked at one another and then at Paul in disbelief.

"Forgive me, brothers. I didn't know what I was doing when I hurt you," Paul pleaded. "I know now I was persecuting the risen, true Messiah and all those who follow him. Forgive me, and please, allow me to prove to you my intentions." He held out his hand for the letters from Caiaphas.

The men handed the letters back to him. Paul took them and walked over to the fire, tossing the letters into the flames. He stood back and watched his past directive turn into ashes. He turned to face the others. "I'm eager to learn how to be a follower of Jesus. Will you please help me?"

The men's eyebrows lifted at this surprising development. They rushed up to Paul and embraced him. "Welcome, brother Paul! You are forgiven. Come, join us!"

Paul humbly embraced the men who welcomed him with open arms. Liz sat up on the wall, her tail curling up and down as she beamed with delight at the scene below. Nigel sat next to her.

"*C'est magnifique!* Paul is attending his first official gathering of believers, and he has been accepted. Jesus must be so pleased with them!" Liz exclaimed.

"Indeed, my dear, I'm sure he is," Nigel agreed. "Although I know this has come as quite the shock to these very ones Paul sent running out of Jerusalem. I doubt he will receive the same welcome from the Jewish leaders of Damascus when they find out that Saul is now Paul. As far as they are concerned, everything is still proceeding as planned. Judas doesn't even yet know what has happened to Paul."

Liz frowned. "*Oui,* and Paul is planning to speak at synagogue tomorrow. Let's hope he doesn't get the same reception Jesus did in Nazareth when he spoke the truth."

Paul sat dressed in his usual blue-fringed robe, looking the full part of the Pharisee he was known to be. He watched as the local elders filed into the synagogue, nodding their satisfaction with his presence here in Damascus. They whispered among themselves that finally the heresy of those followers of the Way would be put to a stop here in Damascus. They even hoped they would get to witness Saul's famed violent roundup of believers who would then be dragged to court for a good flogging.

Ananias and the group of Jesus-followers filed in and sat near the back, catching Paul's eye with affirming smiles. They were praying for Paul, and he could feel their prayers. They were the only ones who knew what was about to happen here in the synagogue. After opening songs and prayers, the *hazzan,* or leader of the Jewish congregation, stood to escort Paul over to the lectern in the front of the room.

Paul unrolled the scroll and read the designated passage for the day. His eyes welled up when he saw that the passage was Isaiah 35. He smiled inside and with a loud voice and perfect inflection read the verses that talked about Messiah. That talked about him. That talked about the Way.

"Strengthen the feeble hands, steady the knees that give way; say to those with fearful hearts,

'Be strong, do not fear; your God will come, he will come with vengeance; with divine retribution he will come to save you.'" Paul paused, a lump forming in his throat as he read the next line.

"Then will the eyes of the blind be opened . . ." He paused and looked around the room, making eye contact with Ananias, who gave him an affirming nod. ". . . And the ears of the deaf unstopped. Then will the lame leap like a deer, and the mute tongue shout for joy. Water will gush forth in the wilderness and streams in the desert. The burning sand will become a pool, the thirsty ground bubbling springs.

"In the haunts where jackals once lay, grass and reeds and papyrus will grow. And a highway will be there . . ." He paused again. Paul looked up and recited the last two lines by memory. "It will be called the Way of Holiness; it will be for those who walk on that Way."

Paul rolled the scroll back up and handed it back to the *hazzan.* He looked around the room and was struck with the divine realization that synagogues like this one were scattered in Gentile cities all over the Roman Empire. He had a platform from which to preach the good news of Jesus in each and every one of them! If he had seen the truth that Jesus was Messiah, then surely these Jews would, too. And it all would begin with him here in Damascus.

Paul smiled and took a deep breath. "Jesus is Messiah. He is the Way, the Truth, and the Life. Isaiah prophesied about him in this passage. Not only did Jesus open the eyes of the blind, such as the man in the temple in Jerusalem, but he opened *my* eyes! For I was once blind as to who he was. But now I see. I see clearly that Jesus is the Son of God, who was crucified for our sins, but was raised to life on the third day."

Shock waves pulsed through the assembly as Paul proceeded to deliver a passionate sermon of how he had met Jesus on the road to Damascus, was blinded but now understood the truth. The synagogue elders looked at one another in disbelief and murmured among themselves. "He was supposed to come here and arrest those who believe this heresy! Now listen to him preach it, to *us!*"

When Paul finished, he prayed over the congregation. Ananias stood up and motioned for him to leave with him.

"He's mad!" Judas muttered under his breath to the priest. "I knew nothing of this! He's been under my roof but I assure you he will be gone this day. And I plan to write to Caiaphas immediately about this surprising development."

Paul walked out of the synagogue, surrounded by his new friends who now knew without a shadow of a doubt that Paul of Tarsus was not just a new believer and follower of the Way. With this bold sermon in the most powerful synagogue of Damascus, he had just become their most courageous champion.

165

DESERT DISCOVERIES

P aul tossed and turned on his bed. His restlessness knew no bounds as he hungered for more firsthand knowledge of his newfound Savior. Daily he sought out conversation with believers who had been with Jesus, wanting to know everything they could remember about him. How he regretted missing those three years of Jesus' ministry on Earth! Oh, to have been one of his disciples! Just the thought of sitting down with Jesus to discuss all the things he taught made Paul crave more understanding. He even wished for those blessed three days of glorious blindness when Jesus had been close to him in spirit, revealing truth to his mind and heart.

It was no use trying to sleep anymore. Paul got up and lit the oil lamp in this room Ananias had provided for him. Once Judas heard Paul's bold sermon professing Jesus as Messiah, he immediately kicked Paul out of his house. Word had it that Judas had written to Caiaphas about what Paul had done at the synagogue, with the approval of the local Jewish leaders. No telling what kind of response Caiaphas would make when the news reached him.

Paul was taken aback by the response of Judas and the other Jews of Damascus. *Moses must have felt this way when his fellow Hebrews first rejected him as the one offering them deliverance from the Egyptians,*

Paul thought to himself as he unrolled his scroll of Exodus in the dim light. Suddenly he realized something he never had before. Moses was zealous to deliver his fellow Hebrews while he was still in the court of Pharaoh, but he wasn't prepared to actually do it. Killing an Egyptian who was beating on a fellow Hebrew didn't win their favor. It had only made Moses a marked man wanted for murder by the Egyptians. No, deliverance of God's people would come by God's plan alone, not the feeble attempts spurred by Moses' zeal. God had to prepare Moses' mind and heart. So Moses fled to Midian in the Arabian desert. He was there forty years before God spoke to him in the burning bush.

"A burning bush with the voice of God instructing Moses to deliver the Hebrews. A blinding light with the voice of Jesus instructing *me* to deliver the Gentiles," Paul said to himself out loud, setting the scroll down on the table. Suddenly his heart started racing. "Like Moses, *I'm* not ready for what I've been called to do, and I'm guilty of murder, thinking I was defending God's people. I must get away and learn. Oh, Lord Jesus, I *need* to learn! But how? I can't yet return to Jerusalem to learn from Jesus' disciples. Just as Moses risked arrest by the Egyptians, I would risk arrest by the Sanhedrin."

He thought for a moment as he stared at the scroll of Exodus. Of course! Arabia! He'd go where Moses had escaped to be alone in the wilderness. "I will go away and be taught by you alone, my Lord." Paul clasped his hands together as his excitement grew over this revelation. Being the son of a trader, he knew how to obtain passage on one of the Nabatean caravans heading south to Midian. Damascus was one of the key trade cities for Arabian myrrh and frankincense from the Nabatean kingdom headquartered in Petra, 250 miles south. Mount Horeb, where Moses encountered the burning bush and where he received the Ten Commandments, was another 165 miles south of Petra, which he could travel on foot if need be. The caravans would be leaving Damascus before sunup to beat the blistering sun. He needed to get to them before they departed.

Paul looked around the room. All he needed to take was his knapsack with the scrolls of Scripture, and a few clothes. He would leave behind his Pharisaic robes. He no longer needed them. Paul took out a piece of papyrus and quickly penned a note to Ananias.

> *Dear Brother Ananias,*
>
> *I am going away to learn from the Master in solitude. Thank you for your hospitality and care of me following my Damascus Road experience. You are my first brother in Christ, and will ever be in my prayers as you keep sharing the good news of Jesus here in Damascus. I ask that you pray for me as I seek truth and the wisdom to know how I am to fulfill the call he has given me. Until I return, I remain your brother in our Lord Jesus Christ.*
> *Paul*

Paul left the letter sitting on the table, picked up his knapsack, blew out the oil lamp, and headed out the door.

⊃⊂

"Now I see!" Max exclaimed, as Clarie lifted him to sit in a saddlebag draped over the camel. "Ye took the form of an Arab lad ta be part of this car-r-ravan heading ta Petr-r-ra."

Clarie smiled and rubbed her coarse beard. "And of course Paul will think nothing of my exotic animals that ride along with me."

"Bravo! It's terribly exciting to think of Mount Horeb and our time there with Moses," Nigel exclaimed, scurrying up to stand between the ears of the camel. "I was quite the camel driver back in the day. Do you remember taking out Pharaoh's chariots, my dear?"

Liz giggled, sitting pretty in the other saddlebag. *"Bien sûr!* How could I forget such a thrilling adventure on our loud camel friend, Osahar? Pardon, but *comment vous appelez-vous?"* she asked the camel.

The camel turned her eyes up to Nigel. "What did she say?" she asked in a very quiet voice.

Nigel and Liz looked at one another in surprise. Never had they heard such a soft-spoken camel. "My, my, my, aren't you the far cry from my previous noble camel transports, Osahar and Lawrence from

Arabia?" Nigel exclaimed with a jolly chuckle. "Liz asked you what your name is, my dear."

"Leena," the camel replied softly, batting her long eyelashes over her big brown eyes.

"Ah, well you certainly live up to your name, no?" Liz said in delight. "Leena means 'softness.' I am Liz, these are Max and Nigel. *Merci* for allowing us to ride you for this journey."

"I'm happy to have other quiet animals to talk to," Leena replied. "The other camels are so loud. And I've never seen a human who could speak camel."

Clarie patted Leena on her sweet face and smiled as she spotted Paul hurrying up the dark road. She had placed a torch burning right where they stood so he would be inclined to talk to her first. "Here he comes."

Paul walked right up to Clarie, recognizing her from standing outside Judas' house on Straight Street. "I am needing transport to Petra. Actually to Mount Horeb in Midian, but I can make it from Petra myself. I am prepared to pay you well."

"I'm sure you are. Come, I have a camel for you." Clarie winked at Liz as she led Paul to another camel sitting on the ground right behind them. The camel had a colorful fringed cloth draped over its hump underneath a leather saddle. "You're just in time. The caravan is pulling out."

Paul slung his knapsack over the camel's hump, patted the animal, and climbed onto the saddle. He nodded gratefully to Clarie once he was set. "Thank you, my friend."

Clarie nodded and patted the camel's backside. "HA!" The camel rose to its feet with a whiny snort. Paul took the reins and waited for the Arab man (Clarie) to mount his camel. Clarie climbed aboard and Leena rose to her feet. They were at the end of a caravan of twenty camels laden with goods from the Roman world going back to southern Arabia. The sound of men chiding their mounts sounded as the caravan proceeded out of Damascus.

Paul looked up to the stars twinkling in the early morning sky above. He prayed a silent prayer as they began their journey, expectant about all that would happen to him before he returned to this place.

⊂×

Liz studied Paul as they rode along through the hot desert. He pulled his white head covering tightly around his face against the burning sun. Whenever the caravan stopped, Paul kept to himself. He didn't seem to want to have contact with anyone. He sat and read his scrolls. He mindlessly watched hot sand blow across the stones. He prayed, and he slept.

"Do you realize that every human the Maker has called to do great things had to spend periods of time alone before they were able to complete their missions? Moses spent forty years in the desert where we are headed now," Liz remembered. "Young David spent thirteen years running from King Saul after he was named Saul's replacement as the new king of Israel. Elijah retreated by the brook, exhausted after his match with King Ahab, to rest before he continued on his mission. John the Baptist spent years in the desert before he began his short ministry."

"And even Jesus himself spent forty days alone in the desert," Nigel added. "Well, I should correct that statement. Alone without *humans*. He did have us, after all."

"Aye, an' he had ta deal with that devil," Max reminded him. "So, Paul be doin' the r-r-right thing in gettin' r-r-ready for wha's ahead. He's got ta learn ta pr-r-reach the ver-r-ry gospel he tried ta silence."

"Paul must be so exhausted, no?" Liz pondered. "He has spent so much energy fighting against the Maker and the followers of the Way. And he has spent a lifetime trying to keep all the laws to perfection."

"The old boy must need a long rest after keeping every jot and tittle of that burdensome law," Nigel agreed. "How Jesus hated all that silly man-made law business! I'm pleased that Paul is finally coming to realize he is free from all that."

"That's going to be one of the main discoveries Paul will make out here in the desert. He needs to fully understand why the law was given and its role in the life of God's people up until now. He also needs to see how Jesus fulfilled the law, not replaced it. He'll need to go back to grasp the promise to Abraham for that," Clarie explained. "When we get to Mount Horeb, I'll leave you to be with Paul as he discovers this and much more."

"But how will we get away with bein' ar-r-round the lad?" Max asked with concern.

"Oh, let's just say a certain mouse will be chased by a certain cat who'll be chased by a certain dog into the desert, which will, of course, be out of my control. I'll have to leave you there, saddened but having no choice but to head on back to Petra," Clarie explained.

"Brilliant! I do love a good chase scene," Nigel quipped.

"For now, leave him be. Allow him his time alone with Jesus. You will be the only witnesses to what happens to Paul out here in this Arabian desert. Keep an eye out for anything that might try to harm him. When it's time for Paul to leave Mount Horeb, you can miraculously show up at his campsite," Clarie instructed them. "Until then, I'll check on things in Jerusalem."

171

Clarie and Paul peeled off from the caravan that made its way on into the city of Petra, proceeding the 165 miles south to the desert of Midian. They stopped at a small oasis of water and date palm trees near the base of Mount Horeb.

"Here we are," Clarie said, setting Leena down so she could slide off the saddle onto the ground. She whispered to Max, Liz, and Nigel, "I'll see you later. This is your cue. Get some water and then start the chase." She gave them a final petting and a wink.

Max and Liz jumped out of the saddle bags and walked to get some water. Paul and Clarie went over to fill their water pouches. Nigel whispered in Leena's ear, "Cheerio, my dear. Until we meet again, ta-ta."

"Bye, Nigel," Leena softly replied.

Nigel smiled and petted her head before jumping down to sneak a drink from the spring. He signaled to Max and Liz that he was ready. Max nodded and nudged Liz, who got the message. Suddenly Nigel darted out and ran right under Paul's legs, causing him to step back a step. Liz took chase after Nigel, and Max took chase after Liz, barking and putting on a good show. Clarie ran a few steps, calling, "Come back, you two!" She smiled as she watched them run off into the wilderness. Then she turned and raised her hands in the air and gave an "Oh, well" look for Paul. "Well, if they don't come back soon I'll have to leave them here. I have to get my spices to Petra."

"Let's rest a while. Perhaps they'll come back," Paul encouraged her. Together they sat in the shade of a date palm tree. Paul leaned his head back and closed his eyes, thankful for having reached his destination. After an hour of silence, Clarie decided it was time to go.

"I don't worry about unexpected delays, do you? The discipline of delay is a good teacher," Clarie said, poking the ground with a stick. "Delays that teach and prepare us for things save time in the long run."

Paul opened his eyes and studied this kind Arab with sand caked in his smile lines. He puzzled over the man's unusual blue eyes. "Wise words. Tell me, have you heard of Jesus? He spoke many wise words as well."

Clarie smiled. "I have heard of him. I even met him," she said, standing up to leave.

Paul's eyes widened at this surprising news. "You met Jesus? Oh how I wish I had talked with you before now. I believe he is Messiah. I believe he is the Savior of the world."

Clarie paused a moment, put her hands on her hips, and looked out at the desert wilderness. "Isn't Messiah a Jewish promise? I'm an Arab, but descended from Abraham just like you. You'll have to convince me the next time we meet."

Paul got to his feet excitedly. "I promise to do so. Thank you for bringing me this far out here. And I'm sorry for the loss of your animals."

"Yes, well, cats and dogs will be cats and dogs. But those two are smart and can fend for themselves. I've never seen two animals travel so far on their own. And they are extremely loyal. No telling where they will turn up, but I'm sure I'll see them again," Clarie predicted, shrugging her shoulders. "Perhaps you and I will meet again as well. I'll look forward to your argument about how Jesus could save an Arab such as me."

"It's a promise," Paul said with a smile. "May God bless you and keep you until we meet again."

Clarie walked over to ready the camels. Paul put his water pouch, bag of food provisions, and knapsack over his shoulder and walked away into the wilderness. Clarie smiled at him as she mounted Leena and rode off back toward Petra.

Max, Liz, and Nigel hid behind a boulder, watching Paul steadily climb to some caves at the base of Mount Horeb. It was then they heard him begin talking to himself. With no one else around, Paul felt completely free to give voice to his thoughts. And he spoke directly to Jesus.

"I will start at the beginning, Jesus. I want to go through all the Scripture I have studied my entire life. But this time, I wish to look at everything with you in mind. Show yourself to me," Paul prayed, climbing some rocks. He began with the first verse of the Torah. "In the beginning God created the heavens and the earth. Now the earth was formless and empty, darkness was over the surface of the deep, and the Spirit of God was hovering over the waters. And God said, 'Let there be light,' and there was light. God saw that the light was good, and he separated the light from the darkness. God called the light 'day,' and the darkness he called 'night.' And there was evening, and there was morning—the first day." Paul suddenly stopped in his tracks. "Day six you said, 'Let us make man in *our* image.'" He shook his head in wonder. "There you are, right at the beginning!" He walked a little farther and sat down on a huge, flat boulder.

173

Paul closed his eyes and pretended he was blind again, reaching out in front of him, pawing at the air. "Darkness. There are two kinds of darkness: physical and spiritual. I had both." He sat there a long while, pondering deeply. The animals quietly watched him. After a time he opened his eyes and held up a hand as if instructing himself as he slowly made out his thoughts. "The God who said, 'Let light shine out of darkness,' has shone in our hearts . . . to give the light of the knowledge of the glory of God in the face of Christ." Paul stretched his hands out and shouted at the top of his lungs, "Amazing, Jesus! You are the Light of the world! And you were there at the beginning of creation with the Father. You had no beginning, and you have no end."

"Looks like he's already learnin'," Max whispered with a smile.

"*Oui,* and he has such freedom in his spirit to shout for joy!" Liz beamed.

"I daresay, we'll be here for quite some time if Paul goes through each passage of Scripture with such thoughtfulness," Nigel said, preening his whiskers. "One cannot replace an entire lifetime of Jewish worldview with Jesus over the course of just a weekend. I suspect this will take years."

"Aye, well Moses had forty years with sheep, an' the disciples had thr-r-ree years with Jesus," Max added, looking at Liz and Nigel. "We best settle in for a long r-r-retr-r-reat, however long it takes."

Paul got up and gazed across the rocky wilderness surrounding Mount Horeb. "It was here you called your servant Moses in the burning bush, and it was here your people wandered in the wilderness and set up the tabernacle." He turned his gaze up to the mountain caves. "It was here Elijah heard your gentle whisper and where your finger wrote the laws on stone tablets." Paul swallowed hard, knowing he was standing in a holy place. "You've called this your mountain, God. However you choose to now speak to me through your Holy Spirit, speak. Show me your glory as you showed the others, so I might do your bidding."

He thought of the Arab man who brought him here and smiled. "And I know an Arab who needs an answer, so please give me the words."

174

PERILOUS PETRA

L ook how dark his face has gotten out here in the sun," Liz whispered. She, Max, and Nigel were hiding in the bushes on the banks of the oasis pool. Paul was bathing in the cool waters of the early evening hours. "I almost wouldn't recognize him."

"Indeed, he looks more like one of the local Bedouins roaming this rugged wilderness," Nigel noted. "But I daresay he is even less like the Saul of three years ago. I'm quite pleased with all he has learned out here on this Arabian retreat."

"Aye, did ye hear wha' he said this mornin'?" Max asked them. "He said that all his upbr-r-ringin' an' all that men thought aboot how gr-r-rand he were as a Pharisee were worthless. Compared with discoverin' Jesus out here, nothin' matters ta the lad anymore."

"*Oui,* and I feel it is time for us to make our presence known," Liz suggested. "He must be prepared to preach the gospel, and he cannot stay here forever. I feel we are to leave soon."

"Well, there be no time like the pr-r-resent," Max said with a grin. "Come on, Mousie. I think ye should come over, too. Let him see ye. This should be fun."

Max trotted out of the bushes and went right up to the waterline,

175

taking a drink and wagging his tail. Liz and Nigel shrugged their shoulders and started out. Liz stopped Nigel and reminded him, "Hide your spectacles, *mon ami.*"

"Right!" Nigel said, removing his glasses. He gripped them in his paw and squinted. "I'm afraid I'll have to ask for a ride, my dear." He climbed up on Liz's shoulders and together they walked over to join Max.

Paul looked over and saw the animals his Arabian traveling companion had lost long ago. A wide smile grew on his face as he waded out of the water. "Will wonders never cease?! Hello, you two!" Paul squatted down next to them, water dripping off his arm as he petted them. Suddenly he saw Nigel sitting on top of Liz. "And I see the hunter has now befriended her prey. What a perfect picture of what has happened to me! The Arab said you could fend for yourselves and so you have."

Max grinned and barked, *"If ye only knew how we've fended for ye, laddie! Snakes, scorpions, jackals, an' wolves couldn't get near ye."*

"It was most important for you not to be interrupted during your study of Jesus and Scripture," Liz meowed, head-butting Paul's knee. *"Protection is our specialty, no? That, and the written Word."*

Paul laughed at the 'talkative' animals. "Well, I am glad to see you. I know that your owner would love to know that you are safe and sound." He stood up and looked at the stars beginning to appear in the pinkish-gray twilight sky. "I've been feeling I need to leave this place. If the Lord confirms this feeling for me tonight, we can head out in the morning, and perhaps I can return you to your Arab. We'll head to Petra. You will give me a good excuse to seek out my Arab friend and tell him about Jesus."

Nigel cheered and squeaked, *"Bravo! It's utterly splendid of you to allow me to be in your company, my good fellow."*

"Come, I'll share whatever I have for dinner," Paul said, picking up his cloak and pulling a hand through his long, wet hair. He proceeded to walk back to his residential cave to light a fire for the night.

Max, Liz, and Nigel trotted along behind him. Once they were seated around the fire, Paul offered them some fruit and nuts. "Not much is available out here, as I'm sure you've discovered on your own. But I've learned to be content with whatever I have."

As the animals graciously ate the tasty morsels, they felt something electric in the air. Suddenly there appeared in the sky above them the most radiant, beautiful cloud Paul had ever seen. "Look at that! It looks like fire! God guided the Israelites by such a cloud through this wilderness."

Max and Liz grinned at one another. It wasn't just a similar cloud. It was *the* cloud—the very same fire cloud that had guided the animals to the Ark, and had guided the nation of Israel across the wilderness. Paul got to his knees in awe of the cloud. He felt the overwhelming presence of God radiating all around him.

"The people wandered needlessly in this wilderness for forty years. If only they had believed in your word, they could have entered the Promised Land in a matter of days," Paul recounted. "I fear they are wandering again, but this time in needless, burdensome laws that will never get them where they need to be. Jesus, *you* are the new Promised Land. Just as you called Moses from this desert to accomplish his mission of leading your people out of Egypt, I feel the time has come for me to spread your word to lead people out of darkness."

177

The fire crackled and popped and the fire cloud lit up the desert sky while Paul, Max, Liz, and Nigel sat in silence. Not another word was spoken until morning, but they all knew Paul's time here in the desert had come to an end. In the morning, they would be on their way to Petra.

∝

"*Petra* is the Greek word for 'rock,' just like *Peter,*" Liz explained to Max as they walked along behind Paul. "The Nabateans built their capital city out of rock in the middle of the Jordanian wilderness hundreds of years ago. King Aretas IV is their current ruler, and he set up a chain of settlements all along the spice trade caravan route. The Nabateans long ago learned how to control water and create oases. I am quite eager to see this marvelous city! I've long heard the carvings are exquisite."

"Indeed, a rose-red city of rock with more than eight hundred tombs and dwellings," Nigel added. "These Arabians remind me of the

Egyptians in their treatment of the dead, but instead of pyramids, they carve elaborate tombs out of the colorful sandstone."

"Do ye think Paul will tr-r-ry ta talk ta the Nabateans aboot Jesus?" Max asked. "They'll be the first humans he's been with in thr-r-ree years, an' I know he's dyin' ta share all he's learned then."

"Most undoubtedly, old boy," Nigel stated firmly from atop Max's head. "I would expect Paul to be quite enthusiastic about sharing the gospel with non-Jews."

"We've arrived at the *Siq,*" Paul announced up ahead. "This is the entrance to Petra!"

Towering almost two hundred feet above them was a winding, narrow gorge of colorful rocks of red, purple, pink, yellow, gold, and brown ochre. This natural geographic *Siq,* or "shaft," was a mile long and led directly into Petra. The animals already felt small, but they were amazed to see how small even Paul looked with the soaring, colorful cliffs above. As they wound their way around each turn, they heard the soft thump-thump-thump-thump of feet behind them.

Max grinned when he saw who it was. "That lass always be r-r-right on time." Clarie rode Leena the camel right up to Paul.

"Hello, my friends," she called. "Welcome to Petra!"

Paul reached his hand up to pat Leena. "Hello! Yes, your animal friends just recently appeared and I was hoping to find you here. It's been a long time but you were right. They fended for themselves well."

"I told you they would," Clarie answered, winking at the animals. "Come, follow me on into the city."

As they neared the entrance, their jaws dropped to see a massive monument carved right into the rock, soaring more than 130 feet high. It was adorned with six Corinthian columns at the base topped by a Greek-style cornice with a massive door in the center. A second level of columns and statues surrounded a circular focal point with an ornately sculpted urn displayed in the center. Hundreds of people milled about in the street below, selling their wares and going about their business.

"*C'est magnifique!* Would you look at this architecture?" Liz gasped. "What a surprise to find such Greek building influence in the middle of the wilderness!"

Paul stood back and marveled at the building carved into the rock. "What is this place?"

"It's called *Al Khazneh,* or "the Treasury," one of the many monuments here to honor the dead," Clarie explained as Leena slowly knelt down on the ground. She hopped off the camel and patted Paul on the back. "King Aretas is having a big banquet tonight to celebrate the newest monument honoring Obodas the god. Obodas was a Nabatean king almost 150 years ago, but was deified soon after his death." She studied Paul's face, anticipating his reaction to such wicked paganism.

Paul frowned. "There is much darkness here. Would you show me around?"

"Certainly. I think you would especially like to see the amphitheater," Clarie answered, leading them down the street, past tomb after tomb hewn into the rock face on either side of them. Soon they stood at the base of a curved amphitheater with forty-five rows of seats rising in an arc to hold ten thousand people. "It was built to have the best view of most of the tombs here in Petra."

Paul's heart was overwhelmed by the stark contrast of this dark place after having spent three years in holiness with the Lord. "I'm sure the acoustics are good here," Paul said, looking around. "Tell me, will the people gather here for this . . . festival?"

"Yes, tonight they will come here before the grand banquet," Clarie told him. "Come, let's go to my home and let you rest. This evening, I will bring you here as the people gather."

Paul nodded, slowly smiling as thoughts ran through his mind. He was eager to share the good news of Jesus, and here in Petra was an amphitheater where he could give his first speech to a large non-Jewish audience. Excitement coursed through him at this opportunity. "Yes, very well, thank you. And I'm afraid I never got your name. I'm Paul."

Clarie smiled. "Call me Clarence."

$\propto$

While Paul was resting, Clarie took Max, Liz, and Nigel for a walk around the city. They told Clarie about Paul's time out in the wilderness, and she caught them up on Al, Kate, and the disciples. Liz and

Nigel gawked at the incredible architectural marvels in this hidden city. Soon they walked down a path and heard the sound of rushing water. Carved into the rock was a huge form of a lion with an open mouth. Water rushed down the mountain and out of the lion's mouth into a large basin below.

"Extraordinary! Utterly exquisite!" Nigel exclaimed, running up to the lion. "Never have I seen such a unique fountain!" His little whiskers quivered with excitement.

Max and Liz stood behind Nigel, feeling the refreshing spray of the water coming off the rock. Suddenly they heard a rumbling sound and the lion's head turned. The water stopped and the lion fountain gurgled out, "Hello, my friends."

"Gillamon! I've never seen ye so HUGE!" Max shouted, his words echoing off the stone.

"Statues come in all shapes and sizes," Gillamon replied with a warm chuckle. "So you've seen some great work sculpted on Paul these last three years. He thinks he is ready to begin his mission, but that is not the case. He still needs many years of training for the work ahead. What happens here tonight will prove that to him."

"But Gillamon, he is so eager to share Jesus!" Liz protested. "Why can't he begin with the understanding he has now?"

"Every human the Maker chooses for a great work must endure periods of disappointment, delay, solitude, or suffering," Gillamon explained. "Paul wishes to imitate Moses, but remember that Moses spent forty years out in this desert. Paul isn't ready yet."

"So what should we expect now?" Nigel asked.

"Be ready to leave here quickly. Paul will experience a series of three rejections leading to necessary escape, starting here tonight," Gillamon said. "He must flee to Damascus. Go with him, but understand you will not be there long. What he does here will affect his ability to preach there. You will then need to help him escape from Damascus. After that, he will yet have to escape even Jerusalem until he fully learns he is not yet ready to serve the Maker."

"Oh, how terribly sad for the chap!" Nigel lamented.

Liz frowned. *"Mais oui,* but Gillamon is right. Others have spent long years getting prepared. Paul's difficult calling requires it."

"Aye, so we'll be with him thr-r-rough it all," Max affirmed. "If we did it for Moses, we'll do it for Paul."

"I can always count on you," Gillamon told them. "Go with Paul. He is an eager statue, but he is unfinished and not ready for display." The lion's head once again became part of the rock face. Soon the water resumed flowing through its mouth.

"We best get going," Clarie instructed them, walking back down the path toward the heart of the city. "The festival will begin soon. And just so you know, I will not be going with you to Damascus. Follow my lead tonight. Things will happen quickly."

The amphitheater filled with the people of Petra. A buzz of excitement coursed through the crowd as the sun began to set. Torches were lit around the theater and along the roads, causing the red-rose rocks' bursting color to glow. Musicians played drums and flutes to fill the air with festive music. Paul walked with Clarie into the amphitheater while Max, Liz, and Nigel stayed as instructed with Leena the camel, just outside. They sat in Leena's saddlebags, watching everything unfold.

"I'm happy to see you all again," Leena whispered.

"I think we'll be spending a lot of time together, my dear," Nigel assured her, tapping her gently on the forehead.

Paul was eager to address the crowd. He turned to Clarie. "Three years ago you asked me how Jesus could save an Arab like you. I'd like to answer your question, but to this audience as well."

Clarie nodded, and held her hand out to the front of the amphitheater. "Be my guest. I suggest you do so before the festivities begin."

Paul smiled and patted the Arab on the back, then walked to the center of the stage. A hush soon fell over the crowd as they wondered who this stranger was.

"I am Paul of Tarsus. I come to bring the people of Petra a good word. I am a Jew, descended from Isaac. You are Arabs, descended from Ishmael. But the father of both Isaac and Ishmael was Abraham. And long ago, God promised Abraham that all nations would be blessed through him, so that means Jew and non-Jew. That means my people and yours," he began, drawing looks of alarm from the crowd, who did not expect a speech delivered to them by a Jew.

Liz looked around the crowd as Paul continued explaining the history of Moses and the Law, the promised Messiah, and Jesus' sacrifice. She told the others, "Jews have not been well received here, ever since Herod the Great sacked this city twice when the Nabateans failed to pay tribute to Rome. They are not listening to what he has to say, even though he is speaking truth."

"Yes, I fear he is to learn a hard lesson on delivering a message to a hostile, unreceptive audience," Nigel echoed. "This could turn ugly quickly if he offends them."

"You have gathered here tonight to pay homage to a false god, Obodas. There is only one God, and he sent his Son Jesus to pay for your sins and offer you eternal life through grace. Yet you spend your days carving elaborate tombs all over this city so you can feast in banquet halls and worship dead humans and false gods," Paul declared. He grew animated and passionate about trying to get these people to see the truth. "Please cease this pagan practice!"

Max furrowed his brow. "Ye mean offend them like that?"

Immediately the crowd rose to their feet in anger over Paul's words. Clarie rushed over to grab Paul and usher him out of the amphitheater as word spread to King Aretas about what was happening. "Hurry, you must get out of here fast, my friend!"

Paul instantly realized he had made a mistake in his timing and delivery. This wasn't the way to approach these people. In his zeal to relay the truth of Jesus to these lost people, he had only angered them. He realized they did not wish to hear the full-blown truth, especially from a Jew, and especially on this night. His stomach sank. He ran with Clarie to where her camel waited. He climbed into the saddle and Clarie pulled on the reins to get the camel to her feet.

"Take my camel and get to Damascus!" Clarie instructed him. "And Paul, despite what this crowd does, I believe in Jesus. Now go!" She slapped Leena on the rump. "HA!"

Leena took off running through the torch-lit streets, past the magnificent carved monuments to the Treasury and the city exit through the *Siq*. Nigel stood atop Leena's head, steering her ears to the left, directing the camel back down the *Siq* and out of Petra at top speed. The only light came from the moon and stars above that cast shadows from the rocks onto the path below. They soon heard the clip-clop gallop of horses echoing off the rocks like thunder behind them on their terrifying escape through this narrow gorge.

Nigel held onto Leena's ears and steered her through the winding, mile-long gorge until they were out onto the open plain. "Hurry! Over to those rocks!" he directed her.

Leena ran as directed and Paul held on tight until they found cover behind some boulders. They stopped and held their breath as they listened for a moment. They soon could tell that the horses were running in the opposite direction.

Paul let go a deep breath and sat back in the saddle. "Well, that didn't go as I had hoped," Paul said, his heart pounding out of his chest. He looked down and saw that Max and Liz were sitting in the saddle bags. "And I didn't plan to take you all away again from your master. But I can't return to Petra. Let's get back to Damascus. From there I'll figure out what to do."

Paul looked up at the full moon. "Moses fled civilization to go to the wilderness. I'm fleeing the wilderness to go back to civilization. But something tells me this won't be the last time I have to flee."

Nigel leaned forward and whispered to Leena as he took an ear in each paw, "To Damascus, my dear! Run like the wind!" Nigel's legs flew up behind him as the camel took off. The little mouse was in camel-driving heaven.

Max and Liz looked knowingly at each other. They knew this adventure was just the beginning. Life with Paul was going to prove to be one chase scene after another, as the hunter had now become the hunted.

183

ESCAPING DAMASCUS

nanias sat alone at his table, cracking pistachio nuts. As he cracked open each one, he marveled at the soft, delicious nut encased in such a hard outer shell. *Some people are a lot like pistachios. Hard on the outside but inside they hold valuable nuggets,* he thought to himself. Squeezing a nut with all his might between his thumb and fingers, he strained to release another nut from its shell. *And some are harder to crack than others.* He thought of people he knew, smiling at his little analogy. *Some people are just plain nuts before they find Jesus.* He popped a nut into his mouth. *Or afterward, for that matter. But in a good way.*

A soft knock came at his door and Ananias looked up in surprise. It was late for visitors. He got up from the table and went over to open the door. There stood a very dirty, tanned traveler, smiling with relief.

"Paul! I was just thinking about you!" Ananias exclaimed, reaching out to welcome Paul with a big embrace. "Come in, come in!"

Paul stepped inside, leaving Leena and the other animals outside by a water trough. "Thank you, old friend. It's good to see you." He pulled off his turban and rubbed his hands vigorously through his sandy hair. He looked around the humble home and the usual fixtures of domestic life: table, bed, chair, cooking fire, baskets of food. "I've lived out in the wilderness for so long, it almost feels strange to see such luxury, but I'd be grateful if you took in this weary traveler."

"Of course, of course," Ananias encouraged, pouring Paul a cup of water. "Please, sit down. Tell me, where have you been these last three years? I haven't ceased praying for you."

Paul eagerly gulped down the cool water and wiped his mouth with the back of his forearm. Ananias refilled his cup, and Paul thanked him. "The Lord led me to Midian, to Mount Horeb. He taught me things in his Word I never understood before, especially in light of Jesus. I had time to walk slowly, think thoroughly, praise loudly, and speak my mind with freedom." Paul leaned forward and struggled to put his experience into words. "Jesus himself taught me, Ananias. He poured revelations into my mind that no man could ever provide."

Ananias nodded slowly, clearly pleased with Paul's sojourn. "Good. That is *very* good! I look forward to hearing all you've learned." He gave Paul an affirming pat on the back. "Things have been quiet here since you left. The Jewish leaders here and in Jerusalem were none too pleased with your change of heart, as you can imagine. But with time, things died down. The believers still meet but in relative peace."

185

"I'm afraid I am unable to keep silent, Ananias. I may stir things up again. I have to share Jesus boldly," Paul insisted. "That is my calling."

"And when God has called you to do something, you must obey," Ananias answered with a hand on Paul's shoulder. "I know the believers are hungry to understand more about Jesus. You must come speak tomorrow."

"And on the Sabbath, in the synagogue," Paul added. "I intend to do as Jesus commanded, and preach to everyone, Jew and Gentile alike. Although my first attempt at non-Jews didn't go well, I'm afraid."

Ananias raised his eyebrows, bringing over a basket of bread for Paul. "Oh? What happened?"

Paul eagerly took the bread and tore off a piece. How delicious it tasted! He chewed and swallowed a big bite before answering. "I stood before several thousand Nabateans in the amphitheater of Petra and proclaimed Jesus as Savior. But I derided their beliefs on the night of a huge festival celebrating those beliefs. They rose up in anger and I escaped the city with my life, riding on a camel back here to Damascus."

"I see," replied Ananias with a wrinkled brow. "We should expect word to reach the Nabatean ethnarch here in Damascus. King Aretas appointed him under the treaty with Rome to keep watch over Arabs here in the city. His role is to protect them and punish violators of their laws, but he cannot arrest anyone inside the walls of this city for crimes committed across the border."

"Well, that's a relief. Although I'm sure the Jewish leaders won't be too happy when I begin preaching in the synagogues again," Paul offered. He sat there a minute, contemplating the reality of his situation with groups he had angered. "It doesn't matter. I must preach Jesus, whatever comes."

"And so you shall, my friend. I know our Lord is pleased with your fervor," Ananias affirmed him, pushing the bowl of pistachios over to Paul. "Nuts?"

186

Liz walked daintily along the city wall, taking in the sights of busy Damascus below. At times she stopped and sat to observe the people, her tail slowly curling up and down. It was her pattern to sit and study humans, learning most about human behavior simply by watching them, especially when they didn't know anyone was looking. She heard an argument erupt in the market and turned her gaze in that direction. A group of Roman soldiers broke up a scuffle after an Arab merchant accused a trader of shortchanging him. The Nabatean ethnarch soon arrived on the scene and settled matters quickly. If there was one thing the Romans excelled at, it was law and order. And with the local rulers such as this Nabatean governor they put in place to oversee the cultural idiosyncrasies of their people, the Roman world was an efficiently run machine.

Liz resumed walking along the wall again, high above the city. She smiled as she thought back to Noah's Ark. She remembered walking around the entire perimeter of the ark's small windows to determine what was happening outside on the day of the flood. She learned that day how helpful it was to scope out her surroundings so she was ready with ideas for situations that might arise. Gillamon had already told them Paul would need to escape Damascus, but they didn't yet know when or what exactly would happen. So while they waited, Liz researched the city.

She came to an unusual-looking outcropping on the wall. A house was built into the wall and its windows extended out over the street below, about ten feet from the ground. *Interesting,* she thought. Liz maneuvered around the window and kept going. Soon she was at the main gate leading into Damascus and to the Temple of Jupiter. Throngs of people poured into the city, a major melting pot of traders and commerce. Scuffles like the one she had just seen were bound to frequently happen. Once the Roman soldiers were gone, danger loomed in the shadows for those who had crossed the wrong people. Word spread quickly if someone stepped out of bounds. No secret was safe in Damascus.

Guards kept watch at all the gates leading in and out of the city, day and night. Liz frowned. *If Paul meets another reaction here like he did in Petra, he will not be able to flee the city without notice. And he will most certainly need to travel on foot.* A caravan was making its way toward the city—camels laden with frankincense and myrrh from Arabia. And she realized with alarm exactly where they traveled from: *Petra.* She quickly made her way along the wall, watching where the traders went. Liz would be sure to especially observe these humans. Between Paul stirring up the Jews again in the synagogue and the arrival of traders from Petra, it was only a matter of time before things heated up in Damascus.

187

∝

Max and Nigel were enjoying a warm, sunny afternoon on the banks of the Abana River outside the city. "He was magnificent!" Nigel cheered. "He out-argued every Jewish leader in the synagogue, leaving them speechless, and I daresay, quite chagrined. Paul expertly laid out the prophecies about Messiah, and showed precisely how Jesus fulfilled them. I must say, his three years of study and revelation in the desert have prepared him mightily for his mission. At least for speaking to Jews."

Max grinned. "That's our lad! An' more new believers keep comin' over ta hear Paul in the houses. I guess he has ta learn how ta speak ta one gr-r-roup at a time." He watched some fish swim by. "If Big Al were here, he'd be starin' in the water with his fluffy tail twitchin', jest waitin' ta gr-r-rab a fish. I miss the lad. I miss me Kate, too."

Nigel's enthusiastic expression suddenly turned solemn. "Oh dear, I just realized something. Judas was there today, the chap who wrote to Caiaphas about Saul's changing his name to Paul, and about all the ruckus Paul caused in the synagogue three years ago. He had rather the smug look on his face, standing near the back with his arms crossed over his chest."

"An arrest warrant!" Liz rushed up to them, shouting and out of breath. "King Aretas has an arrest warrant out for Paul! I just overheard the traders from Petra reporting in to the Nabatean ethnarch."

Max's fur bristled and he furrowed his brow. "Can they jest go ar-r-rest Paul now?"

Liz shook her head. "No, they can only arrest him outside the city walls. I overheard their plan. The king has offered a bribe to whoever catches Paul when he tries to leave the city. They are to carry him off and . . . slit his throat."

Nigel put his paw up to his own throat. "How dreadful! We must act immediately! I was just telling Max that today I saw Judas looking rather smug as he listened to Paul win every argument in synagogue today. I shall go at once and find out their intentions. If Judas and the Jews are plotting to capture Paul *inside* the city . . ."

"And the Nabateans are plotting to capture Paul *outside* the city . . ." Liz continued.

Liz and Nigel looked at each other and exclaimed, "We have to help Paul escape them both!"

"He can't leave through the gates," Nigel offered as he began to pace back and forth. He stopped and looked at the water rushing by. Parts of the Abana River broke off in streams that snaked through the city. "Paul frequently tries to imitate his hero, Moses. Could we perhaps pull a Moses and set him adrift in a basket?"

Max, Liz, and Nigel walked over to study the river. "While the water is deep here, it may not be deep enough inside the city," Liz surmised, now turning her gaze up to the city walls.

"Aye, an' he's not a wee laddie like baby Moses were when we pushed his basket thr-r-rough the r-r-rushes," Max offered. "I don't think Paul would float easy."

"Right you are, old boy," agreed Nigel, pushing his spectacles up on his nose.

"But he is small enough for a fish basket!" Liz suggested excitedly. "And I know just the right spot! Nigel, go find out what you can about the plot of the Jews. Max, go retrieve a fish basket from the market. We'll meet back at Ananias' house tonight while the humans are gone."

Max and Nigel looked at one another with puzzled expressions as Liz ran off quickly, calling back, "I have a letter to write!"

Paul and Ananias laughed easily as they walked down Straight Street. It had been a wonderful evening of fellowship with the believers of Damascus. Their joy overflowed with the understanding that grew daily as they studied the Scriptures, discussed them, and prayed together. Paul was ecstatic to have so many followers already seeking him out on a daily basis. Hearts were responding to the good news of Jesus! Although he had failed in his delivery in Petra, here in Damascus things were looking up.

When the men arrived, there on the doorstep was a large, moldable fish basket. Ananias picked it up and puzzled over why it was there. He opened it to see if someone perhaps left them some fish for dinner. But the only thing inside was a piece of rolled papyrus. Ananias looked both ways up and down the street. "Let's get in the house."

"I'm glad Josiah was able to return the camel to the Arabian traders for me," Paul said, sitting on the floor by the low table, picking up a handful of pistachios. "I know I can't go near them myself. I hope Clarence's animals can find him again."

Ananias unrolled the papyrus and scanned the contents of the letter. He looked up at Paul in alarm. "You have to leave. Tonight!" He handed the letter to Paul.

Paul quickly read the letter and dropped his hand to the table. "More trouble, now here in Damascus." He shook his head sorrowfully. "I don't want to leave, Ananias."

"But you *must!*" Ananias insisted, gripping Paul's arm. "One of your followers has taken a great risk to bring us this information. And he has provided a brilliant plan. I know the very house he speaks of in this letter. Its windows jut out over the city wall. We can lower you down in this fish basket and you can escape on foot."

Paul clasped his hands behind his head and let out a loud breath. "Very well. Let me gather my things."

While Ananias gathered together a long rope, Liz and Nigel hugged one another in the shadows of the room. "Good work, my dear!" Nigel cheered quietly. "And just in time. The Jews, along with the Nabateans, are out to kill Paul. Now he can give those murderous plotters the slip!"

"Hurry, let's join Max," Liz whispered as the two men quickly left, carrying the fish basket and the rope.

Max's tail was erect and he stood at attention behind some bushes, watching for signs of movement up and down the street below the house that jutted out over it. He glanced up occasionally, looking for anyone appearing in the window.

Liz and Nigel came running up. "They're coming," Liz reported breathlessly.

"Liz's plan will work," Nigel added with balled fists. "It must!"

"Aye, if I see anyone tr-r-ry ta head this way, I'll sound the alarm," Max offered.

The three animals gazed up at the window as they heard whispers and movement. They caught a quick glance at two men looking out the window and down to the street, likely trying to determine if the rope was long enough. They disappeared for a moment and soon the fish basket was hanging by a rope from the window.

"I see movement in the basket," Liz said. "Because it is a shapeless basket, it will fold around him, no?"

Ever so slowly, the basket started inching its way down. Suddenly Max's ears went up as he heard voices coming down the road. "R-r-romans!" Three Roman soldiers were walking toward them to reach the gate two hundred yards away. They would see the basket if it were lowered any further. A low growl entered Max's throat and he started barking while running toward the soldiers.

Liz and Nigel snapped their eyes up to the basket, hoping the men would stop lowering it. They breathed a sigh of relief as the basket stopped, swinging slightly as the men struggled to hold onto the rope while Paul quietly hung there, hidden inside.

Max kept barking and ran right by the soldiers. The Romans laughed at the little dog blazing past them, clearly on the chase after something. They turned their heads to try to get a glimpse of what he was chasing, just as they passed the wall where Paul's basket hung there in the darkness.

"Probably chasing a rat," one of the soldiers offered.

"Yes, the dog probably figured out the rat had cheated him at gambling," another soldier countered, shoving his fellow soldier jokingly. "Rats cheat."

"I won fair and square!" the third soldier protested, hitting the second soldier in the chest with the back of his hand. "Don't cry to me if you can't beat the odds."

191

Beads of sweat covered Paul's brow as he heard the soldiers carry on about the dog and the rat. He could feel the tension of the rope, and prayed it would hold his weight. He could hear the men groaning above trying to keep the basket steady.

Finally the voices of the soldiers faded as they passed by. One of the men looked out the window and gave the all clear to lower the basket. Liz and Nigel held their breath and clung to one another as Paul was lowered over the wall. When at last the basket hit the ground with a thud, Paul rolled out of it awkwardly, grabbed his knapsack, and ran off into the night. Ananias leaned out the window and hugged the other men, rejoicing that Paul had escaped. They hurriedly pulled the empty basket back up through the window.

"*Ooh-la-la!* But that was stressful, no?" Liz said with a paw over her heart. "We did it, *mon ami!* Paul is safe!"

Nigel wiped back his whiskers, trying to regain his composure after Paul's nerve-wracking escape. "Indeed. I say, this has given me an entirely new perspective on fishing for men!"

"Two escapes down, one ta go," Max said with a big grin as he walked up to them. "So I guess we'll be headin' back ta Jerusalem now. We'll get ta see Al an' Kate!"

"*Oui,* but we must decide when and if we'll make our presence known to Paul there. We don't know what kind of reception he will receive in Jerusalem, either from the Sanhedrin or from the apostles," Liz offered as the three animals started walking down the darkened road in the direction Paul had fled. "This next mission may require an inside job. And I know just the noble, brave warrior to pull it off."

UNWANTED
FOR MURDER

"LIZ! Oh, me beauty!" Al excaimed joyfully, enveloping Liz in a tight embrace. "How I've missed ye, Lass!"

Liz struggled to breathe for a moment, but kissed Al on the cheek. "*Cher* Albert, I am so happy to see you!"

"Max, me love!" Kate exclaimed as she and Max shared a loving embrace. "The days have been so long without ye."

"Aye, 'tis gr-r-rand ta see me bonnie Kate," Max said with his eyes closed.

They didn't hear the flapping of wings as Nigel landed. He hopped off Naomi, his faithful pigeon, giving her a loving pat on the head. "Thank you, my dear." Nigel stood to the side and grinned, giving the two sets of lovebirds their privacy. He clasped his paws behind his back and rolled up and down on the balls of his feet, humming. Earlier he had sneaked in to give Kate and Al the news that they were in the city, arriving ahead of Saul, now turned Paul. Immediately Kate and Al ran to have this touching reunion in the Garden of Gethsemane.

"How have things been in Jerusalem?" Liz asked. "Who is left here after all this time?"

"Peter, John an' his brother James be the three left from the Twelve,"

Kate told her. "The other nine disciples left ta share the good news like Jesus told 'em ta do. Mary an' Jesus' brother James also still live in Jerusalem. He's been takin' the lead with the church here since Peter an' John travel aboot. Al an' me don't go with the lads on those short trips. Sometimes Barnabas stays with us. I love Barnabas! He's such a kind-hearted lad."

"*Bon!* I'm so happy to hear this!" Liz cheered. "Has there been any more persecution?"

"I've made sure everythin' stays calm and peaceful," Al reported with a goofy grin. "Sure, and our mission here be easy. The church be growin' and Peter gives me all the fish I can eat."

Liz giggled and patted Al's plump belly. "*Oui,* I see this. The church isn't the only thing that is growing."

"So how long will ye be here?" Kate asked.

Max frowned. "Not too long, Lass. Gillamon told us Paul would have ta escape Jerusalem, jest as he did Damascus. After that, I think we'll be goin' wherever he goes."

Kate nudged Max again. "Well, I be grateful for any time I have with ye."

Nigel rejoined the group. "Might I inquire as to who is in the city now?" he asked. "Paul is on his way and we need to determine the situation at hand."

"John and his brother James took Jesus' mother, Mary, with them for a visit to Nazareth," Kate reported. "So of the disciples, only Peter be here right now. Clarie comes an' goes, but we haven't seen her lately."

Liz thought a moment. "Hmmm, if Clarie isn't here, I can think of no one better to greet Paul than Barnabas. He may be the only one who would allow Paul to get close to him at this point. Kate, where is Barnabas now?"

"He's in the city, helpin' with buyin' food for the church," Kate replied. "Peter told him ta be careful with Al gettin' into the fish at the market." Al gave a sheepish grin.

"I believe a fishy encounter can be arranged," Nigel told the group, sharing a knowing grin with Liz. "I'll maintain aerial reconnaissance to watch for Paul's arrival."

194

Liz nudged Al with her cheek. "And you, my noble, brave warrior, will guide Barnabas right to him."

Jerusalem. The beautiful walled city stood high on the hillside, firm and resolute. The city was as solid in its traditions as it was in its structural foundations. And for every threat that sought her destruction, Jerusalem eventually answered with a resounding comeback. God made his people a tenacious lot: stiff-necked and disobedient against God on one hand, and passionate about revering God on the other. They were passionate but misguided in their zeal. Just like Paul had been.

Paul walked up the road leading into Jerusalem, remembering who he was the last time he rode out of this city on horseback almost four years ago. He shook his head as he thought back to his arrogant rage that had made him want to smother the new movement called the Way. How he had *hated* the followers of Jesus! Anything that threatened the established laws and other customs of Israel needed elimination, and he had been the man for the job. He would wield his sword and strike down this "threat" to Israel. *How foolish I was!* Paul thought. "Oh Jesus, thank you for blinding me to show me the truth that *I* was the threat, not you. You, not I, are the salvation for Israel. You are the salvation for the entire world."

His heart pounded and his palms began to sweat as he entered Jerusalem. Paul knew the Jews had tried to kill him in Damascus. *Would they try to kill me here?* he wondered. *This is my city! I know everything about how Jerusalem lives and breathes and moves. I know our laws inside and out. I know how the system works. If anyone can convince these people that Jesus is Messiah, surely I can. I was one of the insiders, but now I know the truth. Surely my incredible changes of heart and mind will impress the people!*

Paul stood in the bustling street for a moment, wondering where he should go first. *Do I go directly to the Sanhedrin?* The thought made the blood drain from his face. He didn't want to risk being arrested and locked up without first being heard. Better to ease his way back into their good graces and convince them of Jesus once he was secure in the church here in Jerusalem. He pulled his cloak high over his head and

195

around his face and took a deep breath. *It won't be easy, but I'll go to the disciples. Yes, at least there I pray I will find welcome.*

Paul headed to one of the gathering places where he knew the followers of the Way frequently met for study and fellowship. At least they had four years ago. Paul wondered if the persecution he ignited here in Jerusalem was still aflame, or if it had died down these past years without him here. He would soon find out.

"Come here!" Barnabas scolded Al, who ran ahead of him in the street. "I had to pay extra for that fish!"

Al carried a fish in his mouth, watching for Nigel's signal. Nigel flew up ahead on Naomi as he followed Paul through the streets of Jerusalem. Once Paul stopped, Nigel circled around and gave Al the thumbs up. Al looked to make sure Barnabas was still running after him, but was careful to stay just out of his reach. When he saw the group of people, he darted under a shady tree and dropped the fish, sitting there like a good kitty. Winded, Barnabas stopped under the tree and put his hands on his knees to catch his breath. He then grabbed the fish and shook it at Al. "Just wait until I tell Peter what you've done, Ari!" Al innocently gave him his best "Who, me?" look.

A group of believers and skeptical hellenized Jews were there in the courtyard near the synagogue, debating a troubling passage in Deuteronomy. Barnabas plopped down under the tree to rest and Al sat next to him. Paul made his way over and quietly sat down in the back of the group.

Seeing the dress of these hellenized Jews made Paul's heart ache as he thought of Stephen. Although he knew he was forgiven the blood on his hands, he would carry the blood of Stephen on his heart for the rest of his life. He would use it to spur him on for good and to be courageous himself. He prayed a silent prayer of gratitude for grace and turned his attention to the discussion.

"In chapter 21, Moses clearly wrote, 'Anyone hung on a tree is under God's curse.' Jesus was hung on a tree," one of the hellenized Jews argued. "How could he possibly be Messiah? If anyone is cursed

196

by God, surely he could not be Messiah!"

Murmurings of agreement rippled through the group. Paul bit his lip. This had been his exact stumbling block over Jesus' claim to be Messiah. While in the desert, however, he got to the bottom of this issue with Jesus, and finally understood what it meant with the revelation of Jesus' perspective. When none of the believers offered a ready rebuttal, Paul cleared his throat and decided to speak up.

"If God spoke through Moses to write these words, we must of course stay true to believing them. Indeed, anyone who hangs on a tree is cursed by God," Paul began. "The problem of assuming that Jesus couldn't be Messiah because he hung on a tree comes from misunderstanding the purpose of the promised Messiah."

The people in the crowd turned around to see who was speaking. Someone immediately recognized him and whispered in the ears of the people around him. "That's Saul of Tarsus! He's back in Jerusalem! He must be here to spy on us!"

Word spread quietly and quickly through the crowd as Paul continued to speak. "Jesus indeed became cursed when he was nailed to the cross. He became cursed and at the same time wiped out the curse. That was the point of his coming as Messiah. He came to redeem us from our self-defeating, cursed life by absorbing it completely into himself. Jesus became sin—our sin—while on the cross."

Suddenly the people started getting up and dispersing in every direction. Paul stopped talking and watched as the group left him sitting there, alone. He hung his head and drew his legs up into his chest. He had been rejected by former friends. Now he was rejected by former enemies. He was unwanted by both. He was unwanted by the believers because he had committed murder, and he was unwanted by the Jews because he now would *not* commit murder.

Sitting in the shade of the nearby tree, Barnabas quietly watched Paul. He had witnessed this entire scene, and was just as shocked as the other believers who fled, leaving Paul sitting by himself. They ran away in fear, but Barnabas remained where he was in curiosity. For anyone to say the words that Saul of Tarsus had just uttered, something radical must have happened. The Saul that Barnabas knew a few years ago surely wouldn't have bothered to engage these believers in discussion. No, he would have rounded them up and taken them to jail.

The apostles had been wondering what exactly happened to Saul and his tirades that led to the dispersion of so many of the believers fleeing in fear. Saul's fate was a mystery, but he mattered little as reports of the spreading gospel came back to the church in Jerusalem. The believers rejoiced over God turning Saul's persecution into a force for good. Like an eagle kicks its young out of the nest, Saul's persecution had kicked believers out of Jerusalem. But that's when the gospel found its wings. Barnabas raised his eyebrows as he realized they should actually *thank* Saul for that.

Paul slowly stood and brushed the dust off his cloak. He looked around the deserted courtyard. The once domineering, powerful Saul of Tarsus had nowhere to go. Barnabas studied the defeated-looking man, and something deep inside told him to speak to Saul. They had long ago been students together under Gamaliel, but over time, their beliefs drifted apart. Now, however, Saul didn't look so threatening.

198

"Your insights were quite profound, Saul. I wonder if Gamaliel would agree," Barnabas said loudly from under the tree.

Paul spun around, startled to hear someone address him as Saul—startled to hear someone address him at all. He squinted as he walked slowly to the shady spot under the tree, trying to determine who had spoken to him. Age had changed the man's face, but not his eyes. Paul smiled. "Barnabas, my old friend. I know my presence here is quite unexpected, but so are my words, aren't they? And I no longer go by Saul. Please . . . call me Paul."

Barnabas slowly nodded his head, feeling a connection in spirit with his old schoolmate. "Paul? Your Roman name." He held out his hand to invite Paul to sit with him. "What has happened to you?" Al sat there grinning. The arranged meeting was taking place as planned.

Paul sat down and picked up a stick to twirl in his fingers. "On my way to Damascus, I met Jesus. He appeared to me, and blinded me for three days. He called me by name, saying, 'Saul, Saul, why do you persecute me?' I asked who he was, and he told me he was Jesus." Paul poked the stick into the palm of his hand. "He said, 'It is hard for you, this kicking against the goads. But get up and go into the city, where you will be told what you must do.' I saw his nail-pierced hands, Barnabas. It was Jesus."

Barnabas's eyes grew wide at hearing Paul's report. His mind swirled with confusion at this shocking turn of events. He didn't quite know how to respond. "Go on. What happened next?"

Paul tossed the stick on the ground and wrapped his arms around his knees. "I was led into Damascus and for three days I didn't eat or drink. I remained in darkness and I prayed. I briefly had some unknown visitors, but finally a man by the name of Ananias came to me. He put his hands on me so I could see again. He baptized me, Barnabas, and he introduced me to the believers in Damascus."

"I'm sure they were shocked to see you there as a believer instead of as their persecutor!" Barnabas exclaimed in shock and wonder at this news. "How did Ananias know to come to you?"

"The Lord spoke to him in a vision, and told him he must come help restore my sight," Paul told him. "When he rightfully expressed his fear, the Lord said, 'This man is my chosen instrument to proclaim my name to the Gentiles and their kings and to the people of Israel. I will show him how much he must suffer for my name.' I spent three years alone with the Lord in the Arabian desert to understand all of this, Barnabas. I returned to Damascus with a price on my head, and fellow believers had to help me escape over the city wall in a fish basket. And now . . . I've come here."

"His chosen instrument. Gentiles? Their kings?" Barnabas wrinkled his brow, trying to process Paul's incredible story.

"Yes, and to the people of Israel," Paul said hopefully.

"And you escaped in a fish basket with the help of the very people you went there to arrest," Barnabas repeated slowly. He rubbed his eyes and let his hands drop into his lap. He stared intently at this transformed soul in front of him. "Paul, no one believed in people like Jesus did. He didn't hold their past against them. Peter could tell you that. Peter grieved to the point of despair over having denied Jesus the night he was arrested. But Jesus forgave him. Yes, he forgave him and he restored him, charging him to lead the disciples."

Paul's eyes now widened. "Peter *denied* Jesus?"

Barnabas nodded and held up three fingers to emphasize his point. "Three times. Denied he even knew Jesus. His fear got the best of him that night. Peter understands regret for past mistakes. But once he was restored, nothing has been able to stop him from preaching and healing in Jesus' name."

"Praise God! So the persecution has stopped here in Jerusalem?" Paul asked hopefully.

"For the most part, yes. Once you left, things settled down," Barnabas explained. "We've been meeting in freedom and peace without interference from the Sanhedrin. When they lost their main henchman—you—they retreated and have left us alone."

"I'm so relieved to hear this, more than you could possibly know," Paul said. "And I wish to establish bonds of fellowship with Peter and the church here. I've come to Jerusalem to see if they will see me and hear what I have to say."

Barnabas studied Paul's face for a moment and saw nothing but genuineness and humility. "People tend to think the best or the worst of others. I choose to think as does Jesus. He believes the best and sees what people *can* be. I've found that people usually live up to the expectations you give them." He stood and picked up his walking stick. "Ananias believed you in Damascus. And I believe you in Jerusalem. Come, I'm taking you to Peter."

Paul quickly got to his feet, gripping Barnabas's shoulder with joy. "Thank you, my friend. Thank you for believing in me. I promise to live up to your expectations."

"I expect you to surpass them!" Barnabas chuckled, looking at Al as he realized this cat had made this chance encounter with Paul possible by running right to this tree. He reached down and mussed the fur on Al's head. "Just like Peter's cat here."

Paul smiled at Al, who pawed after Barnabas's satchel of fish. "I recently had the company of a beautiful black cat. I forgot how much I missed her until seeing this one. He's a bit larger than she was, though."

TWO WEEKS LATER

Clarie sat under the grove of olive trees, smiling as Max, Liz, Kate, and Al joined her. She was now dressed as a Jewish man of Jerusalem, posing as one of the new believers in the church there. "I'm happy to see you all! I hope the four of you have enjoyed a nice long visit together."

"*Bonjour, mon amie!*" Liz exclaimed, rushing up to her. "*Oui*, it has been heavenly to be together. I did not know if we would be able to see you here in Jerusalem."

"You did very well with arranging for Paul and Barnabas to meet," Clarie told them. "Paul has been visiting with Peter and Jesus' brother, James, and of course has been able to roam about freely here in Jerusalem."

"Aye, they've been sharin' up a storm," Kate piped up. "Paul's shared all he learned from Jesus while in Arabia, an' of course he's wanted ta hear stories of their time with Jesus."

Nigel suddenly flew in on Naomi for a landing. "I bring dreadful news!" he said as he jumped off the pigeon. "I've uncovered another murder plot!"

Max growled. "Against Paul, I take it? Which r-r-rascals be schemin'?"

"Quite the surprising turn of events, as the same chaps Saul hired to arrest Stephen have now turned on Paul! Lander is the ring leader," Nigel explained, straightening his spectacles. "He gathered together chaps by the name of Egan, Talus, and Xeno to discuss how and when they would kill Paul. Dastardly planning, I assure you, wanting to take him by night and kill him away from the eyes of Jerusalem. They consider Paul a traitor to their lost cause."

"I knew he would cause trouble again," Liz said with a frown. "*Lander*—'the lion.'" He oversaw Stephen's arrest and death, and now this plot to kill Paul." Her tail swished back and forth as she thought this through.

"It's time for us ta leave," Max lamented. "Clarie, can ye tell Peter an' the lads all aboot the plot?"

"Yes, I'll suggest to Peter and James that they make arrangements

201

for some of the men to take Paul to Caesarea where he can get a boat to Tarsus," Clarie answered. "Of course, I'll be one of the men escorting Paul. It's almost sixty miles on foot. Max and Liz, you keep out of sight behind us, and I'll get you onto the ship headed to Tarsus."

Nigel cleared his throat. "And where do you wish me to be?"

"You can fly overhead as we head to Caesarea, for you'll need to be on assignment there soon," Clarie instructed. "Exciting things are coming there. Once Paul's ship sets sail, I'll tell you what to do."

"Splendid!" Nigel cheered. "I shall look forward to a trip to the coast. Nothing like a taste of salt air."

Clarie stood up and told the others, "You four can stay here until nightfall. I'll have Nigel come get you as we depart with Paul."

Max and Kate, Liz and Al exchanged somber looks, knowing it was time to say "Farewell" again.

Paul knelt down to pray in the temple, praising God for the wonderful two weeks he had experienced so far in Jerusalem. He was grateful to have been received with open arms into the Jerusalem church, and his time spent with Peter and James was priceless. Paul soaked up stories about Jesus and his teachings, and marveled at how he could share insights before Peter could finish, having heard the same instruction from Jesus in the desert. Paul wanted to prove the validity of his calling to Peter and James, telling them he had received such revelations from Jesus alone. He wanted the authority to preach as an apostle, for he had seen the risen Lord. Jesus, not men, had formed his thinking and his ability to preach. And preach he had.

Paul's heart had led him to preach at the same synagogue of Hellenistic Jews where Stephen had preached. He had even met with the same men he had bribed to arrest Stephen, trying to show them how wrong he had been. He had frequently encountered heated opposition from them, but Paul felt that, with time, he could win them over.

Suddenly Paul's prayer was invaded by a vision. Jesus spoke to him: "Hurry and leave Jerusalem quickly, because the people here will not accept your witness about me."

Paul's eyes remained closed while he answered Jesus in the vision. "Lord, they know very well I went to the synagogues and arrested and beat those who believe in you. And when your witness Stephen was put to death, I myself was there, approving of his murder and taking care of the cloaks of his murderers."

Jesus interrupted him. "Go, for I will send you far away to the Gentiles."

Paul's eyes opened and his heart sank. He couldn't believe it. He couldn't believe that Jerusalem would not accept his testimony. Jesus himself had to tell Paul otherwise for him to believe it. But despite his great ideas of how he would be Jesus' champion in Jerusalem, God had other plans. And he must not argue with God. Paul stood up and looked over his shoulder, wondering if the temple guards he so long ago had called to do his bidding would now come after him. He quickly left the temple complex and made his way back to Peter and James, Jesus' brother.

203

"Good! You're here," Peter exclaimed, shoving Paul's knapsack into his arms. "Some of the brothers overheard the Hellenistic Jews. They're plotting to kill you. We've got to get you out of Jerusalem."

"Yes, Jesus just told me," Paul relayed. "He told me I had to leave Jerusalem and go away to the Gentiles. He said the Jews wouldn't accept my words here."

Peter and James looked in amazement at Paul. They still marveled at the 180-degree turn this man's life had made. Now the resurrected Jesus spoke to him, just as he had appeared and spoken both to Peter and James.

James handed Paul a bag of food to take with him. "Some of the brothers are going to get you to Caesarea, where you can get a boat back to Tarsus."

"Tarsus?!" Paul exclaimed. "I'm to go back to my home? What about our work? When will you call me? And what am I supposed to do now?"

Peter held up his hands to calm Paul's passionate protests. "I don't know when, Paul, but just as Jesus gave you a specific word to leave, he'll make it clear what you are to do next. Jerusalem is too hot to hold you right now. Stay in Tarsus, and when the time is right, we'll send for you."

"Be patient, Paul, just like Jesus," James encouraged him. "My brother maintained a positive attitude that never gave up despite the delays and the opposition he faced. He never rushed into anything, but waited patiently for God's perfect timing." He smiled and put a hand on Paul's shoulder. "Let patience have her perfect work in you, Paul."

Paul clutched his knapsack to his chest, frowning. He reluctantly nodded. "Very well. I will trust your direction and will continue to pray for you all here in Jerusalem. Thank you, my brothers, for welcoming me into your fellowship."

Peter reached over and hugged the smaller man, his new brother in Christ. "Jesus told us to love one another, and to forgive one another. If we're to carry his message to others, we have to do as he told us. Love and forgive."

Clarie, as a Jewish man, knocked at the door and slowly slipped inside. "My men are waiting. We've made arrangements to distract the plotters tonight so we can get Paul out of the city." Turning to Paul, she told him, "I'm Carmi. Don't worry, you're in good hands."

Paul smiled and suddenly had a puzzled expression as he looked into her blue eyes. "Thank you."

James ushered them to the door. "Godspeed until we meet again."

As Paul slipped out the door with Clarie, he stared at her for a moment.

"Is anything wrong?" Clarie asked him.

Paul studied her eyes. "Have we met before? You seem familiar to me. I pray it wasn't when I was Saul."

"Yes, our paths crossed then," Clarie answered honestly as she heaved her knapsack on her shoulder and patted Paul on the back. "But that's all behind us now. Come, let's get you out of here."

Clarie smiled to herself as she led Paul down the darkened streets of Jerusalem to escape once more into the night. Little did Paul know that Clarie had been the temple guard who took him to Damascus and the Arab man who took him to Arabia. Now she was aiding his escape out of Jerusalem and would take him to Caesarea. But she was just getting started in disguising herself to Paul.

24

Passing Ships at Caesarea

The aquamarine waters of the Mediterranean stretched as far as the eye could see. Blue waves crashed into the two large breakwaters along the harbor, sending white sea-spray flying into the air. The massive white stone wall that encircled the grand harbor held a wide promenade where sailors and passengers walked along, loading and unloading cargo from the numerous Roman ships tied to the docks. All along the wall rose enormous statues, a lighthouse, and two large towers that guarded the entrance to the harbor. Massive chains would be stretched across the harbor entrance from the two towers, preventing ships from entering when closed and keeping three hundred wintering ships safe from the boisterous waters brought by menacing southeast winds. Ships entering the harbor were greeted by a massive statue of Caesar Augustus, welcoming them to this, the largest seaport in the Mediterranean, which bore his name—Caesarea.

Rising from the pier was a broad flight of steps leading to the Temple of Augustus, another reminder of the city's namesake. Herod the Great spared no expense at making this Roman capital city of the Judean Province the most elaborate, beautiful city on the coast, second only to Jerusalem in its grandeur. Caesarea enjoyed the typical constructions of a Roman city, including entertainment facilities—a theater, amphitheater, and hippodrome, where chariot races thrilled the crowds. Pink columns of imported Aswan Egyptian granite lined the entrance to the amphitheater, giving the four thousand spectators an exquisite view of contrasting colors with the crystal blue sea behind them.

Dotted all along the harbor were houses made of white stone and paved streets lined with hundreds of columns. But the grandest house of all was Herod's Palace, built onto a natural promontory that jutted out into the sea. Herod built a freshwater swimming pool at the end of the palace so he could bathe with ease in fresh water while he gazed into the salty blue waters of the Mediterranean. Luxury abounded throughout this palace of elaborately tiled floors depicting scenes of animals and fish.

Despite Herod's taste for beauty and his passion for building wondrous places like the temple in Jerusalem and this marvelous city of Caesarea, he was despicable in his behavior and skill for destroying lives. Murder was in the makeup of the Herod family line. Herod the Great ordered the slaughter of all baby boys born in and around Bethlehem when wise men came looking for the new king of the Jews. His son Herod Antipas had beheaded John the Baptist. This left his grandson, King Herod Agrippa I, next in line to kill whoever threatened his rule.

Following Herod the Great's death, his kingdom was divided into three regions to be ruled by his sons, Archelaus, Philip I, and Herod Antipas, but they all answered to Rome. The Roman Senate granted Caesarea and all of Judea to Archelaus, but he proved to be incompetent and was exiled by Rome. From that point on, Rome imposed direct rule over the Judean province. Its governors, called procurators or prefects, maintained this Caesarean palace as their official headquarters. Philip I died and his northern kingdom fell to his nephew, King Herod Agrippa I. Herod Antipas was proving to be such a thorn in Rome's side he was soon to be banished. Regardless of this volatile ruling family, one thing was certain. Wherever any of the Herods ruled, there was sure to be beauty, but in the hands of a beast.

One of Rome's governors appointed to rule Caesarea was Pontius Pilate. He had lived here when he traveled to Jerusalem for that fateful

206

Passover seven years ago. He had returned from Jerusalem to this sea-side palace, greatly disturbed and seeking solace. Pilate roamed the hallways lined with white gauzy curtains blowing in the sea breeze, reliving every bit of his decision-making process in the matter of that mysterious "criminal." He hoped for relief from the haunting events surrounding the death of Jesus of Nazareth, but not even the beauty of this place could give him peace. Despite the fact that he washed his hands in front of those who accused Jesus, declaring that Jesus' blood was on *their* hands, all he saw when he gazed at his own hands was the blood of the scourged and crucified Nazarene.

Pilate was soon replaced by Marcellus, then Marullus, as Roman governors here in Caesarea. But the entire Roman world itself was in a state of turnover with the rise of a new Roman emperor: Caligula. Every city was busy receiving new statues of the flamboyant emperor. He insisted they be placed prominently throughout the empire. And every Roman officer knew he could be called back to Rome at any time.

207

Two aqueducts brought water into the city of Caesarea from the springs below Mount Carmel ten miles away. The beautiful repeating arch structure filled the city with fresh water, and served to remind residents and visitors of the architectural marvels provided by powerful Roman engineering. Herod intentionally built Caesarea as a Roman, pagan city, but it eventually drew Jews and Samaritans with its commercial and cultural offerings. And wherever Jews and other groups mixed, there was bound to be friction.

On this beautiful, sunshiny day, Max and Liz sat atop the aqueduct and gazed at the splendor of Caesarea. The cry of the seagulls overhead made Max turn his gaze skyward. He breathed the salt air deeply into his lungs and smiled. "Jest think, Lass. Those seagulls' line goes all the way back ta Cr-r-rinan an' Bethoo, me friends from Scotland."

Liz curled her tail slowly up and down, also watching the seagulls soaring in the air. *"Oui,* they were dear friends to all of us on Noah's Ark." She spied a pigeon coming in for a landing and smiled as Nigel's tiny paw waved to them from above. He leaned forward to whisper in Naomi's ear, directing her to land atop the aqueduct.

"Utterly splendid day for flying, I must say!" Nigel exclaimed as they landed. The little mouse jumped off the pigeon and gave her a tender pat. "Thank you, my dear. Go enjoy your day with friends and I shall find you later." Naomi flew off again and Nigel took a deep breath of salt air, closing his eyes with delight. "And an equally splendid day for sea travel. Paul should have nothing but smooth sailing to Tarsus."

"Aye, have the humans arrived at the docks yet?" Max asked. "We ran ahead of them ta scope out the city."

"They should be there shortly. I spied them entering the gates of Caesarea not long ago," Nigel reported. "Should we make our way to the docks?"

Liz stretched out long, extending her back leg in a graceful pose. "*Oui,* let's be going. Clarie will direct us to the proper vessel, so we may hide behind cargo until time to depart." She began daintily walking down the aqueduct toward the harbor docks, Max and Nigel following along behind.

208

There was so much activity at the docks that no one noticed the small animals darting in and out of the crates and baskets of cargo, piles of rope, and other shipping supplies. As they huddled around a cluster of Roman jars, called *amphorae,* containing olive oil for transport, Liz spotted a familiar face—her own—on the deck of a ship docked in front of them.

"Libertas!" Liz exclaimed, pointing. "*Voila!* It's the statue that Marcus Antonius had carved with his wife as the model for the Roman goddess and me for the cat at her feet!"

"Aye, an' the statue that Gillamon spoke ta us through in their garden," Max added. "Wha's it doin' here on this ship?"

"Stop it, Theo! That's *MY* lucky marble and you know it!" A young Roman boy, about seven, was chasing an older Roman boy, about nine, who held his fist in the air, laughing and clearly keeping the treasured object away from him. He proceeded to jump onto the older boy's back and tackle him to the dock. They scuffled and the red marble went flying out of the boy's hand and down the dock. The animals watched as the marble rolled and rolled, finally stopping under the sandal of a man on the dock. It was Paul.

Paul leaned down and picked up the marble, smiling as he rolled it around in his fingers. He looked down the dock, searching for its owner when the two Roman boys came running up to him.

"Please, sir, may I have my marble?" the young Roman pleaded.

Paul looked from the younger boy to the older boy. "I see this marble is special to you. Did someone take it against your will?"

The older boy looked at his younger brother and then down at the dock. "Yes, sir. I took it. But I was just teasing him."

Paul held the red marble up to the sun and looked at the beautiful swirled glass. "This is indeed a treasure. I've never seen a marble made of glass. Most are made of fired clay. May I ask where you got this . . . and what is your name?"

"My name is Julius, sir," the young boy answered hopefully. His face lit up to share about his prize. "My grandfather sent this marble to me for my birthday. He was an officer in the emperor's service in Rome. We're going to see him now and he promised to teach me how to be an expert marble player!"

"He sounds like a good man," Paul said with a smile. He looked at the older boy. "And what is your name? You appear to be Julius' guilty older brother."

"Yes, sir, I am. My name is Theophilus," the boy answered. "I am guilty, sir."

"Well you know that if you are guilty of something, you must make it right. The good news is that your brother's treasure wasn't lost in the sea, as it could easily have rolled off the dock here," Paul instructed him. "It's a terrible feeling to be guilty, isn't it? Especially for hurting someone you love."

"Yes, sir, it is," Theophilus replied. He turned to his little brother. "I'm sorry for taking your marble, Julius. I know it means a lot to you. It's just that you're always bragging about it!"

Paul looked at Julius, who frowned in anger at his older brother. Paul leaned forward and looked into Julius' eyes. "The proper response is, 'I forgive you, brother.'"

Julius continued to scowl. "Okay. I forgive you, Theo. But don't do it again, or I'll . . . !" He stopped as he saw Paul looking at him with a frown.

209

"Let me tell you boys something. You are brothers. Whether you want to admit it or not, I know you love each other. So, *act* like it." Paul looked from Julius to Theophilus. "Love is patient, love is kind. It does not envy . . ." He looked back to Julius. "It does not boast, it is not proud. It does not dishonor others, it is not self-seeking, it is not easily angered." He held out the marble to the young boy. "It keeps no record of wrongs. Here is your marble, Julius. Enjoy this treasure that your grandfather gave you in love, but both of you, remember the lesson behind it that is even a greater treasure."

Julius smiled and took the marble. He looked from Paul to Theo and back to Paul. "The red marble lesson."

"The red marble lesson," Paul smiled and said, mussing Julius' hair.

A beautiful Roman woman with green eyes called the boys. They turned and waved at her.

"Yes, thank you, sir," Theophilus added. "We'll remember. You won't tell our mother about this, will you?"

"Good, Theophilus," Paul said, leaning over to whisper in his ear. "Your guilty secret is safe with me, now that you've made it right. Go have fun."

The boys turned and ran back to the ship. Paul watched them, muttering to himself. "When I was a child, I talked like a child, I thought like a child, I reasoned like a child. When I became a man, I put the ways of childhood behind me." He put his hands behind his back and strolled along the dock, deep in thought.

Liz watched as the boys climbed aboard the ship with the Libertas statue tied securely to the deck. "Those are Marcus's grandsons! Did you hear them? They are traveling back to Rome, no?"

Nigel spied two Roman centurions walking toward them. They wore sculpted breastplates made of leather and the red-plumed helmets of their rank. Their red capes blew behind them in the wind as they walked down the dock. "And there is Armandus!"

"Cornelius, my friend, it is good of you to let me stay with you here in Caesarea while I finish up business matters," Armandus said as they walked by. "My servant Caius will safely see Bella and the boys back to Rome. I'll join them there soon."

"I'm delighted to be of assistance to a fellow member of the Italian Regiment," Cornelius replied, patting Armandus' back. "I'm sorry you'll be leaving Judea, but this is an excellent opportunity for your boys to be educated in Rome. And it is fortunate for you to get away from Herod Antipas and your post with him there in Capernaum. Word is that he won't be serving Rome much longer."

"Yes, it *is* an opportunity," Armandus agreed. "Rome indeed offers the best education, but I worry about the pagan influence there. You are right about Antipas, though. It will be good to part ways with that madman."

"Pagan influences are everywhere in the Roman world. Just look at Caesarea! The Temple of Augustus is here to remind us the emperor is god," Cornelius pointed out. "What you teach in the home will have the most impact on those boys. My family believes in one God and we pray to him each day in our home."

Armandus nodded. "You are a God-fearing man like me, Cornelius. You have shown kindness to the Jewish people here in Caesarea as I have in Capernaum. I'm glad we share a spirit inclined to one God." He hesitated a moment. Could he trust Cornelius with his story about Jesus of Nazareth? How he longed to understand more about the man he had crucified and yet had risen from the dead! Jesus told Armandus to find Peter, but the centurion had never encountered the disciple. Now he was heading back to Rome. Perhaps he would never know more about Jesus. Maybe if he discussed this with Cornelius while he was here, he could learn more. Maybe Cornelius had encountered Jesus, too. Yes, he would talk with his Roman friend. He led Cornelius to the ship where his wife and sons waited. "Come, meet my family."

Cornelius saw the Libertas statue with the boys sitting on its base and raised his eyebrows. "Looks like you're taking a piece of pagan Rome back with you, my friend," he jested.

Armandus smiled. "The face of my mother is on that statue. My father had it carved here, and left it in their home, which they gave to me. Now I'm taking it back to Rome. For me, it is no longer a goddess. I simply see this statue as my beautiful mother."

"If we Romans can change from pagans to God-fearing men,

211

perhaps even our statues can change to symbolize good as well," Cornelius ventured with a smile.

Max studied the statue as Armandus and Cornelius climbed aboard the ship to greet the family and make their farewells. Suddenly the statue winked at him and a big grin grew on Max's face. "Looks like Gillamon be headin' ta R-r-rome then."

"That he is," Clarie's voice came as she sat down on a crate next to them. "He is watching over Julius and Theophilus for this mission."

"I say, those boys are the sons of Armandus, the centurion at the cross. And they are the grandsons of Marcus, the centurion who allowed Mary and Joseph to escape Bethlehem with Jesus," Nigel pondered, tapping his chin with his paw. "Might these boys continue the family legacy?"

Clarie smiled and put her hands on her knees. "Time will tell, won't it?"

212

"*C'est magnifique!*" Liz exclaimed, delighted to see these children. "And they met Paul. I am certain neither Paul nor the boys realize how special their encounter really was."

Clarie looked at the Libertas statue and nodded. "Time will tell about that, too. For now, Max and Liz, you have a boat to catch. I've arranged passage for Paul on a ship to Tarsus back down the dock. He's buying food provisions now. Come, I'll get you on board before he returns. You may appear to him when you arrive in Tarsus. He will need you more than you can imagine."

"But why, Lass?" Max asked as they started walking down the dock to the ship.

"You two will be the only friends he has," Clarie replied. "Nigel, you are to follow Armandus and Cornelius back to Cornelius' home."

"Right! And what shall I do there?" Nigel asked, giving a kiss to Liz and a pat to Max in farewell.

Clarie stopped in front of Paul's ship to Tarsus. "Watch them get ready for company."

25

CLEAN SHEETS

"I don't know how or why you travel with me everywhere, Ari," Peter said, tossing Al a last piece of fish. "I do know that all our walking is making us both lose weight, though."

Al gobbled up the fish, burped, and meowed, *"Aye, two fine lookin' lads, that be us!"*

Peter studied this big, orange cat that had been around ever since the first day he met Jesus. There had been four animals in all—two cats and two dogs—and they had belonged to Jesus' friend, Gillamon. Oh, how Jesus loved these animals! One day Gillamon wasn't around but the animals stayed. Peter figured something had happened to the old man, and the animals attached themselves to the other people they knew. The black dog and the black cat had disappeared a few years ago, but the white dog had grown attached to John and Mary. And this orange cat had evidently "claimed" Peter as his human, because lately he went everywhere with him. Peter laughed to himself. "Must be the fish."

Suddenly an insistent knock came at the door of this home where Peter was staying in Lydda. He went to the door and cracked it open. "Yes?"

"Peter? We come from Joppa. We heard about the miracle you performed here with Aeneas who was paralyzed and had not been able to get out of bed for eight years," a Jewish man explained. "We heard you

213

healed him! People all over Lydda now believe in Jesus and word spread to us in Joppa!"

Peter wrinkled his brow. "Let's be clear—*Jesus* healed Aeneas. I only spoke the words over him, just as I saw my Lord do, telling him to pick up his mat and walk."

"Please, our friend Tabitha fell sick and has died. Surely you can also raise Tabitha as you saw Jesus bring others back!" a second Jewish man insisted. "She was a believer and spent all her time doing good and helping the poor by making them clothes. Please come with us, Peter."

Peter thought back to the day he, James, and John were with Jesus when he raised Jairus's daughter from the dead. He knew it wasn't in his power to heal or bring anyone back from the dead. Only Jesus could do that. He nodded. "Very well, I will come with you. Let me get my knapsack and my walking stick." He went over to gather his things and rubbed Al on the back. "Ari, we must leave. Twelve miles to Joppa."

214

Al's face dropped, but he faithfully trotted out the door behind Peter. *Sure, there'll be nothin' left o' me after all this walkin'.*

∞

When they arrived, Peter was taken to the room upstairs where Tabitha's body lay. All the widows crowded around him, crying and showing him all the shirts and coats Tabitha had made while she was alive. Peter gently asked them to all leave the room. Then he knelt down and prayed.

"Oh Jesus, I am just a simple man. But you are God, the giver of life. I watched you bring others back from the dead. I watched you raise Jairus's daughter. If it pleases you, and brings you glory, I ask that you please allow your servant Tabitha to rise." Peter took a deep breath, turned to her lifeless body, and said, "Tabitha, get up!"

The young woman's eyes fluttered open and Peter's heart started racing. Tabitha saw Peter and slowly sat up. Peter smiled at her. "Welcome back, sister. The Lord has more work for you to do."

Tabitha smiled and put a hand to her head. "I can't explain what I've just experienced. But I felt enveloped by light and love."

Peter reached over and took Tabitha by the hand, helping her slowly get up. "There are some people who want to see you."

Together they walked out of the room and met the stunned faces of the widows and believers gathered there. Peter smiled. "Jesus has returned Tabitha to us." Immediately all the widows and believers began praising God, surrounding her with embraces and tears of joy. Peter stepped back and allowed this family of believers and friends to celebrate the incredible miracle of life before them.

Peter quietly slipped out of the house, as he didn't wish to draw attention to himself. He wanted only the Lord to be honored for what had happened here. As he stood in the street, he suddenly remembered his cat. "Ari! Ari, where are you?" He looked all around him in the street and chuckled when he saw Al climbing up the legs of a man who evidently was carrying some fish. He went over and picked Al up. "I'm sorry if my cat is bothering you."

215

"Not at all!" said the man with wiry, gray hair. His face and hands were weathered by the sun but his brown eyes shone with the warmth of the Holy Spirit. "He was keeping me company. I'm Simon."

"I also am named Simon, but go now by Peter," Peter explained.

Simon's eyes grew wide and he pointed a wrinkled finger at the apostle. "I've heard about you!" He drew half a fish in the dirt with his foot.

Peter smiled and drew the other half of the fish with his foot, completing the secret Christian symbol. Al looked down at the fish with a goofy grin on his face. *"Glad to see ye laddies usin' me fish idea!"* he meowed.

"Last I heard some men were going to get you to bring you here for Tabitha. Bless you for coming, Peter! Tell me, is Tabitha . . . does she live?" Simon asked hopefully.

Peter smiled and nodded. "Yes, the Lord needed her to stay with us longer."

Simon grasped Peter's arm with an exuberant face. "Praise God! Thank you for helping our sister. Would you do me the honor of staying at my house? Of course you may find it unsuitable as I am a tanner by trade."

Peter smiled broadly. In the Jewish world, tanners were considered unclean and had to live outside the city as they worked their craft of treating animal hides to make leather. Peter looked into the eyes of this fellow believer and saw not an unclean tradesman, but a brother. "I would be honored to stay with you, brother. That is, if you wouldn't mind having my cat here as well. But I warn you, he will eat you out of fish!"

"I'll gladly welcome you and your cat. Had it not been for him, I might not have met you," Simon chuckled and reached out to scratch Al under his chin. "I can see he is quite the eater. Good thing I live right by the sea. He can have all the fish his little heart desires."

Al looked intently at Peter and meowed, *"I LOVE HIM! Aye, it were worth the trip here."*

Simon laughed. "That settles it. We'll go there now. Mind you, my house isn't grand, but at least I can provide you a bed with clean sheets."

216

Peter and Simon made their way to the outskirts of the city, to Simon's house by the sea. It didn't take long for news about Peter's miracle to spread all over Joppa. Tabitha wasn't the only one saved that day, as many people became believers in the Lord when they heard what had happened.

⌒∝

A gentle sea breeze wafted through the home of Cornelius and he breathed in the salt air. He gazed at the position of the sun and knew it was nigh unto three o'clock. Although not a Jew, he abided by many of the Jewish customs in his desire to serve the one God he had come to believe was the only true divine Being. The Roman centurion had grown weary of Rome's endless stream of gods. Rome had a god for every occasion, every profession, and seemingly every event that needed an explanation. As Rome conquered a new land, she adopted their gods. Cornelius's heart stirred for something more. Something real. The more he learned about this Jewish God, the more his heart and mind were drawn to the idea of a singular Being who was the Maker of everything. Yet Cornelius longed for more. So daily, he prayed at 3:00 in the afternoon.

Cornelius knelt down on a red pillow on his special patio where he met the Lord daily in prayer. Gauzy red- and gold-trimmed curtains hung above him, blowing in the sea breeze. He bowed his head and closed his eyes. "I come with honor and thanksgiving to you, the one and Holy God. I am not one of your chosen people. I am a Gentile, and some would say an enemy of your chosen people. But I pray you will accept me for the offerings I make to support those who are poor and needy. Please, I long to know that I am accepted in your eyes. If there is anything you would have me do, please make it plain and I will do it. I pledge my life and my household to you. If this Jesus of Nazareth is indeed your Son, as I have heard all about from my friend, then I will believe in him. But God, there is much we do not understand. Please, show us the way we should go."

Nigel sat watching Cornelius, marveling at the words coming out of this Gentile man. Like Armandus, this Roman longed for the truth. Nigel smiled as he felt expectant for this household. Clarie had told him to get ready for expected guests, but never specified who. He had listened in on the many conversations Cornelius and Armandus had shared over the past few days. Armandus fully confided in Cornelius, telling him all he knew about Jesus of Nazareth. He told him how kind Jesus' parents had been to his Roman family. He told him about the horrible night of the slaughter of the innocents and how Jesus had escaped the sword of Herod. He shared how Jesus had healed his servant, Caius, just by giving the word when he was in Capernaum. He shared all about Jesus' trial before Pilate and how he had been there when Jesus was sent to Herod Antipas. He wept as he shared how Jesus was scourged and how helpless he was to stop it. He shook his head in regret as he recounted the Crucifixion and how he finally had realized who Jesus was just as he died on the cross. Finally Armandus shared how Jesus appeared to him the morning of the Resurrection, telling the soldier that all was forgiven, and to find Peter, his disciple. Armandus told him he believed Jesus was the Son of God, but he didn't know what to do with this belief. Cornelius' desire to know more only grew after hearing all this from Armandus. He asked Armandus to share with his household all he knew about Jesus and his teachings.

As he fervently prayed, Cornelius suddenly had a vision. A brilliant angel of God stood before him. The angel called his name: "Cornelius!"

The Roman stared at the angel in fear. "What is it, sir?"

The angel smiled. "Your prayers and gifts to the poor have come up as a memorial offering before God. Now send men to Joppa to bring back a man named Simon who is called Peter. He is staying with Simon the tanner, whose house is by the sea."

Right before the angel disappeared, he nodded at Nigel. Then suddenly he was gone. Cornelius's heart was racing and he tingled from head to toe. He opened his eyes and looked around. All he saw were the red- and gold-trimmed curtains blowing in the breeze next to him. He grabbed the front of his cloak with his hand and sat up to catch his breath. "Peter!" he exclaimed to himself.

Nigel's whiskers were quivering with excitement, as he was allowed to see the vision as well. *This takes the biscuit! Peter is the guest coming! I do believe we're in for the monumental meeting. This could absolutely change everything.* He then realized a word the angel had used and saw a deeper meaning behind it. *The angel said Cornelius's prayers and gifts were as a memorial offering before God. Memorial. That is the same word used to mean a statue erected to remember what someone has done in the past. I say, it's as if the angel meant that prayers and gifts rose up as a statue in heaven to stand there and remind the Maker of Cornelius! Brilliant! Prayers are like statues before the Maker! Statues. Gillamon has been speaking to us through statues throughout this entire mission. And why have we been allowed to repeatedly see the Libertas statue? Something must be afoot. I can't wait to tell Liz about this.* Nigel chuckled to himself. *Afoot, like Liz at the base of the Libertas statue.*

Cornelius walked through his house and called for his servants and a soldier who was his personal attendant. "Galenus, Ennius! Come here quickly! Rastus, you come as well!"

The three men hurriedly came to Cornelius. "My Lord? What is it?" Rastus the soldier asked in alarm at his captain's urgency. Armandus was also in the house and came running up behind them.

"I've just had a vision. An angel of the Lord told me God was pleased with my prayers and my charity work. He told me to send for

218

a man who is staying in Joppa at the house of a tanner named Simon who lives by the sea." Cornelius smiled and locked eyes with Armandus. "The man you are to find is named Simon Peter. Go to Joppa and ask him to come back here with you immediately."

"Yes, sir! We'll leave right away." Rastus saluted him. "You two, come with me to ready the horses."

As the servants left the room, Armandus put his hands on his hips and smiled broadly at Cornelius. "Peter? You mean the man Jesus told me to find?"

Cornelius slapped Armandus on the back. "Yes, *Peter!* Looks like you won't have to find him after all. He's coming to us, here!"

I say, the Maker has worked this all out rather well! Nigel preened his whiskers with delight. *I believe I shall fly along and ride back with Al. Little does he know he's in for a reunion with his nemesis, the little boy who used to terrorize the big, orange cat.*

219

The next day, as Cornelius's men were nearing Joppa, Peter went up on the roof of Simon's house about noon in order to pray. His stomach rumbled with hunger as he sat down next to Al, who was sleeping soundly on his back, drool coming from the corner of his mouth. Peter chuckled at the fluffy, orange cat. "Don't worry Ari, lunch is coming. I know you are dreaming about what you'll get to eat."

Peter gazed out at the beautiful blue Mediterranean Sea. The abundant sunshine sparkled off the cresting waves rolling into shore. He looked down the beach to where the wharf was located and thought about Jonah. It was from this very port of Joppa that Jonah had disobeyed God and boarded a ship to run away from his assignment of delivering a word of warning to the Ninevites. Jonah didn't want to obey God and give words of salvation and hope to his most hated enemies. He thought he could run away from God and ignore his assignment. So God gave him three days in the belly of a fish to think about it. When Jonah finally went and preached to the Ninevites the people listened and turned to God. Jonah responded by pouting. He didn't like the fact that God loved the enemies of Israel. But God explained to him that he loved them very much and wished for no one to be lost.

A thought suddenly came to Peter. *Rome is the enemy of God's chosen people now. Could it be possible that God loves Gentiles, too?* Perhaps Israel had twisted the concept of being God's elect into an idea of favoritism God never intended. Peter thought back to how Jesus had treated the Samaritans and even Gentiles they had encountered, like that Roman centurion who asked Jesus to heal his servant. Jesus said that man had more faith than anyone in all of Israel! Peter frowned, suddenly feeling ashamed of how God's people were filled with such racial pride and hatred, calling Gentiles "dogs." The Jews had developed traditions that kept them apart from Gentiles, mainly centered around food and other behavioral customs. A Jew would be defiled if he entered a Gentile's home. But that day the Roman came asking for his servant to be healed, Jesus was willing to go to that Gentile's home. Peter frowned. *Have we had this wrong all along? God said he would bless all families of the earth by choosing and blessing one family, and he chose Abraham. And later he chose to save the Ninevites. Maybe the idea of his chosen people must mean simply* the *way he would accomplish blessing all peoples of the earth. That means the Gentiles are worth saving. That means Jesus died for them, too.*

As Peter thought about these things, he lay back next to Al under the white sheet that served as an awning to block the intensity of the sun. The warm sea breeze was blowing through the white sheet, causing it to flap up and down. Peter closed his eyes and began to pray.

Suddenly a vision filled his mind. He saw heaven opened and something coming down that looked like a large sheet being lowered by its four corners to the earth. In it were all kinds of animals, reptiles, and wild birds. A voice said to him, "Get up, Peter; kill and eat!"

But Peter said, "Certainly not, Lord! I have never eaten anything ritually unclean or defiled."

Al woke up when he heard Peter. He stared at Peter and then up at the awning. *Why is he talkin' aboot food?* the cat wondered.

The voice spoke to Peter again: "Do not consider anything unclean that God has declared clean." This happened three times, and then the thing was taken back up into heaven.

Peter opened his eyes and saw Al staring right at him. "You'd eat anything, wouldn't you, Ari?" He sat up and slowly petted Al as he wondered about the meaning of this vision. "But this isn't just about food. It's about *people*. God is telling me no one is unclean in his eyes." He shook his head, not understanding how this could be. It went against every Jewish bone in his body.

At that moment, the men sent by Cornelius were standing at the gate to Simon's house. Rastus called out and asked, "Is there a guest here by the name of Simon Peter?"

Peter was still trying to understand what the vision meant, when the Spirit said, "Listen! Three men are here looking for you. So get ready and go down, and do not hesitate to go with them, for I have sent them."

Peter ran a hand through his hair and looked up at the clean sheet billowing in the Wind above him. "I think things are about to change, Ari. And unlike Jonah, I plan to obey my Lord the *first* time. I don't think you'd much like to be in the belly of a fish. You'd prefer it the other way around." He chuckled and mussed Al's fur. He stood to lean over the edge of the rooftop, seeing the three men below. "Gentiles," he muttered to himself. He waved to them and made his way down the outside staircase.

221

As Peter walked downstairs, Nigel landed on the rooftop. "Good day, old boy!"

"Mousie!" Al exclaimed in delight. "What're ye doin' here?"

"Guess who's coming to dinner?" the little mouse quipped.

Peter nodded to the men as he reached the bottom of the stairs. "I am the man you are looking for. Why have you come?"

"Centurion Cornelius sent us," Rastus answered. "He is a good man who worships God and is highly respected by all the Jewish people. An angel of God told him to invite you to his house, so he could hear what you have to say."

Peter smiled at God's perfect timing. His vision was being confirmed here and now, just minutes after having experienced it. *I suppose this new world must begin with me.* "Please, come in. You are welcome here. Food has just been prepared. Let us eat . . . together. You will stay the night, and tomorrow we'll head to Caesarea."

JEWS AND GENTS

P eter was most wise to bring along six Jewish believers," Nigel said to Al as they rode along in the saddle bag of the horse that Cornelius had provided for Peter. Nigel stayed hidden from view.

"I'm jest glad we got to ride for a change," Al answered. "Why were he wise?"

"My dear chap, you must understand that what is getting ready to happen at Cornelius's house is historic! Monumental! World-changing! The Maker is getting ready to cut down the veil between Jews and Gentiles by having Peter visit," Nigel explained. "But I'm sure the Jewish leaders back in Jerusalem will need to be convinced, just like Peter. Before Peter could convert Cornelius, he first needed to be converted himself about this Gentile business. So, by bringing six believers, Peter will have fellow Jewish witnesses to report back to Jerusalem."

"Jews and Gents, ye say?" Al said easily. "Makes sense to me. Isn't that what Jesus tried to show the disciple laddies that day the Roman lad asked Jesus to heal his servant?"

Nigel nodded slowly and smiled. "Speaking of that Roman lad, there's something you should know . . ."

"Here we are!" Rastus exclaimed as they arrived at Cornelius's house. "Please, come with me, Peter."

Nigel ducked down in the saddle bag while Peter dismounted his horse. As he lifted Al out of the saddlebag onto the ground, Al meowed,

"I should know what, Mousie?"

Cornelius was waiting for Peter, together with relatives and close friends he had invited, such as Armandus. As Peter was about to go in the house, Cornelius met him, fell at his feet, and bowed down before him.

Peter frowned and lifted Cornelius by the shoulders. He would not treat this man like a dog any more than he would allow this man to treat him like a god. "Stand up. I myself am only a man."

Cornelius locked forearms with Peter and they shared a solid smile. "Welcome to my home, Peter. Come, many people are waiting for you."

As Peter walked into the courtyard, he saw that it was filled with Romans of all ages and ranks. Soldiers, servants, women, and children. Armandus stood in the back and gave Peter an affirming nod as their eyes met. Peter did a double take, as the centurion looked familiar. Peter smiled as he looked around at the others gathered there, still marveling that he was standing in a Gentile home. Paul had told him the Lord called him to take the gospel to the Gentiles. Now Peter understood that in order to support Paul, he and the rest of the Jewish leaders would have to open their hearts to these people as well.

"Please," Cornelius said with an open hand to Peter, encouraging him to speak.

Peter looked around the courtyard. "You yourselves know very well that a Jew is not allowed by his religion to visit or associate with Gentiles. But God has shown me I must not consider any person ritually unclean or defiled. And so when you sent for me, I came without any objection. I ask you, then, why did you send for me?"

Cornelius nodded, understanding that what Peter was doing was just not done in the Jewish world. "It was about this time three days ago that I was praying in my house at three o'clock in the afternoon. Suddenly a man dressed in shining clothes stood in front of me and said: 'Cornelius! God has heard your prayer and has taken notice of your works of charity. Send someone to Joppa for a man whose full name is Simon Peter. He is a guest in the home of Simon the tanner of leather, who lives by the sea.' And so I sent for you at once, and you

223

have been good enough to come." He looked around the room and smiled at his guests. "Now we are all here in the presence of God, waiting to hear anything the Lord has instructed you to say."

Peter's heart welled up with understanding. On the thirty-mile journey here, Rastus had shared with Peter about all they had heard about Jesus, but also about how they didn't know what to do next. God had prepared these Gentiles for the Good News, and he had prepared Peter to share it. Little by little over the years, God had been leading Peter out of his strict Jewish world. Starting with Jesus' encounters with the Samaritan woman and the Roman centurion, then to welcoming Stephen, Barnabas, and the other Hellenist Jews with Greek heritage into their fold, and to visiting Samaria with Philip, God was preparing Peter to accept the Gentiles. Paul had told Peter that the Lord specifically had called him to go to the Gentiles. Even staying in the home of Simon the tanner was part of God's preparation until Peter finally heard the voice of the Lord himself. Jesus told his disciples to take the Good News to the ends of the earth, but that wouldn't be possible without the very first Gentile believer.

Peter continued, "I now realize that it is true that God treats everyone on the same basis. Those who fear him and do what is right are acceptable to him, no matter what race they belong to. You know the message he sent to the people of Israel, proclaiming the good news of peace through Jesus Christ, who is Lord of all. You know of the great events that took place throughout the land of Israel, beginning in Galilee after John the Baptizer preached his message in the region of the Jordan River. You know about Jesus of Nazareth and how God poured out on him the Holy Spirit and power. He went everywhere, doing good and healing all who were under the power of the Devil, for God was with Jesus. We are witnesses of everything he did in the land of Israel and in Jerusalem. Then they put him to death by nailing him to a cross," Peter said, pausing to look at the anguished face of the Roman centurion in the back of the courtyard. Peter recognized the regret written on the man's face, remembering his own regret over denying Jesus the night of his betrayal. But Peter smiled—there was good news to tell. "But God raised him from death three days later and caused him to appear, not to everyone, but only to the witnesses God had already chosen, that is, to us who ate and drank with him after he rose from death. And he commanded us to preach the gospel to the people and to testify that he is the one whom God has appointed judge of the living and the dead. All the prophets spoke about him, saying that all who believe in him will have their sins forgiven through the power of his name."

While Peter was still speaking, a rush of Wind filled the courtyard. The curtains blew and Peter knew in an instant what was happening. The Holy Spirit came down on all those who were listening to his message, and they immediately began praising God's greatness. It was Pentecost all over again. Only this time, for Gentiles.

Cornelius lifted his hands to heaven. "Thank you, Lord! Thank you for answering my prayer!"

Armandus closed his eyes as tears streamed down his cheeks. "You are the one true God, Maker of heaven and earth! And Jesus is your one and only Son, sent to die for me!"

225

Peter and the Jewish believers who had come from Joppa were amazed that God had poured out his gift of the Holy Spirit on the Gentiles also. Peter smiled as he realized that God had accepted these Gentile believers. Now so must the church accept them. "These people have received the Holy Spirit, just as we also did. Can anyone, then, stop them from being baptized with water? Let them be baptized in the name of Jesus Christ!"

"Yes! Please, follow me!" invited Cornelius as he led everyone to the large pool of water just off the courtyard. He quickly took off his red robe and stepped into the water.

Peter directed the six Jewish believers from Joppa to also step into the water so they could baptize everyone in Cornelius's home. He would once again stand back and allow others to perform this honor, so as not to draw attention to himself.

Armandus eagerly stepped into the pool to be welcomed by one of the Jewish men with open arms. Armandus closed his eyes and allowed himself to be submerged in the waters symbolic of grace and new life in Christ. As he rose out of the water, Nigel hugged Al. "He's done it! Armandus is saved!"

Al's eyes grew wide. "Armandus? Ye mean that Roman be Armandus? He were the little boy who . . ."

"Yes, yes, yes, but let bygones be bygones, old boy!" Nigel stopped Al mid-sentence. "This is a happy day!"

Armandus stepped out of the pool, radiating joy, and ran into the open arms of Peter. They hugged for a moment and then looked each other in the face. "Jesus told me to find you, Peter. He told me you would help me find the way. But you found *me.* I'm so grateful."

Gratitude welled up in Peter when he heard that his Master had given this Gentile a word to find him. "Jesus told you to find *me?* Praise God, I am humbled to have been the one to share the Good News with you. Tell me, we've met, haven't we?"

Armandus nodded. "Yes, in Capernaum. Jesus healed my servant."

Peter's eyes widened. "Of course! I knew I recognized you! Jesus said you had more faith than anyone he had met in all of Israel. Oh, my brother, I am honored to know you!"

"There is more, Peter," Armandus said. "I was the centurion at the cross. I've long carried the burden of Jesus' dying by my hand. He told me that morning of the Resurrection when he came to me that I was forgiven. Now I see I was honored to be there. I was honored to be near my Lord the day he saved the world."

Peter grabbed Armandus again in a tight embrace and wept. "Indeed, my friend. You were witness to the greatest moment in human history. That day the veil was torn in the temple from the top to the bottom." He released his new brother and gripped him by the shoulders. "And this day, the veil is torn between Jew and Gentile!"

"Indeed!" Cornelius exclaimed, coming over dripping wet to join Peter and Armandus. "Thank you, brother. Thank you for daring to cross the great divide between us. I guess this is the first Gentile church?" He smiled as he held his hand out over the exuberant crowd of people gathered there, celebrating this happy day.

"That it is!" Peter exclaimed, slapping Cornelius's back. "I'd say this calls for a feast!"

"Feast we shall!" Cornelius shouted, clapping his hands for his servants. "Fill the tables with food! It's time for us to dine together!"

Al's ears perked up. "A feast! A reunion feast!" Al came running up to Armandus and wrapped himself around his legs, meowing, *"Remember me, lad?"*

Armandus laughed and picked up the big, orange cat. "And who do we have here?"

Peter smiled. "That's my cat, Ari. He goes everywhere with me."

Suddenly a rush of childhood memories came over Armandus with flashbacks of running through his mother's garden, chasing an orange cat around the Libertas statue. He laughed. "I used to chase a cat just like this one. Poor kitty, I tried to pull his tail."

"TRIED!? Ye DID pull me tail, laddie!" Al protested with a meow. *"Aye, but all's forgiven now. I'll even eat fish with ye Jews and Gents to prove it!"*

"Today has seen more than one miracle with the Gentiles." Nigel shook his head and chuckled at Al's reunion with Armandus. "Jews and Gents, indeed, Albert Aloysius. Jews and Gents."

Hard Years for a Heavenly Vision

T HIRTEEN!" the *hazzan* cried as he raised his arm high to deliver the next blow of the heavy whip with all his might. The four-pronged leather strap tore into Paul's shoulder and curled around to cut his chest. Paul gripped the iron rings that held his chains on the stone pillar, gritted his teeth, and moaned in agony as the whip found its mark. Tears rolled down his face as he heard the Jewish leader read the traditional curse for this flogging meant to punish and correct him—a wayward Jew: "If thou wilt not observe to do all the words of this Law that are written in this book, that thou mayest fear this glorious and fearful name, The Lord Thy God, then the Lord will make thy plagues wonderful."

Paul knew what was coming. After the thirteen lashes to his chest, the whipping moved to his back with thirteen lashes across one shoulder and a final thirteen lashes across the other shoulder, each lash cutting across already open, bleeding wounds. He moaned through this, his third scourging at the hands of the Jews in Tarsus who attempted to purge his offenses so he could resume his place in the synagogue. The alternative was to be excommunicated from Israel, which Paul couldn't risk, as he spoke at every opportunity in the synagogues about salvation through faith in Jesus as Messiah. *"You will be hated by everyone because of me, but the one who stands firm to the end will be saved."* Jesus' words filled Paul's mind. *"I am with you always."*

Max growled while Liz wiped her eyes, grief-stricken to see Paul suffer so much for proclaiming Jesus. "This time jest because he dared ta eat with Gentiles an' tell them aboot Jesus."

Liz sniffed. *"Oui.* He has disobeyed the orders from the Jewish leaders to stop preaching Jesus to Gentiles or Jews. How they hate Paul! How they actually hate *Jesus."* Liz shook her head at their blindness. "And they truly think that what they are doing to Paul honors God. *Quel dommage!"*

"Aye. No one will have anythin' ta do with him here anymore. Not even his own family," Max grumbled. "Well, Lass, let's be r-r-ready ta help him back ta his cave."

"THIRTY-NINE!" came the final counting cry of the *hazzan.* He lowered his hand and looked at Paul, whose welts were covered in blood; he struggled to even breathe. The man unlocked Paul's wrists from the shackles and Paul fell to the ground. The *hazzan* shook his head in disgust and walked off, leaving Paul there as the rest of the crowd dispersed, mumbling to themselves about the pitiful condition of this once-honored son of Tarsus. In their eyes, Paul was a disgrace and a blasphemer. They held out little hope for his return to their strict Jewish laws.

229

Paul lay there, unable to move for several minutes. Max carried Paul's small leather water pouch in his teeth, and he and Liz trotted over to where Paul lay. Liz swatted at the flies that attempted to land on Paul's open wounds while Max placed the water pouch next to him. Max then gently licked Paul's face, trying to revive him. Paul's hand shook as he lifted it to rest on Max's back. He licked his dry lips and his voice cracked as he spoke with barely a whisper. "Thank you, my little friends." He struggled to slowly sit up. He lifted the water pouch to his parched lips and took a sip, closed his eyes, and prayed. "Thank you, my Lord, for helping me through again. I am weak, but you are strong."

Paul delicately pulled his torn robe up around his shoulders, wincing as he attempted to cover himself for the walk back to his house. He stood up and held a hand to his balding forehead, feeling lightheaded.

Max and Liz frowned at one another. Paul's body was permanently scarred from the lashings he had received, and he had become bow-legged, a common result of repeated, severe floggings.

As Paul slowly walked away from this familiar place of humiliation and beating, Liz's eyes welled up with tears. She knew that this bandy-legged, half-bald, forty-one-year-old man would be impatient to heal, not for his own comfort, but so he could once again go out and preach Jesus. "He has lost all confidence in the flesh here in Tarsus. He carries every scar as a badge of honor for his Lord. Between losing his home and comforts, his position, and getting beaten, one would think he would be ready to give in, no?"

"Not ta mention his thr-r-ree shipwr-r-recks jest tr-r-ryin' ta pr-r-reach in little villages along the coast," Max added. "When he came back bedr-r-raggled from that day tr-r-readin' water at sea, I thought he would give in. Paul may be a wee lad, but I never met a br-r-raver one."

"*Oui,* but I know his heart is heavy," Liz lamented. "He knows that Jesus told him he specifically was to preach to the Gentiles, but he hasn't heard a word from Jerusalem in over seven years for an appointed mission." Liz's tail whipped back and forth as she thought this through. She looked at Max. "*Seven.* Something tells me he may finally be ready. And the world may finally be ready."

"Aye, seven means completeness," Max agreed hopefully. "The lad has pr-r-roved himself ta me, if not the Maker then. An' Nigel told us the church were havin' good years of peace an' gr-r-rowth. Maybe it's time, Lass."

"Well, let's help him get through this night," Liz suggested as she and Max followed along after Paul. "If the Maker has decided it is time for Paul to fulfill his mission, we'll know soon enough."

∝

The oil lamp flickered against the wall of the cave Paul used as his home. Situated on the outskirts of Tarsus, he was able to operate his tentmaking business here. Even though he didn't have friends in the synagogue and had lost his place in religious society in Tarsus, he stayed busy supplying tents to the travelers at this trading crossroads city. And this was a quiet, snug place for him to stay, study, and meditate with his Lord.

Paul would go into town and spend time with Gentiles. He would read Plato with them and try to engage them in conversation. He enjoyed watching their athletic competitions and discussing anything that opened a door to relate to them. He listened to their concerns, problems, and fears. And he always shared Jesus, whether his message was repeatedly rejected or not.

Paul squeezed the water out of the rag and dabbed it lightly on his wounds, taking in a quick breath against the pain. He shut his eyes tightly and forced himself to apply oil to his wounds. He refused to let infection get hold of him. Nothing would stop Paul of Tarsus. Even though he awaited word from the Jerusalem church for an assignment, he did what he could in his own little world. He refused to allow discouragement to set in. But his heart longed for a word.

"It's been so long, Lord. Please allow me to do your work—work that will make a real impact in the world," Paul said out loud, followed by a grunt of pain as he treated his wounds. "But whatever you bring me here and now, that I will be content to do."

231

Max and Liz sat quietly on Paul's bed, waiting for him to lie down. There was little they could do to help him physically, but at least they could be here with him to provide quiet companionship. And Paul never failed to express his love and gratitude for their company just as he had that surprising day they "miraculously showed up" on the streets of Tarsus. He couldn't explain how they had traveled more than four hundred miles from Damascus to Tarsus, and how in the world they had found him, but he remembered the Arab man telling him how loyal these two little animals were. Perhaps they had bonded so much with him through their time in the Arabian desert and in Damascus that they instinctively knew how to find him. Perhaps even God had sent them. After the cold reception of his family, an explanation of how they had done it mattered little to Paul. To see the smiling face and wagging tail of the dog and the purring, affectionate rubs of the cat gave Paul a touch of love he needed as the outcast of his once beloved home. He never had known the animal's names, but figured he needed to call them something. He named Max "Gabriel" after the archangel who brought messages directly from God. He named Liz "Faith" for what his entire journey was about. Paul knew he depended on messages from God and the faith to carry them out. These little animals served as steady reminders.

Paul gingerly lay on his side to find the least wounded part of his body where he could comfortably rest. He was so exhausted, however, even his wounds couldn't keep him awake. He felt the warmth of Max and Liz near him, but they knew he shouldn't be touched in his condition. "Thank you, Gabriel and Faith, for always being by my side," Paul groggily muttered as his heavy eyelids closed.

Max and Liz put their heads down and closed their eyes as well, praying for Paul's healing, and a word from the Lord on his behalf.

A rush of Wind came into the cave and Max and Liz's fur stood on end. They lifted their heads and felt an electrifying presence. The flame of the oil lamp danced off Paul's face. Liz noticed that his eyes were moving rapidly back and forth under his eyelids. His breathing was labored and his mouth was open, as if he were terrified.

"He must be havin' a dr-r-ream," Max whispered.

"It's more than a dream," came Gillamon's voice. "Break the seal."

Liz's heart jumped and she saw the Seven Seal appear on the wall. She looked at Max with her green glowing eyes. "Nigel isn't here, *mon ami.* Can you break the seal with your teeth?"

Max stared at the seal and then back at Liz. "Aye, Lass."

The flame from the oil lamp was dancing furiously now as Max walked over to the red seal with the "7" in the center. He furrowed his brow and reached his mouth over to break it with his teeth. Instantly the IAMISPHERE enveloped them and Gillamon stood there in his original white mountain goat form to greet them. The IAMISPHERE was the place that captured the Maker's view of time. Past, present, and future were seen all at once, depicted in swirling panels of scenes across time. The Order of the Seven were allowed to use this portal to revisit past moments in time, or for visions as the Maker deemed necessary for their missions. Dark panels were portals to the future, and the animals had never been allowed to enter those scenes. Sometimes they came here to simply review or learn about points in history. Other times they actually would step into the scene of history they needed to revisit. They could only enter the IAMISPHERE by breaking a Seven Seal that would appear on paper or objects, as it had appeared tonight on Paul's wall. Nigel usually nibbled the seal for the team, but without him here Max had done the honors.

Gillamon smiled at them with his warm, blue eyes. "Welcome. You two will be witness to what Paul is experiencing. He will never be able to write or speak about what he sees, but you will understand. He has been taken up to heaven for this vision. Neither of you will be able to speak, for what you see is in the realm of paradise."

The panels swirled with images and names and titles for Jesus. Max and Liz could hardly breathe, given the holiness and power of the moment. One center pane suddenly came into view. Paul was encased in light and stood before Jesus, who sat on his throne at the right hand of God. Thousands of angels hovered around the throne. Unspeakable riches filled every visible inch of space. Omniscience and omnipotence filled the air around them. Fierce, undeniable love was the heavenly oxygen Paul inhaled.

233

Suddenly Paul dropped to his knees and began praising Jesus. "King of Kings! Lord of Lords! There is no other beside you! Only begotten Son! Creator of all things! Giver and Sustainer of life! Great Physician! Wall of fire! Friend of sinners! God of all comfort! Pearl of great worth! Ark of safety! Rock of ages! Right hand of God! Higher than angels! Stronger than death! No beginning or end! The Way! The Truth! The Life! The True Vine! The Strength of Israel! The Root and Offspring of David! Bright and Morning Star! Faithful and True! Author and Finisher of our Faith! Firstborn of all Creation! Exact representation of God! Sun that enlightens! Our Peace! Captain of our Salvation! High Priest! Wonderful Counselor! Mighty God! Everlasting Father! Prince of Peace! Good Shepherd! Lord of the nations! Lion of Judah! Living Word! Righteous Servant! Lord of Hosts! Man of Sorrows! Light of the World! Son of Man! Bread of Life! The Door! Prophet, Priest, and

King! Sabbath rest! Eternal spirit! Ancient of Days! Messiah! Savior! Spotless Lamb of God! THE GREAT I AM!"

Jesus reached out his hand and touched Paul's head. Paul was now weeping in ecstasy. "You can do all things through me. I will strengthen you every step of the way."

Paul lifted his gaze and locked eyes with Jesus. He felt as if he would die from the power and exquisite love emanating from those piercing green eyes. Jesus smiled and nodded. "It is time. Remember what you see here to steel yourself for your mission. But to keep you from pride . . ." Jesus touched Paul's chest and light exploded the vision.

Instantly, Max and Liz were back on Paul's bed, and Paul was lying there next to them, covered in sweat. Their hearts were beating out of their chests and they couldn't speak. But Paul's face was now serene.

Liz looked at Max and they shared a moment of wonder and awe. She reached her dainty paw to softly touch Paul's chest and couldn't believe what she saw.

234

Paul's body still bore scars, but he was completely healed from his wounds—save the new thorn he had just received in heaven.

WHO ARE THESE PEOPLE?

Nigel flew high above the road as Barnabas made his way toward the entrance to Antioch. "Ah, there he is, my dear," he said to Naomi, pointing to the much beloved man known as "Son of Encouragement." Nigel scanned the breathtaking city below them. "And here we are! Antioch!"

"It sure is a large city," Naomi replied.

"Third largest city in the Roman Empire, behind Rome and Alexandria, with half a million residents," Nigel explained. "Antioch has a fascinating history as well as a simply dastardly culture. Would you care for me to elaborate, my dear?"

Naomi soared over a river that flowed into Antioch. She grinned, knowing that Nigel was dying to share his vast knowledge with her. "Of course, Nigel!"

"Splendid," Nigel happily replied, straightening his spectacles. "Below is the Orontes River. Antioch is fifteen miles upriver from the Mediterranean Sea, so naturally it is a huge trading city with the world, even with distant *China*. Caravans of camels bring silk, spices, and other exotic goods here. The city is filled with Romans, Persians, Indians, and even *Chinese*, whom I find utterly fascinating. I haven't gotten the knack of their language, I'm afraid." Nigel paused for a moment as he recalled listening to two Chinese men in the street. He shook his head, remembering how he was at a complete loss to understand them.

"Now where was I? Oh yes, Antioch was founded as a Hellenistic city (of Greek culture) in 300 BC by Seleucus Nicator. He was a general for Alexander the Great and was awarded the Syrian territory after Alexander's death. He named the city after his father, Antiochus. It's known as 'Antioch the Beautiful' or 'Antioch of Syria' to distinguish it from the fifteen other Antiochs, you know," Nigel explained, assuming that Naomi would of course be familiar with these other cities. The pigeon politely listened to Nigel's lecture, trying to keep up with his vast knowledge of history, geography, and Roman architecture. She grinned. How in the world a tiny British mouse knew so much was beyond her.

"If you look closely you can see that Antioch is divided into four quarters, each with its own wall, while the entire city is surrounded by a common wall. It's filled with grand mansions, temples, theaters, racecourses, aqueducts, baths, et cetera, et cetera, et cetera," related Nigel, spinning his paw. "They take chariot racing so seriously here that the rivalry between the blue and green chariot teams sometimes ends in riots and death. I hear the green team even had Caligula wearing their colors!"

"Caligula? The crazy emperor?" Naomi asked. "Do you think the blue team was behind his assassination?"

"I wouldn't put it past them, my dear!" Nigel quipped. "Such is the passion here in Antioch for their teams. No doubt the blue and green teams will seek the favor of the new emperor Claudius now. But Antioch also has a passion for art. Some of the world's finest mosaics adorn the buildings here. And would you believe that the wealthy citizens of Antioch even have swimming pools, indoor plumbing, and *heat* in their homes? Extraordinary!" Nigel enthused. Naomi wondered what *plumbing* was. They were flying along the four-mile-long main street. "Herod the Great used polished stones to pave this street, and lined it with columns, trees, and fountains."

"Ooooh, fountains!" Naomi cheered. "My favorite!"

"I'm sure you'll have a grand time gathering there with friends."

Nigel chuckled at the predictable life of a pigeon. "Ah, now there in the distance, five miles outside the city is the Temple of Daphne, amidst the laurel grove."

"Who is Daphne?" Naomi asked, doing a flyover of the huge hippodrome. A chariot race was in progress.

"The subject of yet another mythological tale, typical of absurd human fantasy," Nigel scoffed, preening his whiskers. "The story goes that Daphne was a beautiful nymph who captured the heart of the god Apollo. He mercilessly chased her and the poor girl prayed for safety, so she was turned into a laurel bush. The pagans worship and offer despicable sacrifices to Daphne and Apollo, but I very much doubt a laurelized nymph and a make-believe god offer much hope. Despite its grandeur, Antioch is such a wretched, immoral place."

"What? Who *are* these people?" Naomi wanted to know. "And why is Barnabas coming here?"

"I'm glad you asked, for here is the ray of hope for our vile little city below," Nigel enthused. "A small population of Jews have long lived here, enjoying the rights of Roman citizenship, and have developed a large following among the Greeks. After Stephen's tragic death and Saul's terrible persecution, many believers fled Jerusalem and came here. At first they only spoke with their fellow Jews about Jesus. But then other believers from Cyprus and Cyrene arrived and started sharing Jesus with Greeks. I'm thrilled to report that many pagans have now become believers! So, when the Jerusalem church got wind of this, they decided to send Barnabas here to check on things."

"So Jesus has followers here in Antioch? That's wonderful news!" Naomi rejoiced.

"Indeed. Light is once again shining out of a dark place, just as it did in Egypt," Nigel noted. He spied Barnabas talking with a group of men outside the home of a wealthy family. They appeared to be welcoming him with open arms. "If you would be so kind, please deliver me to the fountain outside that dwelling." Naomi came in for a landing and Nigel hurriedly jumped off, following Barnabas inside.

"You're just in time, Barnabas! Please, join us at the table, and take the seat of honor," a man with dark skin encouraged, leading him to

237

the table filled with abundant food. He clapped his hands for a basin of water to be brought over. "I am Simon, from Cyrene."

"Thank you, Simon," Barnabas said with a smile, scanning the faces of Jews and Gentiles from all walks of life gathered around this feast. They eagerly welcomed him. He immediately marveled at the rightness of seeing believers of all races coming together for fellowship. He then realized who Simon was as he studied the man who was washing his feet. "Simon from Cyrene? Are you the man who carried Jesus' cross?"

Simon nodded humbly, wiping Barnabas's feet with a towel. "It was my privilege to do that for our Lord. Of course, I had no idea what was really happening when the Roman centurion told me to carry his cross. Jesus was so weak from the scourging that he couldn't carry that much weight. I didn't realize at that time I was being chosen for a great honor."

"Yes, and father was quite shaken when we finally met back up with him. I'm his son, Rufus," a young man said, extending a warm pat of greeting on Barnabas's back. He plopped down at the table and popped a grape into his mouth. "My brother Alexander and I were terrified by the Roman soldiers. I'll never forget that day. I was just a boy. I remember being so sad about the kind man they were crucifying."

"But now we can celebrate our risen Lord!" Simon exclaimed with a broad smile, handing the basin of water to a servant. "And he has come to Antioch! We are growing so fast here, Barnabas. The people are hungry for the truth of Jesus and are responding in droves."

"Tell us, what is the word from Jerusalem?" Rufus asked him.

"This good news has reached the ear of the church in Jerusalem. They send their blessings and asked me to come see how you are getting along," Barnabas offered. "I am here to serve with you and help in any way I can."

"God be praised!" Simon cheered. "My friend, we will keep you busy, I assure you. We need help with solid preaching to the intellectuals, and assistance with helping our widows and orphans here in Antioch just as they've done in Jerusalem."

Nigel sat high up on a windowsill and listened to all the needs of this infant movement of believers here in Antioch. He remembered Peter and Cornelius and the enthusiasm of those in Caesarea to spread

238

the gospel. He smiled as he recalled Al's words. "Jews and Gents." The mouse thought to himself, *With so large a Gentile and Jewish population here, they need someone with a double background who understands the cultures of both. They need someone who is brave and skilled in argument to speak intelligently to such a pagan population, and who will not easily back down. They need someone who is 'street-wise' in such a modern city. Barnabas can of course help with the charity work, but they need someone else to lead the preaching charge here.* Suddenly it dawned on the little mouse. *By Jove, they need Paul!*

Max and Liz sat outside with Paul, who was sewing a new tent for a customer. It was a warm day, and the sunshine provided the light Paul needed to work with his needle and thread. Paul wore a sleeveless tunic and sweat dripped down his face. He picked up a cloth and wiped it away.

239

Suddenly a shadow passed overhead. Liz looked up and smiled. She turned to Max and whispered, "Nigel is here!" Naomi made another pass and Nigel waved.

Max looked straight ahead and saw a man walking up the road toward them. "Aye, an' so be Barnabas!" He stood, wagging his tail and giving a single bark of welcome.

Paul looked up to see what had gotten the dog's attention. "What is it, Boy?" As he squinted, he slowly recognized his old friend Barnabas. He smiled and set his tent-making project aside. Barnabas lifted a hand in greeting as he neared them. "I don't believe it," Paul said and smiled as he stood to greet his long-lost friend.

"I've looked everywhere for you, my friend!" Barnabas exclaimed, walking up to give Paul a big bear hug. "Finally, I found you!"

Paul leaned back and smiled, gripping forearms with Barnabas. "Well, I'm glad you have! Tell me you haven't been wandering around Tarsus for seven years, though. I was beginning to think I had long been forgotten."

"Never could I forget you, my brother." Barnabas frowned as he suddenly spied the scars all over Paul's arms and shoulders. "What has happened to you?"

"The Jewish leaders here in Tarsus were none too pleased with my revolutionary claim of Jesus as Messiah," Paul explained with a sad smile. "I'm proud to suffer for my Lord. I haven't stopped talking of him, Barnabas. I talk to Jews and Gentiles—whomever I can get to listen. They'll have to kill me before I stop preaching Jesus."

Barnabas was stunned at the clear evidence of suffering and persecution Paul had experienced. But he smiled broadly and put his hand on Paul's shoulder. "I know Jesus is proud of you, Paul. I know *I* am. And I'm glad you are so eager to preach. That's why I've come. Antioch needs you."

Paul's eyes widened. "Antioch? Has Jerusalem approved preaching to Gentiles?"

"There's much I need to tell you about, beginning with Caesarea," Barnabas shared.

Together he and Paul walked into Paul's cave to have a long discussion about all that had transpired with Peter and Cornelius, Peter's report to the Jerusalem leaders about spreading the gospel to Gentiles, the growth of the church in Judea, Galilee, and Samaria, and the explosion of the gospel in Antioch.

Nigel scurried up to Max and Liz. "Hello, my friends! I bring exciting news!" He kissed Liz's extended paw.

Liz brightened with seeing their mouse friend. *"Bonjour,* Nigel! Do tell us everything!"

"Aye, looks like Barnabas has news for Paul," Max added.

Nigel tucked his paws behind his back and lifted his chin in delight. "I'm pleased to report that the time has finally come. Paul is to accompany Barnabas back to Antioch to begin leading the new church there. Gentiles are flocking to the Antioch believers, and they simply must have a strong leader such as Paul."

"Bon! We knew the time was near," Liz exclaimed. "Did Jerusalem tell Barnabas to come get Paul?"

"Not exactly," Nigel said with a grin, twirling some of his whiskers. "But he did get help from a certain learned mouse."

Max grinned widely, showing his white teeth. "Wha' did ye do then, Mousie?"

240

"Oh, I simply sent him a note from an anonymous believer, detailing the exact needs of the Antioch church. I asked if he could please think of *anyone* who was an intellectual, well- schooled, a gifted preacher and scholar, a man with determination and grit, unafraid to face conflict and danger, and who could speak Hebrew, Greek, and Latin."

"In other words, you wrote out Paul's résumé but left off his name, no?" Liz asked with a grin.

"Precisely," Nigel said with a chuckle. "Of course, our dear Barnabas didn't truly need my help, as it became clear to him very quickly that the Antioch post called for someone with greater qualifications than he possessed. He knew Paul was the perfect man for the job. I just helped bring him to mind a little sooner, perhaps. How did you know Paul's time had come?"

Max and Liz shared a knowing grin. "Let's jest say, heaven made it loud an' clear. Paul had a vision an' Gillamon invited us ta see it in the IAMISPHERE."

241

"Max broke the Seven Seal," Liz reported. "Nigel, we were honored to see Paul stand before Jesus. Jesus told Paul it was time."

Nigel's eyes widened. "Brilliant! Well, I certainly hope Paul keeps his head about him. Most men would be quite proud to have such a stellar commissioning service by Jesus himself."

"Aye, that's why Paul were given wha' he calls 'a thorn in his flesh' then," Max explained. "He's asked the Maker thr-r-ree times ta r-r-remove it, but the Maker told him his gr-r-race were enough ta help him."

"Jesus told Paul he would give him the strength he needed for all things," Liz added.

"Splendid. Well, that's good to hear," Nigel said. "I suspect that Paul is going to need all the strength he can muster."

"It makes complete sense that the Greek believers here do not refer to Jesus as the Jewish Messiah," Liz observed as the huge gathering of believers filed out of the large home after Sunday service. *"Messiah* has long been understood as a Jewish term for the Jewish people. The

Gentiles better understand him as their anointed Savior and Lord, calling him *Christos.*"

"Ergo, these believers observe 'the Lord's day' on the day of Jesus' resurrection," Nigel added. "They worship on Sunday rather than the Jewish Sabbath of Saturday."

"It's like the Way be findin' its own identity then," Max suggested. "It's no longer jest a Jewish gr-r-roup anymore. Even Paul be callin' Jesus 'Chr-r-rist' now."

Paul and Barnabas filed out of the house, bidding everyone good-bye. People were smiling, hugging, and enjoying one another's company. The love and joy they shared among themselves was evident to outsiders.

"Twenty new believers in Christ just today," Paul exclaimed happily, gripping Barnabas's arm. "That makes more than one hundred new believers this week alone! Just think, Barnabas, if we keep up this pace, we'll have a major church established here in Antioch in no time." He was ecstatic to finally be preaching regularly, and to crowds who welcomed his message.

Barnabas smiled and patted Paul on the back. "The Lord knew what he was doing when he chose you for this assignment, Paul. There is no one more perfectly suited to reach the Gentiles than you."

A group of Greeks were standing behind Paul and Barnabas, listening to their conversation. They had watched all the people come out of the house, and knew they regularly gathered there.

"Who are these people?" one man asked.

"They are the people who are always talking about Jesus the Christos," a woman answered.

"You know, Christ-people," another man replied.

"Christians?" another woman asked. "Is that what you call them?"

The other man nodded and shrugged his shoulders. "Yes, that sounds right. Christians."

Paul and Barnabas smiled as they overheard the people talking about them. "'Christians,'" Paul whispered with raised eyebrows. "I like it."

Barnabas grinned. "It has a nice ring to it, doesn't it?"

"I believe our Greek brothers and sisters have awarded us a brand new title," Paul pointed out with a pleased expression.

Max, Liz, and Nigel watched as Paul and Barnabas turned to go introduce themselves to the group of Greeks who had given the followers of the Way a new name.

"*C'est magnifique!*" Liz exclaimed. "*Christians!* I love this name."

"Aye, I think Jesus will be glad with the lads an' lassies usin' his title like that," Max echoed.

Nigel was drawing in the dirt, spelling out 'Christ' in Greek letters. He clapped his paws once in discovery. "Brilliant! Do you remember our discussion with Gillamon long ago when we were in Alexandria, assisting with writing the Greek Scriptures called the *Septuagint?* He told us the Messiah would someday be called 'Christ.' And if you recall, X—Chi—in the Greek alphabet is the first letter in *Christos.*"

Max and Liz looked over Nigel's shoulder and saw what he had drawn:

243

ΧΡΙΣΤΟΣ

"X marks the spot!" Max remembered. "The Gr-r-reeks know Jesus by the X."

"Not just the Greeks, but now the entire world," Liz added. "X isn't just Chi in the Greek alphabet, it's the symbol of the cross."

Max nodded. "Aye, somehow when ye think aboot Jesus with the symbol of the cr-r-ross, it doesn't seem like such a hor-r-rible thing anymore. When ye think aboot wha' it means, it almost seems like somethin' . . . good."

Nigel tapped a finger thoughtfully on his chin. "Have you noticed how we keep witnessing things changing and taking on new meaning when Jesus is involved?"

"*Oui, mon ami,*" Liz agreed. "People like Saul, places like Antioch, words like Christ, and now even symbols like the cross."

"And perhaps, statues," Nigel added. "All by a factor of X."

HEARTACHE AND JAILBREAK

"They've taken James!" cried Rhoda. The servant barreled into the house belonging to Mark's mother, Mary. Rhoda was out of breath, having run all the way from the temple area.

Peter, John, Mark, Paul, and Barnabas rose to their feet in alarm. "Taken him? Where?" Peter demanded.

Rhoda rested her hand on her stomach to catch her breath. "Herod ordered the arrest of James and some of our fellow believers, and they've been carried off to the Antonia Fortress for trial. Word is spreading that they are going to kill James!"

John's eyes grew wide with fear and anguish. *Kill my brother? I must get down there!*

Paul, with a furrowed brow, put his hand on John's arm. "If Herod Agrippa is on the warpath, he might seek to round up more leaders of the Jerusalem church. I would caution you against going, John."

"I can't just sit here!" John protested, grabbing his cloak. He ran out the door.

"I'll go with him," Peter said. "I hear you, Paul, but I need to be with John should the worst happen."

"Then we will pray for your safety," Paul promised.

"I'm glad you've come to Jerusalem," Peter said, hurriedly putting on his cloak. "I know the Antioch church sent you and Barnabas with money to help us through the famine, but I think we most need your prayers."

Paul nodded as Peter turned and ran after John. "Our brothers need us. Let's get on our knees."

The group of men and women assembled there immediately began to pray. Kate, Nigel, and Al looked at one another in distress. Max and Liz had stayed behind in Antioch while Paul and Barnabas made this short trip to Jerusalem.

"Oh dear, I think we best go and see what is happening," Nigel suggested.

Al put his paws up to his mouth in fear. "I don't handle violence well."

Nigel put his paw on the scaredy cat's arm. "They might need us, old boy. Buck up now!"

Al gulped and nodded. "Aye, Mousie. I'll go then."

"I'll stay here an' pray with the group," Kate offered. "An' I'll be prayin' for ye two ta know wha' ta do."

"Right!" Nigel replied. "To the Fortress!"

245

✕⊃

Jerusalem was filling with crowds, as the Passover was about to begin. Nigel rode on Al's back as Al darted through and around the thousands of people in the street. When they reached the courtyard where James and the others were taken for trial they met a sea of people shouting and shoving their way toward them. Al stopped and Nigel studied what was happening. James was in chains and being escorted by four Roman guards through the streets. He was being led outside the city.

"He deserves to die!" shouted some in the crowd. "These Christians think they can take over our Passover and make it their own!"

"We're too late!" Nigel lamented. "They're leading James to his death!"

Al suddenly saw Peter and John being carried along with the rioting crowd. "There be Peter and John!" He took off after them, trying to keep from getting stepped on.

As they reached the city gate, Peter held John back and let the crowds pass them by. "There's nothing we can do for him now. Stay here with me."

John was weeping as he looked on the scene with horror. An executioner wore a black mask over his face and stood waiting by a wooden block, sword in hand. The Roman soldiers made James kneel and place his head on the block. He didn't resist them but calmly did as they ordered. The executioner lifted his arms high and John quickly turned his gaze away as the sword came down and found its mark.

Cheers arose from the crowd to see Roman justice carried out. The Roman soldiers took note of the response of the crowd. A group of fellow believers quickly surrounded James's body and carefully wrapped it for burial. Peter supported John with his arm tightly around the man's shoulder. "Come, before this mob grabs us as well. Let's not allow them more bloodshed today."

Nigel and Al also had looked away as James was beheaded, but now Nigel took note of all that was going on. "Jesus told James and John that they would indeed drink from the cup of his suffering when they asked to sit on either side of him," Nigel remembered with a heavy heart. "So one Son of Thunder was the first disciple to die."

Al ducked into the shadows as two Roman soldiers walked by. "Herod wanted a report, so let's get to his palace," one soldier said with a smile. "I think he got what he was after."

"Those Roman laddies seem glad aboot all o' this." Al's lip trembled with sadness but he suddenly recognized two of the soldiers. "Mousie, don't they look familiar?"

Nigel frowned and studied the soldiers. Suddenly his eyes widened. "Velius and Ulixes! They are the same two Romans who attended Jesus' crucifixion with Armandus." The little mouse crossed his arms. "Still doing their dirty work with glee, I see. Well, I intend to find out what they're up to next. Al, you head back to the house. I'm going to Herod's palace."

"Aye, I'll let Kate know," Al replied sadly. "John will need the lass now."

With that, Nigel went one way and Al went the other.

Weeping filled the house as Peter and John reported James's death. Paul embraced John and got one-on-one with him to offer support and prayer. Kate went over and sat next to John, trying to bring him comfort in the loss of his brother. Peter talked with Barnabas, Mark, and Jesus' brother James about the situation.

"Herod Agrippa is out to persecute the Christians in order to gain favor with the Jewish leaders," Peter explained. "They brought James up on flimsy charges of causing a riot while trying to preach. The verdict and the execution were swift."

"Herod is desperate for the approval of the people," Jesus' brother James observed with a frown. "All the Herods want to be liked. They know the people don't consider them as their true Jewish kings, so they will go to extreme measures to get their favor. Herod the Great built the Jews a magnificent temple."

"And now the Jews want Herod Agrippa to tear down the Church," Barnabas said, shaking his head.

The group sat quietly for a while and entered into a time of prayer. They once again felt the grip of persecution tightening around them, but this time it wasn't Saul leading the charge. It was the grandson of Herod the Great.

The next morning found Peter pacing around the outer courtyard of the house. He had hardly slept all night. Everyone was grieving over James, but more was bothering Peter. As Mark stepped outside to see where Peter was, Al slipped out the door to listen in on their conversation.

"I'm going back to see about the release of the other brothers they've locked up," Peter told Mark determinedly, grabbing his cloak.

"But Peter . . ." Mark began to object.

"I have to go to their aid," Peter interrupted. "If the Lord deems this the right time for me to die like James, so be it. If not, well, perhaps I can help our brothers. But you stay here. Tell the others."

Peter left Mark standing there and headed down the outside stair-well. Mark put his hands on his hips and frowned. After a moment he slipped back inside the house. Al sat there, torn whether he should fol-low Peter. He was scared to death with what was happening.

Suddenly Nigel scurried over to where Al sat. "Dreadful news!"

Al jumped and his face grew fearful. "What news, Mousie?"

"When Velius and Ulixes reported to Herod that executing James met with approval among the Jews, Herod told them to seize Peter also!" Nigel reported. His voice turned sarcastic over the hypocrisy of the situation. "But that scoundrel will carry out his despicable plan *after* the religious festival. They plan to keep Peter in jail and bring him to trial after Passover, which is of course the *lawful* thing to do."

Al grabbed Nigel and held him up to his face. "Mousie! Peter jest left! He were goin' to go right to the Fortress to help the poor laddies still stuck in there!"

Nigel wriggled to get his paws out from Al's embrace. "Peter took the bait! Herod thought he could lure the church leaders to come to their fellow believers' aid."

"So what do we do now?" Al cried. "We can't jest let the bad laddies take Peter!"

"I suggest we go after him," Nigel said with a balled fist in the air. "Would you be so kind as to place me on your back?"

"Aye," Al replied, putting Nigel onto his shoulder. "Peter needs us." Once Nigel was in place, he took hold of Al's fur and Al took off run-ning down the stairs.

They arrived just as Velius and Ulixes grabbed Peter. "Come on, Christian! If you insist on following the path your Christ took, Herod is more than happy to help you on your way," Ulixes sneered.

Peter resisted the men as they struggled to put the shackles on his wrists. "What are the charges?" Peter shouted.

Velius and Ulixes looked at one another. "Interfering with Roman justice. We know you are the ringleader who organized stealing the body of Jesus," Velius responded sarcastically.

"But no one will be able to get to you and steal *you* away like last time," Ulixes added. "Four squads of four soldiers each will be watching you at all times."

Peter's eyes grew wide and he stumbled as the Roman soldiers roughly handled him. They each grabbed an arm and led Peter away to the Antonia Fortress.

"This is intolerable! These men saw the angels at the tomb!" Nigel fumed, jumping off Al's back. "They saw the stone rolled away and Jesus' body gone. They were told to lie about falling asleep at the tomb and the disciples stealing Jesus' body!"

"Maybe they jest started believin' their own lies," guessed Al. "But Mousie, somethin' tells me I got to go with Peter."

"I must say I am quite taken aback by this surge of bravery, old boy!" Nigel exclaimed. "But you've been in jail before. And you had lions to deal with as you guarded Daniel. I'm sure you can handle these Romans."

249

"Aye, I dunno what's come over me then," Al said with a gulp. "I'm still scared but Max isn't here so I gots to be the brave one. Plus, last time Peter were in jail, he didn't stay there long. Clarie and the angel showed up."

"Hear, hear! You can do it!" Nigel cheered, hitting Al in the leg with his tiny fist. "And right you are. Perhaps Peter shall have another angelic jailbreak! I shall go tell Kate what is happening and check in on you back at the Fortress."

◁

Al stood near the iron gate leading into the Antonia Fortress, watching for the changing of the guard that took place every three hours. Suddenly he heard a new squad of four soldiers approach the gate to relieve the other four soldiers inside. He swallowed hard, and his whiskers were quivering with fear. *I must be daft,* he thought as he fell in line behind the soldiers as they opened the gate. He proceeded to trot down the corridor behind them. The sound of their metal-soled shoes on the stone echoed loudly. They came to the first Roman soldier guarding the corridor. One new soldier traded places with him while the other three soldiers proceeded to Peter's cell.

A soldier was posted outside the door to the cell and Peter sat between two Roman guards inside, one chained to either side of him. As the soldiers busied themselves with the changeover, Al slipped past them and into the cell. He hadn't thought far enough ahead to know if he should let Peter and the soldiers see him or not. So for now, he hid over in a dark corner behind a bale of hay, which was used to line the floor of the cell. Al peeked around the hay and saw Peter lift his heavily chained arms to take a drink of water. *Well, at least I be here. What I'm supposed to do exactly I dunno. But I be here, Peter lad.*

In the house where the Jerusalem church often met, believers had gathered to mourn for James and to wait out this new wave of persecution. They brought word of Peter's arrest and that he was in prison. The women made food and kept everyone as comfortable as possible.

"I knew I shouldn't have let him go by himself!" Mark spat, angry at himself.

Barnabas put his hand on Mark's shoulder. "Listen, little cousin, Herod was going to find and arrest Peter no matter if you were there or not. There's nothing you could have done. And if Herod's soldiers came here looking for him, we could all be in jail right now. It may still come to that."

"Which is why we need to pray continually for Peter and this situation," Paul interjected. "The Lord can release Peter as he did before, but we must pray against this darkness."

Kate's eyes welled up with tears as she heard the news. She had not left John's side until Nigel arrived. "They've got Peter, too? Oh, Nigel, I jest can't take it if we lose him *an'* James!"

"We must keep the faith, my dear," Nigel consoled her. "You stay at your post with John and I shall keep you informed. And chin up. Our fearless feline is with him."

Kate smiled at the thought of Al's surprising bravery. "Liz would be so proud."

Nigel preened his whiskers. "Indeed. He wasn't told to go to the jail, but is facing the unknown with remarkable nerve. I daresay the Holy Spirit is already doing the impossible!"

Al jumped awake as he heard the creak of the iron door lock for the 3:00 a.m. changing of the guard. He rubbed his eyes and saw that Ulixes and Velius were the two guards coming into the cell to relieve the soldiers chained to Peter. Peter yawned. He had been in a deep sleep.

"Looks like you're not too worried, Christian," Velius teased Peter as he clamped the shackle on his own wrist and jingled the short chain that attached to Peter.

"You should be. Your trial is tomorrow," Ulixes informed him. "And you know how your friends' trials went."

Peter looked at the ruthless Roman soldiers. "My God will judge what is right."

251

"Ha! Like he did for your Jesus? Or for James?" Ulixes mocked. "Well, so far it seems your God has been on Rome's side in court."

"Yes, looks like we'll be busy with carrying out more Roman justice on you tomorrow," Velius added. "Sleep well with that in your head, Christian."

Peter ignored them and shut his eyes, lying back down. The two Roman guards rested their heads back on the stone wall. It wasn't long before they were all sound asleep. All except for Al. He was worried sick. *Why did I think I could do anythin' in here? Rome be bigger than this kitty.*

"Yes, but not bigger than God," came a whisper behind Al.

Al turned around quickly and saw a beautiful blue butterfly hovering over him. It landed on his nose. "Time for you to get to work."

"Clarie? Ye be mighty small then. How're ye supposed to help Peter out o' here dressed like that?" Al asked, looking at her with crossed eyes.

She moved her wings up and down. "I'm not going to. *You* are, with an angel's help of course. Show me your claws."

Al held up his right paw and made his claws stick out. "Don't tell me

I got to stick 'em in those soldiers! They be scarier than lion beasties!"

Clarie studied his claws and landed on his "pointer" claw. "This one will do. You're going to pick the locks on Peter's wrists."

Al's eyes widened as he studied his paw. "With me claw? Lass, I hate to tell ye this, but me claws aren't as strong as iron shackles then!"

"Normally, you're right," Clarie replied with her sweet butterfly smile. "But you've earned a new skill with your bravery. Your pointer claw will become like iron to pick locks."

A goofy grin appeared on Al's face as Clarie flittered to land on his head. He slowly tiptoed over to where Peter lay sleeping between the two guards. His paw shook nervously as he sprung his pointer claw and slowly lowered it to the lock on Peter's left wrist. He stuck his tongue out as he dug around in the lock until he felt something move.

Just then Velius snorted a loud snort and Al jumped.

"You're doing fine, Al. Keep going," Clarie whispered.

Al nodded and tiptoed over to Peter's right wrist, sticking his pointer claw into the other lock. As soon as he felt the lock click, a bright light shone in the cell and lit up the walls with sparkling glory. Al fell back onto the stone floor in fear as an angel appeared.

The angel nodded with a smile at Al before striking Peter on the side to wake him up. "Quick, get up!" he instructed him, and the chains fell off Peter's wrists.

Al held up his paw and looked at it in awe. "Iron claws," he whispered to himself.

Peter opened his eyes but wore a dazed and confused look on his face. He wrinkled his forehead and sat up, lifting his hands to see the shackles on the floor next to him. He slowly rubbed his wrists as he looked at the two guards, who stayed sound asleep. He saw Al sitting there and displayed a slight smile, but said nothing.

"Put on your clothes and sandals," the angel instructed. "Wrap your cloak around you and follow me."

Peter stood and did as the angel instructed, getting dressed while Al trotted out of the cell. Clarie flew above him and landed on the sleeping guard outside the cell. "Sleeping like a baby," she whispered. Let's check on the other guard."

Al trotted down the corridor as Clarie flew along and there they found Nigel reciting Plato to the fourth sleeping guard. The little mouse winked and gave Al a salute but kept up his monologue so as not to break the hypnotic trance. Nigel paced back and forth, lifting his paw for emphasis. *"Music is a moral law. It gives soul to the universe, wings to the mind, flight to the imagination, and charm and gaiety to life and to everything."*

The angel and Peter walked right by them and out toward the iron gate that led to the city. Al trotted along behind them. "It don't look like Peter knows what be really happenin'," Al whispered to Clarie. "He looks like he's sleep walkin'."

"He thinks he is seeing a vision," Clarie replied, flitting along above.

Suddenly the iron gate opened for them by itself, and they walked right on through. When they had walked the length of one street, the angel suddenly left Peter alone in the darkened street. Peter came to himself and shook his head. "Now I know that it is really true!" he said as he leaned against a wall and let go a relieved breath. "The Lord sent his angel to rescue me from Herod's power and from everything the Jewish people expected to happen." Peter suddenly felt Al rubbing up against his legs. A blue butterfly flew by his head. He reached down and picked Al up. "How did you get here, Ari?"

"Had to break ye out o' jail, lad," Al meowed. *"Jest call me 'Iron Claw Al!'"*

"Let's get back to Mary's house to let them know I'm free," Peter said, holding the meowing cat close to his chest and looking both ways in the street. The sun would be rising soon. "Then we've got to get out of Jerusalem before Herod gets any more ideas."

253

JUSTICE

eter's breath rose like mist in the cool spring morning air as he climbed the outer staircase leading to Mary's house. He placed Al on the ground and carefully looked around the outer courtyard before going to the door. When he tried to open the door he found it locked. "They must be fearful of the Romans coming here," he whispered to Al. He looked around again to make sure no one was watching him. "We have to be quiet."

Peter softly knocked at the outer entrance, grimacing as the sound seemed as loud as thunder. After a moment he heard Rhoda's voice on the other side of the door. "Wh-wh-who's there?" she asked fearfully.

"It's me, Peter!" he answered in a hoarse whisper.

Rhoda's eyes lit up when she recognized Peter's voice. Without opening the door, she ran back to some of the others who were awake. "Peter is at the door!"

"You're out of your mind," one of the men said wearily. He and some of the others had taken the fourth watch of the night to pray. Everyone was exhausted from keeping up the unending prayer vigil for Peter.

Rhoda leaned over and pointed back to the door. "I'm telling you, it's Peter! It's his voice!"

"It must be his angel," another of the men offered up as an explanation.

"His angel?" Kate growled. *"Ye believe a guardian angel appears after someone dies but I never heard such a loud angel, an' trust me lads, I've seen a lot of angels in me lifetime!"*

Peter kept on knocking. Kate looked around and frowned at the tired, fearful humans. *"Wha's wrong with ye!"* she barked, waking John. *"That's the sound of wha' ye been prayin' for all night! Are ye not goin' ta open the door ta yer answer then?!"* She ran over and nudged John, who rose to his feet, along with Mark, Paul, and Barnabas. James had gone back to his house to hold a prayer vigil with another group of believers.

Mark ran to the door and quickly opened it with the others bunched up behind him. "Peter! It *is* you!"

Kate and Al saw each other and rolled their eyes. *"Daft humans!"* she mouthed. Al nodded.

Peter quickly held up his hands for them to be quiet. "Shhhh! There's no time. I'm not coming in. Listen, the Lord sent an angel to break me out of prison. My chains just fell off and I followed the angel past the guards and out to the street," Peter recounted.

Al held up his iron claw to Kate, pointing to it excitedly with his other paw. He wore a huge goofy grin. Kate cocked her head to the side and grinned back, wondering what Al had done.

"Praise God!" Paul exclaimed behind Mark. The others started hugging one another and murmuring excitedly.

Peter looked to see who was there at the door and noticed James was missing. "Tell James and the other brothers and sisters about this," Peter said. "I'm leaving Jerusalem. I'll send word to you as soon as I can."

Al saluted Kate and turned to trot off behind Peter, who hurried down the stairs. Together they made their way down the darkened streets as a faint ribbon of pink appeared in the sky. Sunrise was coming and they had to get out of town before all hell broke loose in the Fortress.

Nigel sat in a corner of the prison cell, waiting to see everything unfold. Clarie fluttered her wings next to him.

255

"I daresay, these two scoundrels are in for a rude awakening," Nigel whispered, looking at Velius and Ulixes. "This time they really *were* asleep at their post, unlike that rubbish they claimed about sleeping while guarding Jesus' tomb."

"Yes, and *this* time they'll suffer the real consequences of doing so," Clarie replied. She took off and started flying around Ulixes's face, bothering him to wake him up.

Ulixes swatted at her with his eyes closed. He subconsciously realized that he was able to raise his arm up a little too freely. He opened his eyes with a start and saw that Peter was gone. Instantly he panicked and his heart tried to race out of his chest. "Velius! Where's the prisoner?!"

Velius sat up in a stupor and looked around the room. He quickly grabbed the chains that had been attached to Peter and held them up in disbelief. "How could this be?" he screamed.

Both the soldiers got to their feet and ran to the cell door, finding it securely locked. "Open the door!" Ulixes shouted at the sleeping soldier outside the cell. "You fool! How did you let the prisoner escape?!"

The third soldier shook his head and scrambled to his feet. He put his hand on his hip and felt the key ring attached securely to his loin belt. His eyes grew wide as he saw Ulixes and Velius grabbing the bars of the cell door from the inside. "Where is the prisoner? I haven't opened this door!"

The fourth soldier, posted down the corridor, came running up behind them, along with the four soldiers for the 6:00 a.m. changing of the guard. Everyone started yelling and screaming, each one trying to blame someone else for Peter's escape. No one claimed responsibility. Finally a centurion came running down the corridor to see what all the commotion was about. As Ulixes, Velius, and the other two soldiers shouted blame, the centurion ordered them all into the cell, grabbing the key ring and locking them inside.

"The prisoner is missing and you four were on guard!" the centurion shouted. "You are ALL responsible!" He turned to the new squad of soldiers. "Guard these men with your lives while I report to Herod." He looked back to the now imprisoned Roman soldiers who clustered around the cell door in fear. "Knowing Herod, he'll order their immediate execution for sleeping on their watch and allowing the prisoner to escape."

"NO! PLEASE!" Ulixes and Velius screamed.

"I can't help but be astounded at how the tables are now turned on these two men who so cruelly mocked and tortured Jesus. Once again David was spot on in his psalm," Nigel said, clucking his tongue and shaking his head. "*Evil will slay the wicked; the foes of the righteous will be condemned.*"

Clarie nodded. "What a pity evil men arrogantly think their sins will never catch up with them. When the Enemy has used them for his purposes, he inevitably turns around and destroys them."

"Indeed," Nigel agreed with a frown. "And if the Enemy doesn't destroy them, the Maker himself will see to justice. They were given a chance to believe and turn to Jesus. They would have been forgiven for everything." He cleared his throat and lifted a paw in the direction of the door. "Shall we depart, my dear?"

257

"Yes, we must sadly leave these men to their fate," Clarie replied, lifting off to fly through the cell door.

Nigel scurried along behind her. They passed squads of soldiers looking everywhere for Peter. "Search all you wish, old chaps. Your prisoner has cracked on."

FOUR MONTHS LATER: AUGUST 1, AD 44

The balmy sea breeze gently blew the gauzy white curtains of Herod's palace in Caesarea. Herod Agrippa breathed in the salt air while he held out his arms for his servants to dress him. He saw the early morning stars begin to fade with the approaching sunrise.

"HURRY! The sun will rise soon and I want my entrance to be spectacular!" he snapped.

"Yes, my liege," the servants fearfully replied as they fiddled with pulling the heavy silver robe over the layers of fat around the rotund king. Herod had this robe made just for this occasion honoring Caesar's birthday.

"Such a waste of perfectly good cloth to adorn such a perfectly loathsome creature," Nigel muttered to himself with his arms crossed over his chest. He stood by a column in the open courtyard of Herod's chambers.

"The amphitheater is filled with people from Tyre and Sidon, my king," reported Blastus, Herod's court official. "From my extensive discussions with their representatives, they are eager to win back your favor. One could say they are *hungry* for it."

A wicked grin grew on Herod's slimy face and he held up his hand in a balled fist. "You see, Blastus, you must hold the vermin captive with a merciless grip. I keep their food supply in my power so they dare not defy my authority."

Blastus nodded and grinned. "Indeed, they won't make that mistake again. And how clever of you to offer them your gracious forgiveness in the middle of Caesar's birthday festival! They will see your extravagant splendor and power, backed by the authority of Rome."

258

"Exactly," Herod laughed, pointing a finger at Blastus. He then slapped away the hand of the servant who was straightening his silver robe one last time. "ENOUGH! Give me my crown!" He snapped his pudgy fingers and the servant quickly placed a matching silver laurel leaf crown on his head. "We go! Alert the trumpeters for my arrival."

Nigel watched as Herod stormed down the marble corridor of the palace to his waiting chariot for the short ride to the amphitheater. His entourage of servants hustled down the hall behind him. Suddenly an owl landed right next to Nigel.

"Would you like a lift to the amphitheater?" the owl asked, blinking its blue eyes.

Nigel studied the bird, holding his spectacles. "Clarie? I'd be delighted," he said as he climbed aboard her back. "My dear, you never cease to amaze me! Why an owl today?"

Clarie took off soaring above the gorgeous blue-green water surrounding the palace. "Way back when Emperor Tiberius threw Herod Agrippa in prison following a disagreement, Herod leaned against a tree where an owl sat. A fellow German prisoner told him that the bird was a sign of an early release, followed by good fortune, but if he ever saw it again, Herod would only have five days to live."

"Do you mean to tell me that Herod's death is imminent?" Nigel said with wide eyes. "Were you the owl or the prisoner that day?"

"I was the owl. Gillamon was the prisoner," Clarie explained, circling above the amphitheater. "And if Herod acts as we expect him to here today, the answer is 'yes.'"

Nigel looked down to see Herod taking a seat on his throne. Just then the sun peeked over the horizon and its staggering bright rays lit up his silver robe with dazzling brilliance. The people gasped in awe of Herod's appearance. The crowd erupted in applause as Herod stood and addressed the crowd. Clarie swooped in for a landing on a rope right above Herod's head.

Voices in the crowd began shouting out praises to Herod: "This is the voice of a god, not of a man. Be gracious to us, our king! Hail King Agrippa!"

259

Herod smiled and lifted his arms out in arrogant reception of their words, looking around the amphitheater at the eager people firmly in his control. He puffed up his chest as the people called him a god. He looked up and suddenly saw the owl sitting above his head. His smile quickly faded and panic made him break out in a heavy sweat. Nigel and Clarie saw an angel unseen by the humans suddenly appear in front of Herod. The angel's face looked fierce and he struck Herod in the gut before he quickly disappeared. Herod gripped the front of his silver robe and leaned over in pain, falling off his throne. Immediately Herod's attendants rushed to his side.

"Because Herod did not give praise to God while the people called *him* a god," Clarie explained as attendants carried the arrogant king out of the amphitheater, "he will indeed now die."

Nigel marveled at the swiftness of God's judgment on Herod's arrogance. He quoted more from David's Thirty-Fourth Psalm: *"The eyes of the Lord are on the righteous, and his ears are attentive to their cry; but the face of the Lord is against those who do evil, to blot out their name from the earth.* Tell me, how will Herod die?"

"He'll suffer with being eaten by worms and die in five days," Clarie replied.

"How revolting!" Nigel exclaimed with a look of horror on his face.

"The ears of the Lord were indeed attentive to the cries of those who prayed for Peter when Herod sought to kill him. It looked like Herod had triumphed after killing James and throwing Peter in jail," stated Clarie.

"Hear, hear! Now Herod is dead, Peter is free, and the *church* is the one triumphing," Nigel cheered with a fist of victory raised high in the air. "Justice has been served by the Maker himself!"

"HOOT-HOOT, Nigel!" Clarie agreed, lifting off the rope and soaring above Caesarea. "As long as I'm a bird, allow me to take you to your next stop."

"Splendid! Might I request Antioch?" Nigel suggested. "I can't wait to see Max and Liz and give them all the news."

"You better make it quick. Their big journey awaits!" Clarie exclaimed.

"Oh? Where are they headed?" Nigel inquired.

Clarie smiled to herself, thinking of all that was coming. "To the ends of the earth."

PART THREE

To the Ends of the Earth

FIRST WORDS,
FIRST JOURNEY

L iz and Nigel sat on the table in the house where Paul, Barnabas, and Mark were staying in Antioch. The soft glow of the oil lamp lit up the papyrus scrolls Mark had brought from Jerusalem.

"This is excellent, no?" Liz whispered to Nigel. "Mark has captured so many things Peter related to him that Jesus had done. This work is invaluable for Paul and others who were not with Jesus themselves. They will be able to read these stories aloud as they travel."

"Yes, Peter was brilliant to encourage Mark to take notes on these events as he shared them," Nigel agreed readily. Suddenly his eyes lit up and he placed his paw on the pages. "My dear, do you realize what this is? I do believe we have the beginnings of our New Testament!"

"*Oui!* You are right, *mon ami!* Gillamon said the apostles would write down the stories of Jesus. We knew Matthew would be doing this, but I never dreamed young Mark would capture Peter's stories as well!" Liz's tail curled up and down and her eyes were on fire with the possibilities. She rolled out the scrolls, taking summary note of what was there. "Of course, Mark's notes are not in any kind of order. This needs much work."

Nigel could see Liz's mind reeling with possibilities. He smiled and preened his whiskers. "Once again I see our passion for the pen coming into view! How thrilling to see these very first words of the New Testament that will be read by generations of believers to come! And to think this begins as Paul, Barnabas, and Mark set off on their first journey tomorrow."

Liz embraced Nigel with an endearing hug. "The disciples have done as Jesus asked. They have taken the gospel to Jerusalem and to Judea and Samaria. Now they'll begin the journey to the ends of the earth, beginning with Cyprus." Liz wrinkled her brow in thought. "And we must do as we've been asked, Nigel. We are to assist with the writing of the New Testament."

"Aye, an' me part be ta pr-r-rotect it," came Max's voice, with his paws up on the table. His large square head and triangle ears peered at them over the edge of the table. "So wha's the plan, Lass?"

Liz put her paw on Mark's scrolls. "These are the beginning writings, and as we start this journey tomorrow you must guard them, *mon ami.* Paul and Barnabas brought Mark with them from Jerusalem to assist in their journey. Paul is anxious to travel first to Cyprus, where Barnabas is from, but then to sail over to Perga and head north to Antioch of Pisidia."

"Which is one of the most treacherous roads in the Roman Empire, I might add," Nigel piped up. "Steep terrain, bandits, and the like, you know."

"Not to mention the dangers of malaria common to the coastal area," Liz added. "I suspect this journey will be filled with danger."

"Aye, but seein' how we be pr-r-rotected by the Holy Spir-r-rit, the dangers will have ta get thr-r-rough him first," Max suggested with a determined look. "Then thr-r-rough me!"

The salty, turquoise water lapped against the hull of the ship as they pulled into the harbor of Salamis on the island of Cyprus. Max, Liz, and Nigel stood on the bow and scanned the beautiful shoreline where the first missionary journey was set to begin. The seagulls cried out in the clear blue sky above. Abundant sunshine bounced off the white buildings dotting the bustling coastal town.

"What a splendid place to embark on such an historic quest!" Nigel exclaimed with his fists raised in excitement. "I daresay the church at Antioch was brilliant to catch the first vision of carrying the good news across the sea, beginning here. It was quite the blessed send-off for these three chaps."

"Paul wants ta tr-r-rot all over the island, shar-r-rin' in the synagogues," Max reported. "Barnabas said they'll go ninety miles, east ta west."

"Cyprus is known as 'The Happy Isle' because it has the most perfect climate anywhere, and has everything anyone might need to have a happy life," Liz explained. "Just think how happy they will truly be as they hear about Jesus!"

"Indeed! While some here have heard the Good News already from those who fled Saul's persecution in Jerusalem fifteen years ago, he intends to blanket the island," Nigel offered. "But I believe he sees this first stop as a prelude only. His eyes are set on areas where no one has heard about Jesus at all."

265

Liz studied Paul's beaming face as the ship docked and the men got ready to set foot on Cyprus. He couldn't wait to begin. *"Oui,* he is confident the Maker will reveal the best strategy to seize opportunities as they arise."

"An' the Enemy will be r-r-right there ta tr-r-ry an' stop 'em," Max cautioned, trotting along the deck behind the men, keeping his sights on Mark's bag.

The little band crossed the southern wooded hills above the bay and preached in synagogues with surprising ease. They never stayed long in one place but kept moving. Max continually kept guard, and chased off snakes and tarantulas that came near their campfire. They finally arrived at the grand harbor of the Roman capital city of New Paphos. The proconsul, Sergius Paulus, had invited Paul and Barnabas to lecture in his palace after hearing of their teaching tour around the island. So on this breezy spring day, the men walked up the processional way to the ornate, granite palace. Legionnaires stood at attention to welcome them. The animals stayed well hidden as they sneaked into the palace compound filled with the images of pagan Rome.

"First the Greek gods roamed this island, now Roman gods fill the hearts and minds of the pagans here on Cyprus," Nigel observed. "Homer wrote that from out of the sea foam here, Aphrodite the goddess of love emerged, full grown and full of power. I'm so very glad we bypassed her temple area. Such a dastardly place, like Daphne's temple in Antioch."

"All this false god stuff be ever-r-rywhere we go!" Max complained. "I hope Jesus takes over this island someday."

Liz smiled. "That makes me think of my dear Albert. He said that if Rome invited the God of Israel to their city as they do the other gods of conquered people, he would take over the place. But this is just the point, no? With every pagan reached, the tide will begin to turn."

"Let's see if Paul has success today with this Sergius fellow. He's quite the intellectual, I hear, but very superstitious. His court magician is never far away," Nigel noted as they entered the elegant audience hall lined with marble pillars. The animals hid behind massive pots of tropical plants trailing over the sides.

Paul, Barnabas, and Mark were greeted warmly by Sergius, who sat in his red chair of golden scrolled arms fitted with eagles at the base. He was dressed in a white toga with a red sash, and his short brown cropped hair was combed forward around his face. He was eager to hear what these men had to say. Paul began sharing about Jesus, explaining who he was and why he had to be a suffering Savior. As Sergius listened intently, the magician kept interrupting Paul and whispering in the ear of the proconsul, mocking what Paul was trying to say.

Liz's tail whipped back and forth quickly as she spied the magician. "He's called 'Bar-Jesus' or Elymas," she spat. "He is a Jew who claims to be a prophet. Pfft! He is no prophet! He works for the Evil One, and it is very clear he fears losing his influence over Sergius with this talk of Jesus. Paul is trying to keep his cool, but I think his patience is wearing thin."

Suddenly Paul was filled with the Holy Spirit and boldness entered his soul. He looked straight at Elymas and pointed his finger at the magician. "You son of the Devil! You are the enemy of everything that is good. You are full of all kinds of evil tricks, and you always keep trying to turn the Lord's truths into lies! The Lord's hand will come down on you now; you will be blind and will not see the light of day for a time."

At once Elymas felt a dark mist cover his eyes, and he walked around trying to find someone to lead him by the hand. The crowd of court observers gasped and put their hands on their mouths, fearful of Paul's ability to speak with such power.

Sergius slowly rose to his feet in awe of what was happening. He stared at Elymas, then at Paul. "You indeed must serve the one true God and his son Jesus," he said, motioning for his servants. "Take the magician away. I wish to hear more about . . . Jesus." He and Paul shared a smile.

Mark fiddled in his bag and handed Paul a scroll. Paul unrolled it and smiled. "Let me tell you a story." He began reading from the scroll. "Once as Jesus and his disciples entered a city there was a blind man there named Bartimaeus. Many rebuked him and told him to be quiet, but he shouted all the more, 'Son of David, have mercy on me!' Jesus stopped and said, 'Call him.' So they called to the blind man, 'Cheer up! On your feet! He's calling you.' Throwing his cloak aside, he jumped to his feet and came to Jesus. 'What do you want me to do for you?' Jesus asked him. The blind man said, 'Rabbi, I want to see.' 'Go,' said Jesus, 'your faith has healed you.' Immediately he received his sight and followed Jesus along the road."

267

Paul handed the scroll back to Mark. "Sergius, the false man-made gods that you worship are dark, without life and without answers. But Jesus is the Way, the Truth, and the Life. He is the Light of the World, and he will show the way. Elymas has been temporarily blinded to teach him truth, just as I was before I found Jesus. But search your heart, Sergius. You are blind also."

Sergius nodded slowly. "Yes, I am blind. And I now wish to see Jesus."

"*C'est bon!* He believes!" Liz cheered as Paul led Sergius to Christ. "The Maker is opening the door to the Gentiles! Just think of all the possibilities as they travel on!"

Nigel grinned. "Splendid success! And I believe that Barnabas realizes that Paul must be the one to walk through the Gentile door ahead of them, leading the way."

"I'm going back to Jerusalem," Mark announced, hurriedly packing his knapsack.

"You're *leaving?*" Barnabas asked, grabbing Mark's arm. "How can you quit this journey? We're just getting started!"

Paul shivered with fever. His back rested against the wall, and he frowned at Mark and his decision. Max and Liz lay on either side of him, trying to comfort him.

"Didn't you see the bodies of two more men who were attacked and killed on the mountain road to Pisidian Antioch? Some traders brought them into Perga this morning," Mark reported. He looked at Paul, who was shivering from a terrible case of malaria. "And look at Paul! He's in no condition to travel a hundred miles like that. We'd be easy targets for bandits." Mark leaned in to whisper in Barnabas's ear. "Cousin, *you* should be leading this journey anyway." He straightened up and put his knapsack on his back. "Do what you want. I'm heading back to where it's safe."

Barnabas looked at Paul with burdened eyes as Mark stormed out of the room where they were staying. "Let him go," Paul said with a wave of his hand. He wrapped his blanket tighter around himself and squinted from the stabbing headache. "He's lost his heart and he clearly doesn't have the nerve to press on. He's not ready for this."

Barnabas looked at the floor and nodded. He threw up his hand. "I'm sorry, my friend. I thought my cousin was up to the challenge."

"People will stay with you when things are easy," Paul said, closing his eyes. "But they show their true colors when things get tough." His hands rested on Max and Liz and he slowly stroked their fur. "We will keep the faith and press on with God's message to the Gentiles."

"Rest now," Barnabas said. "I will go get us food." He stepped out of the room and Paul drifted off to sleep.

"It's outr-r-right cowardly desertion!" Max whispered to Liz. "Wha' aboot the scrolls? Should I go after them?"

Liz wrinkled her brow. "No, I know Mark will take good care of the scrolls as he returns to Jerusalem. Perhaps Paul needs the *absence* of them to prod him to write down his own thoughts, no? I've been thinking that someone needs to record the events of this historic journey. We need the stories of Jesus, *oui,* but we also need the stories of what Jesus' disciples do with the mission he gave them to reach the world."

Nigel tiptoed over to join Max and Liz. "Sorry to see the young chap so fickle, but we are getting ready to enter fickle territory in Galatia."

"*Oui,* I'm sorry to say the Galatians come from what the humans like to call the French—the Gauls," Liz agreed, shaking her head. "They are quite a warring, hot-headed people, apt to easily change their minds. Although they are of course very intelligent, I'm afraid they are inconsistent in their resolve and easily steered in the wrong direction."

"Warlike?" Max asked.

"Yes, old boy," Nigel said, twirling his paw. "In the fourth century BC the Gauls invaded the Roman Empire and sacked Rome. From there they crossed into Greece and fought all through Asia Minor to help the king of Bithynia with a civil war. They eventually settled here and became a Roman province. Julius Caesar once said these blond Orientals are 'fond of change and not to be trusted.'"

"An' Paul an' Barnabas be headin' r-r-right inta their lands ta pr-r-reach. Sounds like they've got a challenge before they even get started," Max noted. "It would have been easier if Mark had stayed."

"I believe Mark will come around, *mon ami,*" Liz suggested. "He is but a boy, no? Like his writing, he also needs a lot of work. We will see him again, I am sure."

Nigel tapped Max on the paw. "Agreed. So we must press on. Max, you have kept Mark's writings safe for now. Perhaps your protection is needed more for just Paul and Barnabas for the next leg of the journey."

Max, Liz, and Nigel stared at Paul as he shivered in his delirious sleep. "Aye. The lad be sick an' knows dangers be comin' but he still wants ta go on. He's one determined lad. An' *br-r-rave.*"

269

The days were long and hard as Paul and Barnabas traveled with a caravan heading north. There was safety in numbers from robbers along this treacherous road. Max was on constant alert for dangerous threats, barking when he saw shadows move in the night. More than once he roused the men and scared off would-be robbers. Heat by day, cold by night, and drenching storms kept the weary travelers tired from lack of meaningful rest. Paul refused to stop despite Barnabas's concern. Paul was still weak from malaria, but they pressed on to make fifteen miles a day. Within a week they parted ways with the caravan and came to the exquisite turquoise waters of Lake Limnai, with snow-capped mountains around it and Mount Olympus far ahead in the distance. Farms and cottages dotted the landscape and they sometimes stayed at inns along the way, and Paul was ever eager to share their mission with the innkeepers. Finally, they saw the large city of Pisidian Antioch come into view, its proud gates beckoning.

270

"We're here!" Paul exclaimed with joy, patting Barnabas on the back. "And just in time for the Sabbath."

Paul and Barnabas quickly found a place to stay, and headed for the synagogue. Max, Liz, and Nigel ran underfoot of the city dwellers as the men climbed the steps and through the impressive arches erected in honor of Caesar Augustus and his military victories. Paul gazed up at the white marble Temple of Augustus, who was worshipped along with various local Roman gods. A familiar statue of Augustus with his out-stretched hand was placed on a stacked block platform. Paul clenched his jaw at the blatant lost-ness of these pagan people who worshipped a man.

"Time to be a light for the Gentiles, Barnabas. But first, we go to the Jews," Paul said.

"The synagogue is that way," Barnabas pointed, seeing some Jews heading to the beautiful building with carved Ionic columns depicting Hebrew symbols—the menorah and the Star of David.

Paul and Barnabas walked into the synagogue and sat down in the seats reserved for visiting rabbis. Max stayed outside while Liz and

Nigel sneaked in under the flowing robes of several elders, making their way to a high spot to observe the service. After the reading from the Law of Moses and from the writings of the prophets, the officials of the synagogue sent Paul and Barnabas a message: "Friends, we want you to speak to the people if you have a message of encouragement for them."

Paul stood up, and looked around the room, noticing the large numbers of God-fearing pagans. He motioned with his hand, and decided to sidestep the custom of ignoring the existence of non-Jewish God-fearers.

"Fellow Israelites and all Gentiles here who worship God: hear me! The God of the people of Israel chose our ancestors and made the people a great nation during the time they lived as foreigners in Egypt. God brought them out of Egypt by his great power, and for forty years he endured them in the desert. He destroyed seven nations in the land of Canaan and made his people the owners of the land. All of this took about 450 years.

271

"After this he gave them judges until the time of the prophet Samuel. And when they asked for a king, God gave them Saul son of Kish from the tribe of Benjamin, to be their king for forty years. After removing him, God made David their king. This is what God said about him: 'I have found that David son of Jesse is the kind of man I like, a man who will do all I want him to do.' It was Jesus, a descendant of David, whom God made the Savior of the people of Israel, as he had promised. Before Jesus began his work, John preached to all the people of Israel that they should turn from their sins and be baptized. And as John was about to finish his mission, he said to the people, 'Who do you think I am? I am not the one you are waiting for. But listen! He is coming after me, and I am not good enough to take his sandals off his feet.'

"My fellow Israelites, descendants of Abraham, and all Gentiles here who worship God: it is to us that this message of salvation has been sent!" Paul paused for effect.

"Brilliant!" Nigel whispered to Liz. "Paul has the Jews intrigued and the Gentiles eating out of his hand! I do believe he is using the same pattern of Stephen and Peter. He's given the history of Israel but with the promise for all mankind."

"Oui, he's showing that history is moving in the direction of God's purposes," Liz replied, observing the response of the people. "But he may lose the Jewish leaders with what comes next. It's one thing to present Jesus as the Messiah to the Jews. It's quite another to say in the same breath that the Messiah has come for the Gentiles as well. For the Maker to equally accept Gentiles is blasphemy to the Jews."

"For the people who live in Jerusalem and their leaders did not know that he is the Savior, nor did they understand the words of the prophets that are read every Sabbath." Paul held his hand out over the scrolls that had just been read. "Yet they made the prophets' words come true by condemning Jesus. And even though they could find no reason to pass the death sentence on him, they asked Pilate to have him put to death. And after they had done everything that the Scriptures say about him, they took him down from the cross and placed him in a tomb. But God raised him from death, and for many days he appeared to those who had traveled with him from Galilee to Jerusalem. They are now witnesses for him to the people of Israel. And we are here to bring the Good News to you: what God promised our ancestors he would do, he has now done for us, who are their descendants, by raising Jesus to life. As it is written in the second Psalm,

'You are my Son; today I have become your Father.'

"And this is what God said about raising him from death, never to rot away in the grave:

'I will give you the sacred and sure blessings that I promised to David.'

"As indeed he says in another passage, 'You will not allow your faithful servant to rot in the grave.'

"For David served God's purposes in his own time, and then he died, was buried with his ancestors, and his body rotted in the grave. But this did not happen to the one whom God raised from death. All of you, my fellow Israelites, are to know for sure that it is through Jesus that the message about forgiveness of sins is preached to you; you are to know that everyone who believes in him is set free from all the sins from which the Law of Moses could not set you free. Take care, then, so that what the prophets said may not happen to you:

272

'Look, you scoffers! Be astonished and die! For what I am doing today is something that you will not believe, even when someone explains it to you!'"

"He just demolished the barrier between Jew and Gentile," Nigel marveled. "All are offered God's free grace."

Liz watched as faces lit up with understanding and hope, with eagerness to respond to his message. "*Oui,* but with a warning. Now that they have heard the truth, if they reject God's offer of grace through Jesus, they are responsible for their eternal decision."

Nigel watched the people as Paul and Barnabas left the synagogue. They were surrounded by people inviting them to come back the next Sabbath and tell them more about these things. "They're begging for more, look at them! The Jews have told these Gentiles that they have to abide by their rigorous laws, and here Paul comes and tells them that none of that is necessary. Simple faith in Jesus can give them immediate forgiveness and joy. These people are hungry for this truth they've never heard before."

273

Liz spied the Jewish leaders clustered together with angry faces. "But as usual, there are some who have no appetite for Jesus."

ONE WEEK LATER

"Word spr-r-read like wildfire this week in the market, in the mansions, in the bar-r-racks, an' everywhere in the str-r-reets," Max reported happily. "Antioch in Pisidia be buzzin' with the Good News. Look at all the lads an' lassies filing inta the synagogue."

The animals stood outside as crowds pressed their way into the packed building to hear Paul again.

"Gentiles outnumber the Jews this week," Liz observed. "I wonder if the service will even be allowed to begin." She and Nigel trotted off to sneak inside.

The Jews were furious as they saw the crowds file in, bumping faithful Jewish followers out of their usual places. Jealousy filled the elders with contempt for Paul and Barnabas.

"Nearly everyone in the town has come to hear these Christians!" fumed an elder.

Another leading Jewish elder clenched his fists in anger. "I refuse to allow this to continue!" He motioned for the crowd to settle down and stood in front of the synagogue. "Silence! We ask you to quiet down." He walked over to where Paul and Barnabas were once again seated in the place designated for visiting rabbis. "You are not welcome in these seats of honor. Blasphemers, both of you! We will not hear any more of this heresy! You have mocked our laws in front of the entire city of Antioch! This Jesus of Nazareth was a criminal who railed against our laws and has led you to delusional heresy!" He proceeded to spit on them and a murmur of disapproval rose up throughout the crowd.

Paul and Barnabas calmly stood up. Nigel leaned over and whispered to Liz, "Paul isn't surprised. They've only said the exact same thing he once said."

274

Barnabas lifted his voice boldly. "It was necessary that the word of God should be spoken first to you. But since you reject it and do not consider yourselves worthy of eternal life, we will leave you and go to the Gentiles."

Paul spread his hands out to the Gentiles gathered there. "For this is the commandment that the Lord has given us:

'I have made you a light for the Gentiles, so that all the world may be saved.'"

When the Gentiles heard this, they erupted with shouts of joy and immediately stood to their feet. Paul and Barnabas walked out of the synagogue as the people filed out behind them, hungry to hear the sermon they had come for. The apostles made their way to the square and Paul jumped up on the stacked rectangular base of Caesar Augustus's statue so he could be seen and heard. And there before the sea of hungry Gentiles, Paul fed them the bread of a sermon about Jesus of Nazareth.

Max, Liz, and Nigel stood in the back of the crowd, marveling at the groundswell of support for Paul and Barnabas after they were kicked out of the synagogue.

"It is very clear to Paul that the Jews are not going to listen to him, but he will not give up on them while he pursues his calling to preach to the Gentiles. Just like he was blinded for a time before he believed about Jesus, so too will Israel be blinded while the Gentiles come to the light," Nigel suggested. "Thrilling to see yet more prophecy come true in front of our eyes!"

Liz smiled, happy to see the Gentiles so eager to embrace Jesus. "This is a happy day for them."

Max cocked his head as he studied the Caesar statue. "We're not the only ones happy aboot this day." Max's white teeth appeared in a broad smile as he suddenly saw the stern image of Caesar grow a slight grin. "Looks like Gillamon be happy aboot it, too."

275

STICKS AND STONES

Never had Pisidian Antioch known such joy. For the first time in the existence of the ancient city, there was a buzz of excitement and hope stemming from something that was real. The people learned how God's laws showed them sin against the standard of holiness. But they also learned that now through Jesus there was grace and freedom to live with him as Savior and Lord, no longer burdened by endless man-made laws they could never hope to fully keep. Paul and Barnabas talked all day long, teaching the gospel to the lost, and grace to the saved. Many Gentiles and some Jews responded in droves, but as dusk began to settle in, Paul showed signs of weakness. Barnabas frowned at his faithful friend, concerned that the malaria was coming in for another attack. Paul had been pushing so hard, first to travel here, and then to preach here. Despite his perseverance, Barnabas knew that in spite of all he did, Paul was only human. Finally Barnabas dismissed the new believers with blessing, and told them where he and Paul were staying.

As the people dispersed to go back to their homes, the animals gathered around the statue of Caesar Augustus, waiting until the coast was clear of humans.

"Gillamon? Are ye there?" Max whispered, looking around the empty square to make sure they weren't overheard.

The statue's eyes blinked and Caesar smiled. "Hello, Max. Hello, Liz and Nigel. It has been a wonderful day."

"Might I say you look perfectly regal as emperor?" Nigel quipped with a chuckle.

"I've seen this statue all over the Roman Empire and wanted to try it on for size," Gillamon joked warmly, wiggling his outstretched pointer finger. "Sadly, the people have been told that this statue is not only Caesar Augustus but also a god to be worshipped. Thankfully they received the truth today. I want to prepare you for what is coming as this truth spreads. The newly believing Galatians will be warm to Paul but he and Barnabas are in for intense opposition and fickle hearts from the greater population. You won't believe how fast these people will change their minds about Paul and Barnabas."

Liz shook her head. "Pfft! Fickle Galatians! Gillamon, I am worried about Paul's health. He has been pushing so very hard."

"Aye, the laddie needs a good r-r-rest," Max added.

"Exactly, and this forced rest will show Paul and Barnabas the perfect strategy for establishing churches everywhere they go," Gillamon said. "Before now they have quickly traveled through towns as they did in Cyprus. In the long run, what works best is to settle a solid group of believers in an area. They must learn to stay put long enough for the gospel to take hold."

277

"He *makes* me lie down in green pastures. He restores my soul," Nigel said, quoting the Twenty-Third Psalm. "So the Maker will use Paul's illness to help the gospel spread like a divine epidemic? Brilliant!"

"*C'est magnifique!* Whoever would have thought that being sick could serve the Maker's purposes?!" Liz exclaimed. "So now I see two strategies emerging for how Paul and Barnabas will spread the gospel on this journey. First is the synagogue strategy. They go to a city and visit the synagogue, where they not only present to the Jews first, but where they also find a group of God-fearing Gentiles open to their message. Second is the stay strategy. They will stay in an area until the new group of believers are solid enough for them to move on. Is this correct?"

"*Oui,* Liz, you have it," Gillamon affirmed. "And because these strategies will be so successful, it will anger the Jews."

"'Cause Paul an' Barnabas be stealin' their sheep then," Max offered.

"I been watchin' those jealous Jews all day, scowlin' at the happy people turnin' ta Jesus. But since Paul an' Barnabas be pr-r-reachin' outside, wha' can they do then?"

"They'll stir up the fickle people against them," Gillamon cautioned. "Be prepared, Max. Things will get rough very soon. You've done well to protect them so far, but there are some difficult days to come when you will not be able to help them. Nor should you."

"But why shouldn't I help the lads?!" Max protested excitedly.

"Just as Jesus' sufferings had to happen for the Maker's purposes, so too must the persecution that Paul, Barnabas, and all the Christians face in order to spread the gospel," Gillamon explained. "Remember that things aren't always what they seem at first."

"Gillamon, I wish to ask you about the scrolls for the New Testament," Nigel told him. "Young Mark parted company, as you know, but we are certain his writings have the potential to become a splendid book. Might we have another opportunity to work on his manuscript? And what about the others, such as Matthew?"

"*Oui,* and I have wondered if we should be writing down the events of this journey," Liz added.

"All in good time. The answer to all your questions is 'yes,'" Gillamon replied, his eyes twinkling with his familiar warmth. "Many books will come from not only Mark, but also from Paul and someone you'll need to meet soon. There is a third strategy to round out their missionary endeavor. When you figure that out, you'll start to see the New Testament take shape. And just so you know, Matthew is working on his own book as we speak. You'll see it when the time is right."

Liz and Nigel looked at one another with glee, hugging in anticipation. "So far we have Matthew and Mark," Nigel cheered. "Jolly good beginning!"

"Aye, so for now we'll jest keep pr-r-ressin' on with Paul an' Barnabas," Max offered. "Can ye tell us the news aboot Kate an' Al then? I miss me lass."

Gillamon reached down and gave Max a comforting pet. "I know, Max. Kate is well with John, and brings Mary such joy in Jerusalem. You'll get to see her before long." He tickled Liz under the chin. "Al is happy with Peter, and you'll see him when you return to Syrian Antioch. Clarie goes between them as needed, and sends her love." He raised himself up and resumed the position of Caesar Augustus. "I'm back to Rome. Keep the faith, little ones." The statue's face turned stern and cold once more.

"He's one busy statue," Max said, staring up at the outstretched hand of Augustus.

Liz sat there, curling her tail up and down in thought. "The third strategy . . . hmmmm."

"What do you suppose it is, my dear?" Nigel asked, straightening his spectacles. "Something to do with the pen, I assume?"

Liz shrugged her shoulders. *"Je ne sais pas*, but as always, we will know in time."

⟀

It didn't take long for the word of the Lord to spread everywhere in the region. New believers took the Good News throughout the city, up to the hillsides, and over to Lake Limnai. Fishermen bowed their heads before they pushed their boats out for the day, praying for Jesus to fill their nets as he had done for the disciples. Shepherds sat in fields and discussed the truths of Jesus' role as the Good Shepherd. Women buying grain at the market discovered they were fellow believers, and went home to make bread together, happy to prepare it for the Lord's Supper. And daily, people came to Paul's bedside, where he taught them more and more, answering their questions and shoring up their new faith. Once his health was restored, he and Barnabas went from house to house, teaching and breaking bread. One day they would be with a rich Jewish merchant's family and friends in the city, another day with a group of Roman soldiers camped on the outskirts of town, and yet another day at a Greek farmhouse where slaves sat at the feet of their masters to hear the Good News.

"There is neither Jew nor Greek, slave nor freeman, male nor female; for you all are one in Christ Jesus," Paul taught them.

"This is radical teaching to these people!" Nigel exclaimed at such a gathering in the courtyard of a shopkeeper in the city. "Their world has been conditioned for one class of people to hate or show utter contempt for the other."

"*Oui,* for a slave and a master to hear they are brothers is shocking," Liz agreed.

"Aye, especially for some r-r-rich Gentile lassies who like the Jewish synagogue," Max reported, out of breath as he joined Liz and Nigel. "I jest overheard them talkin' with the Jewish leaders who be set on gettin' the city r-r-riled up. They been tellin' their R-r-roman husbands that Paul an' Barnabas be a thr-r-reat. They're comin' ta punish the lads before kickin' 'em out of the city!"

No sooner were the words out of Max's mouth than Roman soldiers stormed into the courtyard. The people scrambled as they grabbed Paul and Barnabas. The soldiers put them in shackles and hurried them down to the town square where other criminals and runaway slaves awaited their fate. There the city magistrates sat on a raised platform while their Roman-appointed lictors stood behind them, holding their *fasces*—a bundle of birch rods tied with leather straps around a protruding ax. The *fasces* was both a symbol and a tool used for authority, punishment, and execution. A crowd quickly gathered, and Paul and Barnabas were shoved to the front of the line. A whipping post stood ominously next to them.

Max growled and his fur rose on end. "They've got their bunch of sticks r-r-ready. I'd like ta gr-r-rab the whole lot from their hands an' see how *they* like ta get whacked with it!"

Liz gently placed her paw on Max's shoulder. "Steady, Maximillan."

"You are accused of entering our city for the purpose of stirring up trouble between the classes, between slaves and their masters, and denigrating long-standing religious bodies," the Roman magistrate claimed, sharing a nod with the Jewish elders of the synagogue. "Therefore you will be punished and then taken to the outskirts of the city where you will be released after expulsion from the city."

Barnabas hoarsely whispered in Paul's ear, "Tell them you're a Roman citizen!"

Paul sadly smiled at Barnabas. "I will not allow you to endure this alone, Barnabas."

The group of Christians looked on in sadness as Paul was stripped and tied to the pillar. A lictor stepped down and pulled out some rods from his fasces. He lifted his arm back and beat Paul across the back, legs, and feet, drawing muffled cries from the apostle. Moans rose from the crowd as Paul was thrown to the ground in a bloody heap and Barnabas was also tied and beaten. The nonbelieving Jews looked on with smug satisfaction while some of the believers ran to get the apostles' belongings. Paul and Barnabas were then forced to their feet, roughly escorted to the outskirts of town and thrown on the ground, followed by a mixed crowd of sad believers and gloating Jews.

Paul and Barnabas slowly rose from the ground, wincing in pain. They drew themselves up and lifted their chins high. With broken voice, Paul uttered Jesus' instructions, "If any place will not receive you and they refuse to hear you, when you leave, shake off the dust that is on your feet as a testimony against them." Together Paul and Barnabas shook the dust off their feet and turned to walk down the road.

281

The accusing Jews called out a few parting insults before heading back to the city. Several believers huddled around the men, giving them their knapsacks and trying to help them. An elderly Jewish woman came up to them with a young woman and a handsome younger man by her side.

"You will come with us to the inn on the Augustan Way where we will tend to your wounds," the elderly lady fussed, taking Barnabas by the arm. "I am Lois, and this is my daughter Eunice and her son . . ."

Paul suddenly felt lightheaded and the young man reached over to catch him. "Steady there!"

"Thank you," Paul said, relieved to have support to stand.

"I'm Timothy," the young man said, sharing a smile with Paul, who locked eyes with the eighteen-year-old who appeared half-Jew, half-Greek. His curly light brown hair was held back by a traditional Greek headband and he wore a white chiton with red sash. Timothy's jawline was square and he had striking blue eyes.

"Where are you from, Son?" Paul asked him as they slowly made their way to the inn.

"We're from Lystra, about one hundred thirty miles east of here,"

Timothy answered. "These are my grandmother and my mother. I've escorted them here but I'm heading back home. We heard you speak yesterday. My grandmother believed everything you said."

"And you?" Paul asked, gingerly lifting a hand to touch his badly bruised arm.

Timothy shrugged his shoulders. "I like what you said, but I need to hear more to understand, especially after all this," he said as he held his hand up to Paul's bloody wounds.

Paul smiled. "Well, we can certainly arrange that."

Max and Liz came running up to them. *"Are ye alr-r-right, Laddie?!"* Max whined.

"Who's this?" Timothy asked with a smile.

"This is Gabriel," Paul said, pointing to Max, then Liz, "and Faith. They go everywhere with me. Why exactly, I'm not sure, especially when you see the kind of reception I have in these cities." Paul looked at Barnabas and they shared a painful laugh.

"Why do you keep preaching about Jesus then?" Timothy asked as they neared the inn. "And how can you and Barnabas be so cheerful?"

Paul stopped and looked intently into young Timothy's face. "God is always working things out for the good of those who love him, and who are called according to his purpose. Let's go in and I'll tell you more."

Nigel stayed close behind and watched how God immediately provided Paul and Barnabas the help they needed. The women fussed over Paul and Barnabas, applying homemade ointments to their wounds and making them a meal. That night Timothy sat on the floor, cross-legged and petting Max and Liz on either side of him while he listened intently to Paul. This would just be the first night of many conversations they would have. For it wasn't long until Timothy decided he would take Paul and Barnabas to his hometown of Lystra. But first they would have to travel through Iconium.

ICONIUM

Max felt a chill from the late autumn winds as he trotted down a side street of Iconium, Nigel riding on his back. For weeks he had taken it upon himself to keep an ear out for any plots to harm Paul and Barnabas.

"I know Gillamon said I can't pr-r-revent ever-r-y persecution of the laddies, but we can at least warn them if somethin's comin'. An' tr-r-rust me, Mousie, somethin's comin'," Max grumbled.

"Indeed, old boy, Iconium is as divided as its odd little twin peaks," Nigel offered, staring off at the distant pyramid-looking mountains. "Although this second Galatian church is off and running with both Jews and Gentiles in their camp, once again the unbelieving Jews have split this city into those who hate the apostles and those who adore them. I daresay Paul and Barnabas preach with even greater boldness than in Antioch in Pisidia."

"If Al were here, he'd be sayin' it were another *déjà vu* city," Max told the mouse. "Speakin' of *déjà vu*, when we came thr-r-rough this part of the world on our way ta Noah's Ark, we r-r-ran inta some of the most ar-r-rogant cr-r-reatures ye'd ever want ta meet."

283

"Oh, what were they?" Nigel asked.

"Turkeys," Max remembered. "They even thought this land would someday be named after them. Cr-r-razy birds. Maybe the turkeys r-r-rubbed off on the humans here. They act jest like 'em."

Suddenly they saw a group of Jewish elders talking in hushed tones to some Roman officials. Max slowed his pace and tiptoed up to listen in on their conversation.

"So you will turn a blind eye?" one of the Jewish elders asked with a smile as he slipped a bag of coins to the official.

The official took the bag and handed it off to his assistant. "You never know when mob violence will erupt before we can do anything about it."

Another Jewish elder picked up a stone lying in the street and tossed it around in his palm. "Stones can come from nowhere in a situation like that," he said with an insidious grin.

"Hurry, Max! We've no time to lose," Nigel urged. "We must pen a note of warning to Paul and Barnabas immediately!"

⊂✕

"A stoning could easily be fatal, Paul," Barnabas urged. "And no telling how this persecution could spread from us to the new believers here, crushing the church."

Paul nodded and rolled up the anonymous note they had received, warning them that a plot to stone them by mob rule had been set. "I agree. And we've been here long enough to get this church well established. The people here are strong. Antioch is doing well without us, so I'm sure Iconium will manage, too."

"My city of Lystra is only nineteen miles from here," Timothy said, standing to grab his knapsack. "If we leave now we can be there by nightfall. We'll stay in my home."

Liz winked at Nigel and Max. "The power of the pen has saved the day once again, no?"

LYSTRA

"Why didn't Paul start pr-r-reachin' first in the synagogue here like the other towns?" Max wanted to know.

"There isn't one here in Lystra," Nigel explained, looking around the Roman forum where Paul eagerly shared the Good News with the Lycaonians who lived there. "Timothy and his family are but token Jews here."

Paul gazed out at the pagan crowd, trying to assess their response to his message when his eyes landed on a crippled man who sat in rapt attention to every word he spoke. He had seen this man at the same spot each day, begging for alms in the bright winter sunshine. Paul realized this man believed and could be healed, so he looked straight at him and said in a loud voice, "Stand up straight on your feet!"

Instantly the man jumped up and started walking around. The crowds looked at the man and then one another in awe as an audible gasp rippled through the forum. Several young men took off running from the forum toward the Temple of Zeus. A chant started echoing through the crowds, who got to their feet and drew closer around Paul and Barnabas. They started shouting in their own Lycaonian language, "The gods have become like men and have come down to us!" They gave Barnabas the name Zeus, and Paul the name Hermes (messenger of the gods), because he was the chief speaker.

Paul and Barnabas looked at one another with confused grins, not quite sure what the people were doing or saying. "They must be praising God for healing the crippled man!" Barnabas shouted over the din of voices. Paul shrugged his shoulders and hugged the people who came over to touch him.

"Oh dear, this isn't good," Nigel worried. "These poor people think the ancient legend has finally come true here today!"

"And Timothy isn't here to explain," Liz echoed, shaking her head.

"Explain wha'?" Max asked.

"The legend of Zeus and Hermes, old boy," Nigel replied. "Every child here is taught the tale that once upon a time the supreme god Zeus visited Lystra with his faithful messenger sidekick Hermes, but the gods disguised themselves as poor travelers to test the people's hospitality. Only one old peasant couple welcomed the gods into their humble home. Zeus and Hermes responded by turning the rest of the city's people into frogs and the couple's cottage into a gold and marble temple."

285

"And so the people here have awaited the day when the gods would return so they could treat them with honor and respect," Liz continued.

"Ye mean ta tell me these people be makin' all this fuss because they're afr-r-raid Paul an' Barnabas will turn 'em inta fr-r-rogs?!"

"Something like that," Nigel replied. "Pitiful to see the superstitious, uneducated mind run amok."

Suddenly Timothy came running up to Paul and Barnabas. Behind him strode the priest of the god Zeus, whose temple stood just outside the town, bringing bulls and flowers to the gate. "They want to offer sacrifices to you!" Timothy explained, out of breath. "They think you are gods!"

When Barnabas and Paul heard what they were about to do, they instinctively tore their clothes, which was the Jewish response to blasphemy. They ran into the middle of the crowd, desperate for the people to stop what they were doing. "Why are you doing this? We ourselves are only human beings like you!" Barnabas cried.

"Listen to us!" Paul's torn robe flapped in the breeze as he shouted in anguish, "We are here to announce the Good News, to turn you away from these worthless things to the living God, who made heaven, earth, sea, and all that is in them. In the past he allowed all people to go their own way. But he has always given evidence of his existence by the good things he does: he gives you rain from heaven and crops at the right times; he gives you food and fills your hearts with happiness."

The priest hesitated and the people looked at one another with uncertainty.

"They fear offending Paul and Barnabas," Liz explained. "Or offending the living God Paul is trying to share with them."

"Timothy, you and Barnabas go with the priest and take these animals back where they came from," Paul instructed. "Explain that we do not want them to treat us as anything but the mere men we are."

"Right," Barnabas agreed, walking with Timothy to explain things to the priest. They slowly began escorting him back down the road.

286

"Well at least that travesty was averted," Nigel cheered. "How embarrassing it might have been for Paul and Barnabas!"

Just then Max spotted some familiar faces in the back of the crowd. His fur rose on end and a low growl rumbled in his throat. "Those be some of the same Jewish leaders we dealt with in Antioch an' Iconium! Look, they be stir-r-rin up the cr-r-rowd!"

Liz and Nigel watched in horror as suddenly a wave of emotional change washed over the crowd. Those who only moments earlier were praising Paul suddenly grew expressions of fury. A man picked up a stone and hurled it at Paul, hitting him square on the jaw and knocking him to the ground.

"Mon Dieu! They're out to stone Paul!" Liz cried in fear.

A small cluster of believers saw what was happening and tried to stop the pagan crowd but it was too late. Suddenly stones rained down all over Paul, and he held up his arms, desperately trying to shield his head. Blood streamed down his face and he soon passed out. Thinking he was dead, two men from the mob each grabbed a foot and dragged Paul outside the city limits. They dumped his body there and hurried back into town before the Roman guards could identify who was responsible for this mob murder.

"NO!" Max cried as he ran up to Paul. He immediately began licking his face, whimpering, "Ye can't be dead! Wake up, lad, wake up!"

Liz wept as Nigel clung to her. "This can't be happening!"

A group of believers encircled Paul's body, but parted as Barnabas and Timothy came running up to them. They dropped to their knees in disbelief at how quickly the crowd had turned on Paul. Suddenly Paul flinched and Max jumped back, cocking his head. Paul's eyes fluttered open to see the faces of Barnabas and Timothy hovering over him.

"You're alive!" Barnabas exclaimed, putting his hand under Paul's neck to help him sit up.

"This is a miracle!" Timothy shouted with his hands on his head in awe. "How can this be?"

Paul sat up and put his hands on either side of his cut and bleeding head. Timothy handed him his sash to wipe off his face. "I'm alive. God be praised," Paul muttered, looking around at the new believers who were now smiling hesitantly, still grief-stricken over what had happened. "Help me up." Barnabas and Timothy each took an arm and lifted Paul to his feet. "Thank you." He started walking right back into the city.

287

"Where are you going?!" Barnabas protested. "They just tried to kill you!"

"I'm going back into town," Paul calmly replied. "These people didn't know what they were doing. They need to see the power of the living God in action. Perhaps this is the very thing these superstitious people needed in order to understand."

Max stood with his mouth hanging open as he, Liz, and Nigel watched the miraculously saved Paul stride back through the now-deserted streets. The mob had dispersed and people hurried back to their homes so the Romans wouldn't seize them for murder. As Paul strode by their homes, doorways opened and people gazed at him with shock and awe. They couldn't believe that this man they thought they had stoned to death was not only alive, but that he dared enter their city again. Their hearts filled with respect, fear, and a magnetic pull to know about the power of the living God, for surely that was who had saved him.

"One minute they wanted to make sacrifices to him as a god, the next minute they tried to stone him to death," Nigel mused, preening back his whiskers. "Gillamon was right. Fickle Galatians indeed!"

"Oui, but it was the Jewish leaders who traveled all the way from Antioch and Iconium to do this to Paul," Liz reminded them. "So far it has always been the Jewish authorities stirring up trouble, not the Roman or Gentile authorities acting on their own. Nothing has changed since Jesus."

"Aye, an' Paul be anythin' but fickle," Max offered. "He'll keep lovin' the ones who hate him, an' do anythin' he can ta show them the tr-r-ruth. Wha' he's doin' by walkin' back inta town be more powerful than a hundred sermons." He shook his head in amazement at Paul's perseverance and bravery. "It takes r-r-real cour-r-rage ta be a Chr-r-ristian."

288

REUNIONS

So did Timothy leave Lystra with you?" Simon of Cyrene asked, eager to hear more of the magnificent first missionary journey. The entire church of Antioch gathered together on this steamy summer night in the courtyard of his home to hear the report of their missionaries, Paul and Barnabas.

"No, since we felt the need to leave in haste following the attack on Paul, and Timothy was the most solid believer there, we asked him to stay in Lystra and help the other new believers," Barnabas explained. "From there we went to Derbe where we spent the winter. Paul was able to fully recover from his wounds, and the people there showered us with such a warm welcome."

"They would have given me their own eyes while mine were so weak from the malaria and beatings," Paul added, smiling fondly as he remembered the kindness of the believers there. "The people of Derbe didn't show scorn at my poor condition, as would have been the case with the Jewish elite. No, they welcomed us, cared for me, and we led many to Christ there."

"When the snows melted we had a big decision to make," related Barnabas. "Do we head back here through the quick and easy route east? Or do we head west and retrace our steps of this journey before heading home?"

"Surely you didn't go back where you were beaten and stoned!" Rufus exclaimed, followed by murmurs of agreement from the people in the courtyard. Paul and Barnabas shared a knowing grin.

"If Paul were with Daniel back in the day, he would've marched r-r-right back inta the lions' den if it meant savin' the guards!" Max whispered.

Nigel and Liz were seated on the stone wall of the courtyard next to Max. "Indeed, never have I seen such bold determination," the little mouse agreed.

"This is why the Maker chose him, no?" Liz added. "And he is just getting started."

"We decided to go back through all the cities where we had established churches," Barnabas continued. "We went back to Lystra, to Iconium, and on to Antioch in Pisidia. No one bothered us in those cities when we returned. The faith and boldness of the people *grew* because of what we had experienced there. They saw how the Holy Spirit strengthened us, and they understood that he was with them, too."

"Yes, but we learned that it isn't enough to just establish the churches. They need help," Paul explained. "So we strengthened the believers and encouraged them to remain true to the faith, telling them they must pass through many troubles to enter the Kingdom of God."

Barnabas nodded. "In each church we appointed elders. We prayed and fasted with them, and commended them to the Lord. We feel those Galatian churches are in good hands. The Lord opened a huge door of faith to the Gentiles!"

"They are so hungry for the truth!" Paul stressed, looking around at his home church. "I wish you could have seen their faces as they heard the Good News."

"Finally we went back to Perga, where we preached before heading to Attalia and sailing back here," Barnabas reported. He looked around the courtyard at their brothers and sisters in Christ, who were filled with joy at hearing all God had done. "After a thousand miles on foot, it's good to be home."

"Amen, Barnabas. It's good to be home with our church family.

Praise God for all he's done!" Paul exclaimed, lifting his hands.

"We pray you stay awhile," Simon said with a wide smile, followed by a chorus of agreement from the believers.

"AYE!" Max barked. *"I'm r-r-ready for some r-r-rest meself."*

The people laughed at the eager dog's response. "I think Gabriel speaks for all of us that we're home to stay for a long rest," Paul laughed, then added, "but not *too* long. There's a world of Gentiles out there who still need saving."

Liz gazed into the slow-moving waters of the Orontes River, watching the fish swim past. She sighed heavily, knowing how Al would dive in to get them if he were there. "Oh Albert, how I miss you." She closed her eyes and lay down for a nap in the sunshine.

Something started tickling her nose. It smelled sweet. She opened her eyes and saw a flower stuck in her face. "It's not edelweiss but it's all I could find," came Al's voice as he moved the flower and showed his round, orange face, goofy grin and all. "Hello, me beauty!"

291

"Albert!" Liz exclaimed with joy, wrapping her paws around his neck and giving him a big kiss. "You're here!"

"Aye, Peter and me jest arrived," Al responded, handing Liz the flower.

"I'm so happy to see you, *cher* Albert. It's been so long," Liz said, nudging him with her chin and twirling the flower in her paw.

Nigel and Max came bounding down the grassy hillside. "Splendid to see you, old boy! How have your travels been with Peter?"

"Mousie! Max! I love reunions!" Al exclaimed, giving them both a smothering hug. "Me and Peter been lots o' places, puttin' fishes in the dirt everywhere. No more bad laddies after us anywhere, so that's good."

"Gr-r-rand ta see ye, Lad," Max grinned. "How long ye here for?"

"Dunno. Peter wanted to see Paul and Barnabas, so here we be," Al replied. "They already be sharin' stories o' their adventures."

"Yes, the church here is positively thrilled to see Peter, who was actually with Jesus," Nigel relayed. "They're up there enjoying a big feast right now. I must say how delightful it is to see Peter eating and fellowshipping so easily with Gentiles."

"Aye, since some o' the believin' Jews back in Jerusalem still think Jesus belongs to them alone," Al reported. He elbowed Max with a big grin. "Get this, they be callin' themselves *'Christian Pharisees.'*"

"Ye're jestin', Lad!" Max said with a wide-eyed grin. "Those two words go together as much as me an' water before I could swim."

"Oh dear, so the orthodox Jews still cling to the old ways of the Mosaic laws and traditions," Nigel lamented, shaking his head. "Simply dreadful the way they view the Gentiles as despicable sinners."

"Pretty much," Al replied. "I heard one laddie say the only way Gentiles could be accepted into the church would be if they become Jews first."

"This is intolerable!" Nigel fumed. "That kind of thinking is the complete opposite of what Christianity is all about. If this bunch succeeds, they'll turn the Christian movement into nothing more than a Jewish sect."

292

"*Oui*, Jesus set people free from all that," Liz echoed. "Only grace saves, not the Law! This is false teaching, the fourth weapon of the Enemy used against The Way."

"Well, those 'Christian Pharisees' be out travelin' around to tell everybody the way it's got to be," Al told them. "Heard they were even goin' to Galatia."

"Yes, and they're coming here," Clarie said, walking up to them as a little lamb. "Hello, everyone."

"Clarie!" Liz cried with joy, embracing her sweet friend. "Lovely to see you! But what disturbing news, no?"

"Yes, they are causing confusion with all the new churches Paul and Barnabas have worked so hard to start," Clarie reported. "When they get here, things will heat up with Paul and Peter."

"Why those no good r-r-rascals!" Max growled. "Paul aboot died ta br-r-ring the Good News ta those Gentiles an' I'm not aboot ta let some pompous, r-r-rule–cr-r-razy lads r-r-ruin it for them!"

Clarie nodded and smiled. "So, something will have to be done, both here and in Jerusalem, to settle the matter once and for all."

"*Mon amie,* what can we do?" Liz asked. "Does this have something to do with the third strategy Gillamon said would come to help the churches?"

"It does, Liz. Think. How could Paul help the churches he and Barnabas have established in Galatia if people come behind them with confusing teaching?" Clarie asked.

"Well, they cannot use the IAMISPHERE to reach them in a flash," Liz pondered, thinking this through, her tail slowly curling up and down.

"And by the time they *did* travel back there, no telling what shape the churches will be in," Nigel added, tapping his paw on his chin.

"Why don't they jest write a letter?" Al suggested, lying on his back in the grass.

Liz and Nigel looked at one another and exclaimed at the same time, "Why didn't we think of that?!"

"It's so simple, it's obvious, no?" Liz said, kissing Al on the cheek.

Nigel rose up on his tiptoes with his hands clasped behind his back. "Jolly good idea, old boy!"

"So letters be the third str-r-rategy?" Max asked.

293

"*Oui!* Now I see how this will work," Liz answered. "Paul can write letters to the churches he visits, telling them exactly what they need to know, correcting what's wrong, or simply encouraging them."

"*And* if those letters are passed around by the churches, they could become so well known that they merit status as books . . ." Nigel began.

"Of the New Testament!" Liz and Nigel exclaimed. "So some books like Matthew and Mark will be historical accounts of Jesus and the apostles, and some will be letters to churches," Liz added.

"Or letters to individuals with truths that can benefit all Christians," Clarie said with her smiling blue eyes. "Very good. You'll need to inspire Paul to write the churches of Galatia first. Once he sees how successful his correspondence becomes, it will become part of his normal routine."

"Right, so they'll visit a city's synagogue, stay a while to establish a church, and follow up with letters to keep them on track," Nigel outlined, summarizing the three strategies. "Brilliant!"

"I believe you have it," Clarie quipped, kissing Nigel's small head. "Now, get ready for a showdown. The Christian Pharisees will be here soon."

Max frowned and grumbled. "Aye, an' fightin' words be comin'."

DEAR IDIOTS
OF GALATIA

Peter was laughing with Paul, Barnabas, and the Gentile believers around the table when he heard someone clearing his throat behind him. He turned to see three orthodox Jewish men from the church in Jerusalem at the entrance to the courtyard, refusing to come in. Peter's eyes grew wide and he swallowed his bite of food, wiped off his hands, and got up from the table. Barnabas even squirmed at the sight.

"Welcome, brothers, do come in," Peter encouraged them.

They looked at Peter in shock and wore faces of judgmental disapproval. "We see you eat with sinners and Gentiles here in Antioch," they sneered.

Peter was suddenly consumed with guilt and slipped into his old way of thinking. "Yes, uh, well, perhaps you're right. I shouldn't be here."

Paul rose up from the table, indignant at both Peter and the Christian Pharisees. He got right in Peter's face in front of the church, and spoke loud for everyone to hear. "You are a Jew, yet you have been living like a Gentile, not like a Jew. How, then, can you try to force Gentiles to live like Jews?"

"You cannot be saved unless you follow as the Law of Moses requires," the Jews insisted.

Paul stepped in front of Peter and now got right in the face of the pompous Jews who towered over him. "Do you dare suggest that someone's salvation is dependent on their ability to keep the Law? That they can win their salvation by their own efforts?!" he shouted, now pacing back and forth.

"Get r-r-ready," Max whispered with a sly grin to the other animals in the courtyard. "Here he goes."

Paul laid into the Christian Pharisees, Peter, and even Barnabas, who was wavering on this issue. "Your Jewish roots are strangling your understanding of liberty and grace! And I was more perfect than even *you* at keeping the law back in my blinded days," he told one of the Jews, poking him in the chest. "NO ONE can ever earn the favor of God! Do you think Jesus' sacrifice meant nothing? Do you actually believe that a Jew could go to God and say, 'Look, here are my good deeds. I've been so good to keep every tiny bit of the law. Now give me the salvation I've earned.'? NO!"

295

Peter stared at the floor with a convicted look on his face, nodding as he realized how right Paul was, and how he had temporarily slipped back into his "Simon" mindset.

"Give them the what-for and all that, Paul!" Nigel cheered with a fist raised in the air.

"It's not about what we can do for God, but what God has done for us," Paul implored, putting his hands on his chest.

"But, the most important thing in the life of Israel is our laws," the Jews protested. "God himself gave Moses that law, and our very lives depend on it."

"*Depended,*" Paul emphasized. "Wait a minute. Who is the founder of our nation?"

"Abraham, of course," they replied with impatience.

Paul held up a finger. "So how did Abraham gain God's favor then? He lived 430 years before the law was given to Moses."

The Jews looked at one another but had no answer.

"It was FAITH that saved Abraham, not the law. And it is FAITH that saves every man, woman, and child today, NOT the law," Paul continued. "The real sons and daughters of Abraham aren't those related by blood but related by faith."

"If this is true, then where does the law fit?" the Jews asked. "What is the law's place in all this?"

Paul paced around as he thought through his response to make it clear to these blind Jews. He stopped and clasped his hands. "First, the law tells us what sin is. If there is no law, we can't break it, and that means there can be no such thing as sin. Are you with me so far?"

The men grudgingly nodded.

"Second, and I would say most importantly, the law drives us to the *grace* of God. We are completely unable to fully keep the law. Has any one of you kept it perfectly? No, you haven't. So, the law shows us how weak we are, and so our despair leaves us with no other option but to throw ourselves onto the mercy and grace of God." Paul stopped and paused a moment. "The Law is like a tutor you need when you're a child, to learn the basics of life. Or like a guardian you need until you are old enough to make decisions on your own. But the tutor was needed only until Jesus came to purchase our freedom from the law. That's how we become sons of God."

Paul looked around the room at the Gentile and Jewish believers. "We all can call ourselves sons and daughters of the most high God through Jesus' sacrifice alone. And until you understand this, I suggest you keep your mouths shut before leading other young believers astray."

"Hear, hear!" Nigel cheered. "Bravo!"

"*C'est magnifique!* Paul has told them exactly what they need to hear," Liz applauded. "And I believe *we've* just heard exactly what he needs to put in his letter to the Galatians. Nigel, I think we need to get word to Paul about how the Galatians have heard that horrible teaching."

"And I know exactly who can deliver our message," answered Nigel, giving Clarie a wink.

Al wrinkled his brow, staring at Clarie. "Sheep mail?"

∝

"I wept when Jesus looked right at me after I had denied him three times," Peter shared, locking eyes with Paul, clenching his jaw. "Once again, I needed to be rebuked for my shaky behavior. Thank you, my brother. I will never waver on this subject again."

Paul nodded humbly. "Thank you for being so open to my criticism, especially in front of the church. This issue is so crucial, Peter. I feel the entire foundation of Jesus' church will either flourish or fall on this issue about the Gentiles. Jesus said he is the only Way. He is all anyone needs to be saved. Not Judaism, not keeping countless rules. Jesus alone."

"I agree, and you did the right thing," Peter told Paul. "The Antioch church is right—we need to have a council in Jerusalem to settle this matter once and for all. I'd like you, Barnabas, and some of the others from the church to come to Jerusalem soon."

297

"A wise move, Peter," Paul said, gripping Peter's arm and nodding. "You can count on us. We'll come soon."

"Good, good," Peter smiled. "Now, I'll be on my way back to Jerusalem and try to stop any more Christian Pharisees from taking this message out to the churches. Come along, Ari."

Al and Liz were saying their farewells and Peter did a double take on Liz. "You know, the Master had a black cat just like that. Ari must love black cats."

"Oh? Isn't that something?" Paul said, smiling down at Al and Liz. "Shalom, my friend. Safe journey to you."

"Shalom. See you soon," Peter answered as he turned and began walking down the road out of Antioch. Al went trotting off with Peter. "He had a black dog, too," Peter called back.

Liz stood in the street and her eyes welled up to see Al leaving once again. *"Adieu, mon cher,"* she meowed.

Paul reached down and picked Liz up, wrinkling his brow. "Why, Faith, you look sad!" He stared after Peter and the orange cat. Suddenly he realized what Peter had just said. *A black dog?* He studied Liz's face. "Were you and Gabriel . . . ?" he started to ask, wondering if this could be the same cat that had belonged to Jesus. "No, that can't be."

"I bring news from Derbe," announced Clarie, now in the form of a young messenger man. She handed the sealed papyrus scroll to Paul.

Paul smiled and nodded, taking the scroll. "Thank you. Please, have something to eat. Simon? Can you help our guest?"

"Certainly," Simon said, bringing a bowl of water over to wash Clarie's dusty feet.

Clarie locked eyes with Liz and Nigel, who winked at her.

"What's the news?" Barnabas asked. Paul's brow was wrinkled and his lips moved as he read the letter. He didn't reply. "Paul?"

Paul slammed his fist on the table. "Why those . . . !"

"What?!" Barnabas demanded.

"Seems some 'Christian Pharisees' decided it would be a good idea to set the record straight with this Gentile issue and the law there in Galatia. They also say I'm not considered an apostle who holds the *authority* to teach the Gentiles about such things since I never was a personal disciple of Jesus," Paul grumbled, tossing the letter over to Barnabas. He stood and paced around the room. "Our dear churches have been swept into another version of the gospel, and with widespread 'success.' Those former pagans who trusted Jesus as Lord and were full of joy are now miserable trying to keep the Jewish law! AHHH!" He clasped his hands behind his neck and paced back and forth.

"We need to get to Jerusalem sooner than we thought and settle this matter before it spreads any further," suggested Barnabas.

"But our churches can't wait that long," Paul said. "No, we must correct this with them immediately."

"You're not yet recovered enough to start on a journey back there, Paul," Barnabas insisted.

Paul plopped down on the bench next to Barnabas, crestfallen. "Oh, Barnabas, I'm heartsick over this! How is it possible our Galatians have so quickly changed course and got off track?"

"Fickle Galatians," Nigel murmured under his breath.

298

Barnabas put his large hand on Paul's small shoulder. "You, my friend, have thick skin when it comes to attacks from outsiders, but your heart is tender for your children in the faith. You love them deeply, and you must put them back on the right course. They must understand that Jesus' sacrifice cannot be dismissed as some secondary issue."

Paul's eyes filled with fiery determination. "Time to write a letter of my own."

The oil lamps were lit up all around the room where the leaders of the Antioch church had assembled. Spread across the table were rolls of fresh papyrus and a penman preparing his pen and ink. Paul looked around the room. "Thank you all for coming. It was important for me to have you here as I dictate this letter in order to carry the authority of the church who sent me as your missionary to Galatia." He turned to face the penman. "Are you ready?"

299

"Yes, Sir, whenever you are," the scribe replied.

Liz, Nigel, and Max sat in the shadows with Clarie, overjoyed with what was happening.

Paul smiled and clasped his hands together. "Very well, let's begin." He cleared his throat and began pacing around the room.

"From Paul, whose call to be an apostle did not come from human beings or by human means, but from Jesus Christ and God the Father, who raised him from death. All the believers who are here join me in sending greetings to the churches of Galatia:

"May God our Father and the Lord Jesus Christ give you grace and peace.

"In order to set us free from this present evil age, Christ gave himself for our sins, in obedience to the will of our God and Father. To God be the glory forever and ever! Amen.

"I am surprised at you! In no time at all you are deserting the one who called you by the grace of Christ, and are accepting another gospel. Actually, there is no "other gospel," but I say this because there are some people who are upsetting you and trying to change the gospel of Christ. But even if we or an angel from heaven should preach to you a gospel that is different from the one we preached to you, may he be condemned to hell! We have said it before, and now I say it again: if anyone preaches to you a gospel that is different from the one you accepted, may he be condemned to hell! Does this sound as if I am trying to win human approval? No indeed! What I want is God's approval! Am I trying to be popular with people? If I were still trying to do so, I would not be a servant of Christ."

Paul paused to allow the penman, writing furiously, to catch up. When he gave the signal, Paul started again, detailing his qualifications to present the gospel. Meanwhile, the animals talked among themselves.

"Stupendous beginning!" Nigel cheered. "I say, he's quite the fireball with this letter."

Liz's eyes were wide at Paul's fervor. "*C'est ça!* He needs to be, no? But I think the Galatians will see Paul's fiercely protective love come through."

300

"He's like a papa cor-r-rectin' his wee lads an' lassies then," Max observed. "But with the kind of lesson that makes ye feel relieved an' loved."

"O you dear idiots of Galatia, who saw Jesus Christ the crucified so plainly, who has been casting a spell over you?" Paul wailed. "I will ask you one simple question: did you receive the Spirit of God by trying to keep the Law or by believing the message of the gospel? Surely you can't be so idiotic as to think that a man begins his spiritual life in the Spirit and then completes it by reverting to outward observances? Has all your painful experience brought you nowhere? I simply cannot believe it of you! Does God, who gives you his Spirit and works miracles among you, do these things because you have obeyed the Law or because you have believed the gospel? Ask yourselves that."

"This is a timeless lesson," Clarie said with a smile. "One I hope future generations will never forget."

Barnabas and the other church members listened to Paul, sitting in awe of how his mind worked and how he was able to articulate such truth in a clear, powerful way. Scroll after scroll was filled with Paul's words to the Galatians until he neared the end. Paul leaned over the table and picked up a piece of fruit. He studied it for a moment and held it up close to his face.

"But the fruit of the Spirit is love, joy, peace, forbearance, kindness, goodness, faithfulness, gentleness and self-control. Against such things there is no law."

He continued a little longer, looking over the penman's shoulder to make sure he was capturing every word. "Please, now, be so kind as to read it back to me."

The penman picked up all the scrolls and placed them in order. He proceeded to read every word Paul had dictated, reaching the final line. "So let us not become tired of doing good; for if we do not give up, the time will come when we will reap the harvest. So then, as often as we have the chance, we should do good to everyone, and especially to those who belong to our family in the faith."

Paul folded his arms and nodded. "Thank you. May I see that last page?"

301

The penman handed it over to Paul and he saw that there was room left on the page for him to add a personal note. He reached over and grabbed the pen, and wrote in his own handwriting a few more lines, ending with:

> *Quite frankly, I don't want to be bothered anymore by these disputes. I have far more important things to do—the serious living of this faith. I bear in my body scars from my service to Jesus. May what our Master Jesus Christ gives freely be deeply and personally yours, my friends. Oh, yes! - PAUL*

Paul put down his pen, and scanned the room for Clarie, the "messenger." "I'm sending this letter with you back to Derbe tomorrow."

"Yes, sir, I'll leave at first light," Clarie replied. Then leaning over she whispered to the animals, "I should arrive in about ten seconds, IAMISPHERE time."

Liz and Nigel high-fived each other. The first letter in the New Testament was complete and ready for its readers—the fickle, dear idiots of Galatia.

35

FROM THE PENS OF JAMES AND ANONYMOUSE

JERUSALEM, AD 49

Nigel sat up high in the rafters of the room where the Jerusalem Council had gathered shortly after the arrival of Paul and Barnabas. The little mouse was slouched forward with his cheeks resting in his paws, shaking his head at the absurdity of it all. After a tiring morning of listening to the Christian Pharisees' argument about why pagans needed to first become Jews in order to be saved, Peter finally stood. Nigel sat up, hopeful. "Come on now, Peter. Be a good chap and bring some sense to this tiresome meeting."

Peter locked eyes with Paul and Barnabas, giving a slight nod of solidarity before he opened his hands wide to address the group. "My friends, you know that a long time ago God chose me from among you to preach the Good News to the Gentiles, so that they could hear and believe. And God, who knows the thoughts of everyone, showed his approval of the Gentiles by giving the Holy Spirit to them, just as he had to us. He made no difference between us and them; he forgave their sins because they believed. So then, why do you now want to put God to the test by laying a load on the backs of the believers which neither our ancestors nor we ourselves were able to carry? No! We believe and are saved by the grace of the Lord Jesus, just as they are."

"Hear, hear!" Nigel jumped to his feet and raised his little fists in the air. "Finally some reason fills this room. I do hope churches don't get into the habit of having such long, laborious meetings."

There was dead silence. No one said a word. With the room quiet, Barnabas and Paul reported matter-of-factly on the miracles and wonders God had done among the other nations through their ministry. The silence deepened; you could have heard a pin drop.

Nigel preened his whiskers and crossed his arms with satisfaction. "Nothing like proof in the pudding to silence the loudmouthed critics."

James broke the silence. "Friends, listen. Peter has told us the story of how God at the very outset made sure that racial outsiders were included. This is in perfect agreement with the words of the prophets: 'After this I will return, says the Lord, and restore the kingdom of David. I will rebuild its ruins and make it strong again. And so all the rest of the human race will come to me, all the Gentiles whom I have called to be my own.' God said it and now he's doing it. It's no afterthought; he's always known he would do this."

303

"Bravo, James!" Nigel approved. "Brilliant of you to quote Amos."

James continued, "So here is my decision: We're not going to unnecessarily burden non-Jewish people who turn to the Master. We'll write them a letter and tell them, 'Be careful to not get involved in activities connected with idols, to guard the morality of sex and marriage, to not serve food offensive to Jewish Christians—blood, for instance.' This is basic wisdom from Moses, preached and honored for centuries now in city after city as we have met and kept the Sabbath."

A murmuring of approval rose up from the crowd. Everyone agreed!

John spoke up. "James, I suggest we send Paul and Barnabas back to Antioch with the letter, along with two of our men who carry considerable weight in the church—Silas and Judas Barsabbas, perhaps?"

"I agree. These are good men to send," Peter echoed. "They will represent us with true authority."

The Christian Pharisees looked embarrassed for having gone out and spread their faulty ideas, claiming they had the authority of the church. Nigel grinned at their reddened faces.

James nodded. "Very well, I will write the letter and we'll send these men with our blessing."

With that the assembly broke up and members went back to their homes. James sat down at his desk and picked up his pen. And Nigel scurried to a shelf to spy over James's shoulder.

> *From the apostles and leaders, your friends, to our friends in Antioch, Syria, and Cilicia:*
>
> *Greetings!*
>
> *We heard that some men from our church went to you and said things that confused and upset you. Mind you, they had no authority from us; we didn't send them. We have agreed unanimously to pick representatives and send them to you with our good friends Barnabas and Paul. We picked men we knew you could trust, Judas and Silas—they've looked death in the face time and again for the sake of our Master Jesus Christ. We've sent them to confirm in a face-to-face meeting with you what we've written.*
>
> *It seemed to the Holy Spirit and to us that you should not be saddled with any crushing burden, but be responsible only for these bare necessities: Be careful not to get involved in activities connected with idols; avoid serving food offensive to Jewish Christians (blood, for instance); and guard the morality of sex and marriage.*
>
> *These guidelines are sufficient to keep relations congenial between us. And God be with you!*

James blew on the wet ink and read it over twice as Nigel nodded with approval behind him.

"Well done. Cordial. Fair. Concise," Nigel whispered to himself. "Your big brother would be proud."

304

As James got up from his desk and left the room, Nigel jumped onto the table that was scattered with rolls of papyrus, pens, and ink. "James is an excellent writer." Suddenly an idea came to the scribal mouse. "By Jove, James could write to the Jewish believers everywhere. If Paul is to be the chief scribe to the Gentiles, surely the Jewish Christians need a good word from the head of the mother church here in Jerusalem."

The little mouse looked around on the desk for a pen that was small enough for him to hold, and took a piece of papyrus. "I wish Liz were here to assist, but alas, this letter will have to be from me alone." Nigel chuckled to himself. "An 'anonymouse' letter."

After James sent the men on their way back to Antioch with the letter that would settle the Gentile problem once and for all, he sat down at his desk to tidy up. As he picked up the pieces of papyrus, he noticed that one was rolled up and placed on the corner of his desk. James reached over and unrolled the mysterious note. Nigel waited expectantly to see how James would receive it.

305

Peace and grace to you, James:

I was privileged to attend the Jerusalem Council, and am grateful for your wise guidance to resolve the issues for our Gentile brothers and sisters. Your letter was well written and I know will bring joy and relief to them. Yet as I considered the letter to the Gentiles at large, the thought came to me that perhaps our Jewish believing brothers and sisters could benefit from your wise counsel as well, especially after having been dispersed everywhere. Perhaps another, universal letter from you would be a source of direction and encouragement for them.

As we've seen from the Christian Pharisees who misled the Gentiles, there could be great confusion among many other Jews who have held to the old beliefs for so long. Jews have long been conditioned to be a 'doing' people. And while faith in Jesus is all that is required for salvation, surely there are things believers must do as they live out their faith. Equally important, believers need to understand the things they *shouldn't* do as the gospel spreads. As we've just seen, it is possible for Christians to believe all the right things but still live the wrong way. This is especially the case as they face trials and hard times for their faith. Jesus said such difficulties would come, but hearing how to face them specifically would encourage everyone.

So my brother, I would ask you to please consider writing a letter to the Jewish believers, helping them understand the right way to go. As the head of the Jerusalem church, no one could speak to them with greater authority than you.

Blessings.

James flipped the letter over, looking for a signature. When he found none he shrugged his shoulders.

"From the pen of Anonymouse," Nigel muttered with a grin.

James sat back and nodded. "A letter to the Jewish believers . . . hmmmmm." He scratched his chin and raised his eyebrows as ideas began swirling in his heart and mind. James bowed his head and prayed for wisdom about what he should write. When he finished, he took a fresh piece of papyrus and dipped his pen in the ink. Nigel's heart raced with excitement and he scurried to a shelf for a better view over James's shoulder.

James, a servant of God and of the Lord Jesus Christ,
To the twelve tribes scattered among the nations:
Greetings.

Consider it pure joy, my brothers and sisters, whenever you face trials of many kinds, because you know that the testing of your faith produces perseverance. Let perseverance finish its work so that you may be mature and complete, not lacking anything. If any of you lacks wisdom, you should ask God, who gives generously to all without finding fault, and it will be given to you.

"Utterly splendid beginning, James!" Nigel squeaked loudly, then quickly covered his mouth. His eyes had widened with joy as he read James's first words. Once James got started, his pen flew across page after page with divine inspiration. His letter was packed with truths to challenge even the most seasoned Christian. The toughness yet appropriateness of James's letter surprised even Nigel. The little mouse realized that James's letter would be invaluable to not just Jewish believers but all believers to come.

Nigel confidently cleaned his spectacles and straightened them atop his pink nose. "I daresay your letter will undoubtedly find its way into the New Testament, even if I have to use my anonymouse pen to make it so."

307

PARTING WAYS AND BLOCKED PATHS

Things are going well here in Antioch now that the people have embraced James's letter. Let's go back and visit all our friends in each of the towns where we preached the Word of God," Paul said, chewing a pistachio. He cracked another nut. "Let's see how they're doing. We'll take them the letter, too."

Barnabas set down his cup, wiped his mouth with the back of his hand, and nodded. "Great idea! We can take Mark with us." He reached his hand into the bowl of pistachios and grabbed a nut to crack.

Paul frowned and shook his head, popping a pistachio in his mouth. "Absolutely not! I'm not about to take along a quitter who, as soon as the going got tough, jumped ship on us in Perga. Mark is out of the question."

"Ooh-la-la, this is not good," Liz warned Max and Nigel.

"Aye, they shouldn't be talkin' an' eatin' pistachios so fast," Max agreed. "They could choke."

"No, old boy, I believe Liz rather means they could choke on their words," Nigel corrected him.

Barnabas grimaced and pressed a hard pistachio tightly between his thumb and forefinger. "And I say he *goes!* You're rather quick to count Mark out, especially after I came to your side when you needed a second chance."

"The lad's got a point," Max offered.

"And I'm forever grateful to you, Barnabas, but our concern here should be the stability of a dependable traveling companion," Paul argued, grabbing another nut. "I predict this second journey will be even more intense. If Mark quit before we even hit the hardest part of our last journey, he will not be up for this new challenge."

"What about *grace?*" Barnabas shouted. "I'm concerned about the boy!"

"What about our *mission?*" Paul shouted back. "I'm concerned about the spread of the gospel!"

Both men stood and got into a heated argument, each giving rational arguments to support his opposing opinion.

"They both have valid points, no?" Liz said. "A disagreement is an issue seen from different points of view."

"Yet sadly, the hotter the argument, the deeper the wounds if they do not find a solution," Nigel worried.

"I'm sailing for Cyprus!" Barnabas finally shouted, slamming his fist on the table, bouncing pistachios out of the bowl. "And I'm taking Mark with me!"

Paul shot his hands up and out. "Go then! I'll take Silas and start in the opposite direction, seeing as how that's where we stand with things!"

Both men stormed off from the table, leaving pistachios scattered everywhere. Liz jumped up onto the table and looked at the mess. Nigel scurried over to join her and Max put his large square head up to the side.

"This is intolerable!" Nigel fumed, pacing back and forth on his hind legs, kicking pistachio nuts everywhere. "I cannot believe Paul and Barnabas are splitting apart, after all they've accomplished together! They must be mad!" He kicked a nut. "Or nuts, as it were."

Max opened his mouth and caught a pistachio as Nigel kicked it off the table. He cracked the shell and spit it out to enjoy the treat inside. "Aye, but jest like these nuts, ye can't get ta the good part unless ye separate it fr-r-rom the shell."

Liz slowly moved the nuts around the table with her paw as she thought through the implications of what had just happened. Her tail curled up and down. Suddenly she looked over at Max, who had his mouth open, catching another one of Nigel's kicked nuts. "What did you say, *mon ami?*"

Max spit out the shell and grinned as he chewed the pistachio. "Ye got ta divide the nut ta get ta the good part."

Liz looked back at the spread of nuts that Nigel continued to pace and kick through. "Division will lead to addition!" she exclaimed. "Don't you see? Although this is sad for Paul and Barnabas to be divided, there are now two teams going out to spread the Good News!"

Nigel stopped and picked up a pistachio. "Brilliant observation, my pet! I say, those two nuts can divide yet conquer!"

"An' the world will get the tr-r-reat!" Max added. "Toss me that nut ta celebr-r-rate, Mousie."

"I must say, this arrangement makes jolly good sense," Nigel said as he rode on Max's back along the road to Lystra. "With Silas also being a Roman citizen, he and Paul can both claim *civis romanus sum*. Paul need not suffer Roman punishment, as he suffered alongside Barnabas, if it comes to that again."

"*Oui! C'est bon!*" Liz cheered. "I shall be happy to see Paul avoid further harm if possible."

Max trotted along listening to Paul and Silas, who were discussing their excellent visit with the church in Derbe. "Aye, so far so good then. No tr-r-roubles yet. There be safety in numbers. Let's hope the laddies get another gr-r-rand welcome in Lystra."

Liz watched as Paul walked along scarred and bandy-legged, carrying his knapsack and heavy bag of supplies. The apostle was in his fifties now, and after his many physical beatings, malaria, and the perpetual thorn in his side, his health wasn't what it used to be. "I am worried for Paul. He seems to be struggling today. If only he could have a physician's care for his many ailments." Her eyes brightened. "Lystra. Safety in numbers. Timothy!" she thought out loud. "I think I shall suggest some addition while we're here."

That night Paul and Silas were enveloped with love by the people of Lystra, who eagerly listened to the letter from James and the Jerusalem Council. They shared with Paul about how the church had grown since his last visit. Liz repeatedly walked back and forth across Timothy's hearth, rubbing his legs.

"Faith likes you," Paul said with a smile, studying the young man who had done so much for the church in Lystra.

"I like Faith," Timothy answered, scratching Liz under the chin. She began to purr wildly.

"You also *have* faith, Timothy," Paul quipped with a play on words. "The kind of faith we need to help us in this work." He looked at Silas. "I think we should take Timothy with us, if he'd be willing to go."

"Willing?! Of course I'd be willing!" Timothy exclaimed. "You mean I can come with you and Silas?"

Silas scratched his thick black beard. "Only if you truly feel called and right about going."

"I do!" Timothy enthused.

Liz winked at Max and Nigel. "The lass knows how ta wr-r-rap those humans ar-r-round her little tail."

Paul put his hand on Timothy's shoulder. "It will be my joy to have you as my son in the faith, Timothy. May God bless you as you join us to spread the Good News."

Timothy nodded. "And I am honored to join you both. Where do we go from here?"

"We'll continue on through Galatia, but our plan is to turn west into Asia province toward Ephesus," Silas explained. "We can follow Rome's established route for imperial messengers."

"Yes, and from Ephesus we can go over to Greece and once we've covered that area," Paul said, his eyes filled with adventure, "we'll head to Rome."

"Rome!" Timothy exclaimed, picking Liz up and holding her close

311

to his chest. "Just think, little Faith, we'll take the Good News all the way to the emperor himself!"

Liz rubbed Timothy's chin affectionately, meowing, *"All roads lead to Rome,* n'est ce pas?"

The sun was beginning its descent as the trio of missionaries headed southwest on the road from Antioch in Pisidia. The little band was anxious to reach new territory with the gospel, so they traveled as far as they could each day. Suddenly the smell of fresh baked bread wafted through the air. Timothy's mouth watered and he pointed to the solitary fire and tent pitched on the side of the road.

"Look! Someone has a fire going," Timothy announced with a relieved smile. "And bread."

Paul and Silas smiled at one another and then at their young partner. "Go ask if we can join them," Silas instructed Timothy with a wave of his hand.

"Come on, boy!" Timothy said to Max, who followed the young man. They went eagerly running ahead of the others up to the campfire. "Hello?" he called, not seeing anyone around. "Is anyone here?"

"Is that your dog?" came the voice of an old woman from the tent. She stepped out and came over to squat down and give Max a pet. "He's a sturdy fellow."

Max wagged his tail and smiled broadly at the woman with twinkling blue eyes. She gave Max a wink. The Scottie knew in an instant who she was.

"Yes, dear woman, he is," Timothy answered. "Gabriel is his name. And I'm Timothy. My friends Paul and Silas are coming up the road. Might we join your camp for the night?"

"Gabriel? Gabriel is a messenger angel. Imagine that," the old woman replied with a smile, glancing down the road. She took a seat on a rock by her fire. "I'm Clarie. Please, you and your friends, join me. I've just made bread."

"I noticed," Timothy replied happily.

"Welcome, friends," Clarie said as Paul and Silas stepped up. "Please, sit down and rest."

Liz joined Max next to Clarie. He whispered in her ear and she immediately smiled, rubbing Clarie's knees. *"Bonjour, mon amie!"* she meowed.

"Thank you for your hospitality," Paul exhaled as he sat down in relief. He winced from pain in his neck and shoulder.

Clarie studied Paul, who was clearly struggling. "You need a doctor." She picked Liz up and whispered in her ear. "Find him."

"And that's Faith," Timothy explained as Clarie held Liz in her lap. Liz turned her gaze to Clarie's face and nodded.

"A messenger and faith. Two things you need, especially for this journey." Clarie closed her eyes as she stroked Max with one hand and Liz with the other. "Dear God, we thank you for this food we are about to eat. Bless these men who travel in your name. May they receive here what they most need from you. Amen." Clarie opened her eyes and motioned toward the bread. "Please, help yourselves."

313

Timothy eagerly took some bread, handing the loaf to Silas. Silas passed some to Paul, who seemed not to notice. His curiosity was up. It was highly unusual for an old woman to be out here all alone on a dusty road, cooking bread in the middle of nowhere. When she prayed, he felt the stirring of the Holy Spirit telling him to pay close attention to her. "How do you know about our journey? Are you a prophetess?"

Clarie smiled and allowed a few moments of silence before answering the question. "The time isn't ripe for you to go to there yet. You must not venture south."

Paul kept his gaze on the old woman while Timothy and Silas looked from one another to Paul to the old woman. "Has the Holy Spirit told you this, my sister?"

Clarie just smiled, gently placed Liz on the ground, and stood up. "Eat your fill, my friends." She looked down at Max and Liz. "Heed the message and keep the faith."

With that she walked into the tent, winking at Nigel, who hid in the shadows, and leaving the men fixed with confused looks. The fire snapped and popped, and embers rose up to the now darkened sky. The night sky was filling with bright stars. Paul turned his gaze upward and studied the heavens. The brightest star in the sky caught his attention. It was the North Star, twinkling as brightly as the old woman's eyes.

"Tomorrow, we head north," Paul declared. "Get your rest."

In the morning, the old woman and her tent were gone.

Liz sat by the fire and watched Paul's restless sleep as Nigel proceeded to give a mini-lecture on Homer's *Iliad*. They had traveled north to Mysia, and hoped to enter Bithynia tomorrow. Paul's health continued to suffer and Liz continued to ponder Clarie's directive about a doctor: *"Find him." Who and where?* remained Liz's continual questions.

"Of course the historical Mysia where we currently are encamped is much larger than Homer's mythological Mysia," Nigel schooled the others, twirling his paw. "Right, now Homer staged a minor scene of the Trojan War here at Mysia, where the Greeks actually mistake Mysia for Troy." He chuckled heartily. "Can you imagine, mistaking *this* place for *Troy?*"

Max furrowed his brow, slowly shaking his head sarcastically. "No, laddie, I r-r-really can't. *R-r-really.*"

"Where was I? Oh yes, so Achilles wounds Telephus their king after he slays a Greek, and later Telephus begs him to heal the wound," Nigel continued. "So Homer presents the Mysians as allies of Troy. Of course, you'll remember that Achilles is the Greek hero and main character of the *Iliad.*"

"I thought he were Armandus's horse," Max replied.

Paul tossed and turned and began moaning in his sleep.

"Shhhhhh," Liz demanded. "Paul needs his sleep."

"Or he's havin' a d-r-r-ream, Lass," Max suggested.

Paul finally settled down and calmly said one word. "West." He rolled over and remained still.

"West? I wonder if Paul has received new directions," Liz wondered to Nigel. "Speaking of Troy, isn't that west of here?"

"Indeed, my pet, but so as not to confuse Troy and Troas, the people commonly call that city 'Alexandria Troas'," Nigel explained. "Oh dear, that dreadful Temple of Apollo Smintheus is there."

Liz giggled and Max furrowed his brow. "Wha's so funny, Lassie?"

"Smintheus—the *Mouse* Slayer," Liz jested at Nigel. "Another Greek legend, *mon ami*. Apollo's powers include the ability to send famine and disease, usually with *mice*, to anyone who crosses him. Yet he can be persuaded to kill the plague-carrying mice with the proper sacrifice, so the pagans built him a temple at Troas to take care of the evil rodents."

"Simply dreadful myth," Nigel shuddered.

"Aye, well I'd like ta know the r-r-real story of where *we* might be headed!" Max protested.

"*Bien sûr,* Max," Liz replied. "One of Alexander the Great's generals named the city after their fearless leader. Alexander's full name was Alexander Troas, and his family tree is spread across this region. Just across the sea from Troas is Philippi, named after Alexander's father, and beyond there lies Thessalonica, named after Alexander's half-sister."

Max shook his head at all of this mythological and historical information spewing out of Nigel and Liz. "So Troas be a r-r-real place, an' that's where ye think we be headed?"

Liz looked at Paul, who was sleeping soundly. "If what Paul muttered in his sleep is true, Troas it is."

"We came from the east, and have been blocked from going south," Silas recounted. "So now you're telling me our way north has been blocked as well?"

"Yes, Silas," Paul answered, patting his faithful companion on the back. "Jesus came to me in a vision last night and blocked our path north. We must trust the blocked paths as much as the open ones. We head west to Troas." Paul started walking west, his stumbling gait evident to all. He was in a great deal of pain.

Timothy came alongside him and took his knapsack. "Let me carry this for you. I can tell you are hurting."

"Paul, don't you think you should rest?" Silas asked the eager apostle.

Paul shook his head and kept on walking. "I'll rest when we get to Troas."

The animals trotted along behind the trio, expectant about this new direction.

"Seems all this heavenly dir-r-rection means there be somethin' specific waitin' on us in Troas," guessed Max.

"*Oui,* and I have an idea that some*thing* is a some*one,*" Liz suggested. "Clarie said to find him. To find a doctor. But it seems quite the diversion to block travel south and north just for Paul to get medical attention, *n'est ce pas?*"

"I quite agree," Nigel replied. "Do you recall what Gillamon told us when we asked him about writing down the details of this journey? He said, 'Many books will come from not only Mark, but also from Paul and someone you'll need to meet soon.' Could it be that we need to meet that 'someone' in Troas? Could he be both a doctor *and* a writer?"

"Aye, but before we can meet that someone, we need ta figure out who he be then," Max added.

"*Oui,* and figure him out, we shall." Liz smiled. "Unlike Achilles and Apollo, this doctor-writer hero will be *real.*"

37

DOCTOR LUKE

our old wounds have become irritated all over again, Paul," Silas said softly, frowning with concern over Paul, who lay on his bed in pain. "You've rubbed them raw by carrying the heavy bags. From now on, you must let Timothy carry them all the time."

Timothy wrung out a cloth from a bowl of cool water and knelt down on the floor by Paul's bed. He gently dabbed Paul's shoulders with the cloth, wincing as Paul moaned at his touch.

"Th-th-th-thank-k-k-y-y-you," Paul struggled to say as he closed his eyes tight from the pain. He also was running a fever.

"Shhhhhh, my friend. Don't talk. Just rest," Timothy whispered, frowning to see Paul suffering so.

"He's worse," Silas whispered.

"Ye *think?*" Max grumbled, frustrated with the humans. "Why can't these humans jest figure out some way ta help sick people? Some place ta take 'em when they be like this!"

"Unfortunately they do have places to take sick people, but Paul wouldn't want to go there," Nigel offered. "Asclepius is the god of healing, and there are temples to Asclepius scattered all around the Mediterranean. Those needing medical care travel to these temples and make prayers and sacrifices, bring monetary gifts, and even spend the night in the temple."

"*Oui,* the patients lie on pallets before the statue of Asclepius, who holds his staff, which has a snake wrapped around it," Liz interjected. "The patients hope to be visited in their dreams by the god, and believe they can even be healed by him. They tell a priest their dreams in the morning and he then prescribes a cure, which may be nothing more than visiting the baths or a gymnasium. They even use nonvenomous snakes to slither around the floor to promote healing."

"Or even dogs to lick the patients' wounds," Nigel added. He looked at Max, who was horrified by the thought.

"That's it? Snakes slither-r-rin' ar-r-round the floor, an' lickin' dogs?" Max questioned. "They all be daft!"

"We must go find him," Liz determined, her tail swishing back and forth quickly. "We not only need this mystery doctor for our mission's purpose. Paul simply cannot continue with *his* mission until he receives medical attention." She got up and ran out of the room, followed by Max and Nigel.

318

Liz looked up and down the busy street of coastal Troas, and decided to head to the marketplace. "Keep an eye out for anyone who looks as if he might be a doctor."

The animals walked up and down the streets of Troas, but didn't see anyone who could provide help. They saw merchants galore, but no one offering medical aid.

"Blast it all! Why don't physicians have places where people could go see them besides those dreadful pagan temples?" Nigel fumed, riding on Max's back. "I for one think it would be a brilliant idea."

"Perhaps you can suggest it, *mon ami,*" Liz answered back over her shoulder. "When we find . . . him."

Just then she spotted a young Greek man with a book under his arm and a cluster of bright orange berries on thorny stems in his hand. He stopped, winced, and pulled back his hand, looking at a nick in his thumb caused by the thorns. He put his hand up close to his face and studied the blood running off his thumb. Liz inched up close to see what book he was reading. "Pedanius Dioscorides, *De Materia Medica,*" Liz read. Her eyes lit up when she recognized the plant that had nicked his thumb. Suddenly he started walking again, turning a corner, which led him up a winding street.

"He's got *hippophae rhamnoides!*" Liz exclaimed, running after him.

"I hope it's not catchin'," worried Max, following along after her.

The winding street took them up and up until they reached a grassy, beautiful hillside overlooking the sea. The man entered a small cottage and Liz stopped, waiting for Max and Nigel to catch up.

"Wha's the poor laddie got, Liz?" Max asked.

"*Hippophae rhamnoides,* or 'shiny horse'! Also known as 'Sea Buckthorn,'" Liz explained. "The Greeks feed it to their prize racehorses. It makes their coats shine and keeps the horses healthy. Supposedly even the mythological horse Pegasus ate these berries and was able to fly."

"I see, so do you think these berries have medicinal benefit for humans as well?" Nigel asked.

"I need to study this more, but I believe that is exactly what this young man is doing, no? He has a medical book but I do not recognize the author," Liz reported. "He may be our doctor! There's only one way to know. I'm going in."

319

Liz casually walked inside the cottage and saw the young man sitting at a table filled with pens, scrolls, herbs, bowls, and, "*A medical kit!*" she meowed excitedly.

The man heard the little cat meow as she immediately hopped up onto his desk, batting her beautiful eyes and purring loudly. "Well hello," the man said. "Where did you come from?"

"*If you only knew, monsieur,*" Liz meowed, rubbing his chin affectionately. She looked down to see what he was reading from the book he had under his arm.

The man pushed his dark, thick, curly hair out of his eyes, picking up a piece of string to tie it back. A single wisp of long curl escaped and hung down his cheek. His light blue eyes smiled at the curious cat that appeared to be reading his book. "Have you read his work, curious kitty?" he chuckled. "Pedanius Dioscorides, a fellow physician I recently met at the medical school. He's just written this first volume about the uses for aromatic oils, salves and ointments, trees and shrubs, and fleshy fruits." He picked up the stem of orange berries. "I'm eager to learn new uses for this plant." He set it down and stroked Liz as they both read about Sea Buckthorn.

Liz's eyes scanned the page, and her eyes caught this passage: "Oil from the berries applied topically can speed the healing of burns, cuts, ulcers, and slow-to-heal wounds." *"Monsieur, not only are you the doctor I was supposed to find, I have your first patient waiting for you. Do not be angry, but you must follow me now!"*

She grabbed the stem of berries in her mouth and jumped off the table, running out the door. She ran past Max and Nigel, yelling through her clenched teeth, "Make sure he keeps up with me!"

The young doctor jumped up from the table and ran out the door, shouting, "Come back here with my berries!"

A chase scene ensued with Liz blazing down the winding street, followed by the young doctor, and Max running close behind. Nigel held onto Max's ears, his legs flying up in the air as he exuberantly exclaimed, "Tally-ho!"

"Hang on, Mousie!" Max shouted when a pair of donkeys pulling a cart moved into the street ahead of the young man, blocking his way. Max picked up his speed and ran ahead of the man, shouting at the donkeys, "Clear the r-r-road! Ur-r-rgent business! Move this car-r-rt!" He nipped at their heels and the donkeys hee-hawed, stepping to the side just as the young man got there.

"Cheeri-o! Thank you for your cooperation!" Nigel called out to them as he and Max once again took off running behind the man.

When they finally reached the inn where the three evangelists were staying, Liz hurried inside and up the stairs, the young doctor almost catching her by the tail. Silas and Timothy heard a ruckus on the steps and then saw the little black cat dart into the room. She dropped a twig of berries by Paul's bed and sat down, waiting.

The young man stumbled to the doorway and saw a man lying on the bed with his companions standing by. And there he saw the little black cat, sitting innocently by the bed, her tail curled around her. He bent over and put his hands on his knees to catch his breath.

"What's all this? Who are you?" Silas shouted. "Don't you see we have a sick man here?"

The young man stood up straight and strode over to Paul's bedside, where the evangelist lay on his stomach. "And I'm a doctor," the man told them. He immediately looked at Paul's oozing wounds. "My name is Luke." He turned to gaze down at the little cat staring up at him with a coy grin on her face. He reached down and picked up the berries and his face filled with confusion, excitement, and mystery.

"God be praised!" Timothy exclaimed. "Can you help our friend? He has old wounds that will not heal."

"Yes, I can," Luke answered with a smile at the little cat, holding up the twig of berries. "With this. Please, bring me a small bowl." He proceeded to pull off several of the berries while Timothy hurriedly got him a wooden bowl. "Thank you." He made quick work of squeezing the oil from the berries into the bowl. Liz watched him, purring.

"Faith led you here," Paul said, his hand reaching down to scratch Liz under the chin.

"I don't know about Faith, but your cat led me here," Luke said, squeezing a few more berries.

"Her name is Faith," Paul explained. "She is . . . very special."

"Indeed she is," Luke said, shaking his head in wonder. "She stole these berries right off my desk and I chased her here. I don't know how, but she must have known you needed this medicine."

Max and Nigel sat in the doorway. "Brilliant!" Nigel whispered in a grinning Max's ear.

"Now, I've just been reading . . . we've just been reading," he chuckled, "that the oil from these Sea Buckthorn berries aids in the healing of wounds. Stay still while I apply it." Luke gently and methodically applied the ointment over Paul's wounds. Luke frowned as he looked over the many scars all over Paul's back. "May I ask how you came by these?"

Paul winced but smiled. "I bear on my body the scars of Jesus Christ."

"Someone named Jesus did this to you?" Luke implored. "He should be found immediately!"

Silas and Timothy snickered in the corner and Paul joined in their delightful laughter. "You're right, Luke my friend. Let me tell you how to find him."

"I must say I have never seen such an enthralled new believer in my life," Nigel cheered. "Our dear Doctor Luke was immediately captivated by the story of Jesus. Well done, my dear."

"Aye, Lass, ye did a gr-r-rand job of gettin' the lad ta Paul," Max agreed. "Looks like the Holy Spir-r-rit got hold of his heart."

Liz smiled shyly. *"Merci, mes amis.* I only did what the Maker showed me to do. I, too, am most pleased that Luke's mind and heart were open to the Good News. He is extremely intelligent and studies everything in depth, from what I've seen so far."

"He's our type of human, my pet," Nigel said, preening his whiskers. "He possesses a curious mind, exhibits a relentless passion for knowledge, and is an impeccable researcher. He is ravenous to learn from Paul, posing endless questions these past two weeks."

"Aye, an' he's always wr-r-ritin' in his journal then," Max added. "Did ye see how he were wr-r-ritin' aboot Jesus' healin' mir-r-racles? Paul had ta stop a few times since Luke didn't want ta miss anythin'."

"Which means he can be the one to capture the history of Paul's journeys," Liz enthused. "Of all the acts of the apostles for that matter!"

"He must travel on with us then," Nigel offered. "He has no apparent ties here. And I must say how terribly convenient it will be for Paul to have his own personal physician."

"Oui, especially if Paul suffers further injuries or beatings," Liz suggested cautiously. "I fear the Maker leading us to Luke might be timely . . . in a bad way."

38

LASSIE POWER

The man's deep grey eyes projected a lifetime of pain and bitterness. A long scar ran down his face from his right eye to his chin. His rugged face filled with genuine desperation as he started to stretch out his rough, calloused hand, pulling it back into the folds of his dirty brown cloak. He swallowed hard, fighting back the tears as much as the pride that had given him such a tough exterior all these years. "Please . . . please," he begged with a broken voice, dropping his hand to his lap. He lowered his head and shook it side-to-side as he knelt on the stone floor. He suddenly heard something and lifted his gaze. Wiping back his tears, he cleared his throat and slowly rose to his feet. Once again he stretched out his weathered hand and implored with greater urgency, "Please . . ." Hanging from his wrist was a shackle, indicating his bondage. He took one determined step forward. "Come over to Macedonia and help us."

Paul's eyes immediately fluttered open and he sat straight up in bed, breathing heavily. He looked around the room, halfway expecting to see the man, for his dream had been so real. There at the foot of his bed sat Liz, watching him. He reached down and pulled her to his chest. "I finally have our map, little Faith. God is sending us across the sea." He gently stroked her soft fur. "We leave in the morning for

Macedonia." He set her down and rolled over on his side. Letting out a sleep-dazed yawn, he mumbled. "We'll head to the main city."

As Paul drifted back to sleep Liz walked over to Max and Nigel, who both stirred awake. "The Maker has given Paul a vision. Tomorrow we go to Europe. To Macedonia."

"Europe! How delightful!" Nigel cheered. "I say, Macedonia is where the fate of the world was decided in the battle of Philippi. Octavius defeated the assassins of Julius Caesar and sealed his position as emperor. He became Caesar Augustus, ruler of the greatest empire the world had ever known."

Liz smiled, her tail curling slowly up and down as she pondered the light dawning upon a new continent. "I have a feeling the fate of the world will once again be decided, but this time, the King of kings will take that territory."

"Aye, he'll take the whole continent," Max added excitedly. "When the Word gets ta southern Eur-r-rope, it's only a matter of time 'til the Good News spr-r-reads north all the way ta yer homeland of France, Mousie's England, an' me Scotland!"

"*Oui*, and from Scotland across the water to my Albert's Ireland," Liz followed excitedly. "*Ooh-la-la!* And from there, the Good News could cross the ocean to that mysterious land we heard so much about from Patrick and Sally, the raccoons on the Ark: America."

Nigel's whiskers quivered with excitement. "Splendid! This shall be quite thrilling to watch the spread of the Good News from one land to another. But I daresay we must not get ahead of ourselves."

Max nodded his large square head. "Aye, we need ta focus on the city that be in fr-r-ront of us next."

"*Bien sûr*, you are right, *mes amis*," Liz agreed. "Tomorrow we begin taking Europe for Jesus—beginning in Philippi."

"The Maker has sent us favorable winds for this journey," Nigel remarked, breathing in the fresh salt air. "We're cracking on in record time. This journey normally takes five days but at this rate we shall make it in two."

"Wha's that island over there?" Max asked as they neared a small island off the coast of Troas.

"That would be the island of Tenedos," Liz replied. "Homer wrote about that island in his *Iliad* and he wrote that the Greeks hid there, hoping their massive wooden horse would trick the Trojans."

"Right, and don't forget how Virgil later penned that event with greater detail in his sublime epic poem, the *Aeneid,* my dear." Nigel cleared his throat and held his hand up with dramatic flair as he broke out in recitation:

> "'*O unhappy citizens, what madness?*
> *Do you think the enemy's sailed away? Or do you think*
> *any Greek gift's free of treachery? Is that Ulysses's reputation?*
> *Either there are Greeks in hiding, concealed by the wood,*
> *or it's been built as a machine to use against our walls,*
> *or spy on our homes, or fall on the city from above,*
> *or it hides some other trick: Trojans, don't trust this horse.*
> *Whatever it is, I'm afraid of Greeks, even those bearing gifts.*'"

325

"So the Tr-r-rojan lads were fooled by a big wooden horse packed with Gr-r-reeks who br-r-roke out of the beastie an' attacked their city?" Max asked. "I wouldn't tr-r-rust them either, after that."

Liz giggled. "Remember, Max, these are myths and epic tales. I think we can at least trust *our* Greeks, like Doctor Luke." She looked out to the horizon, searching for the next island they would come to. "There is one mythological item we can actually see, however—the Winged Victory of Samothrace."

"Ah yes, a sublime statue, from what I've heard!" Nigel echoed. "We shall harbor at Samothrace tonight. I'd be up for a nighttime excursion, my dear."

"*Bon,* Nigel! Let's go see her!" Liz agreed excitedly.

"Now wait jest a minute! Who be this flyin' lass?" Max wanted to know.

"*Nike*, or 'Winged Victory,' is an exquisite statue made to honor the goddess Nike following a victorious sea battle in the second century

BC," Liz explained, standing on the tip of the bow of their boat, spreading out her front paws in glory. "She is perched on a pedestal resembling the prow of a ship, much like this." Liz put one paw up to her mouth. "While her wings fly gracefully behind her and her robes look as if they are billowing in the sea breeze, she cups a hand to her mouth to announce the victory and honor due the Greek warriors."

"Yes, yes, yes, you give a splendid description, my dear! Nike is utterly magnificent in her beauty, and reminds the beholder that victory is fleeting, and can fly away at any time," Nigel added, holding up a tiny fist in the air. "Warriors must remain vigilant to hold on to their victories!"

"Aye, but she's still a false god," Max noted with a worried look. "Ye don't want ta be takin' her seriously then, pr-r-raisin' her false lassie power!"

"Of course not!" Liz and Nigel protested together.

"We simply wish to appreciate the intricate artwork of this piece that has drawn admirers for two hundred years," Nigel explained.

326

Liz put her dainty paw on Max's shoulder. "Remember that Gillamon told us 'the Maker can take anything—or anyone—and bring good out of them, even when it looks as if they are set in stone.'"

"Well, if ye think Gillamon might show up in the Nike lass, I'll go with ye ta see her tonight then," Max said. "As long as we don't miss the boat in the mornin'."

$\propto$

When the humans had retired for the night, lulled to sleep by the gentle waves lapping against the hull, Max, Liz, and Nigel quietly left the boat, docked at Samothrace. Together they climbed the city's hillside to reach the Samothrace temple complex filled with buildings and statues honoring the great Greek gods. The entire complex was lit up with votive lights, oil lamps, and torches, with people milling about and offering sacrifices.

"How pitiful that these humans actually believe that these statues are living entities," Nigel remarked from atop Max's head. "Alas, there is such darkness in the pagan world."

Liz walked ahead of them through the long portico, trying to locate

Nike. "She is said to be located in a niche near the open air theater." Liz's night vision was of course superior to that of Max and Nigel. When they turned the corner there in the distance stood the statue. *"Voila!* There she is!" Liz ran ahead of them to reach the statue. She sat there gazing up at the beautiful sculpture of Winged Victory. Max and Nigel soon joined her.

"*Ooh-la-la,* but this truly is a masterpiece of sculpture!" Liz exclaimed. "It looks as if the wind is actually blowing her robe!"

Suddenly a huge breeze came up and they heard a sound like the furling of sails slapping in a stiff sea breeze.

"Uh, Lass, I think the *Wind* r-r-really *be* blowin' her r-r-robe," Max announced with a grin. "That can only mean one thing."

Nike's sculpted robe fluttered in the breeze, flowing elegantly as the statue came to life. The statue lowered its hand from its cupped mouth and looked down at the animals. "Hello, my little ones. I'm pleased to see you this evening."

"*Bonsoir*, Gillamon!" Liz replied happily. "I just had to see this statue, but I am delighted you are here!"

"Aye, seein' ye makes it worth the tr-r-rip up here, lad!" Max chimed in.

"Indeed! Lovely night for strolling among the statues, especially when they come to life," Nigel quipped good-humoredly.

"I had a feeling you couldn't resist coming up here," Gillamon said with his warm chuckle. "So, you are off to Europe. From here things will never be the same for the continent again. Many significant things will happen when you reach Philippi. Look for the man with the scar on his face. He will not only be important for Paul, but for Luke as well. An entirely new idea for missions depends on it."

"Who is he, Gillamon?" Liz inquired. "And what must we do when we find him?"

The Nike statue grew more animated, now gently flapping its wings. "You'll know when you see him. Paul will recognize him, as he is the man from his dream. But you must take Luke to the scarfaced man quickly before the moment flies away. Do not worry. You will know when the time is right."

327

"Aye, we'll be r-r-ready," Max affirmed.

The statue reached into the folds of its flowing robe and pulled out a scroll made of an unusual, shimmering, airy material. "Here, this will give you the clues you need. It's the latest entry into Matthew's gospel account. His book is coming along nicely. Read it quickly, for this scroll will not last."

Liz eagerly took the strange scroll and unrolled it while Nigel jumped down to read it as well. The moonlight danced off the glowing words:

> "Then the King will say to those on his right, 'Come, you who are blessed by my Father, inherit the Kingdom prepared for you from the creation of the world. For I was hungry, and you fed me. I was thirsty, and you gave me a drink. I was a stranger, and you invited me into your home. I was naked, and you gave me clothing. I was sick, and you cared for me. I was in prison, and you visited me.'
>
> "Then these righteous ones will reply, 'Lord, when did we ever see you hungry and feed you? Or thirsty and give you something to drink? Or a stranger and show you hospitality? Or naked and give you clothing? When did we ever see you sick or in prison and visit you?'
>
> "And the King will say, 'I tell you the truth, when you did it to one of the least of these my brothers and sisters, you were doing it to me!'"

"Splendid penmanship! Matthew captured Jesus' words perfectly!" Nigel enthused. "I remember Jesus explaining this when the disciples asked him about the final judgment."

"*Oui*, I remember it as well," Liz agreed. "Gillamon, Nigel is right. It is remarkable how Matthew has remembered every word. This can only be the Holy Spirit guiding his pen, no?"

Nike smiled. "Of course. Every word in the New Testament, as well as the Old, is inspired by the Holy Spirit guiding the pen of each scribe." The statue spread out its arms before cupping its mouth once

328

more. "Liz, I'm glad you got to see this statue in its original form. One day you'll see it again, in your homeland of France. Until then, *adieu.*"

Liz's eye's grew wide. "In France?! How can this be, Gillamon?"

But the statue had returned to its cold, white marble state once more. "Maybe the lass will fly there with her lassie power," Max teased.

Suddenly the scroll dissolved into a million tiny, glittering pieces. Liz and Nigel jumped back as the Wind lifted the glitter and carried it off on the breeze.

"Remarkable," Nigel said as they watched the sky twinkle with the remnants of the scroll. "How thrilling to have a sneak preview of Matthew's gospel!"

Liz's eyes reflected the twinkling glitter. *"Oui,* so we must think about what this passage means specifically for Luke and missions."

"Must have ta do with helpin' hurtin' humans," Max suggested. "I'm sure we'll know aboot it soon. For now, let's be on our way then."

329

Liz wore a look of absolute delight as she gazed at the beautiful statue one last time. "I cannot wait to see this statue again, but I simply do not understand how or why she will get to my beloved France."

"We shall all look forward to that brilliant occasion," Nigel said, straightening his spectacles. "But Max is right. For now, we best get back to the boat so *we* can make it to Europe ourselves."

"Aye, come on then, Lass," Max said, giving Liz a gentle nudge with his square head. "Let's be goin'."

Liz nodded slowly in agreement. She reached her paw up to blow a kiss to the beautiful statue. "Until we meet in France, *chérie!*"

The next day the beautiful blue Aegean waters bid them welcome, parting in front of their boat as they glided into the port of Neapolis. Max, Liz, and Nigel stood at the bow of the boat, eyeing the coastline. Liz held her arms out again, striking a pose like Winged Victory, enjoying the sea breeze.

"From here it's a short walk along the Via Egnatia to Philippi," Nigel offered, grinning at Liz.

"Where we'll turn the world upside down," Liz added, dropping her paws to the deck with a shy smile.

"Aye, so we best be expectin' the Enemy ta show up," Max cautioned, frowning. "That's the last thing he wants ta see. I'll be r-r-ready for him then."

Paul, Silas, Luke, and Timothy all had a spring in their step as they walked along the Via Egnatia. They chatted excitedly about breaking new ground here in Macedonia, where the Good News had not yet been shared. Paul was especially happy about getting closer to Rome, where he longed to preach. Soon they saw Philippi's granite buildings gleaming in the late July sun and Paul stopped to observe the city.

A six-mile-long wall surrounded Philippi, a city named for the father of Alexander the Great. The *acropolis,* or elevated citadel, was positioned on a hillside looking down upon the city. The *agora,* or public square, was filled with buildings for trade and commerce. Wealth flowed through this city established in close proximity to gold mines. Two temples stood on the northern corners of the *agora*, and in the center was the *bema,* or court, where trials were conducted and where people held public debates. As in every Roman city there was a huge open-air theater and bathhouse, with luxury abounding at every turn.

"For now, we'll preach in this 'little Rome' of Philippi," Paul offered.

Luke nodded. "This city is Roman to its core, being a self-governing province. Two military officers appointed by Rome called *duumviri* govern the city, and are careful to follow the letter of the law to maintain their status with Rome. We'll see the military presence of Rome, from young legionnaires to old veterans who've chosen to settle here with their families."

Paul considered the man in his dream. He looked like an old soldier bearing the scars of war. Feeling a sense of urgency to see if this man was real or simply an image relaying God's direction, Paul resumed his quick, bandy-legged gait. "Come, let's get to the city."

They found an inn where they could stay, and decided to stroll around the city. Statues to pagan gods were everywhere, and the busy Roman marketplace was buzzing with commerce and trade. Thousands

330

of people from all walks of life roamed the streets of Philippi, and not one of them had ever heard of Jesus Christ.

"I don't see a Jewish synagogue anywhere," Timothy remarked after a while.

"They must not have even ten Jewish men in Philippi to form one," Paul explained. He put his hands on his hips and surveyed the city. "Very well, we'll seek out any God-fearing people outside the city walls on the Sabbath. New situations call for new strategies."

A gentle breeze rustled the lush canopy of trees that arched over the road leading to the Gangites River. Sunlight danced through the leaves onto the road as they walked a mile and a half outside of Philippi. The animals walked behind the men, and Max chomped off a bite of deep green grass.

"So why come out here ta find people?" Max said, spitting grass out of his mouth.

331

The corners of Nigel's mouth turned downward as he picked off a blade of grass that flew onto his spectacles, dangling it with two fingers before shaking it off onto the dusty road.

Liz wrinkled her nose, ever appalled at Max's disregard for good table manners. "Please do not talk with your mouth full, *mon ami.*"

"Right, well per Jewish custom, if there is not a synagogue in a city, any Jews or God-fearing followers will meet for Sabbath worship outside the city walls where there is water for ceremonial washing," Nigel explained, picking off another piece of grass from his shoulder. "Ergo, we are going to the river. Perhaps you could join them, old boy. Cleanliness is next to godliness, you know."

"Paul is eager to see what God-fearers are here in Philippi. I heard him describe the man in his dream," Liz relayed. "He wonders if the man is real. Gillamon already told us he was, so let's keep an eye out."

As they came to the river bank, the cool air created by the fast moving, narrow river greeted them with welcome refreshment. The riverbank was lush with green grass, and slender trees hung with silvery foliage in an arch over the water. Yellow flowers dotted the bank and large rocks were clustered in a small grove at the water's edge. Max's face broke into a wide grin. "R-r-reeds! That's a good sign if ye want the Holy Spir-r-rit ta speak. At least for this Scottish lad, it is."

Paul noticed a group of women gathering around the rocks, getting ready to pray. He made his way down the bank, and the others followed him. "Grace and peace to you on this blessed Sabbath. May we join you?"

A strong-looking woman with a pronounced jawline and deep green eyes stood and surveyed the approaching men. She wore a purple tunic and her brown hair was tied back in a long braid. She was obviously very wealthy. "You are welcome here. I am Lydia." She held out her hand to the other women sitting there. "These are members of my household. Please, sit with us."

"Thank you. I am Paul, and these are Luke, Silas, and Timothy," announced Paul, introducing each man with a gesture. "We hoped to find God-fearers here today. We have good news."

332

"Oh? And what might that be?" Lydia asked.

"The One who was long ago promised to save the world has come. His name is Jesus, and he asked me to come tell you about him," Paul began with a smile.

Liz, Nigel, and Max sat on the bank as Paul shared about Jesus coming to Earth to die for the salvation of the world, yet rising from death to offer new life to all who believe.

"Well, Scarface isn't here," Max noted, looking around. "Jest lassies."

"*Oui*, but look at Lydia's face. She is taking in every word Paul says," Liz observed. "So are the other women from her household."

"I must say, this lady of gentility certainly believes!" Nigel cheered. "And I do believe we are seeing our first European convert. Who would have thought it would all begin with a woman?"

"Doesn't everything begin with us?" Liz teased.

"Aye, that Eve lass started a whole bunch of tr-r-rouble in the garden," stated Max, chomping off more grass, spitting it again as he spoke.

Liz frowned at Max's comment as much as his manners. "I seem to recall that *Adam* also bit into the forbidden fruit. So perhaps women can get it right and help reverse Eve's bad decision, no? After all, it was a woman who Jesus first told he was Messiah."

"That's true, Lass," Max agreed.

"Look, Paul is baptizing the ladies right on the spot," Nigel observed with a grin. "Brilliant!"

Paul set foot in the river and Lydia joined him, her purple tunic swept behind her with the current. Luke, Silas, and Timothy assisted the other women, who also wanted to be baptized, after genuinely grasping Paul's message of salvation through Jesus. Luke was amazed to see house slaves and free women all come together as equals in the waters of grace.

When Lydia rose from the water, Paul was filled with joy to see his first Macedonian convert. No, she didn't have the rugged face of the man in his dream, but he knew that this influential woman needed help as much as anyone who is lost. Paul felt she would soon become a powerhouse for God in Philippi. "The Lord has begun a good work in you, Lydia. He will continue that work as you grow in your faith."

333

Lydia wiped back her hair and nodded. "If you consider me a believer in the Lord, come and stay at my house."

Paul held up his hands. "We are grateful for your offer, but I never wish to impose or intrude on anyone. I do not want to give anyone cause to believe that our motives are anything but pure in preaching the Good News."

Lydia folded her arms and frowned at Paul. "If the Lord has begun a good work in me, I think that includes allowing me to give of what he has blessed me with to support his servants. You will come to my house. All of you." She stubbornly pushed past Paul and took Luke's hand as he helped her out of the water. "Tell him, won't you? Lydia of Thyatira does not take "No" for an answer. I run a large trading business throughout this region, selling my purple dye and cloth. I am organized, strict in my business, fair and honest in all my transactions. Your motives are pure, as are mine. I wish to serve my Lord, and you will not deny me the privilege of blessing you. This matter is settled."

Luke shared a grin with Paul. "I think we need to listen to her."

Lydia squeezed out the water from her tunic and flapped it in the wind. "Of course you do. Besides, I wish to hear more about Jesus, and I will not stay out here in wet clothes. My servants will provide food and we will fellowship and learn together. Agreed?"

She didn't wait for an answer but immediately began giving orders to the other women coming out of the water, instructing them to prepare a feast and lodging arrangements for these men of God.

"Now that's *r-r-real* lassie power!" Max exclaimed with a wide grin.

"For once Paul is speechless," Liz observed with a grin, swishing her tail back and forth. "I like this woman, no? I like Lydia very much!" She leaned in to get right in the faces of Max and Nigel. "So the salvation of Europe begins with a *woman,* who I believe has not only just offered a place for the men to stay, but a place where the first church in Europe can meet." She trotted off after Lydia with her tail high in the air, the tip of it curved in her cute question-mark way.

Max and Nigel sat on the riverbank and watched the men proceed behind the women, as instructed. Max looked at the green grass and wrinkled his nose. "Lassie power can be a good thing. No more gr-r-rass for me. Let's get ta Lydia's house for some r-r-real vittles."

"Hear, hear," Nigel agreed, climbing aboard Max's back. "Purple lassie power, ho!"

As Max trotted along the road back into the city, he felt a chill run up his spine as they passed a cluster of trees. He stopped and looked around, a low growl coming from his throat.

"What's wrong, old boy?" Nigel asked, also cautiously looking around.

"Jest a feelin' like I've felt many times before," Max replied, his eyes narrowing as he started walking again, keeping a lookout. "That feelin' of somethin' evil in the air."

After Max had walked away, a young woman came out from behind the cluster of trees. Her eyes darted back and forth rapidly, and around her neck she wore the necklace of a slave. Her hair was black and messy, but her colorful clothes were richly adorned with charms. She began to tremble and the bracelets on her arms and ankles jangled. Slowly a yelp grew from the back of her throat until she shrieked wildly and went running down the road back toward the river.

334

39

No Ordinary Day

TWELVE DAYS LATER

The men were gathered around the low table in Lydia's house after another bountiful, delicious meal. Light flickered from torches on the wall and the women were busy clearing the dishes. Lydia poured some table scraps in a bowl for Max and Liz, giving them each a little pet and a warm smile. When she left, Nigel scurried over to enjoy the tasty morsels. In the bowl tonight was some bread dipped in honey, and Max proceeded to smear some of the honey all over his long nose.

"I think we could really put down roots here for a while, establishing a church here," Paul told his companions. "These people are hungry for the Good News. So far we've received nothing but positive reception from the people here."

"I agree," Silas replied with a nod. "Lydia is indeed an influential member of the community and her reach to the wealthy as well as the poor is powerful. With her generous support we could stay here and focus on ministry for an extended time."

"What about that slave girl who keeps following us as we go to the river, though?" Timothy asked. "She keeps shouting about our mission, but in an eerie way." He raised his voice to imitate the high-pitched voice of the girl: *"These men are servants of the Most High God, who are telling you the way to be saved!"*

"She's a Pythoness, possibly from Delphi," Luke offered. "Or she could be from Pytho, the shrine of Apollo. The myth goes that a python guards Apollo's temple and it embodies the spirit of the god. His power is given to oracles such as that poor girl to become fortune-tellers, and they make great sums of money predicting the future. Word here in Philippi is that this girl is so valuable she is owned by a group of men, not just one individual. She must make them a fortune in a pagan city such as this."

Paul's look grew serious. "Yes, she's been going at it for several days now. That poor girl is clearly possessed and being used by those greedy men for their selfish gain. I must put a stop to it, as I do not want evil spirits mocking the Lord by telling about our witness. Peter told me Jesus experienced the same thing and renounced the demons that spoke about him as the Son of God."

336

"She even has sores on her arm, probably from scratching herself, caused by the demons. I truly hate seeing people suffer like that." Luke leaned forward and wrapped his arms around his knees. "I wish I could help her."

"Her body needs healin', aye, but wha' the lass r-r-really needs be spiritual healin'," Max told Liz and Nigel as he tried to lick the honey off his nose with his long tongue. He noticed a bee flying into the room. "The lass needs Jesus."

"Oui, she needs both," Liz agreed. Then her face lit up with an idea. *"C'est magnifique!* And Luke can provide both!"

"Go on, my pet," Nigel urged, cleaning his spectacles with a swatch of Lydia's purple cloth.

Liz's tail swished back and forth as she thought this through. "When the men first arrived here in Philippi and didn't find a synagogue, they had to adopt a new strategy to reach people. Well, why couldn't medicine be a new way to reach these Gentiles? If Luke can offer them help for their bodies, I feel they would be open to hearing how they could receive help for their souls."

"Jolly good idea!" Nigel cheered. "I say, Doctor Luke could not only bring credibility to medicine, but preach the gospel while he's at it. Far better than those dreadful pagan temples that sick people go to in the dark of night. He can bring light to body and soul instead!"

Still licking his muzzle, Max watched the bee buzz around the torch mounted on the wall. "Aye, but bug beasties also fly r-r-right ta the light, an' sometimes they be the stingin' kind, jest like that poor fortune-tellin' lass." He stood up and furrowed his brow, already feeling protective of Paul. "Mar-r-rk me words, *that* kind of lassie power be nothin' but tr-r-rouble." The bee swooped down over Max's head, causing him to duck. "An' if Paul takes away the bees' honey-makin' queen, they'll swarm in for the kill."

"Please, please help me. May I have some water to pour over my wrists?" the prisoner begged with a broken voice. His puffy, manacled hands grabbed the iron bars of the prison door. His wrists were bleeding and cut from the shackles, which were too tight for his large wrists. "Please, anything to ease this pain."

337

The jailer wore a scowl on his face, and his mouth curved in a permanently downturned position. His knuckles whitened as he gripped the rod in his hand. He lunged and shouted at the begging prisoner, hitting the metal bars and the prisoner's fingers. "Shut up, scum!"

The prisoner pulled his hand back and cried out in fresh pain from the blow, sinking to his knees by the prison door, unashamedly crying like a baby. The jailer reached for a wooden cup and dipped it in the water bucket riddled with floating dead flies. He threw the water through the prison bars all over the prisoner's head. "There! Water is for drinking, you worthless maggot. Not to help you criminals 'feel all better,'" he mocked, drawing laughter from some young Roman soldiers sitting outside the main prison chamber. "That's all the water you'll get today to remind you not to ask me again." The jailer tossed the cup into the bucket, splashing dirty water over the sides, and walked out to join the two soldiers. They sat next to a fountain in the prison courtyard that flowed with fresh, abundant water.

"They don't call you Arcadius for nothing," one of the soldiers joked, chuckling at the jailer. "You act just like a mean, old bear."

"Yes, a bear who was roused from his sleep at that!" the other soldier followed. "You're ruthless, Arcadius."

The jailer got right in the soldier's faces and pretended to growl at them with his hands up like bear claws. A slight smile—which is all the jailer was capable of—was barely detectable at the corners of his mouth. He picked up a metal cup and dipped it in the clean water of the fountain, put one hand on his hip and lifted a toast to the miserable prisoner sitting inside. "To you, scum. Here's to your poor health." He then tossed the metal cup aside and splashed cool water from the fountain over his rugged face and cropped silver hair to wash away the grime. He grabbed a cloth sitting there and held it to his face for a moment as he grunted from the toil of the day.

Arcadius threw down the cloth and turned to face the soldiers, who looked upon him with respect. "You'll learn in the Roman army, just as I did, that discipline and ruthless adherence to the rules is the only way to manage people. And when it comes to criminal scum like these prisoners, show them no mercy. They don't deserve it. And I'm not going to waste my time doing more than the bare minimum to keep them alive. They're all destined for hard labor, torture, or death. It's a waste of Rome's money to keep them alive, as far as I'm concerned."

"How long were you in the army?" the first new soldier wanted to know, awed by the rugged authority this old soldier possessed.

"Thirty years," Arcadius replied.

The two young soldiers looked at one another in surprise. "Why did you stay in longer than was required?"

"I stayed longer than required because I loved it. But the wife got tired of waiting on me to stay home for good." The jailer pointed up the hill to his house just a stone's throw away. "Now I've got a house full of kids to provide for."

"So you became a jailer. Do you miss life in the army?" the second soldier asked.

The old jailer was getting irritated with all these personal questions, and stood to leave. "Of course I do. I miss the discipline and the thrill of battle."

"Can I ask you one last thing?" the first soldier inquired as he stood. "How did you get that scar?"

When Luke and Timothy offered to help Lydia carry some of her goods to market, Liz and Nigel followed them to learn more about Lydia's purple cloth business. Luke needed to get some supplies to make his ointments. Max went with Paul and Silas, who decided to head to the place of prayer at the river. As they neared the gate to exit Philippi, they heard the distinct jingle-jangle sound of bracelets. Max's fur rose on end. Then they heard the high-pitched voice of the demon-possessed girl behind them.

"These men are servants of the Most High God, who are telling you the way to be saved!" she screeched, pointing at the men with a wild look in her eye and a sinister smile on her face. Her red garments dragged along the ground as she followed Paul and Silas, shouting at them repeatedly. Several bystanders gathered in the street to see what would happen. The girl's owners stood smugly in the back of the crowd, with arms crossed and hoping to pick up some new customers wanting to know their fortunes from this girl. Meanwhile, they were amused by the antics of their slave.

339

Max growled against the evil behind them. Paul clenched his jaw, visibly annoyed to hear this girl's continued rant as her owners looked on. He stopped and turned around to look right at them. Then his gaze went to the girl. He lifted his hand and pointed at her, but spoke to the spirit: "In the name of Jesus Christ I command you to come out of her!"

At that moment the spirit left her. Suddenly her eyes softened and she blinked hard several times, almost as if she had been sleepwalking, and woke wondering where she was. The wild look was gone and she wiped back the messy hair from her face, now aware of her bedraggled appearance. She slowly turned and looked around her as the crowd began muttering in low voices. "Look at her. She's lost her gift. She'll be useless now."

The girl's owners pushed through the crowd, fury rising in them as they, too, realized what Paul had done. Their moneymaking slave was gone. All she was now was a normal, powerless young woman who could do no more than scrub floors for them. The crowd recognized these owners, for they were wealthy, influential men in this city. It was shocking to see them lose their power.

"Troublemaking Jews! Get them!" they cried as men seized Paul and Silas and dragged them along the dusty street to the marketplace to face the authorities.

Max barked as a riot broke out among the crowd. People were yelling and screaming at Paul and Silas, and Max ran underfoot, trying to stay close to them.

From the *bema,* the *duumviri,* or magistrates, looked up to see the approaching crowd. They were trying to finish up the court cases for the day. Despite the fact that they didn't want another issue to resolve today, the last thing they wanted was a threat to public order. The lictors stood behind them with their rods at the ready to administer discipline.

Liz and Nigel were standing in the *agora* when they also heard the commotion. Liz jumped up on a large statue base to see what was happening and caught her breath. *"Oh, no!* It's a mob! They're dragging Paul and Silas through the streets." She took off running, with Nigel close at her heels.

Luke, Timothy, and Lydia soon realized what was happening, and rushed over to join the growing crowd assembled around the magistrates. "We've got to help them!" Timothy shouted.

Wise Lydia slowly put her hand on Timothy's forearm, holding the young man back. "Remain calm, Timothy. I don't want you and Luke arrested, too."

Luke pulled his fingers through his dark, curly hair and exhaled loudly, clasping his hands behind his head in a moment of exasperation. "Lydia is right. We best observe from here and then take action once proceedings begin. This mob is out of control."

The slaveowners shoved Paul and Silas to the ground. "These men are Jews, and are throwing our city into an uproar by advocating customs unlawful for us Romans to accept or practice."

The crowd joined in the attack against Paul and Silas, and yelled their agreement with the owners. Mob rule was taking over and some people were shouting without really understanding what they were even shouting about.

Max ran over to Liz and Nigel and shouted above the din. "Paul healed the demon-possessed lass, so the owners gr-r-rabbed him an' Silas!

"They have no case!" Liz shouted. "Paul broke no law in healing her."

"Paul and Silas are both Roman citizens," Nigel shouted. "They simply need to make that clear when the *duumviri* ask for a defense!"

The magistrates looked at one another, and one leaned over to speak in the other's ear. The crowd was so loud they could hardly hear. "Emperor Claudius recently expelled all Jews from Rome. We should do the same. If their religious practices are undermining public order, we need to stop it immediately."

The other magistrate nodded in agreement. "Many citizens here have powerful connections in Rome. If word of this chaos gets back to Rome, and we do nothing about it, our positions could be in jeopardy." He turned to the two lictors and waved one of them over. "Strip and beat them to set an example of Roman order. Then let them spend a night in jail to think things over."

Immediately the lictors stepped down from the *bema,* each handling one man, and stripped Paul and Silas before roughly dragging them to the flogging posts. The din grew as the slaveowners looked on with eerie satisfaction to see justice done to the men who robbed them of their moneymaking slave.

"This is illegal!" Liz cried. "They did not ask for a defense, which is Paul and Silas's right! They did not get to explain that they are Roman citizens!"

"This is intolerable!" Nigel echoed. "Nor did the *duumviri* announce a formal sentence."

"This be dumb! Dumb *duumvir-r-ri!*" Max added, growling and wanting to chomp at their legs.

As soon as the lictor tore off Paul's shirt, he raised his eyebrows when he saw that his back was covered in scars from previous beatings.

"So, this obviously isn't the first time, you troublemaking Jew!" He proceeded to beat Paul mercilessly with the rod, causing Paul to cry out in pain as blood splattered on the flogging post. Meanwhile the other lictor beat Silas to a pulp.

Timothy was about to go mad with the injustice of what was happening. Luke and Lydia held onto his arms and prayed silently for their friends, grief-stricken at what they were witnessing.

Finally one of the magistrates held up his hand for the lictors to stop. "That's enough. Take them to the jail. Citizens of Philippi, this is over. Calmly disperse and go back to your homes." The two officials then got up and left the *bema*.

Luke grabbed his medical supplies. "Let's get back to Lydia's house. We need to gather believers to pray for Paul and Silas. Meanwhile, I will make some fresh ointment for their wounds. God will provide the time and place for me to tend to them."

As Luke, Timothy, and Lydia left the *agora,* the animals made their plans.

"What can we do?" Liz lamented, wiping her eyes.

"I'll head ta the pr-r-rison since I know me way ar-r-round jails an' jailers," Max told Liz and Nigel. "Liz, ye stay with Luke an' the others. Mousie, ye can go between us then, lettin' us know wha's goin' on."

"Right," Nigel agreed. "Come, my dear, let's see how we can console the others. There's nothing more we can do here."

"*Oui,* and as Luke said, we need to pray," Liz replied, nodding and following Nigel as Max took off after the men.

The lictors picked up the clothes belonging to Paul and Silas and dragged each of the men by the arm the short distance to the jail. It was located in the hillside below the acropolis, near the open-air theater. Arcadius saw them approach and opened the main door of the prison for the lictors.

"You need to guard these men carefully, per the magistrates," the lictors ordered Arcadius, huffing as they dragged Paul and Silas along. "They caused a riot in the city with their religious practices."

"I'll put them in the inner cell. Follow me," Arcadius replied, leading the lictors through the main prison area and back to the more secure cell, which was a cave. As they entered the prison, Max ran in right behind them, staying out of sight.

When they got to the inner cell the lictors threw the men onto the floor. Paul and Silas groaned as their faces landed onto the cold, dank stones. Their bodies screamed against the searing pain from their beating. It was all they could do to breathe.

"Put them in the stocks," Arcadius instructed, seemingly indifferent to the horrible condition of their backs, but angry to see more lawbreaking vermin brought to his jail. "It will provide added security," he said, his grey eyes narrowing as he studied these Jews, "and painful discipline."

The lictors tossed their clothes on the floor and yanked on Paul and Silas to put their feet in the stocks. The rough wooden bars were clamped tightly on their feet and the two men lay on their bloodied backs on the cold stone floor. When the lictors turned to leave, Arcadius knelt down to inspect the stocks on their feet, pulling roughly at the locks. Satisfied they weren't going anywhere, the jailer lifted himself up and stood over his two new prisoners. "So look where your misguided religious zeal has brought you. Maybe you angered one of the other gods by singling one out to follow."

Silas struggled to turn his head, but answered, "We serve the one true God."

The jailer raised his eyebrows and put his hands on his hips, amused. "And what god might that be?"

Paul slowly raised up on his elbows and gazed at Arcadius, suddenly noticing the long scar that ran down his face. "The Savior of the world. Jesus Christ."

"Ha! Well, that's a new one I haven't heard of," Arcadius answered, walking out of the inner cell and slamming the creaking prison door, turning the lock.

"I know you haven't. That's why we're here," Paul replied.

Arcadius's eyes narrowed at this strange remark. "You're *here* because you broke the law. So if your god wanted you in here, you better hope he wants to get you back out!" The jailer turned and stormed off, jingling his keys as he left Paul and Silas without so much as a cup

343

of warm, dirty water.

Paul slowly lay back down and closed his eyes, wincing from the pain. Silas started shivering from his wounds resting on the cold, damp floor. "This was no ordinary day for you I know, my friend," Paul said. "But it's becoming quite so for me, I'm afraid."

Suddenly the men heard a soft clicking sound in the shadows behind them. It was Max, and in his mouth he carried their clothes. He placed them down next to Paul.

"Gabriel? How did you get here?" Silas asked. "He must have followed us from the *agora.*"

Paul took Silas's cloak and smiled weakly, giving Max a soft touch. "Thank you, my little friend." He handed the garment to Silas. "Here, put this over you." Paul struggled to sit up and carefully pulled his own cloak around his shoulders. He looked at Max, growing even more suspicious about the dog's origins. "I think he followed us here from much farther away than the *agora*. You're no ordinary dog, are you, Gabriel?"

344

Max snuggled up to Paul and began to gently lick his wounds. *Aye, an' that were no or-r-rdinar-r-ry jailer. It were Scar-r-rface hisself,* he thought to himself. *An' ye two lads didn't get here in an or-r-rdinar-r-ry way. So somethin' tells me this will be no or-r-rdinar-r-ry night.*

MIDNIGHT RESCUE

D o you hear that?" a prisoner asked.

A group of prisoners in the main chamber sat with their backs against the wall. Two of them were shackled to iron rings embedded in the jail cell wall.

The manacled prisoner who had begged Arcadius for water lifted his gaze. "It . . . it sounds like singing."

I waited patiently for the Lord to help me, and he turned to me and heard my cry.

He lifted me out of the pit of despair, out of the mud and the mire.

He set my feet on solid ground and steadied me as I walked along.

He has given me a new song to sing, a hymn of praise to our God.

"It's coming from the inner cell," a prisoner noted.

Many will see what he has done and be amazed. They will put their trust in the Lord.

Oh, the joys of those who trust the Lord, who have no confidence in the proud or in those who worship idols.

O Lord my God, you have performed many wonders for us.
Your plans for us are too numerous to list. You have no
equal.
If I tried to recite all your wonderful deeds, I would never
come to the end of them.

"How can they be singing such joyful words? Did you see the horrible shape they were in when they got here?" another prisoner asked, his heart aching to have that kind of joy and peace in this hellish place.

"Those men are Jews who've been talking about some God they follow named Jesus," the manacled prisoner answered, rubbing his tender wrists. His mind raced with confusion. These men were worse off than he, yet they weren't complaining or begging. They were *singing*. "It sounds like they're praising their God. Why? Who is this God? And why sing after what happened to them?"

346

I have told all your people about your justice.
I have not been afraid to speak out, as you, O Lord, well
know.
I have not kept the good news of your justice hidden in my
heart; I have talked about your faithfulness and saving power.
I have told everyone in the great assembly of your unfailing
love and faithfulness.

"Saving power," repeated one of the prisoners chained to the wall. He coughed with a rattling chest. He was terribly sick with a fever. Tears filled his eyes. "Unfailing love and faithfulness. That doesn't sound like any god *I've* ever heard of."

Lord, don't hold back your tender mercies from me.
Let your unfailing love and faithfulness always protect me.
For troubles surround me—too many to count! My sins pile
up so high I can't see my way out. They outnumber the hairs on
my head. I have lost all courage.
Please, Lord, rescue me! Come quickly, Lord, and help me.

"Please, please, come and help us," the manacled prisoner whispered under his breath.

May those who try to destroy me be humiliated and put to shame.
May those who take delight in my trouble be turned back in
disgrace.
Let them be horrified by their shame, for they said, "Aha! We
have him now!"

Max sat with his head resting on his front paws as Paul and Silas sang the Fortieth Psalm. They weren't singing to keep up their spirits. This singing naturally poured out of their hearts following hours of prayer. They prayed for God to be glorified through what was happening to them. They prayed for Philippi. They prayed for their friends, who, they knew, were sick with worry over them, and who no doubt were lifting them up in prayer right at this moment. They prayed for the slave girl whom Paul had freed from the clutches of demons, praising God for her release and the resurrected power of Jesus that was theirs. They prayed for the slaveowners who were so lost in their depravity. They prayed for the *duumviri* who illegally condemned them to torture and imprisonment. They prayed for the lictors who beat them. And most of all, they prayed for the jailer, the man with the scar on his face from Paul's dream.

The more they prayed, the more they felt the presence of Jesus there in the cell with them. Soon their bloody wounds, searing pain, and unspeakable discomfort in this cold, dank cell just seemed to dissipate. The more they prayed, the less they saw their condition and the more they saw Christ. They felt his loving approval for how they chose to respond to their abuse. The more they emptied themselves of themselves, the more they were filled with the light and supernatural joy of their Savior. Prayers slowly grew into song as Paul and Silas lifted their hands in praise to God, learning to be content even in this horrible state.

Max felt something like the floor moving beneath his belly, and his ears shot up as he scanned the cell. Just then Nigel scurried in. His

347

face lit up with joy to see Paul and Silas praising God as their beautiful voices filled the cave with heavenly music.

"My, what pleasant sing- . . ." Nigel stopped in mid-sentence, the smile falling off his little face as he also felt something.

Max and Nigel looked at each other in alarm. "Wait for-r-r it . . ." Max advised to the little mouse. "Mousie, the jailer be Scarface."

"The chap from Paul's dream?" Nigel's eyes widened. "If what is happening is what we think it is . . ."

But may all who search for you be filled with joy and gladness in you.
May those who love your salvation repeatedly shout, "The Lord is great!"

348 The manacled prisoner's eyes filled with tears. "The Lord is great!" he whispered.

Max got to his feet and looked up to the ceiling. "Wait for-r-r it . . ."

"This must certainly be the moment we've awaited!" Nigel said nervously with a paw to his mouth.

As for me, since I am poor and needy, let the Lord keep me in his thoughts.

Max furrowed his brow. "Get r-r-ready . . ."

Nigel ran over to the prison door and clung to the iron bars. "I must get to Liz!"

You are my helper and my savior. O my God, do not delay.

"EAR-R-RTHQUAKE!" Max barked.

Arcadius sat straight up in bed. His wife and children began screaming as the violent earthquake rattled their small house. The jailer's heart was trying to beat out of his chest as he waited for the shaking to stop.

He could hear pottery breaking as it fell to the stone floor, and dust fell from the ceiling. After a few minutes, all was still. He immediately jumped out of bed, dressed in his brown cloak now dirty with debris. Once he made sure his family was safe, a sickening thought flashed across his mind.

"The jail!" he screamed, grabbing his short-sword and running out of the house.

Nigel raced through the streets of Philippi as fast as his legs would take him after he scurried over the debris of fallen shackles and stone blocks strewn about on the prison floor. Once out of the prison, he could tell that the rest of the city was intact. "I say, a localized earthquake! Extraordinary!" It wasn't long before he reached Lydia's house and slipped through her front door, which had been left ajar.

Liz sat next to Luke, giving him as much comfort as she could, simply with her presence. Luke, Timothy, Lydia, and a houseful of new Christian believers were on their knees, having kept up this prayer vigil all night for Paul and Silas. Nigel took advantage of their closed eyes and scurried right up to Liz, pulling on her tail. Liz turned quickly and saw her mouse friend harried and out of breath, his spectacles askew on his head. She got up and together they moved away from the humans.

"What has happened, *mon ami?*" Liz whispered, straightening Nigel's spectacles for him.

"Thank you, my dear," Nigel replied, holding his paw over his chest and catching his breath. "An earthquake, but just at the prison. All the prison doors flew open, the stocks holding Paul and Silas fell off, and the iron shackles holding the prisoners simply fell onto the floor! Everyone has been freed!"

"*Mon Cher Dieu!* A divine rescue!" Liz exulted. "Did Paul and Silas leave? Are they on their way here?"

"No, everyone is staying put. I passed the jailer in the street as he was running to check on them. My dear, he is *Scarface!*" Nigel told her, clasping her arm.

"The man from Paul's dream? This must be the moment Gillamon

349

talked about!" Liz replied with wide eyes, looking quickly back to the humans, who remained in prayer. "We must get Luke to the prison before the moment flies away!"

When Arcadius reached the flowing fountain, he saw that nothing was disturbed in the courtyard. Confusion ruled his mind. Nothing but his hillside home and the jail had been touched. He looked around at buildings on the far side of the courtyard, and with the light of the full moon he could tell that not one of them showed signs of destruction. He now was gripped with terror and broke out in a sweat as it dawned on him the earthquake was an entirely localized event. Superstitious Macedonians all believed that earthquakes were sent by angry gods, and if one occurred only in his house and in his jail, then an angry god had singled him out. *Maybe the God of those Jews did this!*

The jailer ran to the prison entrance and saw the prison doors were opened wide back on their hinges. *I'm ruined! The prisoners have escaped and I'm doomed by the angry God!* Arcadius fell to his knees and drew his sword, throwing its sheath onto the stone floor with a noisy clamor. He knew that the penalty imposed by Rome for lost prisoners on his watch would be death. The old soldier, ever true to military discipline, didn't expect mercy, nor would he ask for it. He would end his life right here, right now.

Arcadius put the sword up to his chest and was ready to fall forward on it, to plunge it into his heart, when he saw movement out of the corner of his eye. A small, black dog ran up to him, barking. Startled, he hesitated for a moment before he heard an authoritative voice come from the darkness of the prison.

"Don't harm yourself! We are all here!" Paul shouted.

"The Jewish prisoner?" Arcadius muttered, visibly shaken at hearing the prisoner's voice and his message, coupled with almost having taken his own life. His hand shook as he slowly placed the sword on the floor. "How can this be?"

The jailer's nervous, wide-awake servants came rushing into the prison. "Hurry! Bring me a torch!" he ordered them as he got to his feet. His knees felt weak from the trauma of the last five minutes. A servant handed him a torch and he hastened past the opened main prison cell, where he saw all the prisoners sitting down. His mind swirled with mad confusion. No one was attempting to escape!

When the jailer got to the inner cell with its open door and freed prisoners, he fell trembling before Paul and Silas, who stood quietly in the middle of the cave. Max came rushing up next to him and waited to see what they would do. He couldn't believe they had not fled the jail, just as Peter had done when the Maker sent an angel for his release. Max was ready to hold on to the jailer's leg if need be.

Paul reached down and touched Arcadius's shoulder. "You see, we're all here."

Arcadius slowly rose to his feet but couldn't utter a single word, he was in such shock. He motioned for the men to follow him, and led Paul and Silas out of the jail and into the courtyard. The jailer's wife, children, and servants now were all gathered in the courtyard by the fountain in the panic of the night.

351

His lip trembling, the jailer asked with a broken voice, "Sirs, what must I do to be saved?"

Paul smiled. "Believe in the Lord Jesus, and you will be saved."

"You and your household," Silas added, looking around at the jailer's fearful family.

"How do you propose we get Luke to the jail?" Nigel asked.

"He followed me once before," Liz said, eyeing Luke's new bag containing the ointment he had concocted. It was sitting on the table next to a stack of small clay bowls, and was small enough for her to carry in her mouth. "He'll simply need to follow me again."

"Brilliant!" Nigel cheered. "I'll run ahead of you once we're en route."

Liz sauntered over to Luke and began meowing, *"Monsieur, you must follow me this instant!"*

Luke's eyes remained closed as he continued to pray, although he heard the cat meowing.

When Luke didn't move, Liz grew irritated and thought quickly about how she could get his attention. She jumped onto the table next to the ointment bag and the stack of bowls. "A feline must do what a feline must do," she muttered to herself before she pushed her shoulder into the stack of bowls, sending them crashing to the floor. With that, Luke and the others looked up in alarm. *"Allons-y, Docteur Luke!"* Liz grabbed the ointment bag, jumped off the table, and went running out the door.

Luke got to his feet when he saw what the cat had done. "The cat stole my medicine!" His mind raced back to that moment in Troas when the cat had grabbed his stem of berries. *She's leading me back to Paul again!* he surmised. "I'll be back! Stay here!" Luke instructed the others as he bolted out the door after Liz.

352

Never in a million years would Max have thought the plan would be for the Maker to send an earthquake at midnight to open the prison so Paul and Silas would stay and share Christ with the jailer and his family. But here they were under the light of a full moon, new believers getting baptized in the prison courtyard fountain. Not only that, but the jailer Scarface himself had dipped a cloth into the fountain to tenderly care for Paul's and Silas's wounds. Max had marveled as he watched. "Aye, I knew this would be no or-r-rdinar-r-ry night."

Max saw Nigel scurry through the courtyard, followed by Liz, followed by Luke, who stopped in disbelief at the fountain as Paul and Silas baptized the last of Arcadius's servants. Liz dropped the ointment bag at his feet and casually walked over to sit next to Max, winking at Nigel tucked behind him.

"Brilliant plan to use the *déjà vu* maneuver," Nigel chuckled. "I say, this is quite the unexpected scene. Max, do enlighten us, old boy."

"Well, the short stor-r-ry be that it were the jailer who needed ta be rescued. Paul an' Silas not only didn't r-r-run out of the jail, they shared Chr-r-rist with the lad. Now he an' his household all believe. Scarface washed their wounds an' Paul an' Silas washed him an' his family with baptism."

"*C'est incredible!*" Liz exclaimed. "Perhaps the scar on his face was simply the first chisel mark of the Maker, no?"

"Splendid observation!" replied Nigel. "I say, it appears our jailer will be sculpted into a fine, new living statue!"

"Paul, Silas, I can't believe what I'm seeing," Luke said gawking at the transformation of the entire situation.

"The Lord sent an earthquake to release us, but we had to release these people," Paul replied with a smile. "Meet our new brother in Christ—Arcadius. This is Luke, our beloved doctor."

"I'm honored to know you, Luke," Arcadius said in a joyful, humble voice. "Please come to my house with Paul and Silas. We're going to provide a much-needed meal for them."

"Thank you, brother. I'm happy this night turned out much differently than any of us could ever have imagined. God be praised," Luke replied warmly. "I'd be happy to go to your house, but first please let me look at their wounds." Luke bent down and picked up his ointment bag and glanced over at Liz, who sat there batting her eyes affectionately. He winked at her and shook his head in yet more amazement at this mysterious little feline.

353

Arcadius instructed his servants to get the meal ready for their guests. Then he watched as Luke tended Paul and Silas, applying ointment to their wounds. When Luke was finished, the jailer asked him, "I don't suppose you'd have some of that to spare? One of my prisoners is hurting pretty badly around his wrists."

"Certainly. Let me see him," Luke replied, following Arcadius into the jail.

"Mission accomplished, no?" Liz exulted, stretching out her paws like Nike. "We seized the moment before it flew away."

"Indeed, my pet!" Nigel enthused. "Now I wonder what tomorrow will bring."

In the morning, Paul, Silas, and the jailer walked back down the hill to the prison. They had spent the entire night eating, fellowshipping, and celebrating what God had done for all of them. Luke was back in the prison, tending to some of the other prisoners who needed medical attention, especially the man with the raspy cough and the fever. Paul and Silas went into the cell with the other men to answer their questions of why they were singing the night before, and to help them better understand this wonderful God of theirs.

Arcadius stood outside the main prison cell, watching in awe as these Christians ministered body and soul to his prisoners. He glanced outside and saw the two lictors heading his way, bringing orders from the magistrates. "Release those men we brought you yesterday."

The jailer turned with the good news for Paul and Silas. "The magistrates have ordered that you and Silas be released. Now you can leave. Go in peace."

Paul stood up and came to the prison door, shaking his head. "They beat us publicly without a trial, even though we are Roman citizens, and threw us into prison. And now do they want to get rid of us quietly? No! Let them come themselves and escort us out."

The lictors looked at one another in fear at this news.

Arcadius put his hands on his hips and grinned. "Well, what are you waiting for? Go tell the magistrates what Paul said."

The lictors quickly left the prison and hurried back to the *duumviri*.

"Jest wait 'til they find out how dumb they r-r-really were ta tr-r-reat R-r-roman citizens like that," Max said with a grin.

"*Oui,* a Roman citizen can only be flogged if he has disobeyed direct orders from magistrates, and even then only after a fair trial and formal sentencing," Liz noted. "The *duumviri* are the lawbreakers here, not Paul and Silas!"

"Ergo, they could be in big trouble with Rome should Paul and Silas lodge a complaint against them," Nigel added, straightening his spectacles.

It only took moments for the wide-eyed, now humbled, magistrates to arrive at the jail, followed by several citizens of Philippi who gathered in the courtyard, wondering what was happening.

"Please accept our most humble and heartfelt apologies," they cried. "We didn't know you were Roman citizens! Had we only known, this never would have happened."

Paul and Silas made no reply, but allowed the magistrates to squirm. Max chuckled. "They're makin' the dumb laddies sweat."

"Please, may we escort you out?" the magistrates groveled.

Arcadius smiled, took his key ring, and winked at Paul and Silas as he opened the cell door, letting them out. Luke followed them.

"May those who try to destroy me be humiliated and put to shame. May those who take delight in my trouble be turned back in disgrace," the manacled prisoner said with a smile, quoting the Fortieth Psalm he had heard Paul and Silas sing the night before.

The magistrates looked chagrined and humiliated as the onlookers watched them personally escort from the prison the two men they had mercilessly flogged the day before. "May we please beg a favor of you? As you can imagine, the uproar yesterday was upsetting to the good people of Philippi. We need to request that you please leave the city so the issue can die down and we can maintain the peace here."

Paul stopped and looked both men square in the face. "We will leave, but mind you we leave behind many friends here. Many. Friends." He turned and looked at Luke and then back at the magistrates. "We will hear of it if they are mistreated."

Relief flooded the faces of the magistrates, who each let go a heavy sigh. "Yes, yes, certainly, and we'll make sure your friends are always treated with the utmost respect."

"Very well," Paul agreed, motioning for Silas to come along. Together they walked away from the prison, leaving the magistrates feeling as if they had just escaped their own imprisonment.

"Bravo, Paul!" Nigel cheered with a fist raised high. "He gave them the what-for but in a firm, turn-the-other-cheek way. He has given the young Christians here some power with the leaders of Philippi, who wouldn't dream of giving them grief now."

"*Oui*, the church in Philippi has a bright future!" predicted Liz happily.

"Aye, but it sounds like they'll be livin' it without us," Max said. Liz watched as Luke got into a very animated discussion with Paul and Silas on the way back to Lydia's house. "But there may be one of us who ends up staying behind."

⋉

Lydia's house was buzzing with happy voices, abundant food, and fellowship. All the brothers and sisters of the budding church of Philippi gathered to praise God for answering their prayers, and Paul and Silas gave them tremendous encouragement for the days ahead. Even Arcadius came to join them so he could see Paul and Silas off. But before they left with Timothy, there was a big decision to be made.

"So it's settled. I will stay here and help the church get better established while I begin a medical practice to help the sick," Luke declared. "I feel the Lord will open up many doors to reach the lost as I'm tending to their hurting bodies."

"And I'll help provide you with a place where those needing medical help can come see you," Lydia offered. "Then we'll invite them to join us when we gather for worship."

356

Arcadius put his hand on Luke's back. "Doctor Luke here will still have to come to my jail to care for my prisoners. But the good news is that as he shares Jesus . . ." a big, mischievous grin broke out on the old soldier's face, making his scar appear as if a deep smile line on his cheek, ". . . he'll have a captive audience."

41

Jealous Jews and Trading Tents

A r-r-re we ther-r-re yet?" Max huffed, his paw pads feeling sore. "I need some of Luke's or-r-range ber-r-ry stuff. Seems like we've walked a million miles fr-r-rom Philippi."

Nigel sat atop Max's back as he and Liz walked down the dusty Via Egnatia behind Paul, Silas, and Timothy. The men were discussing the possibilities that awaited them in Thessalonica, as they knew there was a Jewish synagogue there. Paul could once again launch his ministry with Jews and God-fearers in that city. "Actually, we've only traveled roughly one hundred miles, old boy: thirty-three miles to Amphipolis, another thirty miles to Apollonia, and thirty-six more to Thessalonica—I estimate one more mile and we'll be there."

"Aye, the longest mile always be the last one," Max panted. He looked behind him. "*Only* a hundr-r-red miles. Hope you've enjoyed the r-r-ride up there, Mousie."

Nigel petted Max's shoulder with a jolly chuckle. "With you as my noble steed, how could I not?"

"I smell the sea," Liz remarked happily as she breathed in the salt air. The curve of the road opened to an expansive view below the slopes of the Kortiates Mountains down to the blue waters of the Gulf of

Thermae. "Thessalonica is a bustling harbor town. I believe it is the second largest city in all of Greece, no?"

"Indeed it is, my pet," Nigel chimed in, straightening his spectacles as the three animals gazed out at the city below. "The city boasts two hundred thousand humans, and was named for Alexander the Great's half-sister. And if you look out in the distance across the bay you can see the fabled Mt. Olympus."

"Where all the cr-r-razy Gr-r-reeks think their gods live?" Max snorted.

"*Oui,* but the Greeks are believing that less and less," Liz replied. "Still, they cling to their statue gods."

"Let's pray that Paul and his band of merry men help the pagans believe in Jesus more and more and their statue gods less and less," Nigel suggested. "How thrilling to think of those exquisite works of art becoming simply that—*art* and not *idols!*"

"Aye, but it's goin' ta take a while for that," Max added, looking out at the vast expanse of Thessalonica. "Two hundred thousand lads an' lassies be a lot of pagans."

Liz nodded. "But at least here, Paul can get a head start with the Jews."

⊂×

Paul noticed two young Jewish men sitting in the back of the synagogue, whispering and nodding their heads as he spoke. Invoking his privilege as a visiting rabbi, Paul read the Scriptures and then proceeded to make the case for Jesus as Messiah, proving verse by verse that Messiah had to suffer and rise from death.

"This Jesus whom I announce to you," Paul announced with a sparkle in his eye, "*is* Messiah!"

"Some of them look convinced," Liz offered, spying the two young men as well as some leading women and a large group of Greeks who worshiped God. She and Nigel sat up in a window of the synagogue while Max waited outside.

"Indeed, and while the elders do not appear to be jumping out of their prayer shawls with excitement, at least they have been polite," Nigel answered. "Paul has an open door to return next Sabbath."

The synagogue began to empty and the two young Jewish men came up to Paul. "Thank you for speaking today, rabbi. I'm Jason and this is Aristarchus. We hoped you and your friends might come to my house."

"Yes, and share more about Messiah," Aristarchus chimed in, then quickly added with a big smile, "about Jesus."

Paul placed his hand on Jason's shoulder. "We'd be honored."

As Paul, Silas, and Timothy followed the two Jewish men, a few more God-fearing Gentiles joined them along the street. The Jewish elders stood on the steps of the synagogue and noted the eagerness with which this group of people embraced the newcomers with the radical message that Messiah had come. "They wish to hear more from Paul," one elder remarked.

"So do I," another elder agreed. "I plan to hear much more. We must know all that Paul is claiming with this Jesus. We'll keep an eye on him."

The elders walked off and Liz's tail whipped back and forth. She furrowed her brow. "And we will keep an eye on *you, messieurs.*"

‹×

"You mean they actually *beat* you without so much as a trial?" Jason asked, wide-eyed, setting down a bowl of bread in front of his guests.

Silas nodded, reaching for a piece. "Yes, and the roar of the crowd was so loud we couldn't even shout that we were Roman citizens. Then they threw us in jail for the night."

"So what happened then?" Aristarchus eagerly asked, mumbling with olives in his mouth. "Did you get justice? Did you report the magistrates to Rome?"

"He reminds me of Albert," Liz whispered, looking at Aristarchus. She sighed, missing her love.

"Aye, talkin' with his mouth full," Max agreed with a fond grin.

"First an earthquake opened the doors of the jail, and then God helped us save the jailer and his entire family," Paul explained.

"Did the prisoners get out?" Jason wanted to know. "Wait, *save* the jailer?"

Paul closed his eyes and nodded with a warm smile. "The jailer was ready to take his life, but because we didn't run, the open doors of the jail led to the open door of his heart. Just as you have accepted the Word of God from us today, not as the word of men, but as what it really is—the Word of God—that Roman jailer did the same that night."

"We're learning that the Lord will use whatever means necessary to reach the lost, even an earthquake!" Timothy added with joy.

"And although there was every reason to run that night, God gave us courage to stay in the jail and share the Good News. In the morning, the magistrates let us go and once they discovered we were Roman citizens, they were fearful we'd report the gross injustice to Rome," Silas continued. "But Paul handled them with firm grace. We feel the believers in Philippi will be given fair treatment as a result."

"And now God has given us the courage to come here to Thessalonica and tell you the good news that comes from him," Paul continued. He looked around the room at the group of eager people who were here to know about Jesus. "Our appeal to you is not based on error or impure motives, nor do we try to trick anyone. Instead, we always speak as God wants us to, because he has judged us worthy to be entrusted with the Good News. We do not try to please people, but to please God, who tests our motives."

Jason nodded. "We are glad you've come, and I wish to offer my home for your stay. We don't have much here, as we are not rich like your Philippian friends, but we offer it to you freely."

Paul nodded slowly. "Thank you, Jason. We would be pleased to stay with you, but we will not impose on you in any way. We must earn our keep. The man who will not work shall not eat."

"Very well. What kind of trade do you do, besides preaching?" Jason asked.

"I make tents," Paul answered. He smiled and patted Silas and Timothy on the back. "And tomorrow, so will they."

∝

"Jason's house has become the epicenter of the Way movement here," Nigel enthused, watching another packed prayer meeting come to a close. "I say, there are more Greeks than even Jews now coming to hear Paul. His tentmaking business is thriving and the second church in Europe is off to a smashing start!"

"*Oui.* Jason, Aristarchus, and the other new Jewish believers here have gained courage from Paul to go out and share with not only fellow Jews but even pagans in the marketplace," Liz agreed.

"Aye, the lad don't flatter anyone here in the city. Paul sells tents ta pagans an' shoots str-r-raight with 'em aboot their little house idols an' their gr-r-rand temple idols," Max noted. "He's honest an' the people be r-r-respondin' ta Jesus. So, some of those statues be changin' from idols ta art, Mousie."

Nigel preened his whiskers. "Nothing pleases me more."

"The Jewish leaders are far from pleased, however," Liz said in a serious tone. "I have studied them closely these past three Sabbaths when Paul has preached. They are jealous of Paul and Silas taking away so many of their Greek followers and convincing so many Jews that Jesus is Messiah. And Paul, Silas, and Timothy hope they can settle in Thessalonica to get this church strong while they support themselves. But something tells me jealous Jews and trading tents will not mix for long."

"We best be on the lookout for tr-r-rouble," Max warned. "An' this time, Luke's not here ta do the doctorin'."

Liz walked ahead of Max and Nigel through the *agora,* studying the goings-on of this bustling city. It was filled to the gills with trade, and with the huge volume of traveling merchants, Paul's tents were selling well. He, Silas, and Timothy were off this morning delivering a huge order of tents to a merchant from Corinth. "Thessalonica is in the center of the main Roman road crossing east to Asia and west to Rome. Countless Greek ships come in and out of this harbor. *Ooh-la-la,* but the possibilities for the Good News traveling from this city by land and sea are incredible!"

"Now we simply need to train a fleet of pigeons to carry the Good News by air," Nigel quipped with a jolly chuckle. "I agree, my dear.

Thessalonica is vital to founding Christianity as truly a world religion. Brilliant for Paul to have come here."

Max didn't seem to be paying attention. His gaze was fixed on the Jewish leaders, who were talking to a group of men who did nothing but hang around the marketplace all day, doing nothing. "Wha' could those lads be up ta?"

Liz and Nigel studied the unlikely group of pious Jews and lazy pagans. "From the looks of it, no good," Liz replied.

Suddenly the lazy men nodded and began yelling in the market-place, drawing a crowd of people around them. Soon the whole city was in an uproar, fists were raised in anger, and a mob went down the street.

"Wor-r-rthless loafers!" Max growled. "They be headin' ta Jason's house!"

"Ill-kempt ragamuffins!" Nigel fumed. "I presume they are after Paul. What shall we do?"

362

"Pray that Paul, Silas, and Timothy have been delayed by trading tents," Liz answered, watching the Jewish leaders headed to the *bema,* where the court was currently listening to trials. "Jealous Jews want them silenced, once again."

Soon the mob came dragging Jason, Aristarchus, and some other believers before the city authorities. The Jewish leaders frowned, as their desired prey had not been caught.

"That r-r-rabble got Jason but not Paul!" Max noted, angry but relieved.

"Praise God for those tents!" Nigel echoed. "Still, let's see what they plan to do with the others. I pray no rods are used on our budding Thessalonian believers."

The city magistrates looked out at the yelling, angry mob and had their armed lictors come from behind them to settle the crowd merely with their intimidating presence. Once they could hear, a magistrate asked, "Now what is this all about?"

A filthy man clung to Jason's upper arm and spat, "Those who have turned the world upside down have come here too! Jason has kept them in his house." He threw Jason to the ground.

"They are all breaking the laws of the emperor, saying that there is another king, whose name is Jesus," another loafer accused, pushing Aristarchus and some of the other believers out next to Jason, who slowly got to his feet.

"This is intolerable!" Nigel shouted. "They are accusing Paul and Silas of being part of those militant messianic Jews stirring up trouble all over the Roman Empire. They are the reason Claudius expelled the Jews from Rome!"

"*Oui*, but Paul and Silas always teach respect for Roman law and order," Liz pointed out, shaking her head. "Since they preach about Jesus as King, these Jews are using the same angle the Jerusalem Jews used against Jesus."

Max nodded. "The jealous Jews keep twistin' their words aboot Jesus bein' put ta death by R-r-romans for bein' the King of the Jews. Ther-r-re be weapon number four again."

A fresh uproar erupted from the mob while the magistrates conferred with one another. One of the magistrates leaned over and pulled out a letter that Claudius had sent to the Jewish community in Egypt. "I've just heard from a magistrate in Alexandria who recently dealt with some Jewish freedom-fighters from Judea who were trying to cause trouble there. This came straight from the emperor himself:

363

> Do not bring in or invite Jews who sail to Alexandria from Syria or down the Nile from other parts of Egypt. If you do, this will make me very suspicious, and I will punish them severely for fomenting a general plague throughout the whole world.

One of the magistrates raised his eyebrows. "We must keep this riotous plague from touching *our* part of the world. But let's make these Thessalonian citizens keep the plague under control for us." He raised his hands and calmed the crowd once more so he could speak. He looked at Jason and the others standing before the court. "You will be released on bond, provided that those troublemaking Jews Paul and

Silas leave Thessalonica immediately. If they are seen again, you will be arrested and pay mightily."

Jason and the others breathed a sigh of relief as the lictors stayed put. There would be no beatings of punishment or warning. Only the threat of a hefty fine if their guests didn't leave. The jealous Jews, however, were fuming.

"I say, at least these chaps have a bit of *sanity*, unlike those *duumviri* in Philippi," Nigel noted.

"Aye, these lads seem a wee bit smart," Max agreed.

"But the outcome is still terrible, no?" Liz swallowed a lump in her throat. "Paul and Silas must leave."

Max let go a grunt. "On the r-r-road again."

The September moon was high overhead as Paul and Silas quickly made their way through the Augustan Arch and out of Thessalonica down the Via Egnatia. They headed toward the Axios River, where they would catch a ferry and then turn southwest off the main Roman road toward Berea, some sixty miles away.

"Do you think he'll be okay here?" Silas asked as he looked behind him to make sure they weren't being followed.

"Timothy will be fine," Paul assured him, "as you and I were the ones targeted for our preaching. He'll follow us soon to Berea, but I want him to minister to the believers here who are upset with what has happened. We had no choice but to remove the threat to Jason and the others by leaving town." The aging apostle sighed heavily. "My heart aches to leave this young church. I pray the Lord helps it stay the course, and I long to return here as soon as possible."

Max and Liz kept up the pace, also keeping watch behind them.

"Do you think he'll be okay here?" Liz worried.

"Lass, after all the danger-r-rous tr-r-ravelin' that little mouse has done over the centur-r-ries by hisself?" Max huffed. "Aye, he'll keep an eye on young Timothy an' we'll see him soon enough."

TWO WEEKS LATER

"Oh dear, this isn't good," Nigel muttered to himself as he sat high in a nook of the elder chambers at the synagogue.

"Paul is preaching about this Jesus in *Berea* now?" one of the elders demanded angrily, slamming his fist on the table. Some messengers had just returned from Berea with the news.

"Yes, and apparently the Jewish leaders at the synagogue there are very open to him," the messenger claimed. "They eagerly listen to Paul and then search the Scriptures to verify the truth of his words. Many Jews and Greeks have believed his message."

"Enough!" the jealous Jew shouted, standing to head out of the room. "We leave in the morning."

"Where are we going?" another elder asked.

"Berea! If those Jews there won't stop this blasphemy, we will!" he announced, slamming the door behind him.

BEREA

"Incoming!" Nigel called to Max and Liz below with a paw cupped around his mouth.

They looked up in the late afternoon sky and saw Nigel on a pigeon, swooping in for a landing. He hurriedly got off, gave the pigeon a parting pet, and scurried immediately over to where his friends were in the courtyard of the synagogue.

"Bad news, I'm afraid," Nigel gushed, out of breath.

Max's tail was up in alarm. "Wha's wr-r-rong, lad?"

"Those confounded jealous Jews are on their way here! They want Paul's head, I tell you!" Nigel related quickly. "Word reached them about Paul's ministry here and they are determined to put an end to it."

"They're coming all the way from Thessalonica after Paul?" Liz asked, wide-eyed. "And here we thought things were going so well after Timothy's arrival last night. He told us that Jason, Aristarchus, and all the other believers were staying solid in the faith, pressing on in the city."

"Yes, yes, yes, that is true. The church is thriving, but the Jews are conniving, I say!" Nigel rhymed. "They should be here soon."

"Looks like Paul has ta pr-r-reach an' r-r-run again," Max growled. "It's jest like wha' happened ta Jesus. Jealous Jews hounded him wher-r-rever he went."

"Yes, but in doing so, they are helping to spread the gospel to the next town," came a voice from behind. "And the next town is the grandest one of them all."

"Clarie?!" Liz cried, surprised to see a Greek young man, whom she assumed was their friend wearing a green tunic and brown headband.

"Hello, all," Clarie replied, her blue eyes twinkling with joy to see her friends. She squatted down and petted them. "Al and Kate send their love, and are doing well, aside from missing you."

Max wore a happy grin. "That's gr-r-rand news, Lass. But things here be gettin' r-r-rough."

366

Clarie gave a wave of her hand. "As I said, those troublemaking Jews are just helping to spread the gospel by moving Paul along. Jesus is taking ground with every mile his servants are forced to run."

"Where are we headed next?" Liz wanted to know. "You said the grandest city of them all?"

"The cradle of democracy, the intellectual capital of the world, the city of architectural marvels, and sadly, the home of more statues of gods than the rest of Greece combined—twenty thousand at last count," Clarie replied.

"Athens!" Nigel exclaimed. "I haven't been there since the glory days of Socrates, Plato, and Aristotle, long before Greece fell to the Romans."

"Twenty thousand statues!" Liz marveled. "No wonder they say it is easier to meet a god than another person in Athens, no?"

"Gr-r-reat," Max said sarcastically. "So the laddies will be up against the idol capital of the world then."

"Lad, not laddies," Clarie corrected him. "Silas and Timothy will stay here in Berea while Paul escapes to Athens alone. But then they will part ways. Timothy will return to Thessalonica to support the believers there while Silas stays here to strengthen the Berean church. Later they'll all meet back up in Corinth."

"Clarie, might Luke also join them?" Liz wondered. "I had thought he would be the one to write about Paul's journeys, but I do not know anymore. It does not seem possible now."

"Time will tell," Clarie teased them with a smile. "When are things ever what they seem at first?"

"So how are we to be of assistance, my dear?" Nigel asked.

A crowd of people came down the street murmuring. The Jewish elders from Thessalonica had arrived. They were already stirring up another mob to capture Paul, this time killing him if need be. Anything to silence the effective preacher.

"Go with Paul to Athens, and help him find the unknown god." Clarie rose to her feet. "I must rescue him from this mob. I'll grab some other Berean believers to escort Paul to a ship bound for Athens."

"Unknown god?" Max asked. "Lassie, if the god be unknown, how're we supposed ta find it in a city of twenty thousand statues?"

Clarie smiled at Max. "Even an unknown god has a place in Athens. Think of the real me and you'll find it. It's exactly what Paul will need to make his point to the most prestigious court in the world." She turned to leave. "Get to the edge of town. I'll meet you there." With that she went running toward the growing mob, leaving the animals in the street.

367

42

THE UNKNOWN GOD

Paul felt a hand grip his right arm, pulling him out of harm's way from the growing mob. "Come with us, now," a man named Nikolas told him. He was a new Berean believer Paul knew well. Sopater, another of the new Berean Christians, came along Paul's left side. "Let's get you out of here." Paul grudgingly agreed and went with the men to a side street.

"Macedonia has gotten too hot to hold you, my friend," Sopater said. "We'll escort you to Athens, where you'll be safe."

"What about Silas and Timothy?" Paul asked.

"We've got them away from the mob, but they'll be safe here in Berea. They can meet you later," Nikolas assured him. "For now, let's be on our way."

Together the three men secretly ducked down alleys and back streets until they reached the outskirts of town. There Clarie waited for them with a horse and cart. Max, Liz, and Nigel were already sitting in the back, along with Paul's knapsack. Paul smiled when he saw how well his Berean brothers were taking care of him, thinking of all his needs. "Thank you, my friends," he said, climbing into the cart and patting Max.

"It's twenty miles to the coast, so we'll be at the docks in plenty of time for you to catch an early morning ship bound for Athens," Clarie said. Once Sopater and Nikolas climbed into the cart, she took the reins and the horse galloped off into the night.

THREE DAYS LATER

"Paul is pensive," Liz remarked as the animals gazed along with the evangelist at the first distant sights of Athens and the surrounding mountains made of limestone and marble. The 500-foot massive white granite rock of the Acropolis rose from the city center, announcing to the world its national glory and worship of the gods. Sitting on top was the pride and joy of Athens that had stood for five hundred years: the Parthenon.

The Parthenon was 238 feet long, 111 feet wide, and 65 feet high. Eight Doric columns graced its short sides and seventeen its long sides. This massive temple rose over the course of ten years, then sculptors worked another fifteen years on the exquisite decoration alone. Magnificent friezes depicted warriors atop horses, elegant Greek bodies were draped in flowing robes, and great bronze rosettes painted in red and blue adorned the temple.

369

"Wha's that big buildin' for?" Max wondered, seeing something through the Parthenon's massive columns. "An' wha's that big shiny thing in the middle?"

"The Parthenon was built to house a forty-foot-tall gold and ivory statue of the warrior goddess, Athena," Nigel explained. "She wears an elaborate helmet adorned with a Sphinx and griffins. Her ivory breast-plate is carved with snakes and Medusa's head in the center. In one hand she holds a miniature statue of Nike, offering "victory" to the people of Athens, and in the other hand a spear. By her feet lies a shield and near the spear is a serpent. I've heard that the tip of her spear can be seen from forty miles away."

Max's jaw dropped. "She's a big, scary lassie idol, ain't she?"

"Indeed, and although she is highlighted in the Parthenon, all the other gods of Olympus are present in Athens in one form or another," Nigel said with arms crossed across his chest.

"Twenty-thousand statues," Liz reminded them. "No wonder Paul is deep in thought. Not only did he have to leave Silas and Timothy behind, he is concerned for the welfare of his young Macedonian churches and is getting ready to walk into the most idol-ridden city on Earth—alone."

"Not to mention being submerged in the intellectual and philosophical hub of the empire," Nigel added. "These Athenians will challenge Paul on every level. He is in for quite the showdown, I daresay."

Paul gripped the rail of the ship as it carried them into the port of Piraeus. A short walk up the bustling road and he would be immersed in a city that to the eye and to the mind was full of light, but to the spirit was drowning in darkness.

"Once we get you settled in Athens, we'll head back to Berea," Sopater said, joining Paul at the rail. "Is there anything we can do for you once we return?"

"Yes, I've been thinking Timothy needs to return to Thessalonica to strengthen the believers there. I'm so concerned about that church breaking under the strain of the angry Jews. Please tell him to encourage the Thessalonian believers to stand firm and not to be unsettled by the present troubles. Silas can remain in Berea for the time being, helping you and the other believers there. But please tell both of them to join me here in Athens as soon as they can."

Sopater put a hand on Paul's arm. "We will. The Lord will honor the good work you've begun. And we'll pray for you while you are here in Athens."

"Thank you, brother," Paul smiled. "I should leave my children in the hands of God, but I remain the worrisome parent nonetheless. I must learn to be anxious for nothing."

As their ship glided through the blue Aegean waters to dock below Athens, they felt the weight of the darkness they were getting ready to enter.

The days passed in pagan Athens, and Paul felt very much alone. Although he went to the synagogue to reason with the Jews and with the Gentiles who worshipped God, he found no welcoming audience there. Not only were they uninterested in Jesus, they were apathetic

370

about their pagan neighbors, having written off the intellectual Athenians as hopelessly blind. They had turned inward, worshipping the one true God in isolation while surrounded by a sea of lost souls.

So Paul then headed to the *agora* to reason with the people who happened to come by. He came here day after day, speaking boldly about Jesus and the resurrection, using the question-and-answer method of Socrates to engage them. But the people did little more than curiously observe the short, balding, bandy-legged man as a newcomer oddity, giving him no serious thought, and certainly no positive response. They were shallow and scoffed at the supernatural ideas about Jesus, debating with Paul on every point he tried to make. So although the Athenians wanted nothing more than to discuss whatever was new, Paul's new words were just not making any headway.

"Blast it all! Why can't any of these know-it-alls be open to the *possibility* of Paul's words?" Nigel fumed.

"There are two schools of philosophy here in Athens used for discussing the topic *du jour,*" Liz said, twitching her tail back and forth as she watched their respective groups huddle around each other. "Stoics and Epicureans. They look at whatever is discussed through the lens of their outlook on life."

371

"I'm almost afr-r-raid ta ask aboot wha' kind of lens they got," Max said, lying on his belly in the cool green grass.

"Stoics believe that everything, down to the smallest atom, is God," continued Liz, "and that everything that happens is the will of God, no matter how harsh. They believe in a unified world based on reason, and never show joy or sorrow. People must naturally accept things without resentment, and be unafraid and proud to accept the universe as-is. They believe the soul lives after death, but the Epicureans do not."

"'Eat, drink, and be merry, for tomorrow we die' is the Epicurean's mindset," Nigel chimed in. "Quite the opposite of Stoics, they teach that pleasure and happiness are the supreme goals of life, and that the gods may exist but have no interest in the lives of men. Everything happens by chance."

"Sounds like both gr-r-roups be tr-r-ryin' ta figure life out, especially when life gets tough," Max noted. "If they'd only listen ta Paul."

Liz saw a group gathering around Paul. "They listen, but they do not hear," she said, walking over to them.

"What is this ignorant show-off trying to say?" one of them demanded.

"He seems to be talking about foreign gods," another replied.

"Rubbish! He's just picking up bits and pieces of ideas from myths and putting them together."

"I, for one, find it amusing!"

"I find it dangerous, if he's introducing foreign gods and ideas that might harm the people."

"He needs to come to the Areopagus and prove his case. If the court finds him acceptable, he can stay. If not, we can expel him as an unsuitable philosopher."

"Very well," said a man with silver hair and a cut jaw line. "That's what we'll do." He stepped up to Paul. "I am Dionysius. We wish to invite you to attend the Areopagus to present your ideas."

Paul's face lit up. Finally, a group who would sit and listen to him! "Of course, I will gladly come."

"We shall see you tomorrow morning when we convene," Dionysius said.

Another man leaned in behind him and added with a smirk, "We'll be, um, most *intrigued* by what you have to say." He turned and raised an eyebrow to the others as they walked off, leaving Paul standing there.

"*Bon!* This is a wonderful opportunity, no?" Liz exclaimed to Max and Nigel.

"Aye, but he needs ta figure out wha' he's goin' ta say," Max replied.

"Clarie told us he would speak to the most prestigious court in the world!" Nigel reminded them. "The Areopagus comprises thirty of the most brilliant, elitist minds in Athens!"

"*Oui,* and she said we needed to lead Paul to the statue of the unknown god," Liz said. "But first we must find it ourselves. Clarie told us, '*Think of the real me and you'll find it.*'"

The animals grew silent as they thought through what she had meant. Paul started walking, deep in thought about what he was going to say to the Areopagus. His footsteps slowed from grief as he walked through the *agora* of Athens, hands clasped behind his back and a seemingly permanent frown on his face. He was sickened by what he saw and heard. So many young minds were being led astray by the godless philosophies being pumped into them in this intellectual capital of the world. But godless though its soul may have been, Athens was anything but godless—it was full of gods, albeit false ones. Temples, statues, and monuments abounded in a 360-degree view from any place one stood. The animals trailed along behind Paul, hearing him grunt and sigh as he read the monuments and listened to the discussions going on among the supposed learned elite.

Nigel stopped in the street and slapped his paws together. "Of course! Epimenides's sheep!"

"Epimeni-who?" Max asked.

"A poet from Crete, old chap," Nigel answered matter-of-factly. "Six hundred years ago, a horrific plague spread through Athens. Epimenides suggested a plan to make sure they had not offended any of the gods by accident. Although they had many gods represented, they assumed they missed one with all that nasty plague business. But how to know which one?"

"Oui, go on, *mon ami,"* Liz encouraged him.

"The Athenians starved and let loose a flock of sheep throughout the city from the Areopagus, a hill that the Romans now call 'Mars Hill.' The Areopagus court takes its name from this hill, and this is precisely where Paul has been invited to speak. But I digress." Clearing his throat, Nigel continued. "Knowing it would be unnatural for hungry sheep not to eat the lush green grass surrounding the Areopagus, whenever a sheep lay down without eating, it was sacrificed there to the 'unknown god' and an altar was erected to mark the spot."

"Bon, Nigel! You have figured out Clarie's riddle," Liz enthused.

"So ye're sayin' we need ta think like unhungr-r-ry sheep an' figure out where they would lay?" Max asked, shaking his head. "Cr-r-razy Gr-r-reeks. Did they make sheep idols ta mar-r-rk the spot?"

"No, Max, we need to simply look for a marker that reads 'To an Unknown God.' Since it's been six hundred years, we can assume that

373

many of these markers have fallen into disrepair. But according to Clarie, at least one still stands."

The animals split up and ran around from monument to monument, trying to find the marker. Before long, Liz walked by a monument and noticed the letters were glowing. She cautiously walked up to it, and read aloud the inscription:

TO AN UNKNOWN GOD

As she stood there, more letters appeared on the marker:

BONJOUR, LIZ.

A smile grew on Liz's petite face. *"Bonjour,* Gillamon. This is a new kind of statue for you, no?"

The previous message dissolved back into the stone and was replaced with new words:

INDEED. THIS REMINDS ME OF WHEN I CAME TO YOU IN THE TALKING SCROLL.

Liz's eyes danced with delight to be communicating with Gillamon this way. *"Bien sûr!* I remember it well, on our mission with Isaiah!"

"To whom are you speaking, my dear?" Nigel asked, walking up to her.

GOOD DAY, NIGEL.

"By Jove, it's Gillamon!" the little mouse exclaimed with a paw to his spectacles. "This takes the biscuit, old boy! Splendid to 'read you!'"

The letters disappeared again as Max joined them. "Did ye find the sheep stone then?"

"More like a *goat* stone," Nigel quipped, wiping back his whiskers and chuckling.

HOW IS MY FAVORITE SCOTTIE DOG TODAY?

Max jumped back and then walked up to sniff around the marker with his big nose. "Gillamon? Ye don't look much like a statue. I thought all idols looked like statues then."

374

IDOLS CAN TAKE ANY FORM. WHATEVER MAN USES
AS A SUBSTITUTE FOR GOD CAN BECOME AN IDOL.

As the letters streamed across the stone before dissolving, Liz nod-ded. *"Oui,* pagans like to put up statues to represent their gods, but idols can truly be anything that people set on a pedestal in their lives: money, fame, power, other people, food."

"Then ye best have a chat with Big Al aboot his love for food when we see him again, Lass," Max suggested.

YOU MUST BRING PAUL TO SEE ME. IT WILL INSPIRE
A SPEECH GREATER THAN EVEN DEMOSTHENES
PRESENTED TO THE GREEKS OF HIS DAY.

"Demosthe-who?" Max asked with a wrinkled brow.

"Ah, *oui,* the master orator and statesman," Liz remembered. "His first public speech was a disaster but Demosthenes kept working until he became known as the most compelling speaker Greece had ever heard."

375

AND LIZ, YOU MUST REMEMBER EVERY WORD TO
HELP LUKE WHEN HE WRITES IT DOWN.

Liz's face beamed with excitement that Luke could, indeed, be the writer she hoped he would be.

"Right! How do you suggest we assist Paul in this quest?" Nigel asked, glancing up at Max and Liz, who looked at one another with grins before turning their gaze to the little mouse.

"It's a per-r-rfect day for mouse-chasin'," Max said.

Liz put her dainty paw on Nigel's shoulder. *"Cher* Nigel, allow Max to chase and corner you, *s'il vous plaît."*

Nigel's shoulders sagged. "Very well, just as we did in Egypt with Joseph. Paul will not wish to have his pets make a loud scene in this refined place, no doubt." The little mouse removed his spectacles and handed them to Liz, squinting. "Please take care of these, my dear. And Max, do be a good chap and let me know if I'm about to run into an idol."

Liz replied, "Of course." She looked around to see where Paul had gone and saw him examining a statue dedicated to Apollo. *"Bon,* there he is. Okay, *mes amis,* you may begin."

"Let's crack on," Nigel said, taking off running in the direction of Paul.

"Ta the left, Mousie!" Max barked. "Now ta the r-r-right!" He guided the visually challenged mouse so he wouldn't run into one of the forest of statues. "Paul be jest up ahead. Let's do a lap ar-r-round his legs an' head back ta Gillamon!"

Paul heard Max barking and turned to see what the commotion was about. Max came running up and chased Nigel around his legs, barking loudly. Paul ran after them.

"It's working! Paul is following them!" Liz cheered.

VERY GOOD. I'LL GO SILENT NOW. TELL MAX AND NIGEL "WELL DONE."

"I shall," she replied, but the letters had dissolved back into the stone.

Nigel came running up to the monument and hid behind it while Max joined him, "fake barking" at the little mouse. Paul soon stopped and saw Liz sitting there calmly with her tail curled gracefully around her feet. Max scooped up Nigel in his mouth and came around to show Paul his prize.

Paul stood with his hands on his hips, catching his breath. "You better make sure these pagans don't have a mouse god, Gabriel. They might come after you." He chuckled and mussed the fur on Max's head.

"Please read this marker, monsieur," Liz meowed.

"What is this, little Faith?" Paul asked her, his eye having caught the marker. "'TO AN UNKNOWN GOD.' Hmmm. They don't even know what god this is for." His eyes suddenly lit up. "They don't know the ONE, TRUE God. He is indeed unknown to them! This is exactly what I need to use to address the court!"

Max set Nigel down and beamed at Liz. Tomorrow, Paul would take on the intellectual elite of Athens, armed with the knowledge they hungered for but were too blind to see.

⚯

Paul climbed the steps cut into the craggy rock that led up the 377-foot-high hill of the Areopagus, glancing over at the Parthenon. The statue of Athena stood in that temple, offering victory to Greece. But the idol's promises were hollow. The Romans had defeated Greece, and had reduced even this once powerful court to one that only oversaw educational and religious matters. It was still filled with some of the most brilliant minds in the world, but it held little power.

"So this won't be a trial then?" Max asked as the animals followed Paul at a distance so as not to disturb him.

"No, not per se, but they will determine if Paul can continue to speak at will," Nigel replied. "Back in Socrates's day they had the power to put Socrates himself to death for trying to introduce dangerous ideas into the culture. Made the poor chap drink hemlock."

Max stopped in his tracks. "Cr-r-razy Gr-r-reeks. Paul best not dr-r-rink anythin' they offer him."

The thirty men greeted Paul and took their seats while he stood on the white 'Stone of Shame' reserved for the 'defendant,' or one arguing his ideas. Max, Liz, and Nigel hid behind a column behind the court so they could see and hear everything that would happen or be said.

377

"Let us see if *these* hungry sheep of the Areopagus will eat the lush green grass of truth Paul offers them," Liz remarked.

The 'prosecutor' stepped up to the 'Stone of Pride' and held out his hand to Paul. "We would like to know what this new teaching is that you are talking about. Some of the things we hear you say sound strange to us, and we would like to know what they mean."

Paul stood up and couldn't wait to get started. As a lawyer he was in his element, and his mind raced with excitement to present his case. "I see that in every way you Athenians are very religious. For as I walked through your city and looked at the places where you worship, I found an altar on which is written, 'To an Unknown God.' That which you worship, then, even though you do not know it, is what I now proclaim to you."

"Bravo!" Nigel cheered.

"Tell 'em who it be!" Max added quietly.

"God, who made the world and everything in it, is Lord of heaven and earth and does not live in temples made by human hands," Paul continued, pausing to lift a hand toward the Parthenon, with its massive Athena statue, behind them. "Nor does he need anything that we can supply by working for him, since it is he himself who gives life and breath and everything else to everyone. From one human being he created all races of people and made them live throughout the whole earth. He himself fixed beforehand the exact times and the limits of the places where they would live. He did this so that they would look for him, and perhaps find him as they felt around for him. Yet God is actually not far from any one of us; as someone has said,

'In him we live and move and exist.'

"He's quoting Epimenides!" Nigel commented. "Brilliant maneuver!"

"The sheep poet?" Max asked.

"Yes, in his poem about Zeus," Nigel replied.

"Shhhh, I'm trying to listen," Liz hushed them.

Paul continued. "It is as some of your poets have said,

'We too are his children.'"

"Now he's quoting Aratus," Nigel whispered. "He's grabbing their intellectual attention by quoting their own poets. Brilliant!"

"Shhhhh!" Liz shushed him again. "I must remember every word of this speech."

"Since we are God's children, we should not suppose that his nature is anything like an image of gold or silver or stone, shaped by human art and skill. God has overlooked the times when people did not know him, but now he commands all of them everywhere to turn away from their evil ways," stressed Paul, looking around the assembly of men gathered there. "For he has fixed a day in which he will judge the whole world with justice by means of a man he has chosen. He has given proof of this to everyone by raising that man from death!"

At the mention of the Resurrection, the assembly broke out in laughter and sarcastic insults, with some of the men standing as if to walk out from such ridiculous statements. Paul stood there quietly as they ranted.

The prosecutor raised his hand to bring order to the assembly. "We want to hear you speak about this again."

"Pfft! That is the polite way of saying, 'This meeting is adjourned,'" Liz spat.

"Just like that?" Max asked. "He's finished? I thought this were supposed ta be a gr-r-rand speech ta be r-r-remembered like that Demosthe-who lad."

"Sadly, yes. Paul has been dismissed," Nigel confirmed with a frown. "It appears the unknown god of Athens will stay that way for now."

As Paul left the meeting, one man got up and followed him out, catching Liz's attention. "Unless one solitary, silver-haired sheep decided he is hungry after all."

Gillamon and Clarie stood inside the IAMISPHERE, watching this scene in Athens unfold while panes of past and future history swirled around them.

"Not only will Luke someday write about this speech, but entire *books* will be written about it," Clarie noted with hope, spying a library scene. "They just can't imagine all of this now."

Gillamon looked up at a scene of the future that the Maker allowed him to see, way up high in the IAMISPHERE. A man passionately addressed a room full of fellow statesmen, pretending to plunge an ivory letter opener into his heart for dramatic flair. "And another Demosthenes will study what Paul said here today, long after the Parthenon becomes a Christian church."

379

43

AQUILA AND PRISCILLA

O ut of thir-r-rty men in that court, Paul only r-r-reached one," Max lamented as they walked along the road. "That Diony-sius lad."

Paul had decided they needed to leave Athens. He wouldn't be silenced by a court that didn't plan to take him seriously. He'd head fifty miles west to Corinth, the largest city in Greece, and Silas and Timothy would now meet him there.

"Indeed. And in all of Athens, he only made a handful of believers, with no church founded to support them," Nigel added. "I daresay Paul's spirit was crushed more by the polite amusement of those Greeks than by the rods of the lictors in those other cities."

"Aye, now he's weak an' afr-r-aid," Max continued. "The lad's been thr-r-rough some r-r-rough times. I think he needs a br-r-reak."

"Paul seems determined never to take a break when it comes to sharing the Good News," answered Nigel. "By my calculations we have traveled approximately four thousand miles already, and the old boy is just getting started."

"Pfft! Stop all of your negative talk," Liz scolded them. "The Maker will use what Paul started in Athens for his own purposes, in his own time. And he will give Paul the strength to press on. What he really needs now are some good friends."

They heard the sound of horses behind them and turned to see who was coming down the road. Liz studied the passengers and noticed an ornate chariot followed by a group of well-trained athletes running along behind. The runners' faces were set and determined, oozing with the discipline that had given them sculpted bodies along with speed and endurance.

"The games, of course!" Liz cried. "The Isthmian games are scheduled to take place next spring, only six miles from Corinth. This will be perfect for Paul!"

Max observed Paul's slow, bandy-legged gait as the athletes went blazing past him. "Lass, have ye lost yer mind? Paul's no athlete, especially no r-r-runner."

Liz frowned. "No, no, no, *mon ami.* Not to run. To make tents!"

"There be tent-makin' contests at the games?" Max asked in disbelief. Liz rolled her eyes at him.

381

Nigel's eyes widened as he understood where she was going with this. "Of course! Thousands upon thousands of people descend on the area during the games and must stay in tents. Not only is Corinth one of the greatest trading and commercial centers in the world, the games will only increase the number of people here whom Paul can reach *whilst* he is busy making tents."

"Aye, so we need ta find some tentmakers for Paul ta meet when we arrive," Max suggested.

Nigel patted Max's shoulder. "Precisely, old boy."

Liz began to ponder the humans and their games. "The Olympiad is a four-year series of games that open with the Olympic Games. The Isthmian Games are held in years one and three, the Pythian Games in year three, and the Nemean Games in years two and four."

"And such games even include music and singing," Nigel remarked happily.

"Singin'?" Max asked. "I thought they competed with r-r-runnin', wr-r-restlin', boxin', an' the like."

"*Oui*, sports are the main competition, but singing and poetry reading are also part of the Isthmian games," Liz explained.

Max snorted a laugh. "Poetr-r-ry r-r-readin'? Wha' kind of sport be that?"

"The sophisticated kind, old boy—exercising the mind, you know." Nigel cleared his throat and pointed to his head. "I say, I could jolly well be a contender with all the practice I've had reciting Plato."

Another group of chariots went racing by, and Liz spied a brown capuchin monkey swinging by one arm, grinning a mile wide. He blew her a kiss and screeched happily while a small, green plumed basilisk lizard sat next to him, doing bicep curls with a rock. The lizard maintained his serious look of discipline, shaking his head at the swinging monkey who didn't appear to give a serious thought about anything.

"That lizard looks to be an athlete, no?" Liz puzzled out loud. "Those animals come from Central America. Yet they are here in Greece?" Her mind flashed back to the time on the Ark when she and Kate organized Talent Night and Flamingorobics to keep the animals from all over the world entertained and fit while aboard. This got her to thinking. Perhaps they could organize something like that again.

Corinth sat on a four-mile wide isthmus, and due to its geographic position it, not Athens, was the capital of the Achaia Province. It was known as the "Bridge of Greece." Flames from its great lighthouse and Temple of Poseidon guided ships into the twin ports of Cenchrea on the eastern Saronic Gulf and Lechaeum on the western Corinthian Gulf. Slaves unloaded cargo and pulled ships on rollers across the four-mile neck of land in order to avoid a treacherous two-hundred-mile journey around the southern Cape Malea. Because of this, all north-south traffic had to go through Corinth. The city's *agora* was always filled with exotic goods from around the world—Indian spices, Chinese silk, Syrian linen, Turkish marble, and Italian timber, to name a few. The city had swelled to seven hundred thousand people, including sailors, merchants, Roman army veterans, adventure seekers, and also pleasure seekers. Corinth was the most Romanized city in the Greek world—full of noise, excitement, wealth, and rampant wickedness.

Two gods were near and dear to Corinth: Poseidon, god of the sea, and Aphrodite, goddess of love. The Corinthians honored Poseidon with the Isthmian games and Aphrodite with their lifestyles. Immorality was the norm, and if you were from Corinth, your reputation preceded you.

Paul frowned as he entered Corinth, already feeling the darkness of this pagan city that thrived on devoured lives. His heart ached to tell these people about Jesus. They were thirsty for hope and truth, and the eager apostle couldn't wait to share the Good News with them. He suddenly realized *he* was thirsty from the long walk, and headed to the city's water source, the Peirene Fountain.

"There are two legends about this place," Nigel lectured as the animals followed Paul through the fountain's gate. Six arched openings led to a huge, beautifully tiled rectangular water basin. People gathered to drink and fill their pouches and water jars. "One myth says a woman named Peirene became a spring from the tears she shed for her son Cenchrias, who was unintentionally killed by Artemis. The other myth says Pegasus struck the ground with his hoof to create this fountain. Pick your myth, as it were!"

383

Max rolled his eyes. "C-r-razy Gr-r-reek pagans! They can't even decide which nonsense ta believe."

"Exactly, *mon ami,*" Liz replied sadly. "Instead of pursuing truth they make up things to explain life. But truth is truth, no matter what tales they weave."

"Well, the tr-r-ruth aboot this fountain be that some laddies carved it with tools ta car-r-ry water here fr-r-rom a spr-r-ring," Max huffed. "I'm goin' ta dr-r-rink some r-r-real water." He trotted over to join Paul, lapping up the refreshing water as Paul filled his leather pouch. Nigel stayed hidden in the shadows so as not to cause a stir among the people.

Liz spotted a Jewish man and woman at the far end of the water basin who stood to leave. As the man slung his heavy bag over his shoulder, out fell a swatch of cloth the man didn't notice. Curious, Liz walked over to inspect the cloth. She gently pushed it with her paw and her eyes lit up. She picked up the cloth in her mouth and ran out of the fountain area after the couple.

The noisy, crowded streets of Corinth made it challenging for Liz to maneuver without getting stepped on. She darted between and around the legs of people from all walks of life but soon feared she would lose the two. She decided to jump up on some crates to try to spot the couple. As she strained to search the crowd, a pair of big brown eyes and smiling white teeth suddenly appeared in her line of vision. Upside down.

"Whatcha lookin' for, beautiful?" came a voice from the upside-down face. It was the capuchin monkey.

Liz jumped back, startled and a bit annoyed, as she didn't want to lose the couple. She continued to look around the monkey who was swinging by his tail, peeling a banana and talking a mile a minute.

"Hey, I saw you on the road! Why are you eating *that?* YUK!" he said as he pushed the banana into her face. "Here, have a banana! It tastes a lot better than goat hair."

Liz strained to look around the monkey and his banana, but the couple had melted into the crowd and were lost to her. She sighed, rolled her eyes, and put the piece of cloth down on the crate. "I am not *eating* the goat hair. I was simply holding it while trying to find the couple this cloth belongs to." She pushed the banana out of her face. "No, *merci.*"

"Suit yourself," the monkey said, taking a huge sloppy bite, and peeling more of the banana. He swallowed and took another bite, continuing to talk with his mouth full. "Why do you want to find the goat hair people?"

"Because hopefully they make tents, and if so, it is very important that I introduce them to my human," Liz explained. She sighed. "But now I have lost them."

The monkey grinned and tossed his banana peel on the street. "Don't think so!" He wrapped his long, skinny arm around Liz's waist and took off flying through the marketplace from stall roof to stall roof, whooping and hollering, "Wahoo-hoo-hoo!"

"Put me down! Put me down this instant!" Liz protested, but the monkey ignored her.

The column-lined *agora* of Corinth was massive, with so many shops it was hard to count them all. As Liz swung along with the monkey, she was able to get an aerial view to see what vendors were selling in their outdoor shops. Suddenly the monkey turned off the main street of the marketplace to travel down a side street, and Liz grew worried about where he was taking her.

Finally the monkey stopped and hung by his tail from a rafter, holding Liz upside down with him. "See, there they are!"

Liz turned her head so she could view them right side up. It was the couple from the fountain! "They *are* tent makers!"

"Yep, goat hair, leather, the works!" the monkey added. "And they even *rhyme.*"

"*Merci* for bringing me here. But can you put me down now please, *monsieur . . .*" Liz requested firmly.

385

"Noah," the monkey introduced himself as he gently placed Liz on the ground.

"And I am Liz. *Oui,* I did see you on the road. Why are you here in Corinth?" she asked.

Noah's face fell and his eyes widened with worry as he remembered he was not where he was supposed to be. "Uh-oh!" He put a skinny arm up on a rafter to take off but turned to give Liz a wink. "I'm available anytime, little lady!" With that he took off swinging, leaving Liz there.

She wrinkled her forehead with a confused grin. "What a funny monkey!" She turned and looked up at the tentmaker's shop. "*They even rhyme?* But what did he mean?" she asked herself. She noticed that above the shop were living quarters. If this worked out as she hoped, Paul would not only have a place to work, he would have a place to stay. Liz walked in the front door, ready to find out exactly who these people were.

Max and Nigel were frantic. They couldn't find Liz anywhere. Paul was concerned as well, but knew she was no ordinary cat. "She'll turn up, Gabriel," he told Max as they walked out of the fountain area.

As they wandered the streets of Corinth, Nigel worried himself silly. "What if some horrid pagans snatched her up?! What if they've taken her off to some foreign land as an exotic pet?"

Just then Max spied only the black tip of a question mark tail walking toward them. "Not a chance, lad. Here she comes now."

Liz brightened to see them. She wrapped herself around Paul's legs and told Max and Nigel the good news. *"I've found tentmakers, mes amis! They are a wealthy Jewish couple with businesses in Rome, Corinth, and Ephesus but had to flee Rome when the emperor expelled the Jews there. And they rhyme! C'est perfect!"*

Paul smiled to hear the little cat meowing so excitedly. He picked her up and held her close. "You must have found some exciting things, Faith."

Liz wriggled to get out of his arms. She was so excited and wanted him to follow her before the shop closed for the night. *"Allons-y!* Bring him along, Max. Time for you to chase *me,* Nigel!" She took off running.

Max took off barking after her, with Nigel holding on and cheering in his ear, "It's a mouse-and-cat—and dog—game, I say!"

Paul chased the animals through the streets, nearly slipping on Noah's banana peel, until they at last stood in front of the tentmaker's shop. He smiled and put his hands on his hips as the Jewish couple stepped outside to meet him.

"What did you mean, 'They rhyme?'" Nigel whispered to Liz.

"Shalom, friend. I'm Aquila," the man warmly greeted Paul. "And this is my wife, Priscilla."

"Voila," Liz replied to her mouse friend.

"Shalom, I am Paul. I'm a tentmaker by trade," Paul smiled and shared. "I've just arrived in Corinth. Might you have need of another tentmaker?"

"Paul? Of Tarsus?" Aquila asked, his face lighting up with recognition. He drew half a fish in the sand with his foot.

"I am." Paul completed the fish with his foot and smiled at his fellow believers. "Grace and peace to you, my brother and sister in Christ."

"We've heard of you, from many Christian friends in Rome," Priscilla told Paul, putting her hand on his arm. "Welcome to Corinth! Please, come inside. You must stay with us."

"Yes, you have a home with us," Aquila added with a pat on Paul's back. "And yes, the Isthmian Games are upon us, so we could use another tentmaker."

As Paul followed them in, Max, Liz, and Nigel remained outside the shop on this quieter side street of Corinth.

"Splendid work, my dear!" Nigel exclaimed.

Suddenly they saw the green lizard blaze past them on two legs, kicking up dust behind him. He didn't even turn his head to look at them, but maintained his determined gaze on the road ahead.

"Weren't that the little green athlete we saw on the way here?" Max asked as they watched the lizard virtually disappear as it sped down the street.

"Indeed, and clearly he is more serious than his friend," Nigel observed. "No monkey business with this one."

"*Oui,* I've never seen an animal so intent on running for the sake of running." Liz curled her tail up and down as she pondered the little green lizard. "I would like to find out why."

44

NOAH AND NATE

P aul immediately began preaching on the Sabbath in Corinth at the synagogue, just as he had done when first arriving in most of the other cities on this missionary journey. And while he was generally well received by the Jews and God-fearing Greeks for now, only a few chose to follow Christ and be baptized. Gaius Titius Justus was a wealthy man who lived right next door to the synagogue, and he and the handful of Paul's converts showed up every week, eager to learn more. But because he had to support himself, Paul only preached at the synagogue on the Sabbath. The rest of his time was spent making tents.

Aquila led Paul around the city of Corinth and the nearby city of Isthmia, which was preparing for the biennial games. Paul looked at the depravity of the lost people all around him, and longed to reach them with the Good News. But until something provided him a wider preaching platform, progress would be painfully slow.

"Have you ever attended any of the games of the Olympiad?" Aquila asked Paul as they walked down Isthmia's energetic main street, now swarming with the daily new arrivals of athletes and tourists. Aquila towered over Paul, being a tall man with long arms, legs, and fingers. His blackish-brown beard was full and his deep brown eyes were almost hidden, tucked under his bushy eyebrows and curly wild hair. He looked like a big bear wearing a light brown tunic. He stopped at one of the temporary stalls in the *agora* and pointed to a golden vase depicting four runners in a footrace, silhouetted in black paint. "Priscilla and I see souvenirs like this at every venue."

"I know of the games, but I haven't attended them myself." Paul reached over and picked up the vase. "They are running the race for the prize. What do they actually win at these games?"

Aquila's long finger pointed to the runners on the vase. "Winning is everything, and there is no prize for second place. Only one of the athletes wins anything, and he wins a crown of pine and celery leaves."

"A crown that doesn't last," Paul replied in amazement, setting the vase down.

The big man chuckled and nodded. "Yes, by the time the winning athlete receives his crown, it's already wilted. But if an athlete is victorious in the games, he receives true rewards once he returns home. Athletes' home cities may give them money, fame, and even a statue erected in their honor." Aquila started walking again. "Come, let me show you where the athletes are preparing for the upcoming games."

389

The two men made their way to the athletic complex, with the Temple of Poseidon positioned in a central, prominent place to remind all the athletes and attendees who these games were meant to glorify. "Athletes come here from all over the Roman world to prepare for a month before the games begin. The games open with sacrifices made to Poseidon. The main competitions include footraces, boxing, wrestling, javelin throwing, jumping, and discus throwing," Aquila explained. He pointed to the different facilities of the complex. "Sometimes they have chariot races. Men and even some women compete in the games. Here you can see a stadium, hippodrome, and theater."

A man with his face buried in a piece of papyrus brushed past them, reciting poetry. Aquila chuckled. "They even have competitive poetry reading, singing, and playing the lyre and flute, if you can believe that."

Paul smiled as he heard a woman with a lovely alto voice belting out a musical scale, filling the air with notes as she prepared to enter the theater that was part of the athletic complex. "Making a joyful noise is an admirable endeavor." His smile faded as they passed the enormous statue of Poseidon holding his trident. "Unless you're singing to the wrong god."

"I especially want you to see the Palestra," Aquila told Paul while pointing to an elaborate building lined with porticoes. "Every athlete has to come here and first check in with the *'hellanodikai'*, the judges of the games." A group of men wearing purple robes walked out of the building and down the steps toward the baths. Aquila motioned toward them. "These judges determine if an athlete qualifies to participate. Latecomers are disqualified from the games, so athletes try to arrive as early as they can. The judges assign the athletes to age categories, give them their rigorous training schedules, lay out the rules of the games, and administer the oath. They cast lots to pair athletes for competition and they determine the winner, making sure no one cheated. They impose fines and punishments on those who break the oath."

"So athletes take an oath to abide by the rules of the games and if they don't, they are disqualified," Paul summarized, pondering the journey of these athletes.

"Yes, winning is more about honor than the wilted crown they hope to win," Aquila explained. "But before they take the oath, they must truly consider the cost involved, for the required dedication to training is steep."

Nigel stood on a low pedestal next to Max and Liz, who had followed Paul and Aquila here the few miles from Corinth. He cleared his throat and raised his paw into the air as he prepared to recite a Greek Stoic philosopher: "'Would you be a victor in the Olympic games? So in good truth would I, for it is a glorious thing; but pray consider what must go before, and what may follow, and so proceed to the attempt.'" The little mouse straightened his spectacles. "That is from Epictetus, of course."

Two muscular men passed them, their knuckles bleeding and wrapped in leather straps. They were boxers and their sculpted arms, legs, and chests bore deep scars, as did their faces. One man's eye was swollen shut and the other's lip dripped blood. Paul knew how they felt. He also bore scars, but from the repeated beatings for sharing the good news of Christ. "I understand boxing to be among the most dangerous of the competitions."

Aquila frowned and folded his massive arms over his chest as they studied the boxers. "It's true. The only rule is that a boxer can't hold an opponent's fist. Aside from that, everything is fair game. They actually *ask* to be severely beaten as they train so they will be toughened and ready for the games. Their gloves are ridged with steel and spiked with nails. For the games a boxing match can go on for hours, until one boxer either gives up," he stated somberly, looking Paul in the eye, "or dies."

"Endless beatings to train, and a fight to the death for a temporary, wilted crown in honor of a false god," Paul observed, shaking his head, gazing out at the throngs of people filling the streets. "My friend, we have some work to do among these athletes and the people coming to watch the games. They need to know there's a race to run, tough training to endure for a good fight, and all for the one true God. But they'll receive a crown that never fades, with heavenly rewards."

"Agreed," Aquila replied, nodding. "The people will come to us for tents to stay in while they're here. Your preaching can extend out here with them."

391

"*Our* preaching," Paul encouraged him, patting the large man on the back. "You and Priscilla aren't just tentmakers anymore. You are on mission for Christ as you do the work he's given you to do. Jesus said to share the Good News and make disciples as you are going. So wherever you are, whatever you're doing in your work, you have a mission field to share Christ. I'm learning that even if I don't have a large platform from which to preach, I can make my daily life a sharing platform everywhere I go, and with everyone I meet."

Liz watched Paul and Aquila walk off to continue their tour of the athletic complex. "The Maker has provided the perfect way for Paul to share with hundreds of people, no? Although he has been preaching in the synagogue and has had a few converts, he is not making as big an impact on the Jews, Greeks, and these pagans as he had hoped."

"Aye, but the lad has ta spend so much time supportin' himself makin' tents," Max added, "he don't have the time ta go aboot pr-r-reachin' ever-r-ry day."

"It would be splendid if he could simply focus on spreading the Good News," Nigel agreed. "The old boy simply must have his team of

Timothy and Silas once more."

Just then the little green lizard went blazing past them in the street and Liz's heart raced. "There's our athlete!" she shouted as she took off running after him. Nigel jumped from the pedestal onto Max's back, and off they ran after Liz.

The animals slipped through legs, around carts, and under horses in the street in pursuit of the lizard.

"He's a fast, wee beastie!" Max huffed, barely missing a cluster of pottery stacked on a curb.

"These plumed basilisks can reach seven miles per hour, old boy!" Nigel shouted, holding onto Max's ears.

Just as Liz nearly caught up to the lizard, he plunged into a long pool of water. A lion fountain head spewed water into the pool and Liz jumped up onto the ledge to try to find the lizard. Nigel joined Liz on the ledge while Max rested his front paws on it and gazed into the water with them.

"Do ye see him, Lass?" Max asked.

Liz squinted and searched the pool but the lizard was nowhere to be seen. "No, he is staying underwater."

Nigel studied the lion fountain. "I say, do you suppose Gillamon is about?"

The three animals stared at the fountain but the lion head made no movement.

"Goin' for a dip, beautiful?" came a voice from behind them.

Liz turned quickly to see the capuchin monkey hop up next to her on the ledge of the fountain. *"Bonjour,* Noah! I am happy to see you here. We were trying to meet your friend."

Noah peered into the water. "How long's he been under?"

"I'd say two minutes, give or take a few seconds," Nigel piped up. "Hello, old boy. Name's Nigel P. Monaco, and this fine canine is Max."

"Hiya, dudes," Noah replied with a wide grin. "Nate could be in there for thirty minutes if he wants to."

"Wha' in the name of Pete be the lizard doin'? Don't he ever stop movin'?" Max asked.

Noah scooped up a handful of water into the air, watching the drops spray the surface of the pool. "Did you see that?! I can make it rain! Wahoo!" The monkey proceeded to repeatedly splash the water into the air and subsequently all over Liz, Max, and Nigel.

Max frowned and looked at Liz as water dripped off his wiry black fur. "Cr-r-razy monkey! Don't he ever *listen?*"

Liz giggled at the funny monkey who was making a wet mess and thoroughly entertaining himself. She placed her dainty paw on his shoulder. "Noah, *s'il vous plaît,* I know you are having fun, but can you tell us about Nate? He is an athlete, no?"

Noah rolled his eyes with a silly grin. "What was your first clue?" He blew a raspberry before he burst out laughing. "Fastest lizard on two legs!"

"We've seen him, of course. But I never heard your answer as to how you and Nate got to Greece from Central America." Liz gazed pointedly at him. "And why?"

393

Noah rubbed the back of his neck with his hand and wore a cha-grined look. "It seemed like a good idea at the time."

"What seemed like a good idea, my dear fellow?" Nigel asked.

"Seeing if that hollowed-out gourd would hold both of us for a short trip across the lagoon," Noah replied with his white teeth showing in an uncomfortable smile.

"But that short trip turned into a *long* trip across the ocean when the tide took us out to sea," came a voice behind them.

The animals turned to see Nate, a bright green plumed basilisk lizard standing with his hands on his hips and a frown on his face. He stood only twelve inches high, with a long, skinny, yellow-and-black striped tail twice as long as his body and curled behind him. Three plumed crests came off his head, back, and the base of his tail. Blue and white spots ran down his side, legs, and onto the skinny toes on his feet. His golden round eyes had big black pupils.

"I said, 'Um, I don't think we should do that, Noah.' But did he listen to me?" Nate recounted, blinking his eyes slowly as he looked at an embarrassed Noah. "He never listens to me."

"Aye, us neither, little lizard." Max looked inside Noah's ears. "Ye got fluff stuck in there, monkey?"

Nate hopped up onto the ledge and walked up to his monkey friend. "Oh, there's plenty of fluff in there, alright."

Noah wrapped his arm around Nate's small form in a smothering hug. "Yeah, but we're best buds! Nate forgave me, especially when he heard about all the athletes here in Greece he could watch."

"*Oui*, I notice that you are very serious about running and also swimming," Liz told Nate, her sweet face getting eye-level with him. "How would you like to compete, just like the humans?"

A big grin slowly grew on Nate's face and he blinked his eyes. "Like in the Isthmian Games? Um, but I'm pretty small. And I'm a lizard."

"Yeah but he's a giant in sports!" Noah exclaimed, holding Nate's two small front legs up in the air. Nate smacked the monkey in the face with his tail so Noah would let go.

"*Oui*, but I am suggesting games just for animals," Liz explained with a smile. "The very first Animalympics."

"Brilliant idea, my pet!" Nigel exclaimed.

"Aye, Lass, another gr-r-rand animal event jest like ye an' Kate organized on Noah's Ark," Max followed with a wide grin.

"Hey dude, I'm Noah, too!" the monkey said, vigorously pointing to himself and stating the obvious. "But I don't have an ark." The monkey wrinkled his brow and scratched his head in thought before his face brightened with an idea. "I've got a gourd, though!"

Nate's eyes grew wide with excitement. "For real? You mean I could actually run to compete? I've always dreamed of doing something like that! But, um, whom would I run against?"

Nigel wiped off his spectacles and held them up in the air for inspection. "It would not need to be other lizards, certainly. We could make a race for any animals that enjoy the sport. Mix things up a bit, if you will."

"Nigel is right," Liz agreed. "We can organize several competitions, depending on the animals we find to participate, and of course depending on their respective skills."

"OOOH! I can help with that!" Noah shouted with his hand up in the air. "I meet lots of animals from all over the place. Can I be one of those judges or somethin' that announces the games? Can I please, can

I, huh?" His little, round, brown eyes pleaded and he cocked his head sideways with an endearing smile.

"If ye can pay attention long enough ta wha's goin' on, Lad," Max carped at the mile-a-minute-mouthed monkey.

"*Bon!*" Liz cheered. "The human games take place in a month. I suggest we begin to research how they prepare for and structure their games in order to learn how to plan for ours. After all, the humans have held these games successfully for centuries. I am certain we could learn a thing or two from them."

"I shall research the games by air, my dear," Nigel offered.

Nate looked doubtfully at Nigel. "Um, mice don't fly."

"This one do, Lad!" Max announced with a smile, nudging Nigel with his nose.

"On pigeons, old chap," Nigel clarified, straightening his whiskers. Nate grinned at the thought.

395

"This is like a dream come true for me," Nate shared shyly, a touch of emotion making his lip quiver. He leaned in to Liz's ear and whispered, "I know this sounds silly, but I've felt as if Maker *needs* me to use my athletic abilities, as if I'm supposed to do something great with them."

Liz beamed and placed her dainty paw on Nate's shoulder. "This makes me very happy to hear, *mon ami*. Especially if the Maker has spoken to your heart to use your gifts for his purposes."

"But I still don't know how he could use my running or swimming for anything," Nate puzzled.

"Ah, but *he* does. Just do the next thing he has placed in front of you to do, and in time he will make it clear," Liz encouraged him. "You'll see."

"Okay, I will," Nate replied. "And, um . . . thanks, Liz. You don't know how much this means to me."

Noah stuck his animated face right in the middle of Liz and Nate's intimate conversation, shaking a banana between them. "Let's start with checking out the discus throw! Bet I could show those humans a thing or two with *this* baby!"

Nigel cleared his throat. "I hate to cut this short, but we must catch up with Paul."

"Very well, we shall see you two soon, no?" Liz asked Noah and Nate. "You of course know where we are staying in Corinth."

"Yep, I do, wahoo-hoo-hoo! See you!" Noah exclaimed, grabbing Nate and swinging him in the air as they left the fountain. *"Now* aren't you glad you got into that gourd?" His voice trailed off as he hugged Nate.

"That monkey somehow r-r-reminds me of Big Al," Max whispered to Nigel.

Nigel leaned in to whisper back to Max with a chuckle, "Indeed, but I do believe Noah is *out* of his gourd."

Liz felt such joy in her heart from meeting Noah and Nate. Noah had led her to Aquila and Priscilla for Paul. Now Noah and Nate would help organize their games. She simply thought she had come up with a fun activity for animals, as she had back on Noah's Ark. Little did she realize that the Animalympics were not only the answer to Nate's prayers, they would somehow fulfill the Maker's plans as well.

45

Shaking the Dust Off

Priscilla smiled at Paul when he came through the door after a long, hard day of delivering tents. "You have guests, Paul," she announced, her hazel eyes twinkling with excitement for her friend. "Timothy and Silas arrived this afternoon. They're waiting for you upstairs."

"They're here?!" Paul cried with a lump in his throat, dropping his satchel of tools on the floor to run up the stairs. He burst into the room as Timothy and Silas jumped to their feet to embrace their mentor and friend. Paul's eyes welled up with tears as he held tightly to Timothy. "Praise God you made it back to me! Oh, my son, how good to see you!"

"It took a while to find you until we saw Faith and Gabriel sitting outside the shop," Timothy reported excitedly. "How grateful I am to see you, Paul!"

Silas beamed with joy as Paul next embraced him. "We have so much to tell you, my friend. God is working and moving in the young churches. Word is spreading all over the provinces of Greece as people are coming to Christ because of these new believers."

Paul gripped forearms with Silas and nodded with great emotion. "After all my fussing and worry at Berea and when I had to flee to

Athens." He shook his head and smiled at his lack of faith. "The Lord is teaching me he is perfectly able to keep those who put their faith in him. He can indeed be trusted. Come, sit and tell me everything!"

The men huddled together as Paul fired question after question about the churches in Philippi, Berea, and Thessalonica. Timothy and Silas shared what was happening not only with each church, but also with how the gospel was spreading throughout Macedonia and Achaia. Liz, Max, and Nigel listened in on the conversation from the corner of the room.

"I am so happy they've finally come!" Liz cheered. "The team is together again, no? And listen to all that the Maker is doing!"

"To hear that all is well is a blessing on top of blessing," Nigel added.

"Aye, but those pesky Jewish leaders still be causin' tr-r-rouble for the wee churches," Max growled. "Wha's it goin' ta take ta get them ta stop?"

Nigel rolled up and down on the balls of his feet. "I daresay they won't stop until Jesus comes again, old boy."

"So the good news is that the Thessalonians are standing firm despite the persecution they must endure and the ongoing attacks from the Jews," related Timothy. "Their love and affection for you is stronger than ever, Paul. Not only that, they are growing in depth and numbers."

"God is able to do more than we even think or imagine, isn't he?" Paul exulted with gratitude for the good news.

"Speaking of that, we've brought you a gift from Philippi," Silas informed Paul, digging in his knapsack for a bag and handing it to him. "Luke and the church sent you a large sum of money so you can focus on preaching and not have to spend all your time making tents."

Paul wiped his eyes with the back of his arm and clutched the heavy bag to his chest. "Father bless them! My dear Philippians. My dear friend Luke. What a joy they are to me! I've been longing to preach more here in Corinth, but earning my keep has consumed my time. I've made slow progress with the Jews as well as with the Greeks and the other pagans here."

Timothy grinned ear to ear. "Well, now you can preach full-time."

"Yes, and we're here now, so we can help Aquila and Priscilla with the tentmaking," Silas assured him with a pat on the back. "And we'll also help you with getting the Corinthian church going."

"*C'est magnifique!* Luke sent the right medicine for Paul once again," Liz cheered.

"Aye, the jinglin' kind," Max agreed.

"Paul, I need to tell you the Thessalonians are worried over some things they don't understand," Timothy continued. "Some of the believers there have died, and those left behind worry that those believers may miss Jesus' final resurrection when he comes again."

"I think you need to write to them, Paul," Silas encouraged him. "A word from you would set their hearts and minds at ease."

"I agree. Very well, I'll write them immediately. I'll write them tonight!" Paul jumped up and gathered some writing papyrus and a pen, and placed them on the table. "Timothy, would you jot it down for me, please? You know how I best gather my thoughts when I pace and speak."

399

"I'd be honored, Paul," Timothy answered, moving to the table.

"Splendid! Looks like another book in the making," Nigel enthused, his whiskers quivering with excitement.

Paul started pacing around the room as he dictated a letter to the Thessalonian church. Timothy wrote as fast as he could, struggling to keep up with Paul:

I, Paul, together here with Silas and Timothy, send greetings to the church at Thessalonica, Christians assembled by God the Father and by the Master, Jesus Christ. God's amazing grace be with you! God's robust peace!

Every time we think of you, we thank God for you. Day and night you're in our prayers as we call to mind your work of faith, your labor of love, and your patience of hope in following our Master, Jesus Christ, before God our Father. It is clear to us, friends, that God not only loves you very much but also has put his hand on you for something special. When the Message we preached came to you, it wasn't just words. Something happened in you. The Holy Spirit put steel in your convictions.

You paid careful attention to the way we lived among you, and determined to live that way yourselves. In imitating us, you imitated the Master. Although great trouble accompanied the Word, you were able to take great joy from the Holy Spirit!—taking the trouble with the joy, the joy with the trouble.

Do you know that all over the provinces of both Macedonia and Achaia believers look up to you? The word has gotten around. Your lives are echoing the Master's Word, not only in the provinces but all over the place. The news of your faith in God is out. We don't even have to say anything anymore—you're the message! People come up and tell us how you received us with open arms, how you deserted the dead idols of your old life so you could embrace and serve God, the true God. They marvel at how expectantly you await the arrival of his Son, whom he raised from the dead—Jesus, who rescued us from certain doom.

So, friends, it's obvious that our visit to you was no waste of time. We had just been given rough treatment in Philippi, as you know, but that didn't slow us down. We were sure of ourselves in God, and went right ahead and said our piece, presenting God's Message to you, defiant of the opposition.

"Do you realize how much this letter will encourage Jason and the others there in Thessalonica?" Nigel posed. "I'm very pleased with it so far."

"Aye, an' if this letter becomes a book, then it will encourage believers ta act jest like 'em," Max added.

Not that the troubles should come as any surprise to you. You've always known that we're in for this kind of thing. It's part of our calling. When we were with you, we made it quite clear that there was trouble ahead. And now that it's happened, you know what it's like. That's why I couldn't quit worrying; I had to know for myself how you were doing in the faith. I didn't want the Tempter getting to you and tearing down everything we had built up together.

"And Paul's reassurance that the troubles they are experiencing should be expected will affirm them, no?" Liz whispered as they watched Paul pace back and forth with animated hand gestures as he spoke.

"Our Tim lad be wr-r-ritin' as fast as he can," Max noticed.

But now that Timothy is back, bringing this terrific report on your faith and love, we feel a lot better. It's especially gratifying to know that you continue to think well of us, and that you want to see us as much as we want to see you! In the middle of our trouble and hard times here, just knowing how you're doing keeps us going. Knowing that your faith is alive keeps us alive.

"Paul is quite right to remind them of proper behavior to please the Maker," Nigel nodded as Paul dictated a section of the letter about living a pure life and treating one another well.

401

"*Oui,* and this will teach future generations of believers how they should act," Liz noted. "*Bon,* now he is addressing their concerns about death and Jesus coming again."

And regarding the question, friends, that has come up about what happens to those already dead and buried, we don't want you in the dark any longer. First off, you must not carry on over them like people who have nothing to look forward to, as if the grave were the last word. Since Jesus died and broke loose from the grave, God will most certainly bring back to life those who died in Jesus.

"Must be hard for humans ta understand dyin' an' wha's comin'," Max said, sharing a knowing look with Liz. "It were no easy thing for us, but there's nothin' ta fear when ye're r-r-right with Jesus."

And then this: We can tell you with complete confidence—we have the Master's word on it—that when the Master comes again to get us, those of us who are still alive will not get a jump on the dead and leave them behind. In actual fact, they'll be ahead of us. The Master himself will give the command. Archangel thunder! God's trumpet blast! He'll come down from heaven and the dead in Christ will rise—they'll go first. Then the rest of us who are still alive at the time will be caught up with them into the clouds to meet the Master. Oh, we'll be walking on air! And then there will be one huge family reunion with the Master. So reassure one another with these words.

"Walking on air!" Nigel exulted with his tiny arms raised in the air. "I simply cannot wait for that day!"

"Well, for now ye'll have ta jest be content with flyin' on pigeons, Mousie," Max teased.

Liz's eyes welled up with tears at the joyous thought of being with Jesus again. "I still miss Jesus so very much, no? I can't wait to be with him for all time. How wonderful to have one huge family reunion!"

"Aye, with no more good-byes," Max added. "It's goin' ta be a gr-r-rand time."

The animals spent the rest of the night listening as Paul finished his letter to the Thessalonians, and the men continued praising God for how he was blessing the movement known as The Way. Thessalonica had been a test case to see if it was possible to make such a lasting impression on a church in as little as a few weeks. Thessalonica passed the test with flying colors. By the end of the night, Paul was so excited about the success of these young churches, he began to dream big. And he had his sights set on winning the entire Roman Empire. But first, he would have to conquer Corinth.

"Not again! No, not again!" Liz lamented. They were sitting in the courtyard outside the synagogue as usual on the Sabbath when suddenly they heard a commotion coming from inside. Soon they saw a mob of Jewish elders dragging Paul out, followed by the congregation. The new believers who attended synagogue were dismayed and confused. But the nonbelieving Jews were bent on stopping what they considered heresy to claim Jesus as Messiah.

"Forty stripes save one!" a Jewish elder shouted as they dragged

Paul to the whipping post. They tore Paul's garment and tossed it on the ground. Then they proceeded to whip him as he had experienced twice before, all the while listening to the *hazzan's* corrective rebuke of this wayward Jew.

"Jest like in Pisidian Antioch!" Max spat. "Now that Paul be teachin' more at the synagogue, these jealous Jews started spewin' all sorts of lies an' evil things aboot him. Now this!"

Nigel scanned the crowd. "But look who is in the back of this mob, clearly struggling with this abuse." It was none other than Crispus, the ruler of the synagogue.

Timothy and Silas did all they could to protest, but once such a punishment began, there was nothing they could do to stop it. All of them had to sit and watch Paul endure yet one more beating for speaking the good news of Jesus to his own people.

Liz shook her head with teary eyes. "How Jesus must grieve for Paul, but how proud he must be that Paul stays faithful time and again, never wavering in his quest to reach the Jews."

When the beating stopped, Paul found supernatural strength to slowly rise to his feet. He picked up his torn garment and shook off the dust toward the Jewish elders and the congregation. "If you are lost, you yourselves must take the blame for it! I am not responsible. From now on I will go to the Gentiles."

"These Jews know full well that Paul is referring to Ezekiel's words that relieve a messenger of responsibility for the death of those who reject his warnings," Nigel pointed out gravely.

"Aye, but at the same time, I know his heart must be hurtin' worse than his back," Max added. "The lad longs ta r-r-reach his fellow Jews. But they jest won't listen."

The new Gentile believer Gaius Titius Justus immediately ran over to Paul, along with Timothy and Silas. "Please come to my house. I'm right next door. Let us care for your wounds there immediately."

Paul felt faint and agreed to go with them to Gaius's house. As the men surrounded Paul to help him walk next door, the Jewish people dispersed, seemingly unaffected by the punishment of another wayward Jew as they saw him. All except for one.

ONE WEEK LATER

"Cr-r-rispus? Ye mean the leader of the synagogue himself?" Max asked in amazement as he joined Liz and Nigel after a morning away with Silas and Aquila. "He an' his whole family?"

"Indeed, old boy!" Nigel reported, straightening his spectacles. "Crispus and his entire family have been baptized this very morning. But first he turned in his resignation at the synagogue, of course. The latest word in the Jewish rumor mill is that some chap by the name of Sosthenes will take his position."

"And now that Paul is preaching here at Gaius's house, many, many other people in Corinth are flocking to hear Paul," Liz added happily. "Timothy has been busy baptizing Greeks and even other pagans Paul met while selling tents. It is wonderful to see good come from such badness, no?"

The animals sat together in the cool shade of trees that surrounded the beautiful lawn and mosaic fountain in the courtyard. Gaius had not only opened his spacious home to Paul for preaching and to start the Corinthian church, he asked Paul to please move into his home for ease of access and the comfort of all. Silas and Timothy stayed with Aquila and Priscilla to continue helping with their tentmaking business, especially as the Isthmian Games approached.

"Someone wants to have a word with you," came a whisper of a voice above them. It was a blue butterfly.

"Clarie!" Liz realized happily, getting up to greet her.

"Follow me to the statue maker's shop," Clarie instructed, flitting away.

Nigel hopped aboard Max's back. Max smiled and trotted after the butterfly. "There can only be *one* someone who'd meet us there."

VISION FOR A FUTURE TIME

The animal friends followed Clarie as she flew down the stone-paved street of Corinth until they reached a courtyard where stood seven headless statues. She lighted on one of them and slowly opened and closed her wings. Max, Liz, and Nigel walked around the statues, looking up to see which one might come to life.

"Why are they all headless?" Liz wondered.

"The statue maker saves time by making statue bodies ahead of time. When someone comes along who wants one made in the likeness of someone, he simply has to sculpt the head and plop it into the waiting neck socket," Clarie explained.

"Brilliant!" Nigel chuckled. "I say, I wonder how my head would look atop one of these."

"There are seven of them," Liz observed, walking around them. "Just like the Order of the Seven."

"I'd like ta see all of us up there, especially me lass, Kate," Max wished, staring up at a beautiful female statue. "Of course, beastie heads on human bodies might be a bit str-r-range then."

"No stranger than some of the Greek gods we've seen in this pagan place, *mon ami,*" Liz pointed out.

"Over here," came Gillamon's familiar voice.

They looked up and there on the back row was the familiar face of Gillamon as a mountain goat, smiling down at them from atop an athletic-looking statue body. "How do I look?"

"Ye look tall, Gillamon, but I think I like ye best with yer own body," Max answered with a grin.

"Are you supposed to be an athlete?" Liz asked him.

"It seemed appropriate with the Isthmian Games approaching," Gillamon replied, flexing his bicep muscle. "I wanted to commend you on all you've done here so far in Corinth. Well done in locating Aquila and Priscilla for Paul. He needed to meet them not only to make tents and have partners, but to be inspired by being around these Isthmian games. His pen will now flow with athletic metaphors throughout the rest of his ministry." Gillamon paused as he looked into the distance, as if gazing into time. "Down to the last words he'll ever write."

"A cr-r-razy monkey helped Liz find the tentmakers," Max chimed in. "He an' his gr-r-reen lizard sidekick."

"Yes, Noah and Nate," Gillamon confirmed with a warm chuckle. "You should have heard the stories Clarie shared with me after she pushed their gourd across the sea to get here."

Max, Liz, and Nigel looked at one another in disbelief.

"You mean Noah and Nate were brought to Greece on purpose?" Liz asked, looking back and forth from Clarie to Gillamon.

"There are no coincidences with the Maker," Clarie answered, gently opening and closing her wings. "He knew those two needed to get here. And he knew Noah would get Nate into that gourd. He is working in every place and at all times to accomplish his purposes with his creatures."

"The Maker is into the details," Nigel mused, amazed once again at God's moving in the animal world.

"Why were the beasties br-r-rought here, Gillamon?" Max asked.

"*Oui*, does it have something to do with the Animalympics?" Liz asked.

"Ultimately, yes," Gillamon replied. "But of course the Maker always accomplishes more than one thing with those who are obedient to follow his lead. Watch what comes with those two." Gillamon stretched his arms above his head, bending the stone of the statue at his will. "The Animalympics will be just as grand as the human games."

"Gillamon, I've been wondering where we can hold our games," Liz replied. "How can we plan if we do not know where we will go next? With Paul's constant travels, this is one thing I have not been able to figure out."

"You don't know?" Gillamon replied to the curious cat with his twinkling eyes and gentle smile. "I'm sure the answer will come to you with time. For now, you need to know some things about Paul." Gillamon leaned forward with his statuesque hands resting on his knees to get closer to the animals. "Although things are looking up for the young churches in the other provinces, Paul's mind is filling with doubt and subtle fear. He is exhausted from this latest beating, and once again he is depressed about being expelled by his Jewish brethren."

407

"Aye, I were worried aboot the lad," Max frowned. "There's only so much one laddie can take, no matter how str-r-rong his faith then."

Gillamon nodded and closed his eyes. "Paul wonders if the same vicious cycle he has experienced in other cities will be repeated here in Corinth: rejection from the Jews followed by acceptance from the pagans, then rage from the Jews followed by being kicked out of town either by the Roman magistrates or an angry mob."

Nigel clasped his paws behind his back and clicked his tongue with a frown. "I say, he must be wondering if he will have to shake the dust off his sandals here in Corinth just as the Good News is taking root in the hearts of the people, who so desperately need it here."

"Indeed. He wonders if he will ever be able to stay anywhere long enough to have a ministry and forge bonds with the people he is able to reach," Gillamon agreed.

"So how can we help him, Gillamon?" Liz implored.

"Comfort him with your presence, as always," Gillamon answered. "Paul will soon receive a fresh touch from the Comforter. You'll know when he comes. But after the Comforter will come the Forger, and Paul will need to write a second letter."

Clarie flitted off into the air as the statue stood back up to its original sculpted form. Gillamon's head slowly disappeared from sight while uttering these words: "Lead Paul to Habakkuk. And beware the Cheetah. Unexpected things will run ahead of it."

Max, Liz, and Nigel stood there among the seven headless statues, awed at Gillamon's comings and goings.

"Where be Habakkuk?" Max asked.

"Habakkuk isn't a place, old boy," Nigel answered. "It's a book written by the prophet named Habakkuk when he preached to Judah before it fell to Babylon."

"Aye, when Daniel an' his fr-r-riends were taken away fr-r-rom Jer-r-rusalem ta live in Nebuchadnezzar's palace," Max remembered. "That were a sad time for the Maker's people."

Nigel preened his whiskers. "Indeed, and when Habakkuk saw their coming doom, his spirit was troubled by why the Maker would allow Judah to have such evil in its midst, and how the Maker could use a sinful nation like Babylon to punish Judah."

"Just when Habakkuk needed to know that the Maker is sovereign and can be trusted in dark days, the Maker showed up in a vision," Liz explained. "I believe we are in for a *déjà vu* kind of night, as my Albert would say."

∝

Sweat beaded up across Paul's brow and he turned his head side-to-side, moaning in his sleep.

"Must be a bad dr-r-ream," Max whispered to Liz and Nigel.

Liz frowned. "His spirit has been so crushed under the load of his calling. He is tired and afraid, no? And he cannot even rest at night."

"I'm sure he longs for those quiet years of isolation in Arabia," Nigel added. "The old boy needs peace in his spirit."

Suddenly the animals felt their fur rise on end. Paul grew very still. And Jesus appeared at his bedside.

"Jesus!" Liz tried to cry in a broken whisper, but nothing came out. She and the others were enveloped in the heavenly vision Paul was now seeing. Jesus looked at the animals and nodded with a smile. Then he drew Paul's attention to his face, just as he had done on the road to

Damascus. But this time, Paul knew exactly who he was, and instead of fear, there was peace.

"Do not be afraid, but keep on speaking and do not give up, for I am with you," Jesus promised with a voice of authority and comfort. "No one will be able to harm you, for many in this city are my people."

A tear slipped out of the corner of Paul's eye to see Jesus himself coming to give him such words of hope and encouragement. "I will press on, my Lord," he whispered in his sleep. "I will not give up."

Jesus' loving smile and silent nod of affirmation made Paul's anguished spirit immediately cast off all doubt and fear. Paul breathed in deeply and entered into a much-needed sleep as the vision softly faded from his mind's eye. He turned over and slept soundly the rest of the night, with Max, Liz, and Nigel curled up at his feet, also plunged into deep, restful sleep.

409

Paul awakened to the feel of sunshine warming his face. Soft rays of the early morning sun peeked through the window into his room. He smiled and stretched long and hard. "Thank you, Jesus," he whispered out loud. He heard rustling in the corner and turned his head to see his cat hiding inside one of his scrolls. Paul sat up, yawned, and pulled his fingers through his graying hair. "What are you doing, Faith?"

Liz kept moving about in the scroll. *"Come and see, mon ami,"* she meowed.

Paul stood and went over to where she was, smiling as he unrolled the top of the scroll. "You're up early. What are you reading?"

Liz beamed at him and sauntered off the scroll so he could pick it up, meowing a *"Bonjour."*

"Habakkuk?" Paul puzzled. "He had a vision as well." He rubbed his eyes and rolled open the scroll to begin reading.

Habakkuk's Complaint

How long, O Lord, must I call for help? But you do not listen!

"Violence is everywhere!" I cry, but you do not come to save.

Must I forever see these evil deeds? Why must I watch all this misery?

Wherever I look, I see destruction and violence.

I am surrounded by people who love to argue and fight.

The law has become paralyzed, and there is no justice in the courts.

The wicked far outnumber the righteous, so that justice has become perverted.

The Lord's Reply

The Lord replied, "Look around at the nations; look and be amazed!

For I am doing something in your own day, something you wouldn't believe even if someone told you about it.

I am raising up the Babylonians, a cruel and violent people. They will march across the world and conquer other lands. They are notorious for their cruelty and do whatever they like. Their horses are swifter than cheetahs and fiercer than wolves at dusk. Their charioteers charge from far away. Like eagles, they swoop down to devour their prey. On they come, all bent on violence. Their hordes advance like a desert wind, sweeping captives ahead of them like sand.

They scoff at kings and princes and scorn all their fortresses. They simply pile ramps of earth against their walls and capture them! They sweep past like the wind and are gone.

But they are deeply guilty, for their own strength is their god."

Habakkuk's Second Complaint

O Lord my God, my Holy One, you who are eternal—surely you do not plan to wipe us out?

O Lord, our Rock, you have sent these Babylonians to correct us, to punish us for our many sins.

But you are pure and cannot stand the sight of evil. Will you wink at their treachery?

Should you be silent while the wicked swallow up people more righteous than they?

Are we only fish to be caught and killed? Are we only sea creatures that have no leader?

Must we be strung up on their hooks and caught in their nets while they rejoice and celebrate?

Then they will worship their nets and burn incense in front of them. "These nets are the gods who have made us rich!" they will claim.

Will you let them get away with this forever? Will they succeed forever in their heartless conquests?

I will climb up to my watchtower and stand at my guard-post. There I will wait to see what the Lord says and how he will answer my complaint.

411

The Lord's Second Reply

Then the Lord said to me, "Write my answer plainly on tablets, so that a runner can carry the correct message to others. This vision is for a future time. It describes the end, and it will be fulfilled. If it seems slow in coming, wait patiently, for it will surely take place. It will not be delayed.

Paul put down the scroll and quoted part of the Lord's reply that grabbed his attention. *"For I am doing something in your own day, something you wouldn't believe even if someone told you about it."* He laid the scroll down and closed his eyes. "Thank you, Jesus, for coming to me with your vision last night. Thank you for doing something now in my own day, just as you did in Habakkuk's day. When the enemy came in on horses swifter than cheetahs, you gave that prophet the courage and strength to live in those dark days. He kept speaking and writing, and so will I. No matter what comes, I will run this race for you."

Liz sat at Paul's feet with her tail curled around her legs. He opened his eyes and smiled at the petite cat. "God is faithful to remind those who do his work, Faith. And I have some pagans to speak to. The Isthmian Games open today, so the city is filled with them." He gave her a gentle rub under her chin before getting dressed to head out the door.

"So accordin' ta Gillamon, now the Forger is supposed ta come," Max recounted as he and Nigel walked over to Liz.

Nigel tapped his paw on his chin. "My dear, did you pick up on that one word from Habakkuk that Gillamon told us to beware of?"

Liz wrinkled her brow as she thought about Gillamon's message and warning. "*Oui, mon ami*—'cheetah." Something tells me we needed to hear from Habakkuk as much as Paul. The Forger is coming against Paul, *oui,* but I think he will be followed by a cheetah that will come against us."

"Paul be headin' ta Isthmia with Aquila, Priscilla, Timothy, an' Silas," Max growled. "We best keep an eye out for tr-r-rouble."

"I shall keep an eye out from above," Nigel stated with a salute, heading to the door. "I have a pigeon to catch."

47

GAMES

Nigel flew all morning above Isthmia on a Corinthian pigeon to survey the athletic complex packed with athletes and spectators. Following the elaborate opening ceremonies of the Isthmian Games, the crowds dispersed to enjoy the first of five days of competitive events. Nigel kept an eye out for any signs of trouble, human or otherwise. The countryside was dotted with countless tents sewn and sold by Aquila and Priscilla's tentmaking shop. "I must say, the humans are terribly efficient in how they've organized these venues. Every event is precisely planned out and scheduled to accommodate the athletes as well as the flow of spectators. Things look very smooth from up here. Let us hope that is the case down below." He spotted two tiny black animals walking over to the discus-throwing area. "Please drop me off over there, my dear."

"Sure thing, Nigel," the pigeon replied as she brought Nigel in for a landing.

"Wahoo-hoo-hoo!" Noah screeched as the discus throwers lined up to, one at a time, heave the flying object, attempting to throw it farther than the competition. "Come on and throw it like I taught you!"

Nate rolled his eyes at his sidekick friend when he saw Liz and Max coming to join them in their choice viewing spot of this venue. The lizard waved at them and pointed to Noah. "He thinks he's an Olympic pro after watching the athletes over the past month. Little does he know that the athletes haven't been paying attention to a screeching monkey swinging a banana."

Liz giggled. *"Bonjour,* Nate. It is good to see you again. Today is an exciting day, no? The Isthmian Games are finally underway. Have you and Noah come up with any ideas for the Animalympics?"

"Oh sure!" Nate answered eagerly. "I was thinking we could include some of the same competitions the humans use, such as footraces, long-jumping, javelin throw, and shot put. But I think we should add water sports. I don't know why humans don't swim in their games. Seems like a no-brainer sport for them to do. I think their bodies could handle it."

Liz raised her eyebrows in delight. *"Bien sûr!* Water sports is a splendid idea, for animals *and* humans! *Bon* suggestion, Nate."

"Brilliant!" Nigel echoed. "Jolly good idea, and if the humans are smart, they'll add swimming to their games in due course."

"Aye, I can honestly say I'd be glad ta compete in water sports," Max chimed in with a wide grin. "I couldn't always say that, lad." He gave Nate a big wink.

Nate smiled shyly. "Um, thanks."

"How about *my* list?!" Noah shouted, getting in their faces. "Wanna hear what I came up with?"

Max, Liz, and Nigel looked at one another with amused grins. "Of course, Noah. What are your ideas?"

Noah rubbed his hands together, then held them up like a picture frame. "Okay, get this. How about lilypad leapfrog, turtle hurdling, synchronized tail chasing, sea cow tipping, and gourd racing?" The monkey grinned broadly, showing his white teeth while awaiting their comments. When they just stared at him, he quickly added, "And we could end it with the triath-lion! Get it? Triath-*LION?* Get it?!"

Nigel's whiskers quivered as he tried to contain his laughter. "I think your suggestions have promise, my young fellow." The little mouse looked at Max. "I'm sure Max here would be among the first to sign up for synchronized tail chasing."

"Very funny, Mousie," Max scowled.

414

"You also have some very creative ideas, Noah," Liz said with a sweet smile. "I especially like your gourd racing idea. This is a new concept for water sports as well, no?"

"You can even ride along with me, little lady," Noah schmoozed with a wink. "I'll win you a crown of catnip or something."

Liz cleared her throat. "Why, thank you, Noah."

Nigel piped up. "I've observed the games from above and think I can adapt the layout for the various sporting venues to the Animalympics. Water sports will add a bit of a challenge, but of course it also depends on where the games will be held."

"Yeah, so when can we start telling animals about our games?" Nate asked. "Noah and I can start spreading the word and getting animals organized. It could take a while depending on how far you want us to travel to find animals from different countries."

Suddenly Clarie came running up to them in the form of a human male athlete. "Hurry and come with me. You need to hear this."

"Who's that?" Noah asked. "And what's a HUMAN doing talking to animals?"

"No time to explain, old boy, but trust us," Nigel urged him. "We must follow that man!"

The animals took off running after Clarie and soon saw they were heading for a very disturbed Paul. He stood there with Timothy, Silas, and a messenger just arrived from Thessalonica.

"They think that letter came from us?" Paul asked concernedly. "We've only sent one to them."

"Yes, Paul, it arrived just after yours," the messenger said. "And just so you know, the messenger who delivered your true letter barely escaped attack by a wild animal."

Paul shared grim looks with Timothy and Silas. They could feel the attacks of the Enemy coming at them from every angle.

"This supposed other letter from Paul has got the church in Thessalonica very confused," the messenger continued. "Some believers are even about to give up, thinking that the Day of the Lord has already come. With the persecution there heating up, some believers have just stopped spreading the Good News."

"Sounds like someone forged a letter to try to destroy the church from the inside," Timothy suggested.

"It could be that same group of Pharisees we encountered before, trying to undermine what we were teaching the believers in Galatia," Silas added.

"The fourth weapon once again!" Nigel recounted. "Remember, Gillamon told us the Enemy would attack the church with four weapons: persecution, moral compromise, distractions, and false teaching."

"You are right, *mon ami,*" Liz agreed with a frown. "And false teaching has now come in the form of forging Paul's letters!"

"Aye, there be more games goin' on here today besides the sportin' kind," Max growled.

Paul immediately recalled what he had read earlier from Habakkuk, and recited it aloud:

416

"Write my answer plainly on tablets, so that a runner can carry the correct message to others. This vision is for a future time. It describes the end, and it will be fulfilled. If it seems slow in coming, wait patiently, for it will surely take place. It will not be delayed."

A group of runners went by them, warming up for the track events that would take place on day two.

"Timothy, I need you to write down a second letter to send to the Thessalonians," Paul requested with urgency. "We're going to clear this matter up immediately, and this time, I'm going to sign it in my own hand so they'll know it's from me."

As the men walked off, Noah and Nate looked at one another. "Um, can someone here tell us what is going on?" Nate asked, looking from Liz to Max to Clarie. "And who *are* you exactly?"

"Yeah, and no funny business," Noah insisted. For once he was serious.

"Very well. We are on mission for the Maker," Liz began. "He has asked us to help this man Paul as he spreads the good news of Jesus to the world. We travel everywhere with him, and we see to his protection."

Nigel held up his finger. "And we see to his *inspiration*. Paul is writing a series of letters to the churches he has founded, and someday those letters will become a very important book for all human believers, for all time."

"So some bad laddies now be tr-r-ryin' ta confuse Jesus' followers with wr-r-ritin' fake letters," Max added. "An' now we hear some wild beastie tr-r-ried ta take out the messenger who delivered Paul's first letter ta the Thessalonians."

"We need to make sure this next letter gets there immediately to set things straight," Clarie insisted. She leaned in close and whispered to Noah and Nate. "I'm really a lamb, but I disguise myself as a human sometimes."

Nate and Noah stood there speechless for a minute, trying to take all of this in.

"Yeah, r-r-r-i-i-i-ght," Noah said, looking at Clarie skeptically. He glanced at Liz. "Is this human playing games with us, Liz?"

"No, Noah, I assure you she is telling the truth," Liz answered quickly. "You can trust every word she says. Clarie really is a lamb. I know this must be hard to believe, but trust her."

"Um, but he," Nate asked, pointing at the male athlete, "is a he, isn't he?" But you're saying he is a she?"

"Precisely, old boy. Clarie can become any creature she needs to at the precise moment she needs to become it," Nigel answered.

"Hey, I met a chameleon once!" Noah exclaimed. He looked Clarie up and down. "Are you a chameleon sheep?"

"Think of me as a sheep in human's clothing," Clarie jested with a wink.

"You say you're working for the Maker? To help others know about Jesus? And the Enemy is fighting to keep you from doing it?" Nate asked. "That sounds like really important stuff. I wish I could do something like that."

"Aye, an' ye best know that the Enemy be tr-r-ryin' ever-r-rythin' he can ta stop us," Max warned them. "We've recently been warned aboot a cheetah."

Nate straightened up and stood tall. "Well, I may not be as fast as a cheetah but I'd run my best to help the Maker and Jesus any day."

"That be mighty br-r-rave of ye, Lad," Max commended him, patting the lizard on the back.

"Well, before the letter can be delivered, it must be written," Clarie noted. "You all go back and see to Paul, Timothy, and Silas writing that letter. Meet me here tomorrow. I'll arrange to be the chosen messenger to deliver the letter to Thessalonica."

"If you go by sea, you can avoid cheetahs," Noah suggested. Everyone looked at him like he had bananas coming out of his ears. "No, really! Thessalonica would be a breeze to get to. Just go south and hang a left after Athens, then cruise north 'til you run right into it."

Nate nodded. "Um, yep, we know the area pretty well after bouncing all over the Aegean Sea in Noah's gourd."

Liz smiled at the two little friends who had travelled so far in a gourd. It was valiant of them to want to help, but such an important mission would only be entrusted to animals such as the Order of the Seven. She didn't wish to squash their enthusiasm, though, so she directed the group to the matter at hand. *"Merci* for your willingness to help, Nate and Noah. But Clarie is right. For now we first need to ensure the letter is written. We'll meet you here tomorrow."

Clarie winked at Liz and nodded. "Noah and Nate, why don't you stay here with me and tell me about your ideas for the Animalympics?"

Liz winked back at Clarie's perfect distraction so they could get back to Corinth. Together she, Max, and Nigel scurried off.

"You know about the Animalympics, too? I've got lots of ideas!" Noah exclaimed, holding up his hands like a picture frame again. "Okay, get this: goat gulping."

LIVE LIKE THAT

One more thing, friends. Pray for us. Pray that the Master's Word will simply take off and race through the country to a groundswell of response, just as it did among you. And pray that we'll be rescued from these scoundrels who are trying to do us in. I'm finding that not all "believers" are believers. But the Master never lets us down. He'll stick by you and protect you from evil."

Paul paced back and forth across the room while Timothy wrote out the second letter to the church at Thessalonica.

"Jesus gave Paul the vision to speak boldly and without fear, just when he needed it," Nigel whispered. "And I believe Habakkuk's words have spilled into Paul's thinking and now his writing."

"I agree, *mon ami*," Liz replied quietly. "Paul has clearly spelled out the correct message and vision for a future time. And he has asked for the most important weapon in a believer's arsenal against the Enemy—prayer."

Max grinned as he listened to Paul. "Aye, an' he's tellin' 'em how to handle the r-r-rascals who need ta be called out there. Tell 'em, laddie!"

Paul rubbed his calloused hands together as he considered how hard he and the others had worked.

"Our orders—backed up by the Master, Jesus—are to refuse to have anything to do with those among you who are lazy and refuse to work the

way we taught you. Don't permit them to freeload on the rest. We showed you how to pull your weight when we were with you, so get on with it. We didn't sit around on our hands expecting others to take care of us. In fact, we worked our fingers to the bone, up half the night moonlighting so you wouldn't be burdened with taking care of us. And it wasn't because we didn't have a right to your support; we did. We simply wanted to provide an example of diligence, hoping it would prove contagious.

"Don't you remember the rule we had when we lived with you? 'If you don't work, you don't eat.' And now we're getting reports that a bunch of lazy good-for-nothings are taking advantage of you. This must not be tolerated. We command them to get to work immediately— no excuses, no arguments—and earn their own keep. Friends, don't slack off in doing your duty.

"If anyone refuses to obey our clear command written in this letter, don't let him get by with it. Point out such a person and refuse to subsidize his freeloading. Maybe then he'll think twice. But don't treat him as an enemy. Sit him down and talk about the problem as someone who cares.

"May the Master of Peace himself give you the gift of getting along with each other at all times, in all ways. May the Master be truly among you!"

420

Paul leaned over Timothy's shoulder to read what he had dictated. Timothy smiled and held the pen up to Paul who took it gladly. "Close it out, Paul. Make sure they know THIS letter is no forgery."

Paul put pen to the papyrus to add the closing remarks:

I, Paul, bid you good-bye in my own handwriting. I do this in all my letters, so examine my signature as proof that the letter is genuine. The incredible grace of our Master, Jesus Christ, be with all of you!

Paul set the pen down and glanced out the window and saw it was nightfall. "We've written the answer out plainly. Tomorrow, a runner can carry the *correct* message to others."

"And that's where the Order of the Seven comes in," Liz whispered excitedly.

Silas held up the small scroll as he gave careful instructions to the young male courier. "Paul is entrusting this letter to you. You've come highly recommended for your swiftness and dependability."

"Yes, certainly, you can count on me," answered Clarie, taking the letter. "I'll get it to Thessalonica posthaste."

"Very well," Silas nodded. "Thank you. And Godspeed, my friend."

Clarie tapped the scroll in her hands and walked toward the hillside where Nate and Noah awaited her. "Godspeed is exactly what we'll need today."

$$\propto$$

Day two of the Isthmian Games was underway, with running as the main sporting event. The air was crisp and clear, with blue skies as far as the eye could see. Max, Liz, and Nigel met up with Noah and Nate, who were watching the footraces from the crest of a hillside above the venue. The beautiful turquoise waters of the Aegean Sea sparkled behind them.

"Hiya, dudes!" Noah greeted them.

"Great day for a race," Nate muttered, preoccupied with watching the games below.

"*Bonjour*, Nate and Noah," Liz replied. "But where is Clarie?"

"That Clarie guy said he'd be back here in a bit," Noah informed them. "AND he said we could go ahead and start telling animals everywhere about the Animalympics!"

"But did she tell you where or when the games will be held?" Liz asked.

"Nah, but he said he would make sure the animals all got the word when the time was right," Noah explained. "We're supposed to just go find good animal athletes and let them know about the games so they can train and get ready."

Liz looked questioningly at Max and Nigel and then back at Nate and Noah. "Well, Clarie knows what she is doing. If she told you to go ahead, then I suppose you can begin the search for animal athletes."

"We're planning to leave after these human games. But today we're enjoying the races," Nate added, keeping his eye on the games. "Did you hear? One runner was disqualified from the last race."

"By Jove, you don't say!" Nigel exclaimed in surprise. "What a scandalous thing at such a prestigious event! What happened, exactly?"

"Turns out that a runner from somewhere in southern Italy arrived here just a couple of days ago, and did not participate in the required training," Nate explained. "He thought because he was so fast he could slip in and get away with it. But then he also cheated *during* the race, knocking another runner out of the competition."

"What a dastardly fellow!" Nigel replied scornfully. "I do hope no other runners follow that scoundrel's lead."

"Serves him r-r-right ta be disqualified," Max growled. "There be no shortcuts an' no cheatin' ta be a r-r-real winner."

"Cheaters never win," Noah declared. "And winners never cheat."

Nate picked up a small scroll that was sitting next to him and pointed to the next race about to start. "Look, they're lining up. Um, I think we can get a better view if we go over there a little bit." The lizard scurried over to a rock about ten yards away.

Nigel straightened his spectacles and followed Nate. "Let's hope for a jolly good, clean race this time."

Noah got ready to join Nate and Nigel but remembered something important to tell Max and Liz. "Guess what?! That Clarie guy told us that as long as we're hitting the road, we can deliver that Paul guy's letter. Isn't that cool?" the monkey remarked happily before running over to join Nate and Nigel. Max's and Liz's mouths hung open in disbelief at what they had just heard.

While Nigel, Nate, and Noah were engrossed in the race, Clarie came up to Max and Liz. "Good morning. I need to share some things with you."

"*Bonjour, mon amie,*" Liz greeted her. "We just heard! Please tell us this isn't true. Are you really going to have Noah and Nate deliver that letter to Thessalonica?"

"Are ye cr-r-razy, Lass?" Max protested. "How are they supposed ta deliver it? Especially if cheetah beasties be aboot! Don't ye need us ta take it then?"

"No, you need to stay here." She pointed over to Nate and Noah.

"The Maker needs *them* to take the letter to Thessalonica. There's more going on here than you know."

"Like wha' exactly, Lass?" pressed Max.

"Yesterday when Nate heard Paul quote Habakkuk's words, his heart's desire was to be that runner. He wants more than anything to use his gift for the Maker," Clarie shared.

"Write my answer plainly on tablets, so that a runner can carry the correct message to others," Liz recited slowly.

Clarie nodded. "This runner just happens to be green."

⊳

"So the little lamb entrusted Paul's letter to a monkey and a lizard?" Lucifer replied with a forced laugh before his face grew sinister. "You can't be serious."

"Swear to . . ." the rat squeaked out in its high-pitched voice, gulping as it stopped short of saying the name of the One who holds power over all. "I heard her ask them to please deliver it to Thessalonica."

423

"Now we can snatch it up anytime we want," said a cheetah sitting there with Lucifer and the rat.

The massive lion got right in the cheetah's face. "You failed at retrieving the first letter when you had all the time you needed. You were outrun by a LAMB! This time you'll get that letter before it ever leaves Corinth. Rest assured this will be your last chance if you fail."

"Well, there's no way a lizard can outrun me," the cheetah laughed.

Lucifer's voice escalated into a spine-tingling roar and he grabbed the cheetah by the throat. "GET ME THAT LETTER NOW BEFORE I CONNECT ALL YOUR DOTS WITH MY CLAWS!"

⊳

"Are you certain you wish to entrust such an important letter to those two little animals?" Liz implored of Clarie with concern. "I do not understand why the Maker would risk such a thing, even if it *is* the desire of Nate's heart."

"Aye, it's not like they be immortal like we be, Lass," Max added.

Clarie looked at her two faithful friends. "How else can faith of the smallest believers ever be tested and proven," she asked as she gazed over at Noah and Nate, "unless terribly important things are entrusted to the most unlikely messengers?"

Liz and Max shared a concerned frown. They feared for the letter that was destined to become part of the New Testament. They didn't understand why they weren't given such a high task, much less why such unlikely creatures were chosen to carry it out.

"Have I ever steered you wrong before?" Clarie asked them.

"Of course not," Liz answered quickly, with her dainty paw on Clarie's shoulder.

"Aye, ye never have because we know where ye get yer orders fr-r-rom then," Max affirmed.

"That's right, so trust HIM," Clarie told them with a wink. "I must be going. I'm sure I'll see you soon."

"Whenever the Maker gives you more orders to send our way," Liz replied with a smile. *"Au revoir, chère amie."*

Clarie nodded. "Now go send those two off with the biggest dose of encouragement you can muster."

"As ye say, little lass," Max replied, turning with Liz to go join Nigel, Noah, and Nate. Clarie immediately vanished from view.

"Well, Max, we must do as directed, no?" Liz asked.

"Aye, even if Clarie herself seems out of her gourd," Max answered with a grin.

Nigel was fully animated, watching the competitors run neck-and-neck as they neared the finish line. He gripped his paws by his side and marched in place, lifting his mousy feet quickly up and down in place. "I say, this is a close one! That chap on the left seems to be making headway on the others."

"Cheetah!" Noah suddenly screeched.

"I must disagree with you, old boy. I believe he is following the rules precisely," Nigel replied. "He is most certainly not a cheater."

"NO!" Noah grabbed Nigel's head with both hands and turned it to see a large cat running straight toward them. "CHEETAH!"

Nigel's eyes got as big as his spectacles and he let out a high-pitched scream. "Cheetah!"

"Gillamon warned us about the cheetah following the Forger!" Liz shouted as she put two and two together. "It must be working for the original Forger himself!"

"Instr-r-ructions or no, ye best be givin' me that scr-r-roll, little lizard." But when he looked down, Nate and Noah were gone.

"Where did they go?" Liz asked, looking around them.

Suddenly they saw the cheetah change course and looked to see what he was chasing. Noah and Nate were running as fast as they could right to the shoreline of the isthmus leading to the Saronic Gulf. But Noah split off and ran right while Nate ran left.

"Nate has Paul's letter!" Liz exclaimed. The cheetah was closing in fast. "Cheetahs run ten times faster than lizards. What is he thinking?!"

"An' wher-r-re's Noah goin'?" Max wanted to know, watching the little monkey running in the opposite direction of his friend down the beach and out of sight. "He be leavin' his best fr-r-riend when he's aboot ta be eaten by that spotted beastie?!"

425

"Write my answer plainly on tablets, so that a runner can carry the correct message to others," Nate's mind played the passage from Habakkuk over and over as he ran with all his might. *"I'll be His runner, if it takes all I've got!"*

"I hope cheetahs never win!" Noah screeched as he tore down the beach.

"The cheetah is quickly closing in on Nate! *Cher Dieu,* please help him!" Liz cried.

Nigel held the sides of his face in his paws, terrified to watch the lizard about to be killed by the fearsome cat. "And Nate is running out of land for escape!"

Suddenly the unimaginable happened. Just as the cheetah reached out its paw to swipe at Nate and the letter, the lizard took off running into the sea—or rather, *onto* the sea—*on top* of the water. The cheetah abruptly stopped at the water's edge in complete shock at the lizard's escape.

Max, Liz, and Nigel looked at one another in disbelief. Not only had Nate escaped, but the cheetah wasn't trying to follow him into the water! It paced back and forth for a moment before running in the direction opposite where it had come from.

"I can't believe me eyes!" Max exclaimed in awe. "That lizard walked on water jest like Jesus an' me did!"

"*Bien sûr!* Of course! Plumed basilisk lizards can run on top of the water when in danger!" Liz explained.

"Brilliant!" Nigel cheered with two fists raised victoriously in the air. "I say, but why isn't the cheetah following him?"

"*C'est magnifique!*" Liz shouted. "Cheetahs can swim when they must, but they hate to get in the water. The cheetah must have known that our athletic lizard would outrun and outswim him both *on* and *in* the water! And if Lucifer sent him to get that letter, he's not about to run back where he came from."

"Look!" Max exclaimed, grinning a mile wide, pointing to the water. "Well, I'll be a monkey's Scottie!"

Noah was way out in the sea, paddling his gourd to pick up Nate.

"Bravo!" Nigel declared. "Well, that puts me in my place. Noah is definitely NOT out of his gourd!"

Liz's eyes welled up with tears of joy as she ran toward the shoreline. "Once again, Noah's 'ark' saves the day!"

Nigel hopped on Max's back to follow her there. "'Noah's gourd' as it were, my dear!"

The three members of the Order of the Seven stood on the beach and gazed out at the crazy monkey who waved and screeched at them happily while the athletic lizard victoriously held up Paul's second letter to the Thessalonians, now safely on its way by sea to the Thessalonian church. In this battle against Lucifer's minion, Max, Liz, and Nigel had done nothing to win the fight. The Maker had used two mortal creatures to accomplish his purposes while the three of them stood still. It was a surreal feeling.

"Truly extraordinary, those two," Nigel exulted with his paws clasped behind his back. "I never would have believed they could have pulled off such a feat with so much reckless abandon."

"Aye, the wee mortal beasties didn't hold back for a second," Max echoed. "They gave all they had for the Maker ta outr-r-run the enemy."

"Just like Paul has been doing throughout this entire mission," Liz added. "Gillamon was right. He said that unexpected things would run ahead of the cheetah, no?"

"If only more mortals would live like that," Nigel suggested.

"Just like Paul," Liz agreed with a smile. "And just like Noah and Nate."

Silent rage poured from the lion's eyes as he watched the letter safely on its way, carried by the two tiny mortal creatures who had bested him. Lucifer's eyes narrowed as he watched the monkey and the lizard cheering in their little gourd, bobbing along in the waves. He could see their hidden escort beneath the waters, and knew they would safely make it to shore and on to Thessalonica. He paced back and forth, angry with once again being thwarted from stopping Paul's correspondence.

"If Paul is so eager to keep running this race, let's see him outrun the authority of Rome," Lucifer scowled.

49

WHERE ALL ROADS LEAD

The bustling crowds thinned out following the close of the spring Isthmian Games, giving Corinth more breathing room with the departing athletes, spectators, tourists, and souvenir vendors. But after the masses left Corinth, a more powerful presence arrived—a new Roman governor. Unlike local magistrates in Philippi or other Roman cities, this position carried the weight of a large province. And he wasn't just any local official. This senator had the ear of the emperor. Any decision made by *this* governor would not just impact Greece, but could ripple throughout the Roman Empire because of the influence he held with Rome.

Lucius Junius Gallio arrived in Corinth on July 1, 51 for a two-year term as proconsul of the Achaia province. Gallio's brother was none other than the highly esteemed philosopher Seneca, who held the favor of Emperor Claudius and was currently serving as the tutor of Claudius' adopted son, Nero.

Gallio's reputation preceded him as a fair-minded, kind man who was pleasant to everyone. As soon as the Jewish leaders of Corinth heard that Gallio had been appointed to their province, they moved into action. This was their chance to finally kill Christianity not only in Corinth, but throughout Greece and anywhere The Way had come against the Jewish establishment.

"Look lively!" Crispus exclaimed, out of breath having run to Gaius's house from the *agora*. Paul and the others were gathered in the courtyard for a morning of teaching. "I overheard some of the Jews from the synagogue. Their anger at losing so many followers to The Way has reached a boiling point. They are coming for you, Paul."

Timothy and Silas immediately got to their feet. "What do you mean, Crispus?" Silas wanted to know.

"Sosthenes, who took my place as ruler of the synagogue, has filed a prosecution against Paul with Gallio," Crispus explained. "The Jews are attempting to outlaw Christianity with the stamp of Rome's approval."

"How can they do that?" Timothy shouted in panic.

"Judaism isn't an official religion of Rome, but it is officially *tolerated* by Rome," Silas explained.

"Yes, and Rome sees Christianity as just a sect of Judaism, not as a separate religion," Crispus added. "The Jews are going to claim that Christianity is outside of Judaism and therefore illegal. If Gallio rules in favor of the Jews, Christianity could be outlawed not just here in Corinth, but throughout the entire Roman Empire. Since Paul is the head of the church here in Corinth, they are bringing Paul up on charges as the chief conspirator against Rome."

"This is far more serious than the threat of a beating," Gaius warned. "This could mean the death of The Way here in Corinth, as well as the death of Paul."

Timothy knelt down next to Paul and gripped his arm. "Paul, do you want us to get you out of Corinth? We could leave right away!"

Paul remained seated with his back against the flowing mosaic fountain in Gaius's beautiful courtyard. He was calm and placed his hand on young Timothy's arm. "No, I'm not going anywhere."

"But what will happen if Gallio rules in the Jews' favor?" Silas implored of Paul. "You could be imprisoned!"

Paul looked at Silas and smiled. "You of all people shouldn't worry about being in prison for the Lord, Silas."

Silas nodded and wore a chagrined look. "Forgive me. You're right of course. So what do you think we should do?"

Paul slowly got to his feet. "We should trust what Jesus told me when he came to me in a vision. He said no attack on me would prosper here in Corinth. He said he has many people in this city. So I choose to believe every word Jesus said."

Timothy, Silas, Gaius, and Crispus looked at one another in half-hearted agreement with Paul. They knew that what Paul said was true in their minds, but the fear in their hearts kept them from realizing the peace Paul clearly had in the midst of such a serious situation. They also had not seen the vision themselves, which made believing all the more difficult.

Liz, Max, and Nigel sat in the courtyard listening to what was happening. But they maintained the same calmness Paul now exhibited. They had been there to witness the vision of Jesus, and they, too, believed every word.

"Bravo, Paul! I daresay, I believe Sosthenes is the one who should be worried," Nigel proposed.

Max nodded. "Aye. If Jesus said no attack here will touch Paul, then whoever leads the charge be in for a r-r-rude awakenin'."

Liz beamed as she studied Paul's face. "Paul isn't anxious in the least. If only believers would take Jesus at his word like this in everything, they would also know peace that can't be explained. *C'est magnifique!*"

A loud bang came at the outer courtyard gate. "Paul of Tarsus, come out immediately! You must answer the charges filed against you."

Timothy stepped forward to stop Paul, instinctively worried for his safety. Paul cupped the young man's face with his hand. "Either Jesus meant what he said, or nothing we believe about him matters. Stretch your faith, Timothy. No weapon formed against us will prosper."

Young Timothy lowered his head and nodded as he realized the truth of what his mentor was telling him. "It's hard to know something and still fight against the emotions that pull in the other direction."

"Yes, it is, so we press on based on what we *know*, not on what we *feel*," Paul assured him with a squeeze of the young man's shoulder. "Open the gate please, Gaius. I'm going to meet Gallio."

Gaius hesitated a moment, but relented and motioned for his servants to open the gate. "Looks like we're all going to court."

As soon as Paul stepped outside, a mob of angry Jews seized him and hurried him down the street toward the *agora*.

The open-air *bema,* or judgment seat, was located in the heart of Corinth's *agora* shops. Covered in white and blue marble, the epicenter of Roman justice for the region stood on an elevated platform to enable crowds to gather and hear the cases brought before the Roman governor of Achaia. Benches lined the sides and back of the prestigious court, which was situated in front of the residence of the governor. The imposing Acrocorinth stood in the distant landscape as a silent sentinel to keep watch over all decisions made in this court. As crowds listened to the cases brought before the governor, their eyes drifted to that towering mountain, reminding them the rule of Rome was as solid as its rock face.

431

Gallio was a handsome older man with piercing blue eyes framed by deep smile lines. His silver cropped hair was brushed forward around his suntanned face. He sat on the judgment seat in the center of the court wearing a white toga pinned up with a crimson sash across his chest. His demeanor was regal and refined, and he quietly watched the approaching mob, taking in every detail of the behavior of the crowd.

He sized up the angry Jews, he sized up the tenuous Greek crowd gathering around the *bema*, he sized up the arrogant chief prosecutor Sosthenes, he sized up the supporters of the accused, and he sized up the defendant himself, Paul. His gaze settled on Paul for a moment as the Jews roughly pushed him forward to stand front and center. Paul locked eyes with Gallio and exuded nothing but respect and complete confidence. Gallio detected no anger, no fear, no resentment. The governor cocked his head to the side as he studied Paul. If anything, Gallio detected in the defendant sadness for what was happening.

Timothy, Silas, Crispus, and Gaius got as close to Paul as they could to offer moral support. Aquila and Priscilla came running from their tentmaker's shop when word got to them about what was going on. Paul was surrounded by his brothers and sisters in Christ. If Paul were taken, they would offer to be taken with him for the cause of Christianity.

Max, Liz, and Nigel darted between legs and hopped up on a low wall so they could hear what was going on.

The court secretary cleared his throat and called the court to order. Gallio nodded quickly and sat upright, folding his hands across his chest as Sosthenes stepped up to present the accusation.

"This man," he began, pointing to Paul, "is trying to persuade people to worship God in a way that is against the law!"

Everyone held their breath. Paul swallowed hard and opened his mouth to speak when Gallio held up his hand to stop him. The governor saw immediately what the Jews were trying to do.

"Gallio is no fool," Liz observed with a coy grin, curling her tail slowly up and down. "He has heard of the repeated attempts by the Jews to come against the sect of Christianity, and he isn't about to be pulled into their internal squabble."

"If this were a matter of some evil crime or wrong that has been committed, it would be reasonable for me to be patient with you Jews," Gallio began, looking around at the faces of the angry Jews. "But since it is an argument about words and names and your own law, you yourselves must settle it. I will not be the judge of such things!"

"Brilliant! This must be the shortest court case in the history of Rome!" Nigel exclaimed, lifting his balled fists victoriously into the air. "Gallio will not interfere in matters where no law has been violated. Good show, old boy!"

"Gallio's decision has just opened the door wide for Paul, the Corinthian church, and for The Way!" Liz cheered. "Jesus was true to his word!"

"Of course he were, Lass!" Max affirmed. "Whatever Jesus says, goes. He made Gallio's decision before Gallio even knew he'd be makin' one today."

"The defendant can go." Gallio stood and motioned for the lictors to remove the Jews. "Get these people out of my court."

Looks of shock and grave disappointment rippled across the faces

432

of the Jews. But looks of anger spread like wildfire among the Greeks who realized the Jews had come against these Christians, who had been nothing but kind to them. Although still pagan, these Greeks saw the difference these Christians had made in this city, for the better.

Suddenly the mob grabbed Sosthenes, the leader of the synagogue, and beat him in front of the court.

"Gallio couldn't care less," Silas shouted as he and the other believers erupted in shouts of praise to God.

Paul rushed over to grab Timothy with a big bear hug, and whispered in the young man's ear, "If we can't trust the One who died for us, whom can we trust?" Timothy wiped away tears of joy over this startling turn of events in Paul's favor. Silas, Gaius, Aquila, and Priscilla gathered around Paul and Timothy, hugging one another and laughing with unspeakable joy.

"Look what God has done and look at all he's taught us," Paul gushed with excitement. "Galatia showed us that Gentiles could be Christians, Philippi showed us that we didn't have to have a synagogue to start a movement, Thessalonica showed us that the Good News could take hold in a short amount of time, and now Corinth has proved that Christianity can come to a great metropolis and spread throughout a Roman province!"

433

"With this freedom, we can look to spread the Gospel in other large Roman cities without fear!" exulted Silas.

Aquila and Priscilla looked at one another and broke out in big grins. "Ephesus! We must go there next! We have a tentmaking business there, too, with contacts already in place."

Paul threw his head back in contagious laughter. "Yes! Ephesus next! I'll go with you there briefly, but I want to go to Jerusalem and report back to home base in Antioch. Then I'll circle back to work with you in Ephesus, God willing. But I don't plan to stop there. After that, we'll head to Rome itself!"

The Christians hugged one another with joy and walked arm in arm back down the main street of Corinth, talking a mile a minute about how they would take the good news of Jesus down every road in the Roman Empire.

"Paul and the believers here are now free to preach wherever they wish with no fear of sudden attacks from the Jews or from Rome," Nigel cheered. "This jolly well takes the biscuit!"

Liz nodded quickly. "The Jews brought Paul here today hoping for Rome's persecution."

"But R-r-rome became his pr-r-rotector instead!" Max exclaimed.

"*Bon!* Paul said he wants to travel to Jerusalem. Do you realize we can see our loved ones again? Oh, how I can't wait to see my Albert!" Liz cried. "It has been too long."

"Aye, I'm goin' ta give me lass a gr-r-reat big hug," shared Max, wrapping his burly paws around his shoulders.

"We can tell Kate and Al the thrilling news about our plans for the inaugural Animalympics," Nigel suggested. "I know they will be most eager to hear all about it."

"If only Kate an' Al could be part of the gr-r-rand event when it happens," Max wished.

"Indeed, as well as Gillamon and Clarie," Nigel added. "The entire Order of the Seven could enter."

Max thought a moment and broke out into a big grin. "Big Al could win the food eatin' competition."

"My Albert would be splendid. He could be an event all by himself, no? The *Al*ympics," Liz giggled. Her eyes brightened and her tail whipped back and forth. "*C'est ça!* We must all be together for the games."

"RIGHT! Team Order of the Seven will compete in the Animalympics together," Nigel cheered, clasping his paws together with enthusiasm. "Now to determine a central location for the games to be held, given our diverse travels."

"We always meet back up in Jerusalem, but somehow that don't seem ta be the r-r-right place," Max thought out loud.

Nigel nodded and twirled his whiskers as he thought this through. "Indeed. And of course, it must be where humans wouldn't suspect us. And where we could hold events at night, preferably in a large arena. We also need ample time to plan, you know."

Liz looked down at the Roman road that ran through Corinth.

434

"Of course! There is a place that meets all of those qualifications, and it also will fall into our mission, according to what Gillamon told us at the very beginning of this quest and what Paul is even now suggesting. Why didn't I think of this before? Gillamon told me I should already know the answer."

"Do tell, my dear," Nigel urged.

"Aye, where would that be, Lass?" Max asked.

The Wind suddenly picked up and encircled the animals, wildly blowing their fur as if to affirm what Liz was thinking. Liz's beautiful eyes danced with excitement. "All roads lead to Rome."

The lion gazed down from the craggy rock face of the Acrocorinth above the city. He seethed at the small band of animals walking behind the tireless apostle who had once again defeated his schemes. "So, you want to play games, do you?"

"Anything you want, Master," the sniveling red-eyed rat eagerly replied, thinking Lucifer was talking to him.

Lucifer rolled his eyes and grabbed the rat, throwing it up in air and playing with it while he thought out loud. "I'll give them games, and in the greatest arena ever built." His dark eyes narrowed as ideas rushed into his wicked mind. "I'll need a place to put my new arena, so I will need to give Rome a facelift. And I'll need an emperor mad enough to do it." The massive lion chuckled wickedly. "Nero. Yes, Nero will do my bidding. And I'll even have him destroy Gallio for his foolish decision here today."

The lion laughed and flippantly tossed the rat on the ground. The rat shook its head but quickly got to its feet, ready to do its master's bidding. Lucifer walked to the edge of the overlook, sending pebbles cascading down the cliff face as he dug his claws into the rocky ledge.

"But I'll also need laborers," Lucifer thought out loud. A thought struck him instantly and a grin covered his face. "Who are the people I've hated the longest?" the lion asked the rat.

"The JEWS!" the rat answered eagerly.

Lucifer grinned and nodded. "So I'll make Jesus' own people, the JEWS, build my new arena. And whom do I hate the most NOW?"

The rat had to think a moment. "Hmmm, that's a hard one. Wait, I know!" It drew a fish symbol in the dirt and pointed proudly to the answer. "The CHRISTIANS!"

The lion sprung its deadly claws and scratched away the fish symbol, seething at the very thought of them. "Yes, the CHRISTIANS. So I'll make Jesus' little followers the 'play things' inside my arena. This will take time, but I am a patient lion. It will be worth the wait when I crush The Way once and for all," Lucifer predicted determinedly, gazing out over Corinth where the Good News was now positioned to break out and spread across Greece despite his best efforts at thwarting it. "If I can't kill it here and now, I'll kill it there and then."

"Kill it where, Master?" the rat asked, gulping as it looked over at the steep cliff below.

"All roads indeed lead to Rome." The lion gave a sinister laugh, thinking of Liz's words. "But for The Way, Rome will be a dead end."

TO BE CONTINUED . . .

THE FIRE,
THE REVELATION,
AND THE FALL

D on't miss the exciting conclusion to this two-book saga that brings to life the events of Acts and the birth of Christianity while showing how each book of the New Testament came to be. *The Wind, the Road, and the Way* covers Resurrection morning through Paul's second missionary journey. *The Fire, the Revelation, and the Fall* (2015) completes the events in Acts, Peter and Paul in Rome, Roman persecution of Christians in the arena, and John's Revelation on Patmos. Watch the miraculous rise of the Church through the fiery trials sent by an Enemy who will stop at nothing to kill anyone who dares to be called Christian.

A Word from the Author

This book almost wasn't. I had complications from surgery right before I started writing, and things were touch and go for a little while. But the Great Physician intervened, people prayed for me around the globe, and I made it. God gave me some amazing revelations while I was recovering. He was deepening my pen through suffering, just as he did with Paul. How could I write Paul's story if I didn't know what it felt like to "despair even of life," as Paul wrote? I had to know what he meant on that and many other issues. This is an occupational hazard of being a writer on God's payroll.

Just as I fully recovered, I had a neck injury requiring weekly treatments for months. Then knee issues requiring painful shots for weeks. All the medical time away from my desk was the *real* pain in the neck. All of this adversely impacted my writing. Normally I'm a writing machine, but writing this book was like long, hard labor. Every time I turned around something slowed me down. I pushed back deadlines twice. Then I finally heard what God was trying to tell me: *Jenny, make this two books instead of one.* So I did, and the floodgates of progress opened.

Originally the book you've just read would have continued all the way through Acts to Rome to John on Patmos, and was entitled *The Way, the Road, and the Fall.* But I was trying to cram too much into one book, and God knew that. So, you'll get to read the rest of it in *The Fire, the Revelation, and the Fall.* Just as Paul was physically blocked from going into Asia—it was because God knew he first had to get Paul to Macedonia to meet Luke. Without Luke we never would have had the book of Acts, which details the incredible account of the birth of the Church. That was also a difficult labor with complications. But the Good News finally took off and spread around the globe, just as Jesus asked. I'm glad Paul's original plans didn't work out for him, and I'm glad they didn't work out for me, either. God knows what he's doing.

So, given that behind-the-scenes look at *The Wind, the Road, and the Way,* I'd like to give you some inside-the-scenes notes about the book. I write fiction based on fact, so it's important for you to know where the fiction enters in, where the unknowns become plot lines, and where I took liberties with the story:

- No one knows what happened in Peter's Resurrection morning encounter with Jesus. Sometimes those "Jesus secrets" indeed are best kept private with him. But I imagine it happened like I wrote it. What better place than inside the empty tomb?

- The other man with Cleopas on the road to Emmaus is unnamed in Scripture, but I named him "Jacob."

- I named the other two of the seven men fishing with Peter the morning by the sea. Only five are mentioned by name in Scripture.

- The 153 fish caught in Chapter 5 – I read several theories on the significance of John stating this exact number of fish caught the morning Jesus restored Peter, from calculating hidden numbers attached to the spelling of words, to the number of people Jesus had restored. I went with the simplest insight I found, from William Barclay's commentary.

- "Before the Spirit can come, the Son must go." This is a quotation from Homer Kent's fantastic book *Jerusalem to Rome: Studies in the Book of Acts* (see the Bibliography).

- When Mary says, "Ah yes, that's him. That's him," after the Holy Spirit comes, this concept was inspired by a sermon by one of my favorite preachers, T.D. Jakes.

- Saul's involvement in Stephen's arrest and death is conjecture. The first mention of Saul in Scripture says Saul watched the coats of the stoners, but I believe he had to have been involved earlier in the plot in order to gain immediate authority to start rounding up followers of The Way.

440

- Judas's character in Damascus – I created his personality and motives.

- Paul's three years in Arabia – I pieced it together from research but a visit to Petra is likely. He somehow angered the Nabatean king, and Petra was their capital, so it's plausible he spoke with offending zeal while there.

- Chapter 33 – The scene of Peter and Paul's showdown with the Jews from Jerusalem happened over the course of time, not in one scene at one meal. I had to compress time here to keep the story moving.

- Paul meeting Luke – No one knows how it happened, so of course I enabled Liz to arrange things.

- Philippian jailer – I took liberties with him being the man in Paul's dream as I created his character, including his name.

- Luke staying behind in Philippi – We're not sure he did but it is certainly plausible that he stayed there for six years, as the "we" statements in Acts resume and Paul picks him up in Philippi on his third missionary journey.

- Noah and Nate – These two characters are based on two precious boys who tragically lost their lives on a lake in Tennessee, July 4, 2012. Noah was my little cousin, and I was heartbroken to lose him, as well as his best friend, Nate. As I sat at their double funeral, I wondered how I could best pay tribute to them beyond dedicating a book to their memory. So I patterned characters after their personalities. Noah was every bit like our lovable capuchin monkey—crazy, silly, full of love, life, and naïve mischief, and ever sweet to the girls. Nate was an athlete, having completed a triathlon. So of course, the "Jesus Christ," or plumed basilisk, lizard was perfect for his character, as the lizard runs on land and water, and swims. Nate would fix his hair in a Mohawk for crazy hair day at school, and this

441

lizard has a natural Mohawk. These boys loved Jesus! Oh, how they loved him! And I'm sure they brightened heaven the day they arrived. But we miss them here. I pray this book blesses their families, and their friends at Cornerstone Academy in Morristown, Tennessee. You'll see Noah and Nate again, in even rarer form in *The Fire, the Revelation, and the Fall*.

- Paul was with Aquila and Priscilla in Corinth during the AD 51 Isthmian Games, and I fell in love with the idea that this is where he was inspired for his athletic metaphors that grace his many letters. You'll see them come out in *The Fire, the Revelation, and the Fall*.

- The Prologue opened up this book with John arriving at Patmos, and I decided to leave it even though I ended the book without circling back to that plot line. You'll get there in the next book. Don't worry; John is in good hands until you arrive.

Thank you for reading. Let's pray my lead-up to writing the next book is just plain boring. But I know I had it easy compared with Paul's suffering: Paul was given a thorn in the flesh that tormented him to keep him from being proud, beaten with rods three times, flogged five times, stoned once, imprisoned, held under house arrest, rejected, persecuted, shipwrecked three times, adrift out in the open sea for a day and night, cold, thirsty, hungry, without clothing, sleep-deprived, worked to exhaustion, in constant danger of thieves, rivers, desert conditions, beasts, betrayals from his own people and others—oh!—and responsible for spreading the good news of Jesus in a hostile, pagan world dominated by the Roman Empire. Then tradition says he was beheaded. So, next time I'm about to complain about my "sufferings," I'll thank God for them instead.

Bibliography

Barclay, William. *The Acts of the Apostles*. Louisville: Westminster John Knox, 2003. Print.

———. *Barclay's Guide to the New Testament*. Louisville: Westminster John Knox, 2008. Print.

———. *The Gospel of John*. Philadelphia: Westminster, 1975. Print.

———. *The Gospel of Luke*. Philadelphia: Westminster, 1975. Print.

———. *The Gospel of Matthew*. Vol. 2. Philadelphia: Westminster, 1975. Print.

Blomberg, Craig. *Matthew*. Vol. 22. Nashville: Broadman, 1992. Print. The New American Commentary.

Bruce, F. F. *Paul, Apostle of the Heart Set Free*. Carlisle, Cumbria, UK: Paternoster, 2000. Print.

———. *Commentary on the Book of the Acts: the English Text, with Introduction, Exposition, and Notes*. Grand Rapids, MI: Eerdmans, 1954. Print.

Cowman, Charles E., and James Reimann. *Streams in the Desert: 366 Daily Devotional Readings*. Grand Rapids, MI: Zondervan Publishing House, 1997. Print.

Cox, Steven L., Kendell H. Easley, A. T. Robertson, and John Albert Broadus. *Harmony of the Gospels*. Nashville: Holman Bible, 2007. Print.

Good News Bible: The Bible in Today's English Version. New York: American Bible Society, 1976. Print.

The Holy Bible: English Standard Version. London: Collins, 2008. Print.

Holy Bible: New International Version. Grand Rapids, MI: Zondervan, 2005. Print.

Holy Bible: New Living Translation. Wheaton, IL: Tyndale House, 1996. Print.

Holy Bible, Red-Letter Edition: Holman Christian Standard Bible. Nashville: Holman Bible, 2004. Print.

Kent, Homer Austin. *Jerusalem to Rome: Studies in the Book of Acts*. Grand Rapids, MI: Baker Book House, 1972. Print.

King James Bible. Nashville: Holman Bible, 1973. Print.

MacArthur, John. *The MacArthur Bible Commentary: Unleashing God's Truth, One Verse at a Time*. Nashville: Thomas Nelson, 2005. Print.

———. *The MacArthur Study Bible: English Standard Version*. Wheaton, IL: Crossway Bibles, 2010. Print.

———. *Twelve Ordinary Men: How the Master Shaped His Disciples for Greatness, and What He Wants to Do with You*. Nashville: W Publishing Group, 2002. Print.

McGee, J. Vernon. *Thru the Bible with J. Vernon McGee*. Vol. IV. Nashville: Thomas Nelson, 1981. Print. Matthew through Romans.

Meyer, F. B., and Lance Wubbels. *The Life of Paul: A Servant of Jesus Christ*. Lynnwood, WA: Emerald, 1995. Print.

———. *Peter*. Fort Washington, PA: Christian Literature Crusade, 1978. Print. Classic Portraits.

"Mount Sinai and the Apostle Paul." *AncientExodus.com*. N.p., n.d. Web. <http://www.ancientexodus.com/topics/index/mount-sinai-and-the-apostle-paul/>.

Paul's Missionary Journeys. N.p., n.d. Web. 15 March 2013. <http://www.welcome-tohosanna.com/PAULS_MISSIONARY_JOURNEYS/0.1WhoIsPaul.html>.

Peterson, Eugene H. *The Message: The Bible in Contemporary Language*. Colorado Springs: NavPress, 2002. Print.

:: *PETRA CITY* ::. N.p., n.d. Web. 01 March 2013. <http://www.visitpetra.jo/>.

"Petra." *Wikipedia*. Wikimedia Foundation. Web. 28 February 2013. <http://en.wikipedia.org/wiki/Petra>.

Phillips, J. B. *The New Testament in Modern English*. New York: Macmillan, 1958. Print.

Polhill, John B. *The New American Commentary—ACTS*. Nashville: Broadman, 1992. Print.

Pollock, John Charles. *The Apostle: A Life of Paul*. Garden City, NY: Doubleday, 1969. Print.

Renner, Rick. *A Light in Darkness: Seven Messages to the Seven Churches*. Tulsa, OK: Teach All Nations, 2010. Print.

———. *Sparkling Gems from the Greek*. Tulsa, OK: Teach All Nations, 2003. Print.

Sanctuary: A Devotional Bible for Women. Carol Stream, IL: Tyndale House, 2006. Print.

"Sermon Series on Acts." *Sermons by Dr. Paul Mims*. N.p., n.d. Web. 08 August 2013. <http://www.csbccl.org/csbccl/Sermons.aspx>.

Stott, John R. W. *The Message of Acts: The Spirit, the Church, and the World*. Leicester, England: Inter-Varsity, 1994. Print.

Swindoll, Charles R. *Paul: A Man of Grace and Grit*. Nashville: Thomas Nelson, 2009. Print.

444

GLOSSARY

Liz's (and Al's) French Terms

Allons-y!	Let's go!
Bien sûr!	Of course!
Bon	Good
Bonjour	Hello/Good day
Bonsoir	Good evening
Bon vol	Good flight
Bon voyage	Good journey
C'est ça!	That's it!
C'est magnifique	It is magnificient/incredible
C'est tragique	It is tragic
C'est très belle	It is very beautiful
C'est vrai	It is true
Chat	Cat
Cher/chère	Dear
Chérie	Dear/sweetheart
Comment vous appelez-vous?	What is your name?
Comprenez-vous?	Do you understand?
Déjà vu	This has happened before
Dieu est bon	God is good
Docteur	Doctor
Du jour	Of the day
Il est ici	He is here
Je comprends	I understand
Je ne comprends pas	I don't understand
Je ne sais pas	I don't know
Je parle français	I speak French
Je vous en prie	You are welcome
Le pain	The bread

Mais	But
Merci	Thank you
Messieurs	Misters
Mon ami/amie	My friend (masc./fem.)
Mon Dieu	My God (please note this is said as a prayerful cry by Liz)
Mon Roi	My King
Monsieur	Mister
N'est ce pas?	Isn't that so?
Non, c'est impossible	No, it is impossible
Oui	Yes
Quel dommage	What a pity
Petit déjeuner	Breakfast
Pour vous	For you
S'il vous plaît	Please
Très bien	Very well, very good
Très jolie	Very pretty

Nigel's British Terms

Cheeky	Flippant / arrogant / smart aleck
Completely mental	Crazy
Cracking on	Proceeding ahead
Crikey	Exclamation of surprise
Ergo	Latin for "therefore"
Fancy	To desire (something)
Jolly	Very, or to emphasize the point
Smashing	Terrific
Takes the biscuit	Outdoes everything else

Award-winning author and speaker

JENNY L. COTE

developed an early passion for God, history, and young people, and beautifully blends these three passions in her two fantasy fiction series, *The Amazing Tales of Max and Liz®* and *Epic Order of the Seven®*. Likened to C. S. Lewis by readers and book reviewers alike, she speaks on creative writing to schools, universities, and conferences around the world. Jenny has a passion for making history fun for kids of all ages, instilling in them a desire to discover their part in HIStory. Her love for research has taken her to most Revolutionary sites in the U.S., to London (with unprecedented access to Handel House Museum to write in Handel's composing room), Oxford (to stay in the home of C. S. Lewis, 'the Kilns', and interview Lewis' secretary, Walter Hooper at the Inklings' famed The Eagle and Child Pub), Paris, Normandy, Rome, Israel, and Egypt. She partnered with the National Park Service to produce Epic Patriot Camp, a summer writing camp at Revolutionary parks to excite kids about history, research, and writing. Jenny's books are available online and in stores around the world, as well as in e-book and audio formats. Jenny has been featured by FOX NEWS on Fox & Friends and local Fox Affiliates, as well as numerous Op-Ed pieces on FoxNews.com. She has also been interviewed by nationally syndicated radio and print media, as well as international publications. Jenny holds two marketing degrees from the University of Georgia and Georgia State University. A Virginia native, Jenny now lives with her family in Roswell, Georgia. Official website: www.epicorderoftheseven.com.

Same Characters, Two Award-Winning Series

The adventure begins with the two-book prequel series: *The Amazing Tales of Max & Liz®*, where the Maker begins building His team of animals to be His envoys through pivotal points of history. Max, Liz, Kate, and Al launch the adventure in book one, *The Ark, the Reed, and the Fire Cloud,* and are joined by their British mouse friend, Nigel, in book two, *The Dreamer, the Schemer, and the Robe.* With book three, *The Prophet, the Shepherd, & the Star,* the team of seven animals is finally complete, and known forevermore as the Order of the Seven in the *Epic Order of the Seven®* series. Working behind the scenes in the lives of Noah, Joseph, Isaiah, Daniel, those in the Christmas story, Jesus, the Disciples, Paul and the early church, the team will pass through Biblical and world history up to modern times with Patrick Henry and the Revolutionary War, and C.S. Lewis and World War II.

Keep up with Jenny and her latest news by subscribing to Epic E-news at www.epicorderoftheseven.com

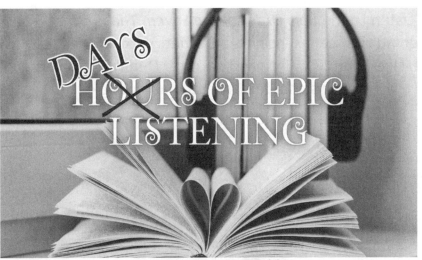

DAYS ~~HOURS~~ OF EPIC LISTENING

AVAILABLE AT AUDIBLE.COM

Listen to the *Epic Order of the Seven, The Podcast* with behind the scenes insights and chats with your hosts Max, Liz, Nigel, Jenny L. Cote and narrator Denny Brownlee as he plays chapters from the audiobooks.

Season One: *The Ark, the Reed, and the Fire Cloud*
Season Two: *The Voice, the Revolution, and the Key*

Tune in here:
epicorderoftheseven.com/podcast
or podcasts on Apple, Google and Spotify

The Epic Revolutionary Saga
Available in Print, eBook, Audio, Study Guide and Podcast

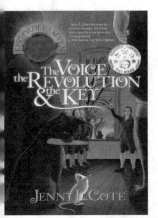  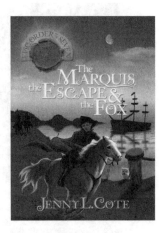

The Voice, the Revolution, and the Key: 1743-75
The founders as kids, events leading up to the eve of Revolution

The Declaration, the Sword, and the Spy: 1775-76
Lexington and Concord, Bunker Hill, siege of Boston through the Declaration of Independence

The Marquis, the Escape, and the Fox: 1776-77
The Battle of New York, Trenton, Princeton, escape of the Marquis de Lafayette from France, and France's secret aid to America

More titles to follow to complete the entire story of the American Revolution and the founding of the United States of America.

Learn more at *www.epicorderoftheseven.com.*

Schedule Jenny L. Cote to Speak to Your Group

Award-winning author Jenny L. Cote opens the world of creative writing and history for students of all ages and reading levels through fun, highly interactive workshops. Jenny has appeared to thousands of students at homeschool groups and conferences, lower, middle, high schools, writing conferences, book clubs, and universities in the US and abroad. Jenny's workshops correspond to her specific books, showing students exactly how she crafts her books, from research to character development to imagery. It gives students real hands-on tools used by an author, with a behind the scenes look at how a book comes together. Surprising grand entrances, fun props, and humorous questions keep students engaged from the first minute, with smiles and hands raised to be chosen to do the next fun thing!

Learn more at www.epicorderoftheseven.com/schools-groups.